Captain Putnam

for the

Republic of Texas

ALSO BY JAMES L. HALEY

THE BLIVEN PUTNAM NAVAL SERIES

The Devil in Paradise: Captain Putnam in Hawaii

A Darker Sea: Master Commandant Putnam and the War of 1812

The Shores of Tripoli: Lieutenant Putnam and the Barbary Pirates

OTHER FICTION

Final Refuge

The Lions of Tsavo

The Kings of San Carlos

NONFICTION

The Handy Texas Answer Book

Captive Paradise: A History of Hawaii

The Texas Supreme Court: A Narrative History 1836–1986

Burleson Century

Wolf: The Lives of Jack London

Passionate Nation: The Epic History of Texas

Sam Houston

Texas: From Spindletop Through World War II

*Most Excellent Sir: Letters Received by Sam Houston,
President of the Republic of Texas, at Columbia, 1836–1837*

Texas: An Album of History

Apaches: A History and Culture Portrait

The Buffalo War: The History of the Red River Indian Uprising of 1874

JUVENILE

Taming Texas: The Chief Justices of Texas
(with Marilyn P. Duncan)

Taming Texas: How Law and Order Came to the Lone Star State
(with Marilyn P. Duncan)

Taming Texas: Law and the Texas Frontier
(with Marilyn P. Duncan)

Stephen F. Austin and the Founding of Texas

Captain Putnam

for the

Republic of Texas

★

JAMES L. HALEY

G. P. Putnam's Sons
New York

PUTNAM
— EST. 1838 —

G. P. PUTNAM'S SONS
Publishers Since 1838
An imprint of Penguin Random House LLC
penguinrandomhouse.com

ISBN: 9780593085110

Printed in Canada
1   3   5   7   9   10   8   6   4   2

Book design by Tiffany Estreicher

*Nearly twenty years ago I published a hefty biography of
Sam Houston, which won a number of important awards and remains
in print. Through several years of certified starving artistry while
I wrote it, my work was underwritten by a generous patron, to whom I
dedicated the work. He and I remained close friends, and it was my
intention to similarly dedicate this Texas-based novel to him, in
gratitude for his many kindnesses during the intervening years. He
passed away shortly before this book was completed, and six weeks shy
of his one hundredth birthday. Therefore, this book now is dedicated:*

*In Loving Memory
Joel Rudd
1920–2020*

As to the state of the seaboard—keep the navy busy.
To it we must look for *essential* aid!

—SAM HOUSTON

CONTENTS

Captain Putnam

for the

Republic of Texas

1

Honor and Conscience

It was like drowning in tepid water, that was the worst—air so
humid it was like sucking in water the temperature of his own
body, so that if it were not for the observed rise and fall of his
own chest, and his own careful observation that he was not, in fact,
suffocating, Bliven Putnam might well have believed he was drowning. He had seen the brawling rivers of the Appalachians, which became the highways of commerce because the mountains were too
steep, too rugged and forested, for wagons to pass through. But here
in Florida the land was untenable for an opposite reason. Here one
must travel on the rivers because—and it was nature's triumphant
irony—most of the land was too soggy upon which to march or ride.
So here he was, in the stern of a longboat pulled by twenty sweating
sailors, with a platoon of marines bristling with rifled muskets and
bayonets like a caterpillar hunkered down along its keel. The oarsmen swept in silence up a sluggish warm river whose name was ex-

hausting to pronounce, followed by three more boats, pulling slowly into a probable Indian war. What in God's name was he doing here, in God's year 1834?

Bliven might have thought that now as a senior captain he would have been assigned a more dignified duty, coursing the deep in a ship of the line or at least in his own frigate. As a youth he would have contested for a prestigious command but now, at forty-seven, quite gray at the temples and his face lined with salt spray and the responsibilities of command, it did not rankle him. He had set out as a boy to see the world, and now he had done so to his satisfaction. It weighed on him as never before that Clarity had spent most of her life waiting for him to come home. He wanted to see his boys: Ben was seventeen now and in his first year at Yale College; Luke was thirteen, bored with school and as restless as he himself had been. Perhaps there was still time to be a father to them and not just some distant memory of awe and a uniform.

Bliven would not say that he was tired—of the Navy, or of command, or of his life. He knew well that in the pecking order of naval officers, it was his own lack of avidity, his lack of competitiveness, for a major command that worked against him. That was well; he was content. The United States now deployed the navy of a major power, and the officers' ranks were full of peacocks to strut and peck at each other. Abruptly he belayed that line of thinking. He should not mock, he scolded himself, for there were fine officers among that top line of command. Isaac Hull, Jacob Jones, and some other old hands were still vigorous and at their duties as they entered their old age. John Downes, now an impeccably experienced commodore, had just taken the fine frigate *Potomac* with her forty-four-long, thirty-two pounders to Malaya and taught those pirates the lesson that Bliven had lacked the firepower to do in 1820. There began to be talk now of mounting an expedition to explore the south polar regions, the last command on earth that he would have wanted, although the chill of an iceberg would be very welcome at this moment. Competition to lead it was sure to be fierce, and his own treasured first lieutenant from his first tour on the *Rappahannock*, Michael Miller, who had advanced to his own creditable commands, was a contender.

The fondness of his recollection of Miller made him question whether perhaps he was tired after all. He had only the barest acquaintance with his present complement of boy-lieutenants, nor did he desire to know them more intimately. They were careerists at the beginning of their ambition, essentially uninteresting, and uninteresting because they were uninterested, lacking in passion for any other pursuit than their own advancement. Indeed, they hearkened back to the species of officer he recalled all too clearly from his boyhood on the *Enterprise*, duelists who tended to their duties only as needed, and not sparing to abuse those who served under them. The obligation to occasionally dine with them made him long for home as never before. Alan Ross, thank God, was still with him, continuing in the service as his steward and continuing now in private employment as his valet when they were not at sea.

Bliven had tried for a time to keep together the core of his companionship from the *Rappahannock* in those days, but he had not been able. Wise Dr. Berend had retired to a town practice in his native Virginia, and so much to refute his complaint of the insufficiency of friends over the family he had outlived, he died much loved by his community and at a far advanced age. Tall Fleming, his wizard of a carpenter, was seized by his family in Roxbury after the Pacific cruise and never permitted to return to sea. Of those he relied upon in earlier years, only Evans Yeakel, his ever-alert bosun, remained. When Bliven had returned to the *Rappahannock* the year before and been piped aboard, Yeakel caught his eye and grinned so fiercely that he could scarcely finish the accolade on his silver whistle. Indeed, he had never left the ship even as Bliven himself had advanced to two other commands, becoming one of those traditional bosuns who attached themselves like barnacles to their vessels and sometimes found themselves at a loss how to carry on after she was paid off or broken up. Bliven had come back aboard to find Yeakel gray as a rat, and thicker, but still nimble despite accommodating the truss that supported his rupture—a new condition for him but a common malady among career seamen.

No, Bliven was content to let other officers climb up each other's backs in quest of better commands like iguanas seeking the sunniest rock. He found himself satisfied to have been placed once more over his dear old *Rappahannock*. Having taken her on her first cruises, to the Caribbean and the Pacific, it seemed poetic, or symmetrical, that he should take her home to Boston from her last cruise. After Malaya and the Sandwich Islands, the ship was assigned to the Mediterranean Squadron, while he was given command of a light frigate and returned to the Caribbean. The Navy wished to take advantage of his experience with the games of pirates, privateers, and newly independent countries. Upon the *Rappahannock*'s return from the Mediterranean, the combined judgment of the Navy was that her hybrid design was not a success, except on the point of her diagonal knee riders that supported the berth deck. That feature was continued into the newer sloops of war, but as the first of her species her list of needed improvements was too long to justify a rebuilding. With her replacement still abuilding, Bliven was given command of her a final time, for a routine patrol of the West Indies, for what should have been the most placid voyage of his career, showing the flag amicably in the British and French islands. Instead, this cruise had transformed itself into an intense and scarifying education on the human condition.

At home, the issue of slavery had become so contentious, so divisive, that he endeavored not to think on it at all. Clarity's abolitionist sentiment had become so militant that she gave him almost no peace, while his renewed correspondence with Sam Bandy, now nearly fifteen years in Texas after his ruin in South Carolina, pummeled him with the opposite considerations: the ruin of the South's economy if slaves were liberated, the desperation that hundreds of thousands of freed men and women must face if they were turned out with no land or employment or skills and, as Sam phrased it, no one to take care of them. While Bliven loved Clarity as fiercely as ever, and missed her, he had looked forward to six months back in the Caribbean as a rest from the issue of slavery as a daily topic.

WHAT HE DISCOVERED there came as a shock, however, and as their three longboats pulled slowly up their Florida river, there was ample time for him to digest the onslaught of unwanted realizations from the previous two months. On every British island it seemed the only topic of conversation was the impending law to take effect on August 1, 1834, that would outlaw slavery throughout the empire. And then discussion would turn in amazement to the almost prophetic tragedy that William Wilberforce, who was the driving engine of emancipation, who had utilized his forty-five years in Parliament to win that day, had died like Moses just short of reaching the Promised Land—but, like Moses, he had been permitted to see it, for he lived long enough to learn that the passage of his bill could not be stopped.

Bliven's next-to-last port of call in the Caribbean was at Jamaica. Kingston Harbour was a hidden labyrinth of shallows, with the first narrowing of its entrance passing beneath the Twelve Apostles battery off to port, a dozen guns whose firing, if an enemy approached, gave ample notice to the sixty-six big guns in the fortification at Mosquito Point, a mile farther in. Those ramparts overlooked a safe channel barely seventy yards wide, through which no hostile ship could survive to approach the city. It was the most brilliant defensive scheme that he could imagine.

Bliven took equal interest in the shallows to starboard, beneath which lay the remains of Port Royal, the infamous pirates' nest that a vengeful God had drowned in an earthquake in 1692, and then suffered the remnant to burn to the ground a decade later. Kingston, on the north shore, was founded by Port Royal survivors and now was a convenient place to hire a carriage for an easy ride to the capital at Spanish Town, fifteen miles to the west, where Bliven would make a courtesy call on the colonial governor. Much of the land along that road was reclaimed marsh, now given to plantations, and between that sight and animated conversation with his driver he learned that sugar was to this colony of Jamaica what cotton was to the American South, the cash crop upon which they depended, and which faced a bleak future without the forced labor of slaves. In the rolling miles between Kingston and Spanish Town, the vast cane fields were yet worked by an unending line of bent black laborers, glared at by overseers armed with whips and muskets and sidearms. Did they truly think that this way of life could be transformed in the darkness that would separate July 31 from August 1? What exactly did they believe it would change into? Of even greater consequence, in Kingston he was told that only one person in four was white and that of the blacks two persons in three were slaves, who would gain their freedom in another two months. What their society would look like in a year's time, after emancipation, God only knew. But their premonitions sounded very much like Sam Bandy's.

From Jamaica Bliven and the *Rappahannock* sailed east to call at Port-au-Prince, in Haiti, to look in on what remained of the several thousand free blacks from the United States whom the American Colonization Society had encouraged to emigrate to that place. The society had recruited them, painted them a pretty picture of tropical life in a whole nation populated by other Negroes, paid their passage— and then turned their attention to other projects. Haiti troubled him more than anything else to that date. At home, the white planters in the South lived in terror of slave uprisings, which of course never actually transpired to the degree they imagined, but this former French colony gave them vivid reason for that fear. They had thrown off the French thirty years before, the only country known in human history to have gained its independence in a slave revolt, and, good God, look what happened: tens of thousands of white people massacred almost to the last crying baby. Then they turned the machetes upon themselves: freeborn black against former slave, native born against immigrant, French speaker against Spanish speaker, in the unspeakable War of Knives. In thirty years of nominal independence, uncountable hundreds of thousands were hacked down.

The United States, which might otherwise have welcomed another country of the western hemisphere throwing off the colonial yoke, reacted to the violent pageant with horror and contempt. Southerners in Congress made certain that Haiti was never recognized; the State Department made a sport of playing all factions, both native and European, against each other; and American banks lent money for ruinous interest to any of the native forces who looted enough gold to justify the risk of a loan. For the past fifteen years the strongman had been Jean-Pierre Boyer, who managed to hold the country together, and he convinced the French to withdraw their army by agreeing to pay an indemnity of a hundred and fifty million francs—an astronomical sum that they could not manage to pay, giving them even a century in which to do it. With so much violence afoot, Bliven counted himself lucky that the bay was so sheltered that he could anchor in its outer roads, where any threat could be seen coming. He obtained an interview with Boyer, whom he found wily and cynical, and dressed in such a fantastical uniform as would justify the most derisive accusation of how slaves would comport themselves if given power. Boyer was acutely sensible of the contempt in which the United States held his country, yet he was determined that Haiti should progress to take her place in the family of nations.

Most of the émigrés sent by the American Colonization Society, Bliven learned, had made their individual and disillusioned ways back home. It was a complex and wretched history. For twenty years the A.C.S. had been funding two colonies of freed slaves, on the claim that it was only right and proper for them to have their own country, before it became clear that the true goal was to separate them and their free example from those still in bondage and thus tighten the South's grip on slavery. The founding of the Haitian colony and Liberia in Africa were now widely recognized as a ruse. And of those who remained here, he found many living in an enclave in the mountains behind the town, clinging to the belief that life in a country of people of their own color must be somehow better than what they had known in the United States. They had not, to his observation, prospered. Indeed, from what he saw of Haiti, he descried no prosperity anywhere, only power held by the very few and the subjection of the destitute mass. These former Americans had not advanced in education; rather, they had assimilated into a society of the most benighted superstition, living in thrall to sorcerers who beat drums and sacrificed chickens and went into trances.

During his days there he offered passage home to several of the former Americans, but as a body they refused, clinging to each other and their fears. Never was Bliven Putnam so relieved to quit a place in his life. In Haiti he had seen a side of the human condition so dark and disturbing that he determined, even as he set his course up the Canal de Saint-Marc, never to relate it to Clarity. One day to relieve his own mind he might write about the horrors there, of the predation of human beings one upon another, of the sorceress who used the diluted poison of the puffer fish to reduce her victims to her own malevolent will, of this nationwide reduction of human beings into jungle creatures. It would be years into his future, however, before he would desire to recall these events.

The British islands offered a different example. No doubt, when they decreed the manumission of their slaves, their design in doing so was humanitarian and laudable, but what he observed in Jamaica and Haiti laid bare how little thought they had given to the consequences. It left Bliven in a quandary of how he should feel about this institution that he had come to loathe as much as his wife did, but whose economic and social realities were forcing him to examine his conscience more closely than perhaps she had done, how it could be ended with the least suffering to everyone.

Now for two hundred miles he must navigate the shallows of the southern Bahamas on his way to Nassau. His orders were to seek an interview with Governor Townley-Balfour and express gently, without raising it to a diplomatic level, America's growing disquiet over the Bahamas' sympathy for harboring runaway slaves from Georgia and Florida.

He threaded a passage through the aptly named Ragged Island chain of cays and sandbars, through which a chart was useless because the bottom was reconfigured by every hurricane. He was relieved on their far side to encounter the deep blue of the Tongue of the Ocean and the straight shot of another two hundred miles to New Providence. Strange islands these were, seven hundred of them stretching some five hundred miles in total from southeast to northwest, but with an aggregate land area smaller than Connecticut. In the previous century they had harbored by rough count a thousand pirates, of sufficient strength that they overthrew British rule and reveled in a Republic of Buccaneers for a dozen years, governed by the pirate code of pure democracy within, and rape and pillage without. Race and class were meaningless to them. Order was restored in large part by offering a royal pardon to the pirates, most of whom accepted it and remained. The Bahamas retained therefore a different complexion of relations between the races, more egalitarian, less tolerant of self-elevated pretense.

Safely anchored in Nassau, what he discovered in the governor was a man ten years younger than himself and not unacquainted with the dubious morality of conquest and subjection, for the Townley-Balfour family were wealthy scions of the Protestant Ascendancy, their fat income produced on estates seized from Irish owners and worked by Irish tenants. Bliven felt his temper rise at the memory of the English captain, Lord Kington, who had slashed him in Naples, and upon whom he had wrought a terrible revenge off the coast of Brazil. That family had also grown rich with their boots on Irish necks.

The governor received him cordially with tea on a sun-splashed veranda. They discussed the wreck of the American ship *Encomium* on Abaco Island the previous February, with a cargo of forty-eight slaves within the legal domestic trade. Captain and crew had been returned to the United States, but the slaves were welcomed and granted their freedom. Along with 165 slaves from the American ship *Comet*, wrecked earlier, and various Seminole Indians who fled the unending violence in Florida, the *Encomium*'s black survivors were settled on the northern tip of Andros Island to build up the new town of Red Bay.

Townley-Balfour frankly admitted the diplomatic morass in which they found themselves on this issue but sought refuge in the fact that it was a matter for the Foreign Office. He was himself merely an officer of the Crown who carried out policy. If a decision should be made to return those people to America, and bondage, he assured Bliven that he would comply, but he had no authority to act without instruction. That was all Bliven needed to hear, and after thanking the governor for his hospitality he set all sail for home.

ROUNDING WEST END OF GRAND BAHAMA
JUNE 20, 1834

My ever dear Love,

I am happy that there are none here to ask me why I am writing to
you, when we have raised every stitch of canvas in a taut southeast
wind, and are flying home just as fast as this poor tired ship can
manage. It seems possible that we will nose into Charlestown even
as I write an affectionate closing to this missive, and I can carry it
home with me. Or perhaps we can make a call, and I can post it, at
that Southern Charleston, in South Carolina, and race it home.
Who would win, do you think?

In honesty, I write you because in doing so I find a small measure
of the solace I take in conversing with you, and in these last months
I have learned much that you will find of the greatest interest, for in
about six weeks' time slavery will be abolished in the British Empire.
While most admit the humanity of this act, I have found a much
wider variety of opinion expressed than we in the U. States might
think they have. Some foretell of horriferous consequences as a
result, where the more high-minded insist that the right thing must
be done, regardless of its results.

I did not think to find—

With no warning whatever Bliven felt and heard a tremendous
jolt in the body of the ship, throwing him from his chair into the
table and causing a bright black jagged streak of ink that trailed to
the edge of his writing paper. The *Rappahannock* seemed to both
slam to a halt and leap upward at the same instant and then come

down and wallow, heavy but free. It felt as though the very fist of God had fetched them a terrific blow under the starboard bow. Ross was in the act of crossing the great cabin, carrying fresh linen to Bliven's berth, when he was thrown from his feet, crashing first into the bulkhead and then to the deck.

"Mr. Ross!" Bliven cried out, vaulting across the room and kneeling over him. "Are you hurt?"

"No, I am all right. Jesus!" Ross got to his feet and arranged his clothing. "Thank you for your attention, sir, but surely you should get topside and see what has happened."

In the instant, Bliven was racing forward down the gun deck to the ladder and grateful to find his bosun waiting for him at its head. "Mr. Yeakel, what in hell has happened?"

He pointed forward. "A wave, Captain! A great giant bastard of a sea came out of nowhere, struck us on the starboard bow."

"But that can't—"

"Sir! It took away our sprits'l and its yard, and when the bow came up out of the trough, the weight of so much water has broken the bowsprit extension. It is still clewed to the jib and forestays'l, and the whole mess has folded back and is hammering the anchor and the cathead. We must cut it all free!"

"Yes, I agree! Bring in all your canvas, quick as you can, and get men—"

Even as they spoke, they heard high above them a sickening, deafening crack. With the forward staysails still clewed up, the weight of the whole wreckage, including the tons of water that the spritsail carried up every time the bow lifted, was too much for the foretopmast. Bliven's and Yeakel's twin gaze shot up at the sound of the explosive split, in time to see it fall the hundred feet to crash onto the bow, smashing the railing and wrecking the camboose's smoke-stack.

"Damn it!" spat Bliven. "Bring in all your sails. Have the carpenter's mate take a sounding, make sure we are in deep enough water to drift. Make sure no one is hurt; get any injured down to the sick bay."

The entirety of the mayhem had taken moments—seconds, really—turning the slightly clumsy but stable *Rappahannock* into a cripple that they would have to fight to control in any but a following wind. Bliven made his way back to the helm, where he found his third lieutenant at the wheel. "Mr. Coleman, you have seen our predicament."

"Yes, sir." He was a redheaded young Vermonter, small but muscular.

"We are bringing in the sails until we get organized again. The wind is southeast. There is little for you to do; just use the rudder to keep the stern into the wind and we will drift to the northwest."

A new thought suddenly seized him. "Mr. Yeakel!" He loped back forward. "Don't let anyone cast the foretopmast overboard. We can do without it better than we can do without a full bowsprit. Once we put in somewhere to make repairs, perhaps you can cut it down to size for a new extension."

"Yes, sir, that is how we will do it."

"Was anyone hurt?"

"No, sir. There was one man crapping at the head, but he doesn't have to anymore. The sight of the mast coming down at him took care of that."

Bliven sought refuge in a thunderous laugh. "Bless his heart! Good for him!" Bliven looked through the rigging as the main topgallant yard was lowered and the courses reefed. "Mr. Yeakel, when you get the bow cleared away, you might set the tops'ls again so we can have a little steerage."

"Very good, Captain."

"Come below and get me if you need me. Oh, and set some men to get the cooking stack back up. The least we can do is feed the men on time."

"Aye, sir."

Who knew where such destructive waves come from? The sounding came in at only twenty fathoms as they rounded Grand Bahama. Perhaps it was storm-driven, from far away, and piled up in the shallows. He disliked, after a third of a century at sea, to encounter some phenomenon that was new to him, whose cause eluded him.

Back in his sea cabin he discovered that Ross had set out charts of the Florida and Georgia coasts, knowing that they would want to search out a place to put in for repairs. They could never tack back to Nassau in their crippled condition, for the southeast wind would be hard against them. Besides, every mile they covered, he wanted it to be a mile toward home. He decided to make north northwest for St. Augustine, that venerable and almost ancient port city in the northeast of Florida, to effect repairs. After twenty minutes he felt the ship begin to move again and knew that the debris had been cleared from the bow and enough canvas set to get them going.

The door to his sea cabin was open, and an hour later Yeakel knocked as he entered. "Excuse me, Captain, there is something you should see."

Bliven rose and followed him. "What is it?"

"I don't know, sir. You must see it."

They went up the ladder and Yeakel strode straight to the starboard beam. "Sir, what do you make of this?"

"Jesus in heaven!" Around them the sea had gone flat but for a long, low, rolling swell that was the color of tea with milk. Everywhere was the hiss of bubbles breaking the sea's surface, and the smell of rotten eggs. "This is unnatural."

Yeakel put a handkerchief over his nose. "Have you any idea what could cause this?"

"No. Is it shallow?"

"No, sir. Carpenter's mate reports no bottom. I thought you should see it, to enter into the log."

Bliven shook his head at the mystery. "You thought rightly. The Sargasso Sea has its mats of floating seaweed, but that is northeast of here, and the currents would keep anything from drifting this way. I have no idea. But I don't like it. Is your bow free of wreckage?"

"Yes, sir."

"Then make all the sail you can; get us out of here. Helm!"

"Sir?"

"We are raising sail again. Continue northwest. We will make our repairs in St. Augustine."

"Very good, sir."

It took two days to reach there, and Bliven was uncertain as he threaded the inlet, past the Salt Run, and dropped anchor at the mouth of the Matanzas River just off the walls of the looming Spanish fortress, whether the Navy would even approve repairs on a vessel that was going home only to be broken up, or else to have a village built on her weather deck and enter into the lugubrious limbo of a receiving hulk.

The American flag fluttered over the walls of this gray-white castle that showed on the old charts as the Castillo de San Marcos, Anglicized since the British assumption in 1763 to Fort St. Mark. Upon being rowed ashore in his gig, he quickly learned that it was now named Fort Marion after the revolutionary "Swamp Fox." He also learned that there was no naval presence in the town; the Navy had determined to establish its Florida base farther north, in the raw lumber of the new village on the St. Johns River just named for the ridiculous Andrew Jackson, that conqueror of an unaware enemy. The garrison commander within the old castle would be able to advise him about any repairs.

He found himself smiling as he approached its cream-white walls. New Englanders like himself were so proud of their aged Pilgrim heritage that began in 1620. Most of them were unaware, and the well-read gallantly declined to recognize, that the Spanish had preceded them on the Atlantic shore by more than a generation. This town dated from 1565, although in this climate nothing could be expected to survive the bugs and decay for so long.

The fort dated from a century later, looming larger as he approached its entrance in the south wall, through a medieval barbican plainly once set off by moats and drawbridges. The whole edifice seemed to have been dropped onto the beach from the Middle Ages: grooves in the walls for a portcullis, a murder hole in the ceiling through which to pour boiling oil or molten lead onto the heads of invaders. The outer walls appeared to be about twelve feet thick, of a rather poor-quality limestone, and the passageway ran about forty feet into a courtyard that looked to be perhaps a hundred feet square. As he passed through the wall he saw on his left what he took for guardrooms and asked a lazy-looking sentry, "Where will I find your commanding officer?"

He saluted and pointed within. "Into the courtyard, Captain. Turn immediately left; his office is in the first casemate."

Bliven returned the salute. "Thank you, Corporal." He continued into the daylight of the court, where to his right an ascending ramp led up to the broad terreplein with its file of heavy cannons along the ramparts. The first door on his left was made of crude vertical planks, with a sign that read HENRY PARKINS, CAPT. U.S.A. COMMDG.

He knocked twice quickly and entered. He saw no adjutant on duty, but an officer entered from a rear room, muscular and very tan, with black hair above dark eyes. "I am Captain Parkins. May I be of assistance?"

Bliven saluted and they shook hands. "Bliven Putnam, Captain, United States sloop of war *Rappahannock*, just now in your harbor."

"Yes, we saw you come in. Please come take a chair." He led the way back into his office, pausing to pour two glasses of wine. "You are welcome, but you know, we have no naval facility or yard or staff."

"I was aware. We were damaged at sea and put in here to make repairs."

"We thought you looked a little snub-nosed. What happened?" Parkins handed over a glass of tawny-colored Madeira.

"Thank you. We were hit by a great, huge sea swell. No idea where it came from; its origin is a mystery."

"I see. How long do you think your repairs will take?"

"Just a few days, I think. We would require a docking facility to repair the foretopmast, but we can do without it. We saved the one that fell to pare down into a new bowsprit. Then we must set new rigging."

"And your men would perhaps enjoy some time ashore, if you are in no great hurry? Your good health." Parkins raised his glass and took a sip.

"That is very kind of you to mention. I am certain that they would."

"Actually, Captain Putnam," he began slowly, "I was not being kind altogether. Your arrival catches us at a particularly acute time, in fact, and I am in need of assistance."

Bliven sat straighter and paid greater attention. "How can we help?"

"You have been at sea for some time?"

"Six months—not long as sailors measure time."

"But a lot can happen on land in six months. Have you heard of our problem with the Seminoles?"

"I have read enough only to know that you have one. My impression is that the Seminoles have been a problem for a long time."

"Indeed, they have, but now the danger of a war has suddenly become very acute and very dangerous."

"Perhaps they want their land back."

"On the contrary, we sent a delegation of their chiefs west to the Creek lands on the Arkansas. These Seminoles are really just Creeks by another name, anyway. We told them we would not make them move if they found those lands objectionable. All those chiefs signed an affidavit as to the quality of the land and their willingness to move. It is the ones who did not go see; they have got their backs up. They have been abusing the Indians who are willing to move, and now we learn they have secretly been purchasing and concealing arms and ammunition and encouraging slaves to flee their plantations and join them in the swamps. Whatever grievance they imagine they have against the government, we cannot brook such defiance on the part of savages."

"Is that the foundation of our objection to them: that they are savages?"

"Of course."

"So that, if they moved into houses, started plantations of rice and cotton, even bought slaves, they would be accepted into society?"

"Well, that is so unlikely that I never entertained the notion."

"That is what the Cherokees have done. Some of them have become whiter than the white people and still they are losing their lands."

"That is different. There is, I believe, known to be gold in Cherokee-held land."

"Oh, well, certainly that does make all the difference, yes indeed."

Parkins ignored this. "Fort King has been reactivated and must be supplied, and quickly. A new agent has been appointed for them, a Mr. Wiley Thompson—perhaps you have heard of him—and the garrison there must have supplies with all speed to protect him and the settlers in that area."

"Thompson? The Georgia congressman?"

"The same."

"Is he not Jackson's man through and through, one of the great shouters to force all the Indians to move west? What good can he do? Why would they listen to anything he has to say? It seems like all he could do is hasten a conflict."

Parkins lowered his gaze in a sour way. "I gather from your accent, Captain Putnam, that you are a New England man."

"Connecticut."

"Then the chances are that your political views would disagree with most of the people in this section."

Bliven sensed a challenge coming. "My personal opinions are of no moment. You and I are military officers, sworn to our duty irrespective of our private thoughts."

Parkins relaxed just a little. "I am happy to hear you say it. But look"—he grinned suddenly, which caught Bliven by surprise—"if that is how you feel, and be honest with me now, you are probably also of the opinion that the United States committed a terrible wrong in wresting Florida away from Spain in the first place. Are you not?"

"I—" Bliven shook his head. "Why would you ask?"

Parkins stood suddenly. "Because there is something I want to show you. Bring your drink." He was out the door so quickly, there was nothing to do but follow him across the courtyard to the northeast corner, where they entered a casemate. "We have been busily engaged in fixing up the fortress into effectiveness. It was quite dilapidated, and the Spanish left it in some disorder. This first room here"—it was dim and cool within—"was called the pennancarra, the place of punishment. Do you see the iron rings in the walls there? That was where they hung prisoners up by their wrists. You see this little hole in the wall? That connects to the old chapel, so the prisoners could hear mass before they were put to death."

Bliven heard this out, stone-faced.

"Last year one of the men noticed this arched doorway that had been rocked up. There was no access from any other direction, so we broke through; let me show you." They ducked through the narrow opening into a room, more dim than the first, in the realm of twenty feet square but irregularly shaped by the parapet above it. "See what we found? Do you know what this ruined old device was?"

Bliven regarded the remains of a wooden frame secured to the far wall and, next to it, a geared, ratcheted wheel on its side, a lever lying on the floor. "Why, it looks like it must have been a rack!"

"It *is* a rack, Captain, of the kind that Torquemada and the priests of the Inquisition would have known very well."

"Well!" Bliven disapproved of the implied generalization that all priests tortured for the Inquisition, but he found himself giving Parkins credit for knowing who Torquemada was. "Captain Parkins, I have long been quite a student of history, but I confess I never imagined to see such an instrument in my own country."

"You know what else we found in here? A skeleton, sealed up, left dead or alive we don't know, decades ago or centuries we don't know. We finally gave him a Christian burial, poor bastard. Come, let us return to my office." He led the way back to the south end of the court. "So, the next time you launch into some self-righteous exposition about poor little Spain losing her empire and how cruel the United States was to take control of Florida away from her, you might remember what you have seen here this day."

"Captain," shot Bliven, "I protest that I never said any such thing."

Parkins turned, smiling again. "No, but you have thought it. Am I wrong?"

In spite of himself, Bliven found himself appreciating this abrupt man, perhaps warily approving of him, and his shortcuts to get to the heart of a matter. "No, you are not wrong. Now tell me: What aid is it that you require in your present exigency?"

"You are an American warship. I presume you have marines aboard?"

"Yes, a rifle company of forty-five, with a lieutenant, a sergeant, and two corporals."

"Excellent. There is a militia company gathering, awaiting my order to proceed to Fort King. They are civilians, each carrying their own arms and with no uniforms. We need to make some impression on the Seminoles of American military discipline, and the presence of a uniformed company would just do the trick. I cannot send my own troops from here without leaving the place open to attack. Therefore, I would be grateful if you would lend me your marines for a few days, escort the militia to Fort King and be present for the council, and help keep order if needed."

"So, what you are requesting is for me to leave my ship here as the bosun and carpenter make their repairs while I detail my marine company to attend the Seminole council and overawe the Indians with their discipline and ferocious demeanor."

Parkins lolled his head from side to side. "Essentially, yes. And be prepared to help in the event of fighting."

"I see." Bliven frowned as he considered his options. Parkins had no authority to order him into the venture, but in this new Navy Bliven's reputation might well be destroyed if he refused his help after the case had been made that lives were in danger. He did not particularly care, but he had Clarity and the boys to think of. "You will understand that I have no authority to let you have them indefinitely. You cannot station them there. We must be back underway as soon as our repairs are effected."

"I understand. They will, however, be very helpful in getting us through what will be a fraught moment."

"Very well, then, Captain, you shall have our cooperation. Now, how do we accomplish this object?"

"Captain Putnam, I thank you. Your supportive attitude will not go unreported. Now, let me explain that forty miles north of here lies the opening of the St. Johns River. At least, they call it a river; it is really more a long, long estuary, brackish water, barely a current, rather like the river Plate in South America."

"Yes, I have been to the river Plate; I know what you are describing."

"Good. So, the St. Johns River goes upstream, almost due south, for seventy or eighty miles. It varies from one to three miles wide and is navigable. Thus St. Augustine, where we are, really sits on a kind of peninsula between the ocean and the river. In your ship's broken condition I could not ask you to sail up to the river mouth and then back down. It would take too long anyway."

"Quite right."

"The river passes southward on its course, fifteen miles west of here, where there is a landing and a settlement. I will ask you to send your marine company overland to this settlement. There is a road, or at least a well-worn trace. They will not have to wade—at least, not very often. They will find boats waiting there to take them to Fort King."

Bliven found himself leery of letting his marines get so far from his control and recall but could not say so directly. Only one solution came to him: "I should lead them myself. Will not the presence of someone of a captain's rank also make an impression on these Indians?"

"Oh, my, yes, it would. I appreciate your initiative so very much."

"Very well. That is how we shall have it."

THAT, THEN, was how Captain Bliven Putnam came to be sweating in the middle of a Florida swamp. He and the marines marched west to the landing on the St. Johns, where they boarded a small steamboat that churned and chugged for over thirty miles upstream before putting in at a landing on the right bank, at the mouth of a river their guide called the Ocklawaha. There they went into camp, a night of endless slaps at mosquitoes, and the frequent curses and dispatching of venomous black snakes they called moccasin snakes. They were of the same family as rattlesnakes but lacking the rattle, and with a wicked disposition, if struck at and not killed with the first blow, to attack.

Their guide was a Creole, white but swarthy, stout, with curly black hair and eyes of bright green, named Shifflette. Bliven and the marine lieutenant found him indispensable in pointing out to them natural features whose sight the men might find demoralizing but which were essentially harmless—such as horned beetles the size of breakfast biscuits—and those that they needed to avoid, such as the moccasin snakes, and leeches if they stepped into water, and they learned to be vigilant for the ridged backs just breaking the surface of gigantic alligators, some of whom it seemed could not have fit into the keeping room of his house without curling their tails, and whose spike-toothed maws could seize a man and drag him under, giving him barely time to scream or thrash.

In the morning they resumed, and the Ocklawaha proved much narrower than the St. Johns, with a stronger current, and was a hard job for their local boatmen to pull against. The farther miles upstream gave Bliven time to stew on this whole kettle of events that was Jackson's doing, him and his implacable determination to throw all the eastern Indians off from their lands and award them to white people.

Yes, Jackson. No one could have any doubt that behind all things

Florida was, and had long been, Andrew Jackson. Gaunt, sour, profane, and violent, he had first slashed his way into the national consciousness, and adulation, during the War of 1812 with an overwhelming defeat of the British at the Battle of New Orleans. Or, rather, it was fought after the War of 1812, for the Treaty of Ghent was signed before the engagement, so it had no effect on the outcome of the conflict except to redeem the reputation of the U.S. Army, which had lurched horrifically from one disaster to the next, while it was the naval victories that kept America in the war.

Jackson revealed much about himself in that battle, including his willingness to accept any aid, whether from friendly Indians or even pirates, in quest of victory. He was a great warrior; there was no denying that. He had nerves of steel, an almost wolflike cunning in planning a battle, and personal bravery amply demonstrated. But he also possessed a thirst for gore, as the story was widely and breathlessly repeated; Bliven hoped it was not true but had himself heard on good authority that it was. When Jackson had crushed hostile Creek Indians who had been seduced by the British at the beginning of that war, he allowed the primitive frontiersmen who made up his militia to roast potatoes in the grease that cooked out of dead hostiles as they were burned inside their redoubt.

Great God, how did such a man ever become president of the United States? In 1818 it was Jackson who had invaded the Spanish Floridas, goaded and spurred by Southern planters—of whom indeed he was one—whose slaves had run away and been harbored by these same Seminoles.

Yet Bliven knew even as he felt his gorge rise at the thought of Jackson that the man did not create the national will, he merely rode it, gave effect to it, used it like wet clay to mold the public perception of himself as a conqueror. It was the nation itself that was changing, becoming more crude, more violent, less educated. Yet even as the democracy included Jackson's Westerners, they had roughened the complexion of the republic. The Founding Fathers, who could debate political philosophy in Latin, had not foreseen them.

And it was Andrew Jackson who had become the champion, the hope—the instrument—of such people. Ten years before, in 1824, Congress had had the vision and found the craft to deny him the ultimate power of the presidency. It was true that he had received a plurality of the popular vote—a testament to the voting power of an uneducated mass. The framers had foreseen some such circumstance and countered it with an electoral college, a barrier they had erected between the mob and the possibility of ruling the country. Since he failed to receive a majority of the votes, the election had been thrown into the House of Representatives for settlement. There Henry Clay, himself a Kentuckian but not one of the rabble, who had finished second to Jackson in the popular vote, brokered a settlement with other factions sympathetic to preserving reasoned government. The House selected John Quincy Adams, son of the second president, who had finished third in the canvass, to become president. He was intelligent, scholarly, and earnest, hagridden to live up to his family's high legacy—a good choice as a caretaker to give the nation a breathing space while considering how to deal with the rising power of the Western section. But then Adams's unfortunate selection of Clay as his secretary of state, after Clay's engineering to make Adams president, ignited a rage of protest and resentment. That Clay was the most qualified man in the country to fill that office was lost in the charge of dishonorable collusion to thwart the democratic majority will.

Those Westerners had some good reason to feel that their majority will had been thwarted; Jackson had become their hero, and their cries of "Corrupt bargain!" gave them the added energy of grievance. In 1828 there had been no stopping them; they swept Jackson into the presidency, this time with no remedy under the Constitution to stop them. The President's House itself was all but pulled down by the horde of frontiersmen invited there to celebrate. They came freely in and out windows, caked the carpets with their muddy boots, pissed in corners and potted plants, smashed crystal and china—and in sum gave Jackson the model for how he had conducted his policies for the past six years.

"Captain?"

"Mr. Shifflette, I beg your pardon, I was in a reverie."

He made a gesture to his right. "This is where we turn up to Silver Spring, Captain. Have your men stay alert now, for the waterway is very narrow. There is no doubt the Seminoles are watching us, but they see how many we are, and how well armed. They have been told that food and supplies are being sent to them, and they see our casks and barrels, therefore they will observe us, but likely they will do nothing."

It was evening when the four boats pulled into the landing, and the boatmen unloaded them at once lest the Indians steal them in the night and discover not the foodstuffs they had been promised, but the powder and lead sent to fight them. Bliven was presented to the agent, Wiley Thompson, and was shocked to discover almost a twin of Jackson: the haughty gaze, the carefully tousled hair, the ruffled cravat spilling out the throat of a theatrically high standing collar.

The next day the Seminole chiefs were summoned to a noon meal, to be followed by the weighty exchanges of a council. Even as he found Thompson costumed for his role, the Seminoles were equal to their parts as well, dressed in a colorful, even gaudy assemblage of bright pantaloons and calico hunting shirts tied down with sashes, their heads bound in turbans, all hung with ropes of beads and chains. The marines stood through the whole proceeding, their rifled muskets at parade rest, the lieutenant and sergeant at the right of the line, the corporals with their platoons.

To Bliven's surprise, Shifflette proved to be not just their guide but also the interpreter between the Seminole chiefs and Thompson. His countenance grew increasingly worried as the tone passed from businesslike to terse to impatient and then to angry. When he saw some of the Indians reach to pull their bows from their shoulders, Bliven said quietly, "Lieutenant."

"Marines, *en garde!*" he snapped in response, and the line in one motion had their rifles in hand, bayonets pointing forward. Calm was restored, and the council dissolved with promises on the part of all to retire and consider well what the other side had said. They would set a future time to meet again.

Bliven walked the agent back to his quarters. "Mr. Thompson, do you believe you will be attacked?"

"No, no. There is little likelihood of that being imminent. They would not mount an attack unless they were in much greater numbers. What they will do is send out runners to the other bands, perhaps as far away as Apalachicola, to send warriors here. Then we will have to see."

"So you have no further need of my marines at present?"

"No. We thank you. I am aware that you must resume your voyage as soon as your ship is repaired."

"Very well." They shook hands. "I wish you luck, sir."

Bliven sought out Shifflette and asked him when they might leave, and he replied, "This instant would not be too soon."

"It is not my custom to run from a fight, but Mr. Thompson just said he did not believe they would attack."

Shifflette let out his breath, measuring how much he could risk saying, before expelling a single harrumph. "Thompson is foolish. Of course they will not attack—not in the way he expects. They will not march on Fort King by companies. Indians fight by stealth, by ambush. An arrow from behind a tree, and there is one less enemy for them to fight. Captain, are you not aware of what the Spanish peasant guerrillas did to Napoleon's troops in the Peninsular War? People will begin to disappear, and it will begin tonight, I do believe."

Bliven thought it a wonder that Shifflette should have an on-point military analogy at hand to justify his opinion. "How do you come to know about that?"

"*Mon ami*, I was there. Now, march your men down to the boats. This is not your fight."

They boarded and pushed off a quarter of an hour later. Aided by the massive surge from the Silver Spring, they made rapid progress, so much faster than going up that the men at the tillers had to be ever alert to keep from running aground in the speed of the current.

"Mr. Shifflette?"

The Creole interpreter joined him in the stern. "Yes, Captain?"

"That one main Seminole chief, the one who got more angry than anyone: What was his name?"

"Ah, that was Mickanoppee. He is one of the chiefs who never signed the treaty agreeing to move west."

"Can you tell me what was said in that great explosion he had? I could not hear you, as you were right in Mr. Thompson's ear."

"Well, let me see. He said to Mr. Thompson, 'You say our chiefs signed the agreement to leave Florida. That is not all the truth. You got them drunk and told them their women and children could not be protected unless they signed. So I say you are a liar.'"

"Is that true?"

"It is, yes. And he said, 'You accuse us of sheltering slaves that run away from you. I say: Who gave you the right to own anybody? I do not know why the great God created different colors of men, some white, some black, some red. But I think it was not so that one color may own another. What kind of heart do you have, to think this way?'"

Bliven raised a hand to his mouth. "Oh, my God."

Shifflette chuckled. "Yes. And then he continued: 'Do you think you have the right to own men because you are the most powerful? Well, then, if my people become powerful, that must give us the right to own you!' He really let him have it."

Bliven sagged and laughed. "I wish I had met him more personally."

"It gets better. Mickanoppee told him that 'seven years ago you moved us from Apalachicola to this place to separate us from the whites. You said you would feed us, and we would live here forever. You have not fed us, and now you want to take this land away. Are you trying to make us your black people? We are not your black people. You have not kept faith with us, and we will live where we choose.'"

"Well, I guess that—"

From the edge of the forest there came the slightest singing whish of a sound, and the oarsman nearest them shrieked as he dropped his oar and grabbed at his shoulder, from which the feathered shaft of an arrow protruded.

"Down!" roared Bliven.

"Marines, *en garde!*" shouted the corporal. "At the tree line, fire!" Flames and smoke obscured the bank, but they heard the balls strike earth and trees.

"Reload!"

Shifflette stood within the smoke and shouted, not sounding frightened but angry, in the Seminole language. He sat again after he repeated it in full.

The boat rocked as Bliven made his way to the injured oarsman, ripped the shirt away from the wound and examined it. "You are a lucky man: it is just a flesh wound. Try to be calm; we will have you to a doctor in a short time. Mr. Shifflette, what did you just tell them?"

"I told them to stop this nonsense, that we are on their side, that we are not going to help those bastards back at Fort King. I told them this is their land, and if they are men, they will fight for it. I wished them good fortune."

Bliven started to erupt in laughter but stifled it into a snort. "You didn't!"

"I did."

"Mr. Shifflette, that is treason."

"Not to me, and damn you if you report me."

"I? Mr. Shifflette, I do not speak a syllable of Seminole. I have no idea what you have said."

"Heh! Very well, then. I like you."

*   *   *

MICKANOPPEE—THAT WAS HIS NAME—and Bliven stamped it into his memory. The whole shameful history that this chief recited of the government's faithlessness to his people, his understanding of the relations among men, that slavery was an offense to God, struck him like a sledge on a great bronze bell. Clarity might argue natural law against slavery, but to hear the same from a man of nature himself was a heavier weight of shot altogether. It made sense to him now. And this whole six months—the Antilles, Jamaica, Haiti, the Bahamas, and now this—it was not possible that God had rubbed Bliven's nose in every aspect and permutation of slavery to no purpose.

And its purpose, he greatly feared, was not just to stoke his revulsion of slavery and other forms of dominating other men that were its functional equal, such as Jackson's treatment of the Indians. Its purpose might not be to make him doubt his own patriotism, for his more than thirty years' service in some of the most godforsaken corners of the globe attested his devotion to duty. But these events with the Seminoles, and knowing Jackson was behind them—indeed, Jackson's very rise to power—had caused him to question where his duty and honor lay when his government had become unrecognizable, when the Constitution he had sworn to protect had been so subverted that the government itself had become a grotesque of itself, led by a strutting egotist who was in it to aggrandize his own lust for power.

His awareness was not that he should find any cure for the nation's ills but that he could, and must, answer for his role in it, or else refuse to take that role. Such a freshness of mind made the following days speed by: Back to St. Augustine and the ship, which he found repaired, after a fashion, with the upper reach of the foretopmast now inserted as a stubby new bowsprit, and the foremast itself shortened, with no fighting top but still able to mount its course and topsail. They stood out into a favorable southerly wind and the push of the Gulf Current, from where it was only eight days home. Never before, as they rose off the port bow, had first sight of the greenfringed white dunes of Cape Cod drawn tears from his eyes. But they did now, and he had a mind never again to see them from this angle, from the sea looking toward home.

2

---•◦•---

The Nunnery

Since Bliven's youth, the harbor in the Charlestown Navy Yard had been deepened and the pilot, notwithstanding their cropped foremast and stubby bowsprit, was able to guide the vessel up to the wharf and make fast the bow and stern lines that arrested the last of their motion while never making contact between hull and quay. It was wonderful to watch such a master in action.

The morning's business was quickly dispensed. His report on their cruise to the Caribbean and unexpected cooperation with the Army in Florida was already written, and a letter to Clarity was ready to post that he would be home in a few days. The purser began discharging the crewmen's debts and paying them the remainder in a mix of scrip and silver, hearing but not listening to their imprecations against his ruinous rates for the slops that he withheld from their pay.

Shortly after midday there were three raps on the door, and Ross entered before being bidden. "Your pardon, Captain, some visitors are coming aboard."

"Am I needed?"

He was already shaking out Bliven's coat. "You will want to come up."

Bliven made it clear from his expression that he expected more, but Ross turned him around to slip his coat on. "By God, Mr. Ross, but you are enigmatic today. A little clarity would be welcome."

"Well, sir, a little Clarity is just what you shall have." He opened the door and gave him a slight push down the gun deck.

As his meaning became clear Bliven walked faster, then broke into a lope to the ladder, which he bounded up in a staccato of hard soles onto the wooden steps. "My God, Clarity!" He seized her and held her tightly. "Oh, my love, what on earth are you doing here?"

"Well, we were just passing by." She pulled back, stretched up, and kissed him earnestly. "Welcome home, Bliv."

"I can't believe it!"

"Dearest, you remember our friend, Reverend Beecher."

Bliven had not noticed him until that moment. "Of course, Reverend!" They shook hands. "I am astonished. I thought you were in Ohio. Have you returned?" He almost added a witty inquiry whether Beecher had come back to renew his warfare with heathen Unitarians, but held back until he should know what new fray he might find himself in.

"Only for a brief sojourn."

My God, how he has aged, thought Bliven. When they first met, a decade before the reverend relocated from Long Island to Litchfield, Bliven was fifteen and a lieutenant, while Beecher was twenty-seven.

At that time he seemed almost old enough to be his parent, but now the dozen years between them seemed hardly worth mentioning, except for the change in Beecher's visage. His mouth had advanced from down-turning to cruel, his eyes from sad to—Bliven could not find a word, but his face, he was sure, had continued to slide, as though melting from the sheer heat of the zeal within.

It was Clarity's voice that brought him back. "We have taken rooms at the old inn on the Salem Turnpike."

"Of course you would. Which half?"

"On Putnam Street, of course."

Beecher let his gaze stray up into the rigging. "It gives your wife pleasure to remind me from time to time of your historic name."

Indeed, it did always give Bliven a surge of family pride to stay on the street that was named, not for his famous great-uncle, Major General Israel Putnam, but for the general's first cousin Seth, known as the Squire, one of Charlestown's leading figures and the early owner of the property.

"Do you know, dearest?" She took his hand. "We shall be among the last patrons there. The property has been bought by Mr. Rice, the shipwright, and it is said he means to restore it to a private residence again."

Bliven winced. "Oh, too bad! But, really, it makes sense. The lot is so small, and there are so few rooms, it could never be very profitable again."

"Do you know, Captain," said Beecher, "this is the first time I have ever greeted you on the deck of one of your ships."

"Why, so it is! Enjoy the sight, for she will be retired presently."

Clarity laid her other hand on Beecher's arm. "Bliv, our reverend friend is staying at the inn as well. The whole city from Boston north is chock-full of people who came to hear him preach. The Salem Turnpike was the only place left with accommodations. Reverend Beecher delivered sermons in three several churches, all on yesterday, and ended up at the Town Hill Church. He is the very talk of the town."

"Indeed, Reverend? Well done. What was your topic?"

Beecher drew himself up. "Popery, its seductions and its evils."

Bliven clasped his hands behind his back in the fashion of officers in conversation. "Oh, my. Then you should have been with me when I was late in Florida. The commandant at the old Spanish fortress in St. Augustine showed me some rooms recently discovered that had been sealed up. One of them was a torture chamber, thoroughly medieval, with the remains of a rack from the days of the Inquisition. You would have found it edifying."

"Good God!"

"He said when the room was first opened, they also found a skeleton within."

"Well, then," said Beecher. "You see what life was like when they held sway. Here and today they are not in power, and they must be more subtle to the public perception, but make no mistake: they are ever at it, laying the foundations to take over. And if they ever do come again to power, look out! And now you know, too, for you have seen the evidence."

Bliven scanned his gaze about. He had known some very fine Catholics, none of whom had evinced any desire to establish Roman rule in America, and thought it better to change the conversation. "Good Lord! Is that still Freddy driving you? Freddy, hello!"

From the open barouche Fred Meriden smiled broadly and waved.

"Whither goest we now?" asked Beecher grandly. "Back to the inn? Are you freed from your duties, Captain, to accompany us?"

"Yes, quite. I have made my report, the crew is mostly discharged, for the ship is to be stricken from the list."

"So you just said," noted Beecher quietly. "One reads that among seamen the retirement of their vessel is an occasion of some emotion."

"So it is, yes, in all honesty. She has seen us safely through many dangers, and I will not deny that I will miss her." His gaze ascended to a gull swooping with a cry between the main and mizzen. "Doubtless she will become a receiving hulk somewhere. If you will go on down and join Mr. Meriden, we will be along in a moment. I must go down and let my steward know that we are leaving."

"Of course." Beecher paused at the boarding gate, eyeing the narrow gangplank as he would an enemy before descending it.

Bliven preceded Clarity down the ladder, holding her hand tightly as she descended after him. When they were out of sight he drew her to himself again, kissing her long and tenderly. "How on earth did you know I was back?"

They began walking aft to the captain's suite. "I didn't!" She beamed. At forty-seven herself, it was astonishing how she had kept the key features of her youth, her high cheeks and merry eyes, even with the gray streaking her honey-colored hair. "I truly didn't. We went for a drive to let the reverend rest from his preaching on yesterday. I knew the Navy Yard was proximate, and I had Mr. Meriden bring us over so I could inquire when you might be expected. They said, 'He is over there, right now, docked early on this morning.' Is that not astonishing luck?"

"So it seems Reverend Beecher is better paid than he was formerly. I thought when he traveled that he accepted the hospitality of his parishioners."

Clarity used their moment alone to draw him close again and threaded an arm around his waist. "Normally, yes, but with such a tour de force of preaching in one day, we thought it well to give him a private place for complete rest and quiet. And with so many people offering to open their homes for him, he could not accept lodging from one without giving offense to a score of others. Besides, the nearest church to this place is the Second Congregational, Reverend Dr. Walker, and he has gone over to the Unitarians. Truly I can tell you there is no truck between him and Dr. Beecher."

"Ah, the dread Unitarians." He looked down at her, never so glad to be with her, and smirked. "My hackles rise. We are paying for his room, aren't we?"

"Yes, dearest. Do you mind?"

"Bah! No, we can afford it." He made the arrangements with Alan Ross that he should follow in about a week's time and bring any letters or papers that needed attention. Bliven and Clarity walked slowly back down the gun deck, empty of crew, their view unobstructed the whole distance to the sick bay in the curve of the bow, so that they could hear their footfalls echo back to them.

"This was a noisy place in a fight, I'll warrant," she said.

"Oh, you have no idea."

"Oh, look!" She indicated the camboose far forward, against the mass of the foremast as it descended to its footing. "Is that where they do the cooking? Oh, please, may I see?"

"You run ahead, I will follow." Here was his wife in the midst of her middle age, but she was still capable of the most instant ignition into passion. It made him smile every time he was reminded how well he had chosen.

She approached it, finding its fire tamped but the stove still warm from cooking the morning's meal for the remaining crew. She tried every box and compartment, opened and closed every flue and damper, assayed the rack of enormous pots and kettles. "Oh, this is incredible, to cook for hundreds on a single giant stove! Polly would be beside herself if she could see this."

He joined her. "How is Polly?"

"She is well. She still misses my mother, of course, but it comforts her to know she will always be in our family. This is made of a very heavy gauge of iron, is it not?"

"Yes. It is used almost constantly for months at a time."

She sated her curiosity and they started back to the ladder. "And these are the pumps here?" She tapped her foot on the side of a large brass bulb bolted to the deck, at the foot of its elm tree. "And those must be the levers stored up there. Oh, if I had been born a man, this might have been the life for me."

"Well, I thank God you were not." He wrapped an arm around her as they walked on, grateful that it appeared she did not blame him for his long absences, grateful that she had found life and purpose beyond being his wife. Surely it was now time to reward her by coming home. "Come, we mustn't keep them waiting any longer. Dear old *Rappahannock.*" He cast his gaze down the ruler-straight file of cascabels of the long twenty-fours, ready to be lifted off their carriages and stored. "It is a queer thing to outlive your ship. I would almost rather take her out and sink her than see her become a hulk." Clarity rested her head against his chest, and he rested his chin atop her head. "My bosun, Mr. Yeakel, has been with her since she first touched water. I don't know what he will do now. He says he may leave the Navy."

They ascended the ladder once more. "Are you thinking to give him a job as you did Mr. Ross?"

"Ha! Not much call for rigging on the farm. He would never do it anyway; ships are all he knows, or cares to know. Doubtless he will find civilian employment. I gave him a letter of introduction."

"That is all well, then. Oh, my! It occurs to me you are going home quite suddenly and shall be without Mr. Ross for some days."

"Yes."

"Will that not be a trial for you? I shall watch with interest to see if you can still dress and undress yourself without your valet."

He placed his lips against her ear. "My love, in a few hours' time you will see how nimbly I can undress myself."

They ambled to the boarding gate. "Well," she said, "if you get confused, I will help you."

He let her pass first down the gangplank. "Mind your footing. I don't want to jump in after you."

It was almost superfluous to be driven to the inn, for it was always the quickest of journeys. At the boundary of the Navy Yard they crossed the turnpike at Adams Street and made a short rightward curl to the near corner of the Training Field. There they turned left onto Common Street, where the second half of the block consisted of one house of the inn, and then turned left onto Putnam Street to the front door of the older portion, the entire trip traversing only about two hundred yards.

The dining room lay in a single-story extension beyond the inn's office and had windows that looked out onto the Training Field, which was the heart of the city and a daily, indeed constant, re-minder of Charlestown's proud heritage. Militia volunteers had drilled on this ground since 1632—two years more than two centuries previous—including those who fell to the British in the Battle of Bunker Hill in 1775, which took place two blocks farther north.

It was nearly nine in the evening when the four of them began their supper, a steaming corn chowder followed by roast beef with parsnips and peas. They were barely half-finished when from the windows of the dining room they saw a stream of people, all walk-ing swiftly in one direction across the Training Field and spilling from its northern corner onto High Street toward Bunker Hill. Voices, excited but indistinct, penetrated the windows.

Bliven raised his hand. "Waiter? Waiter! What is this commotion outside, do you know?"

"Have you not heard, sir? The nunnery is on fire on Mount Bene-dict Hill."

"Oh, my heavens!"

"Well, they have been asking for it, sir, haven't they? The word is that at least one of their students is being held there against her will and forced to participate in all that bizarre kneeling and crossing themselves and whatnot."

"Yes," intoned Beecher, "it has been an outpost of the devil these past seven years. If they are ablaze now it is but a foretaste of their future."

"I am not so certain, Reverend," said Clarity. "I have heard that only very few of their students are of the Roman faith and that the education they receive is of the best quality. You know the majority of them are needy and would otherwise receive no schooling at all."

"Exactly the class that they prey upon!" insisted Beecher. "They are the perfect combination of ignorant and vulnerable—and grateful!"

Bliven gave a single swipe at his lips with his napkin. "Freddy, come quickly. We must go see if we can help. Reverend, will you come?"

Beecher stared down at his plate. "God's will be done."

Bliven stared at him in a moment of disbelief. "God's will be done and the devil take you, then. Come on, Freddy!"

As they sat, suddenly alone, Beecher cut once more into his meat. "My dear Mrs. Putnam, I am shocked. Your husband has not seen you for the greater part of a year, and on the evening of your reunion he not only deserts you but does so to fly to the aid of a nest of papists. I say, I am shocked. Whatever shall you say to him when he returns?"

Clarity rose from the table, so slowly and evenly that she seemed to levitate, her eyes never leaving Beecher's, disbelieving that he would ask such a thing, and he also stood according to custom but uncomfortable in the movement. "He has gone to help fight a fire in the hottest time of the summer," she said. "When he returns, I shall have a basin of cool water waiting for him, and towels. I shall wash the soot from his face and I will say, 'Well done, my dearest love.' Good night, Reverend."

Taken aback, he bowed. "Your servant, ma'am." When she had left the room he observed his unfinished portion, sat again, and tucked the napkin into the front of his collar.

TOGETHER BLIVEN AND FREDDY walked fast across the Training Field to its northern corner, where Adams and Winthrop met to become High Street. They followed the throng as they passed Bunker

Hill and, to their astonishment, heard curses uttered against the portion of it that had become the Catholic cemetery. "Look at that," spat one. "This sacred spot of American freedom, taken over as a burying ground for the damned Romanists. If their convent is burning, it is well and truly done."

They followed on perhaps a third of a mile to the Neck, where Charlestown's principal streets angled together, and saw the two bridges on their right that crossed the Charles River. Ahead of them they could clearly see the glow and occasional lick of flame. The crowd, far from growing tired, quickened its pace.

They reached the foot of Benedict Hill and saw at its low summit an imposing three-story building, fully engulfed in flames. Just inside the property's gate they stopped short and stared in disbelief. "What is this?" breathed Bliven. "I had thought these people were coming to fight the fire. Look: they are making fun and parading and celebrating!"

At forty-seven, Bliven Putnam had never yet seen a riot. He had seen Berber corsairs on the deck of their xebec, hooting and gesturing, and seen the glint of their scimitars brandished to frighten their quarry into a quick surrender. And he had seen Malay Boogis and Hawaiian *kahunas* employing the same intimidation, but these were Americans.

He had always assumed, without actually dwelling in thought on it, that by living under the same government, with similar educations and shared values and experience, riots would never occur to them. Even more so, this was Boston, the center of culture and learning. Yet here they were, with clubs and pitchforks and firebrands hefted above their heads. Several barrels of pitch had been set alight around the grounds to better illuminate the revelry. Some men stood together in groups, smoking cigars. "This is an outrage!" He stepped forward, his hand moving to the hilt of his sword.

Meriden caught him by the arm. "I wouldn't, Captain. I make at least five hundred men to your one. You would be lucky if all they did to you was douse you in tar and feathers and ride you around the grounds on a rail. I could not answer to your wife if I let that happen."

Bliven's shoulders sagged. "You are right, of course. Look, there." He pointed to a bonfire some hundred feet in front of the burning building, around which cavorted a dozen or so men wearing the Ursuline habit over their own clothes. To one side lay a giant mound of books. "It is obvious that they ransacked the building before torching it, which gives ample evidence of the forethought of their actions, and that will weigh against them at their trial."

"Trial?" Meriden looked at him quizzically, his eyes wide. "Do you see anyone here to arrest them?"

"Come, then." He pulled Fred Meriden by the elbow. "We shall mingle in an approving manner, but mark well the faces of the leaders, that we may identify them later."

They approached the book burning and discovered it presided over by one particular man, tall and with an angular face and a beard like a whaling captain. He had draped himself in a black scapular, but not knowing how to assemble the headgear satisfied himself to drape a white underveil over his head. Before a part of the throng, he picked up each book in turn, opened it and announced its title, and asked the mob, "What shall we do with it?"

"Burn it!" they roared, and cheered as he cast it into the blaze.

As they stood there they saw one clot of men enter the chapel, which was a small building that stood a distance apart from the school. Within seconds six of them emerged carrying a coffin, and they came at a run across the hill to the bonfire. There they broke it open and extracted the desiccated remains of a nun in her habit and cast her into the fire.

One of the ladies in the mob cried out, "Burn in hell, you witch!"

Meriden put his lips at Bliven's ear. "How appropriate. Reliving our history."

They heard one woman ask a laughing pall bearer, "I heard that is where they have also buried the babies that were born here. Have you found their bodies?"

"No," he answered. "You may be sure they have been very cleverly hidden. The crypt is full, but rest assured we will find them."

Further men came with a second and third and fourth coffin. Each one they broke open and threw its deceased nun into the flames.

Leaving Meriden to make his own exploration, Bliven stalked around the side of the building, a safe distance from the wall should it collapse. He passed a party of eight or ten men stretched out on the grass, cutting cheese on a plate and eating it on crackers, and stopped to stare at them. "Glass of wine, Captain?" offered one.

"Thank you, no, I am . . . looking for someone."

Continuing to the rear of the building, he saw in the distance a nun standing in the convent garden, gazing at the fire. She observed him when he was yet a distance away. He approached her, giving a quick but correct salute. "Captain Putnam, ma'am, United States Navy. Are you all right?"

"Yes, thank you, Captain. I am Mary Edmond St. George, the Mother Superior of the order here."

"Are your people safe?"

"Yes. There was sufficient warning for all the sisters and the students to escape to the house of a friend of ours, on Winter Hill. It is not far."

"I am glad to hear it."

"Most importantly, we were also able to save the Eucharist." She smiled sadly and pointed to some freshly turned earth in a large patch of tall, feathery green ferns. "It seems the Host is now defended by spears—of asparagus."

Bliven smiled. The asparagus in mention was long past its stage of harvesting the spears, and had been allowed to grow up to flower and seed; he appreciated her presence of mind, and her humor. He shook his head. "Reverend Mother, I am so ashamed of all of them. Did you not see, they emptied the chapel of your dead sisters and cast them onto the fire."

"I did see, my son, and it caused me great pain. I served with those sisters for many years and they were dear friends to me. But the Bible tells us that this corruptible shall put on incorruption. My departed sisters are safe in the arms of the Lord. This vandalism of their bodies does not alter their bliss in paradise."

He stared at her, astonished and searching. "I am at a loss, ma'am. Until this moment I never could have supposed my countrymen capable of such *lunacy*."

"Captain"—she laid her hand on his arm—"did you suppose that just because you live in the United States, with your aspiration to all that lovely equality and democracy, that your people are not prey to the same ignorance and prejudice as people everywhere?"

"Yes. Yes, I suppose I did." Through his coat sleeve he felt her squeeze his arm hard, and he studied her face. He guessed she was fifty, pale and lined. Above her long black scapular her face was framed in the white of her coif and guimpe, her crown band and underveil, all white, either bright or pale according to the rage of the fire. "Is there no one to fight the blaze?" he asked.

"Indeed, yes," she said with a kind of sarcastic enthusiasm. "They are on the grounds at this moment, four different volunteer fire brigades."

He stared at her, his face slack.

"You just passed by one of them: those gentlemen there, lying on the grass, eating cheese on crackers. If they tried to fight the fire—that is, if they had such a disposition—the mob would prevent them, and there might be violence. We would not wish that. The rioters will disperse when they have vented their evil. We can rebuild the convent and we can replace the books. We just give thanks to God that no one has been hurt."

"Your accent is French, Reverend Mother."

"I am *québécoise*, a safely Catholic place. We came here at the call of your bishop in Boston to open the school for the children of your poor, and the immigrants." Her voice took a tone of censure. "Your own wealthy class have done nothing for them."

"Yes, my wife has told me that your school's reputation was—is—quite excellent."

"Your wife? Oh, forgive me, Captain! Is she the famous Mrs. Putnam, the authoress of the adventure novels?"

He laughed quickly and loudly. "Her fame outshines me once again."

"Oh, my goodness! Hers are among the few novels that we allow our girls to read. Her account of your missionaries in the Sandwich Islands was quite thrilling." She shrugged. "They were not Catholic, of course, but the larger lesson was the lengths to which they went to help those poor natives."

"It will not surprise you, Reverend Mother, to learn that my wife was truly there and that she knew intimately the people of whom she wrote. My wife may write stories that are fiction, but she infuses them with so many true events that they could well stand as histories."

Mother Mary Edmond St. George nodded. "I am not surprised." Just then they heard a series of tremendous crashes. Their gaze shot up to the convent in time to see its roof collapse into the third floor, which further collapsed into the second and then the ground floor. The garden grew suddenly bright as day in the tall geyser of flame and sparks that shot up from the burning shell, and they heard a distant cheer rise from the mob.

Bliven thought, *This is ridiculous.* "Reverend Mother, we are standing in the light of your burning convent, and you register no grief, no outrage. You converse as calmly as if you were at a garden party."

She inclined her head at the spectacle. "Things, my son. A grand building, to be sure, with simple but solid furnishings. It is a mistake to attach one's self to things. Attachment to God is the only permanence, and this the mob cannot touch. That is the lesson I am trying to draw from this tragedy." She sighed heavily. "And now I beg you to excuse me, I must get back to our friend's house and see to the comfort of the sisters and the students. We will come look tomorrow"—her face grew ineffably sad—"and we will see if there is anything left to salvage." She extended her hand, and he took it. "Captain Putnam, I thank you for your kindness. Bishop Fenwick shall hear of it."

* * *

IT WAS PAST two o'clock in the morning when he opened the door to their room in the inn on Putnam Street and found Clarity still awake and dressed. "Dearest," she asked, "how was it?"

"I hardly know what to say." He unbuckled his sword, flung his coat into a chair, and sank onto the couch. "The fire was deliberate. It was arson. There was a mob, jeering and hooting. I never saw such a thing in the darkest corners of the world. And do you know what else? Not content with burning the school, they took the trouble to loot their library first and made a separate bonfire on the lawn before it. One of their ringleaders read out the title of each book and was cheered as he cast it into the blaze."

"God in heaven! Please tell me that no one was injured."

"Thankfully, that was a mercy. The nuns and the students all reached safety. I found the Mother Superior in the garden, alone, watching the fire. And do you know? She uttered not one word of condemnation." He felt he was at the edge of weeping but forbade himself. "She regretted their violence but ascribed it to their fear and ignorance. And I have no doubt in my mind that as she says her prayers even at this moment, she is forgiving them."

Clarity wrung a cloth above a basin of cool water and then sat by him, cleansing his face of sweat and soot.

"And shall I tell you the worst of it?"

"Good Lord, what more can there be?"

"The mob, as they burnt the books, called out praises on your Reverend Beecher."

She drew back. "Oh, no."

"Has he never heard that incitement to riot is a serious crime?"

"Dearest, you are shaking. I have never seen you so overwrought."

"No. No, I shake a little. It is a small affliction that I acquired in the Caribbean. It will pass. Now, there is something I must ask you." She quieted and looked at him, worried and expectant. "How many of his sermons did you attend on yesterday? All of them? Did you escort him from church to church?"

"No, dearest, I attended only the last one, here at the Town Hill Church."

"And did he hold forth against the Catholics?"

"Of course. That was his topic; he delivered the same sermon three several times. Dearest, you truly are shaking."

"It will pass. Now, think on this carefully: Did he preach against letting Protestant children be educated in a Catholic school? If so, what did he say, exactly?"

"Yes, of course. He said that a sect so avid for their perversions could not pass by such an opportunity to indoctrinate the young and innocent."

"Oh, good God. Did he utter any call to action? Did he even say something on the order of 'Somebody should do something'?"

"Certainly, Bliv. That was the whole point of his message, that it was up to the people of Boston and Charlestown and the surrounding communities to act, and to act decisively, lest their children be seduced and in time all be led into popery."

"Oh my God. Is it possible that he does not realize what he has done? If he incited them, then he is guilty along with them."

"Oh, nonsense. He had no hand in burning down the convent. And now I am going to insist that you go straightaway to bed and rest. You are clearly not well."

"No." He started to rise. "Which is his room? He must be warned that the law may come for him, even so soon as tonight."

"Oh, very well." She pressed him back onto the couch. "I shall go and speak to him. You get yourself into the bed this instant; I insist upon it."

Bliven calmed and relaxed. "Very well, my love. Send Freddy to the stable to hitch the coach. Tell Beecher that unless he wishes to be arrested, he must clear out tonight—right now. He must not pause or feel safe until he gets back to Ohio. Tell him that we can advise him in future whether he has been indicted, and when, if ever, it is safe to return. Or, if he is so certain that he has done a righteous thing, he may return and stand trial. He might exult in that, for never would so many eyes be on him. And if he is convicted, think of his joy in martyrdom."

Clarity squeezed his hand and kissed his cheek. "I shall return directly."

As soon as the door closed behind her, he stood, pausing to find his balance, and made his way to the bed. He sat on it and laughed softly to himself, perhaps in shock, for just a second. He felt cold, August though it may have been, and unfolded a quilt from the foot of the bed.

Clarity was gone so long that he fell asleep, but was alert again the instant the door opened. "What did Beecher say?"

"I knocked and there was no answer. When I tried the door I found it open and the room was empty, the bed was unmade. I went downstairs and found the proprietor still at his desk."

"At this hour?"

"Yes. It was the reverend who had awakened him. He informed me that Mr. Beecher was called away to urgent business. Two men came for him and helped him gather his things, and they all left together."

Bliven harrumphed. "Well, at least he has an instinct for self-preservation, like any beast of prey."

"How are you feeling?"

"The spell has passed, I think—and better now to know that we did not have to risk our own reputations to aid the flight of a fugitive."

"Now, we do not know that he is any stripe of fugitive, do we, dearest?" She looked to him for a reply but saw he had sunk back into deep slumber.

THE SUN WAS WELL UP when they awakened and washed, and in the dining room downed a gloomy breakfast of eggs, ham, porridge, and apple pie. Bliven ate sparingly, and was still weak, and before the front door Meriden offered his hand to help him up into the barouche. He took it. "Well, this is a hell of a thing. I am too young to be invalided."

"Oh, I know you, Captain, you will be right as rain in no time."

They settled back in the rear of the coach, Bliven relaxing with an arm extended behind Clarity, enjoying the fine summer morning before the heat could settle. Freddy drove the horses northwest up High Street, up which they had run the night before, toward Benedict Hill. "Freddy," asked Bliven, "what are we doing? Did you wish to have a look at what is left of the nunnery?"

"Not especially. I thought you might enjoy to see some new countryside on our way home. We can rest the horses in Framingham and then go on to spend the night in Worcester. Would you rather I turn back to the usual route?"

"No." He settled back, feeling a discomfort in his stomach but determining that it did not merit mention. "Not at all; well done. Do you remember the old days of Mr. Strait's coach? He went all the way down to Long Island Sound and then over. This more direct route will likely save us more than a day."

Very shortly they reached the Neck, where High Street converged with Charlestown's other principal lanes. One route split to the north and the twin bridges over the Charles River, the other to the west, past Benedict Hill. High upon it they saw the ruin of the convent, its three-story shell still standing but hollow within, a pall of smoke still wafting above it. Around it they saw four nuns in Ursuline habits, poking through the cinders and occasionally picking out and wiping off some object too small for them to see what it might be.

Clarity rose a bit from her seat as they passed. "Such an awful sight. Dearest, do you wish to stop and speak with them again?"

"No." He hesitated. "No, the Mother Superior appeared highly competent. I have no doubt they will find a way to overcome all this. She loves your books, by the way. Let us see this new scenery, Freddy." Lulled by the clip-clop of the horses, Bliven barely noticed one sign as they passed it. "What? Did that indicate a lending library?"

Clarity turned her head before it slipped from sight. "Mr. Baker's, yes."

"I thought the lending library was in Warren Hall."

Clarity looked back to the front and settled comfortably against him. "Oh, it is still there. Mr. Baker decided there must be enough people in Charlestown who would pay to borrow books that he would open a second one. I hear he has been whispering allurements to persuade people to switch their allegiance, or at least patronize both, as he has taken pains to acquire volumes that the Warren Hall library does not have."

"Oh, my tired soul," Bliven muttered. "It seems like everything is competition anymore. Did you know, last night we went to help at the fire and we saw—did you notice them?—there are now two toll bridges across the river. They span it in parallel, and so close you could throw a stone from one to the other. Is that not a frivolous waste of resources and effort?"

Clarity smirked and pulled his arm down around her. "Not a waste entirely. The lawyers are profiting, at least. You would not have heard: the proprietors of the first bridge hired the great Mr. Shaw to sue the owners of the new one to put them out of business."

"Hm! And how did they fare?"

"They lost."

"Well, perhaps both will have to lower their tolls now to compete. That will be of some public benefit, anyway."

"Oh, it's not over. Now they have hired Daniel Webster himself to take their case to the Supreme Court."

"Lucky me!" Fred Meriden looked back suddenly at them. "I suppose you could be charging me to borrow books from your library at home. But then, most of them fly far above my poor head."

"Ha!" Bliven reached forward and clapped him on the back. "Yes, old Mr. Marsh was somewhat rarified in his studies, was he not?" He settled back. "Still, my love, I am not certain that there is a call for two lending libraries."

"Well," she allowed, "the town is burgeoning, after all. More than ten thousand now just in Charlestown, one hears."

"Mostly poor laborers, from the look of things. The Catholics and those rich Unitarians, they might support a second lending library, but these people are mostly of Beecher's flock. Who needs books when they have him to tell them what is holy or profane?"

Clarity sensed a renewal coming of his eruption from the previous night. "Now, dearest, let us not reexamine it all. I want you to rest. I am certain that he means well."

"Yes," he said wearily, "but I swear, if your Reverend Beecher were any more full of horse manure, we should have to throw him on our garden. What do you think, Freddy?"

By degrees they had left the town behind for an open country lane. Meriden snapped the reins lightly onto the horses' rumps and they broke into an easy trot. "I would say, bless the libraries for at least trying to bring learning to those that need it."

"Dearest, when we reach Worcester to stay the night, Freddy neglected to tell you that I have made the friendly acquaintance of several of the ladies there."

"Oh? A reading club? Devotees of your novels?"

"It started that way, I confess, but as I got to know them, I discovered them to be ladies of formidable intellect. In fact, whenever they convene, the conversation usually turns to the subject of women and how we deserve the franchise that is now denied us."

"That women should be allowed to vote, you mean?"

"Precisely."

"Oh, fine. So now you have fallen in with a nest of seditionists?"

She looked up at him with some concern but found his eyes merry. "Wholeheartedly. Do you believe that if women could vote, the country would have been saddled with Mr. Jackson as president?"

"Lord, don't get me started on that man."

"Besides, I must have something for adventure, as I can't keep you at home."

Gently he pulled Clarity's head into the crook of his neck and spoke softly. "Well, we shall see about that, in future. We did not have much of a reunion last night, did we, my love? May we make amends tonight?"

She stretched up and kissed the bottom of his chin. "Good news, at last." Concerned, she kissed him a second time, ascertaining a slight heat radiating from his skin. "Dearest, I believe you have a fever. Do you not feel well yet?"

"Not entirely, no. I have a turning in my stomach, and my bones and my joints seem to ache."

"Freddy?"

"Ma'am?"

"When we reach Framingham, may we rest the horses only as long as necessary to reach Worcester without exhausting them?"

"Yes, I believe so."

"We can use the time to buy some bread, and cheese, and ham. We can eat on the road. My friend Mrs. Allison, in Worcester, her husband I judge to be the best doctor within a hundred miles. When we reach town, drive straight to the inn on Grafton Common where I stay. Once we get the captain settled in bed, I will show you where to find Dr. Allison."

Bliven found the road and the countryside new to him, alternately wooded and settled, of the most restful prospect and a welcome antidote for the previous night's mayhem. They crossed the Sudbury River into Framingham, where they bought food and fresh milk, and Meriden rested and watered the horses at the Harmony Grove. There, a blanket spread under a chestnut tree gave them at least as welcome a rest as the horses, for Meriden had to rouse them in an hour to resume the journey.

Grafton, he learned, was a village three miles southeast of Worcester proper and connected to it by a road along the Quinsigamond River. The inn that reposed on the east side of its common Bliven found one of the most symmetrical of buildings: five windows broad, three stories high, white clapboards with black shutters, a chimney at each of the four corners, and a hipped roof beneath a large glass cupola. At first sight he thought it one of the most beautifully designed buildings he had ever seen. He stood to dismount from the coach but quickly sat back down. "Freddy, I'm afraid you will have to help me again. I am dizzy."

With Freddy at one arm and Clarity at the other, they got Bliven's feet on the ground, and he took a moment to glance around the common. He inclined his head to a church on the west side of it. "Let me guess: That would be the Congregationalists there opposite?"

"It would indeed," said Clarity.

"Ah, well, that will explain your choice of lodging, but it appears most convenient. If I expire during the night, you won't have to go far to stage my funeral."

"Don't you even joke about such a thing. You die on me, husband, and I'll beat the living hell out of your body."

Bliven laughed suddenly and helplessly. "My Lord, when did you start swearing?"

"Well, I have heard it often happens to women who marry sailors. Have you got him, Fred? I am going to run in and change my usual room for one on the ground floor. I don't want him going up any stairs."

From the time they got him into bed, Bliven slept deeply. The next he knew, there entered a man of soft edges without being fat, who had thinning brown hair above clear brown eyes, and the most fitting expression of interest and kindness. "William Allison, physician," he introduced himself. "Captain, how are you feeling?" He reached down and took Bliven's hand as though in greeting, but then turned it over and measured his pulse.

"In truth, I have been better."

"Your wife tells me that you suffer chills, and fever."

"Yes."

"Are they constant or periodic?"

"They have set on, but mildly until now, every two or three days." Allison nodded, and Bliven took it that he nodded gravely. "Does that signify?"

"Perhaps. Where have you been in the past months? Anywhere in the tropics?" He lifted Bliven's eyelids and peered beneath.

"Yes, quite constantly, in fact. Jamaica, and Haiti, the Bahamas, and then Fort Fisher, in the interior of Florida."

"Oh, dear, that does sound steamy." From his bag Allison removed a thin tube of wood, with one end flared like a speaking trumpet. "Raise your shirt, please. Now lie very still and breathe normally. My God! That is quite a scar across your belly."

"Yes. I was a very young lieutenant in the Barbary War."

Allison felt along it and could tell that it extended deep beyond the skin. "This would have been a very dangerous wound."

"Yes, but it was expertly treated. You have heard of the eminent Dr. Cutbush?"

"What? The same who wrote the treatise on military medicine? Yes, of course."

"He was the surgeon on my ship. He gave me a silver dollar to bite on while he sewed me up, which I still have to this day."

"Oh, I envy you his acquaintance. Have you heard where he is now?"

"Still retired, I presume. I hope he has not died."

"Ho, far from it. It was just recently in the papers that at his age, when a man has earned the right to do nothing, he has removed to Geneva, in New York, to be professor of chemistry at the new college there."

"I am not surprised, for he so esteemed being useful." Bliven's voice grew wistful. "What happened to him in the Navy was a disgrace and a scandal."

Allison pressed his fingers into Bliven's stomach and lower belly. "There is no tightness or distension; that is good. You refer to his being forced out by Jackson's people?"

"I do—one of many offenses to hang upon his administration."

"Well, comfort yourself, Captain, for Dr. Cutbush is a hero to every physician I know in these parts. But look, now, we must proceed. Lie quietly." He placed the flared end of the tube against Bliven's chest and listened intently by putting his ear on a small bulb at its narrow end. "Do you ever have chest pain?"

"No, never."

"Does your family have any history of diseases of the heart?"

"No."

"No, your heart is quite sound." Allison lowered the shirt again and pressed his fingertips into Bliven's throat and neck. He pulled a chair to the bedside and sat down. "Well, now, Captain. I believe that you have returned home with a case of swamp fever; some doctors now call it malarial fever."

Clarity drew near and listened intently.

"Yes," said Bliven, "I have heard of it. I am not surprised, for the swamps were quite utterly miserable."

"Its name is from the Italian, meaning bad air, because in former times it was prevalent in the marshes around Rome."

Bliven laughed softly. "Now you even sound like Cutbush. Great one for ancient history, he was. He loved citing the works of Galen. I hope that this is not anything that I can pass to my wife?"

"No, I have never heard of such an occurrence."

"Can it be treated?"

"Yes. Do you drink?"

Bliven barked suddenly into a loud laugh that dissolved into a hard cough. "Doctor, if you treat maladies with whiskey, every sailor in the Navy would be as skilled as you."

"Hm! Well, be that as it may, there is a medicine, and it is effective, but it has such a foul and bitter taste that you could never get it down without mixing it with something more palatable."

"What is it?"

"It is called Peruvian bark. It is obtained from a tree in the forest there. I have a small quantity in my bag that you may have, and there is some more in my apothecary that I will send over to you."

Bliven held up a hand. "I often have some rum in my tea in the evening. Would that be a suitable medium?"

"Indeed, yes. Just stir a small spoon of the shaved bark into a cup of tea and rum, and some additional sugar, for I tell you it is very bitter. Let it steep a few moments to draw the medicine out of the bark, and then drink it. In fact, we may start this instant. Mrs. Putnam, can you send for some tea and rum?"

"Yes, right away. Fred?"

"I'll get it. I'll be gone only a moment."

"Also, I will send to Boston, for there is a skilled druggist there who stocks Peruvian bark already drawn into a tincture. It is called quinine water. I will obtain some of that for you."

"For how long must I take it?" asked Bliven.

"If your symptoms abate and you stop taking it, they will return. I would suggest three times a day, with a meal to get the taste out of your mouth. Continue this until I see you again. Perhaps three or four weeks after you feel completely well, we will suspend the treatment and see how you do. That is the devil of the malarial fever—if you continue to treat it, it is not that dangerous, but the spells may recur for many years. Now, listen carefully. While you are taking it, be alert for any chest pain, or if you begin to have trouble with your vision or have any other unfamiliar difficulty. If that happens, stop taking it at once and send for me."

Allison rose to leave, but Clarity caught him by the arm. "Doctor, will you do something for me?"

"If I can, ma'am, most happily."

"I wish you to write to the commandant of the Navy Yard at Charlestown. Tell him that Captain Putnam is most seriously ill with a disease acquired during his last cruise, and he is to be excused from further duty until he should learn otherwise."

"My dear wife!" Bliven roared suddenly from the bed. "The commandant is not a schoolmaster! The situation does not call for a note from home."

"Ease your mind, Mrs. Putnam." Allison laid his hand over hers. "I have written many such letters; I will know how to phrase it."

"Give my very affectionate greetings to Amy."

"I will do so, and I thank you. I will look in on our captain again tomorrow."

3

Highly Important from Texas

I t had been many years since Bliven had been home for the entirety of the apple season, from late summer as they swelled on
their branches, to early fall as they began to turn, and then daily
sampling to determine the right moment to begin the harvest. Then
there was the matter of hiring pickers; in previous years they could
depend on Beecher's tribe of children, who were happy to work for a
wage, but since their departure Fred Meriden had cultivated his own
source of seasonal labor.

It was not an easy summer for Bliven. The swamp fever retained
its grip on him through the hot weather, one of the fiercest sieges of
dry heat that anyone could remember—enough to make him fear
for the apples hanging in the orchard. When the heat finally broke
with sweeps of cool rain, the apples seemed to race to catch up. Their
flavor was not as affected as he feared they would be, but as any
winemaker could testify, not every year produced a fine vintage.

For Bliven himself, Dr. Allison and his quinine water did their office; the malarial fever abated by degrees, until by harvest time he was keen to begin rebuilding his strength. The harvest provided equal measures of growing effort: first by observing the pickers at their work and occasionally scolding one who he saw pick up some windfalls and toss them into the basket. Nothing would ruin cider faster than using apples from the ground after the fruit wasps had gotten to them. Bliven found himself enjoying washing the apples and, when he felt up to it, taking a turn grinding them into the pomace and ultimately operating the great screw press. *Newspapermen,* he thought, *believe they have such a physical job at their printing presses; let them try their hand at this for a while.*

By the time the first succession of frosts had silenced the fields, he was himself again. Since the death of his mother, they had converted his parents' former bedroom into a library, paneled in the finest walnut and supplied, as they had long intended, with the best books from old Marsh's library. Clarity's mother had lasted doggedly into an extended dotage, emerging from her seclusion on enough occasions to retain her position as one of Litchfield's last connections to its earlier days, the last Marsh who could recall much of the revolutionary days and the town's rise to social and cultural prominence. As those days receded, both of the town's former bulwarks of education, the Pierce sisters and their female academy, and Mr. Justice Reeve's celebrated law school, passed from the scene the previous year. Sarah Pierce was now nearing seventy and retired from public life with a sense of accomplishment, and a long roster of women who knew very well that they were among the best educated of their sex in the nation. Old Tapping Reeve passed away soon after their return from the Sandwich Islands, and the law school was kept going by his associate Mr. Gould for another decade. Clarity judged that Reeve had left a far more mixed legacy than the Pierce sisters: two of his graduates, John Calhoun and Aaron Burr, who was also his brother-in-law, she regarded as scoundrels of such ability that they could damage the fabric of the Republic itself. On the other hand, Reeve had set the engine in motion to free the slaves in New England by taking on the cause of "Mum Bett" Freeman of Massachusetts. Even as the revolution was at its most fierce, he won his case by cleverly and successfully citing the words of that rebellious state's daring constitution, that "all men are created free and equal." Sometimes when you stage a revolution, Clarity realized, people will hold you to your rhetoric, and either you acquiesce or you become known as a hypocrite. Then, too, it was old Reeve who had convinced Reverend Beecher to relocate from Long Island to Litchfield. Although she was acquainted with him only through Beecher, she judged his life sufficiently meritorious that when he died at an advanced age back in 1823, she and Bliven attended his funeral respectfully in the rear rank of mourners.

Still, the fall of these two former pillars of Litchfield's culture, notwithstanding that they were succeeded by others equally worthy, left a sense that their past was slipping away, and that the town was sliding slowly down the hierarchy of prominence. At the turn of the last century it had been the fourth largest community in Connecticut, but at the next census in 1840 they might show to be tenth, or twelfth, for the great avenue of commerce developed along the coast, in New Haven and Bridgeport, and the burgeoning new industry of hunting whales for their lamp oil was centered in New London and New Bedford. And there was a spur of business that extended up the Connecticut River through Hartford, which was halfway between

New Haven and Springfield in Massachusetts. From all this Litch-field was removed, and began to blend into Connecticut's restful, rural background, bucolic but not ignorant, unhurried but not indo-lent. Bliven and Clarity found great contentment there, from their shared history but also from its present attitude toward the world. They had no desire to remove, in their mature years, to any scene of greater activity.

The religious atmosphere had moderated since the Beechers de-parted for Ohio, and even the Unitarians gained a foothold—a tell-ing testament to the weight that a single advocate could press onto his community, given he was dedicated and ferocious enough. Lyman Beecher had sold his high, drafty house, where Clarity had encouraged young Harriet in her composition, and where poor Roxana had birthed Beecher children until she died of sheer over-production. After Beecher left for Ohio with Harriet in tow as his scribe, their Litchfield house declined under a careless and distracted new owner, which saddened Clarity to see, and made her feel the more fortunate that they had sold the Marsh manse on favorable terms, salvaging the library, saving numerous fine furnishings or those of sentimental value, and bringing Polly down to the farm as their housekeeper.

Bliven had taken to spending chilly mornings in the library by the Franklin stove they installed, under a blanket in old Marsh's *chaise longue*. It seemed an indolent posture, but in his middle age he had noticed his ankles beginning to swell as a day progressed, and he felt he had earned the privilege of keeping his feet up when he could. Clarity encouraged his time in the library as the most effective in-centive to make him finally retire from the Navy, and she took out subscriptions to newspapers from all over the Northeast to keep his mind from wandering back to sea. The one he came to favor above the others was the *Boston Atlas*; it was in business for only three years so far, but was capably edited, included the most important news, and was strongly Whig in its opinions, which was agreeable to them both.

Bliven did not know that Dr. Allison had fulfilled his promise to inform the Navy of his illness until he began receiving letters inquiring into his health from old friends in the service: Hull, Jones, Downes, even Miller, which delighted him. There was no mention of a further assignment through the winter, but then, he expected none before spring. His sons came home from their respective schools for Christmas—Ben from Yale College and Luke from boarding school in New Haven. He took them hunting on their property near Cornwall, inquired into their studies and their interests. Ben he found as domestically dutiful as his namesake old Benjamin had been; to his surprise it was Luke who reminded him more of himself: restless, inquisitive, unsatisfied. Both seemed deeply happy to have their father in residence, and if they resented his long absences, they said nothing of it. Instead they were enthralled by his moment-by-moment accountings of Barbary pirates, of having the *Tempest* shot from beneath him off Brazil, of having walleyed native priests charge at him in the Sandwich Islands. Clarity observed all this, hoping and praying that he would find this newly discovered domestic bliss more than he could bear to leave again. She would not ask directly but was determined to rekindle their former romance and maintain her own active intellectual life to match his in case she failed.

The spring thaw of 1835 was well underway, with the first green grass and crocuses, when Bliven noticed he had received nothing from the Navy other than monthly drafts for his half-pay. He began to wonder if, perhaps, like old Dr. Cutbush, his opinion of Andrew Jackson had become known and he had been quietly dropped from the Navy's rolls. But then Dr. Allison provided a less political theory of the case when he admitted that after sending them first word of his malarial fever, he had not written anyone news of his improving condition and now apparent recovery. What thrilled Clarity was the fact that he did not seem to mind. He and Meriden and the boys planted heavily that spring, including a new field that he had purchased across the road and farther south. They dug and lined with rocks a second root cellar, so that in coming years they would be all but self-sufficient. They entertained, as Clarity took advantage of the church's less strident doctrine and took a more social part, bringing home those whom Bliven would find the most interesting.

With the first spell of summer's humid heat he felt again the slight dizzy chill and resumed his taking of quinine water with his tea, and as he never gave the malady a chance to take hold, it did not persist. Its mere reappearance, however, prompted Clarity to enlist Dr. Allison as an ally in suggesting that he was not yet ready for duty. Putnam Farm's fields and orchard produced another crop, excellent fruit this year, and Meriden had enough help that Bliven allowed himself on chilly mornings to lie up in the library on the *chaise longue* by the stove once more, with the newspapers, and books, and now with frequent callers.

IT WAS ALMOST NOVEMBER, the harvests were in, the boys were long back at school, and more than once Bliven found himself thinking what a happy thing it would be if this was what life would be like after the Navy. Their *Boston Atlas* came to be the first newspaper that they read each day. The number for the twenty-sixth contained an article that caught his eye especially. It was on the second page, and it was distant news, reprinted from the paper in Cincinnati, but the headline was urgent and declamatory and demanded attention. "HIGHLY IMPORTANT FROM TEXAS! WAR!!" The article had originated in New Orleans, dated October 13, 1835, less than two weeks previous. The news must have been brought by special courier to Cincinnati and been of signal importance.

He looked up at a rustle in the doorway and saw Clarity enter, pushing their wheeled tea cart, laden with a silver service and cakes. After their return from the Pacific, they had sampled various teas from China before settling upon Young Hyson, picked green and tightly rolled without the violence of chopping and roasting. The first time he had tried it, Bliven recognized it as the same golden-yellow tea that Nathan Dunn had served him in China, pungent and grassy. It needed no milk or sugar, but Bliven had grown fond of it with a spoon of honey and just a dash of rum, and when necessary two spoons of honey to offset his reduced dosage of quinine water, which at Dr. Allison's next visit he would inquire about eliminating altogether. The rum, of course, he had learned from Beecher in his youth, but in all the intervening years he had never betrayed the reverend's confidence.

"Tea, dearest," she said.

"Excellent. Thank you. Listen to this." He repeated the article's opening declamation and read further, "'War in Texas. General Cos landed near the mouth of the Brazos with four hundred men.'" He mumbled, "And so on, so on," omitting the journalist's sources and obsequies, then read more deliberately again, "'with the intention of joining the seven hundred federal troops stationed at San Antonio de Béxar, and marching upon the people in Texas. He has issued his proclamation, declaring that he will collect the revenue, disarm the citizens, establish a military government, and confiscate the property of the rebellious.' And so on . . . There is more—ah. 'Stephen F. Austin has written to several citizens of Nacogdoches, that a resort to arms is inevitable.'"

"Oh, dear. That does sound ominous."

"I should write to Sam and make sure he is not in any danger."

Clarity huffed. "Knowing Mr. Bandy, he is likely in the very middle of it, or perhaps the cause of it."

"Oh, pooh. Well, it goes on. There are several dispatches attached to the article. Here is one, a letter sent by one of the American leaders. 'War in defence of our rights, our oaths and our constitution, is inevitable in Texas! If volunteers from the United States will join their brethren in this section they will receive liberal bounties of land.'" Bliven looked up from his copy of the *Atlas*. "Well, there it is. That explains how news got here so fast, they want volunteers."

"Yes, I see."

"'We have millions of acres of our best lands,'" he read on, "'unchosen and unappropriated. Let each man come with a good rifle and one hundred rounds of ammunition—and come soon. Our war cry is "liberty or death." Our principles are to support the constitution, and *down with the usurper!!* Your friend, Sam Houston.'"

"Houston!" Clarity burst out laughing. "Was he not that fellow from Tennessee a few years ago? He was in Jackson's entourage, I think, and utilized that association to win favor and become governor, then had to resign and flee the state after a marital scandal, am I right?"

"Your memory is as accurate as it is unsparing."

"And now he turns up in Texas to lead an American rebellion? How convenient, after Jackson has failed for years to buy the province from Mexico!"

Bliven smiled gently. "We should move to Washington. Your powers of forecast are much wanted in the State Department."

"Bah! If I were a man I would die before I would serve in Jackson's government."

"Yes, a sentiment that I share, but you could prove useful in advising this new Whig Party in how to oppose him."

Clarity inclined her head in acknowledgment. "Thank you, dearest. But come, now, does the timing of all this not suggest that if there is trouble now among the Americans in Texas, it must be Jackson who is pulling the strings?"

Bliven leaned back and took a long, satisfying sip of the Young Hyson. "That may be," he said at last. "But look: that Austin fellow seems in on it, too, and he has been loyal to Mexico from the start, at least until they put him in jail for wanting Texas to have its own statehood within their confederation."

"True," she said, "that was pretty extreme punishment for not much of an offense. That new president they have down there—what is his name?"

"General Santa Anna."

"He sounds like a hard case."

"Yes. Do you remember reading about it? Last spring, he tore up their constitution and began ruling by personal decree. Several states rebelled against him and were crushed for their trouble. Santa Anna allowed his soldiers to sack one city near the capital, called Zacatecas, and they massacred thousands."

Clarity nodded and smiled. "Only you would remember the name of the place. You looked it up in the atlas, I'll wager."

"Yes . . . yes, I did."

"But I do seem to recall it. And I imagine that the Americans in Texas did not take kindly to having their constitution taken away and replaced by military decree."

Bliven sipped more tea. "Right. So, if Jackson is indeed encouraging an American revolt in Texas, Santa Anna is most admirably playing into his hand."

Clarity sagged. "Jackson in Washington and Santa Anna in Mexico. My God, you can't shake a stick on this continent without hitting a tyrant."

"Then let us shake no sticks." Bliven rose and set his cup onto the cart and picked up a cake. "We shall have nothing to do with them, and just now this aging Cincinnatus is going out to the cider mill and see how Freddy is doing."

Further news items received in the coming week described in greater detail how, on the second of October, 1835, several dozen American colonists in Mexican Texas had opened fire on Mexican troops. It seemed that four years previous, the military garrison in San Antonio had lent the community of Gonzales, some fifty miles distant, a small cannon as an aid in defense against Indians. Now, as trouble in Texas threatened, the commander dispatched a company of dragoons to reclaim the gun so that it could not be used against the government if the discontent should grow into rebellion. When they arrived in Gonzales, they were met, on the opposite side of a coursing river, by a flag depicting the cannon, over the legend "COME

AND TAKE IT." It was the American colonists who crossed the river, turned the gun on the Mexican dragoons, and scattered them.

Cos must have sailed long before news of this reached Mexico, and he would have learned of it as he landed his army to march to San Antonio and establish military authority. Volunteers were gathering from all over the American colonies in Mexico, and there seemed now to be no way to avoid a war. Bliven had written to Sam, but he would not expect any reply for at least two months. Of the American newspapers, by and large, those of a Democratic persuasion were elated at the news of an American revolution in Mexico and the accompanying prospect of adding that huge province to the mass of the United States. They pointed out the benighted dictatorship that governed Mexico and the forced conversion of the Americans allowed to live there to the Catholic religion, the denial of their basic political rights, and the staggering wealth that a place as vast and fertile as Texas would bring to the Union. The Whig newspapers, however, cautioned that this was likely the project of American planters in Texas, who had been planters in the South, meant to add slave territory to the Union. This, they pointed out, would wreck the carefully crafted balance between slave and free states in the United States Senate and would be a result that must not be countenanced.

Again, he noticed, all the issues of the day seemed to reduce to slavery. There was no end to it. Ever since his last cruise to the Caribbean, it was omnipresent. That, and Catholicism, always seemed to have a hand in things, with Florida, with Beecher, and now this. At least he could assure himself that a year and a half previous he was not going out of his mind when he perceived that, everywhere he turned, he was confronted by matters of slavery and religion.

There was a knock at the library door, and Polly entered when bidden. "Excuse me, Captain Putnam, there is a Captain Miller here who wishes to see you."

"What! Miller? Here? It cannot be, show him in!" He just had time to kick off the blanket and get to his feet. "Miller! My God! What in hell are you doing here? I had no word."

They shook hands for only a second before embracing like long-lost brothers once thought dead. "Oh, Putnam, it is good to see you. How are you? How is your health?"

"I am in admirable health, sir. Why, did someone tell you that I died?"

Miller laughed. "No. Where is your family? I wanted to meet them."

"The boys have gone off back to school; my wife is attending some charitable meeting at her church. Polly, bring tea! My God, Michael, what brings you out to these hinterlands?"

Miller's smile faded slowly, but his rich hazel-brown eyes with their flecks of green never shied from Bliven's own. "We had best get it over with quick." He reached within his tunic and withdrew a letter sealed with red wax.

Bliven regarded it for a second. "Am I being dismissed from the service? If so, let me assure you that news will not be unwelcome. Polly! Forget the tea; bring brandy! Michael, we will celebrate."

"You may need both, Bliv. Let us sit down. It is true, I am on leave, on my way home to Philadelphia, and I would have stopped to see you in any case. But knowing this"—he handed over the sealed letter—"the Navy used me as their courier. I have orders for you: you are still Captain Putnam, United States Navy. They have allowed you a generous period of recuperation, and now they need you. It is a matter of both the gravest urgency and the greatest secrecy."

Bliven exhaled suddenly, trying to laugh it off, but uncertain how most appropriately to respond. "Will we be back together? That would be some compensation."

"No. They sent me because they know we are friends."

"But where am I going, and on what ship?"

"I cannot tell you. At this moment your orders are to report, post-haste, to Pittsburgh. There is a riverboat there, the *Zenobia*. She is scheduled to depart in five days, but if you are not there in five days, they will wait for you. You will be a passenger on this boat all the way down to New Orleans. Your ship, and your further orders, will be waiting for you there."

"Michael, you will forgive me if I feel somewhat abused."

"I know, and I am sorry; it was not my doing."

"What if I resigned my commission this past week?"

A shadow of shock flickered across Miller's face. "Did you resign your commission?"

"No, but I might, and I might antedate it."

"Hm! As your fellow officer I would be deeply shocked. As your friend, I would understand completely, and I would tell no one."

"Dear Miller. Oh, God, what am I going to tell my wife?"

"I do not envy you the task."

"Five days? That means I cannot tarry a moment. I must leave this afternoon."

"Yes."

"Will you stay and vouch to my wife that I am not inventing this entire business?"

"I will, yes."

There was a knock and Polly entered with the tea tray. "I brought tea, and brandy, and rum, and everything else we had. I didn't know what you might need next."

"Quite right." Bliven shook his head sadly. "Polly, run next door and fetch Mr. Ross. Tell him I need him at once."

Bliven opened his orders and read them, and indeed they conveyed nothing more than what Miller had already told him. Having known of Bliven's fondness for tea with honey and rum, Miller sampled it, but Bliven said nothing about the quinine water. "What about you, Michael? What is next for you?"

"Mediterranean Squadron; at least, that is the word."

"Have you been there before?"

"No, never."

"Try to visit Naples. I loved it there—except for that sword fight, of course."

"Yes. Others have been pressing the sights of Gibraltar on me, where we are sure to put in. Who knows? Perhaps I may send home a Spanish wife!"

"Ha! Yes, my memory is that those Andalusian women surely have their charms." Silence descended. "Shall you have your own command?"

"Yes, a fine new sloop, the *Concord*, twenty-two."

"Excellent. I am happy to see you advanced."

"Captain Putnam—Bliven—I have heard that you wrote some letters in my behalf."

"One or two, perhaps."

"Am I permitted to thank you?"

"Nonsense, you are rising on your own merit." Silence fell once more. "I fear that we are in the calm before the storm."

Miller shrugged and shook his head. "From all you have told me of your wife, she will absorb whatever shot comes at her."

Clarity returned moments later and entered the open library door.

"My love," said Bliven, "we have a most welcome visitor. May I present Captain Michael Miller, late of Philadelphia, of whom you have heard me speak quite often."

The surprise on her face quickly changed to delight; she advanced and extended her hand. "Indeed, Captain Miller! I am so pleased to meet you, having heard so much about you. Bliv, dearest, I had no idea we—" She saw the stricken look in his eyes, the letter with the wax seal in his hands, and guessed everything before another beat of his heart. "Oh no." Her voice was suddenly almost inaudible. "You have been recalled."

"Yes, my love."

She swooned very slightly under the impact. "When must you leave?"

"Instantly, I fear. I am so sorry; I had no idea, either."

She nodded. "That is why Mr. Ross is outside—to help you pack?"

"Yes."

"Then it really is just this sudden."

"I fear so, my love."

"Mrs. Putnam," Miller broke in, "may I say that of my own knowledge, it is a matter of the greatest urgency, and a matter of national importance? Otherwise the Navy would never have acted in so graceless a manner."

Clarity folded her hands before her. "For your own part, Captain Miller, I do not find you in the least part graceless. I find that you fulfill all of my husband's description of you, and I need not tell you of his regard for you. But as for the Navy, no, I do not believe that they care a whoop in high water for people's feelings. But I pray you, do not fret for me. I have much to occupy me until he comes home again. Dearest, will you come to my study to say good-bye when you are ready to leave?"

"Of course."

Turning away, she added, "You will forgive me if I do not offer to help—" She walked quickly back across the parlor and hall, and her fast steps faded into the keeping room. There were the three knocks, always three, and Ross entered.

"Mr. Ross, will you go to the attic for my trunks. I don't need to tell you what to do."

Alone together again, Miller said, "Well, I thought she accepted that very well indeed."

Bliven nodded slowly. "You do, do you? She was shaming me with her goodness. You get married, you will discover how that works. You say you have leave to go home?"

"Yes."

"To Philadelphia?"

"Yes."

"And I must go to Pittsburgh. May we at least travel together? That will take away some of the sting."

"Please do not be offended at my presumption, but I hired two horses in New Haven; I rode one and brought the other along. We can ride them back down and take the coach from there. They change horses so often, we will make better time."

"Mr. Ross has been my steward for so many years, I employ him as my valet when I am at home. He can take one of our horses and I will have it sent back."

THE ZENOBIA, when he and Ross found her, proved to be one of the new species of river packet, small enough at ninety-two feet in length to maneuver the bends of the streams, of shallow enough draft to ascend this far up the Ohio, and not mind any but the most extreme low water in drought. Her steam engine held great interest for Bliven. The boiler consumed a shocking amount of wood, and the steam created within its tubes powered a piston as thick as his leg, which connected to a single stern paddle wheel that he judged to be about ten feet high. This wheel churned them forward with such energy that he was sure that the captain never ran to full power lest he miss a turn and run upon a bank.

On their progress down the Ohio to the Mississippi, Bliven got his first look at Western cities that he had only heard about: Cincinnati, where he wondered if Reverend Beecher was still in hiding after the fiery debacle in Charlestown; St. Louis, which seemed to have become the mid-continental capital of commerce; and then south into a climate that seemed, even in November, perceptibly warmer. By degrees the current slowed, and the Mississippi widened until the bottom forest on either side was reduced to thin green lines above the water. He wore his best uniform to make the acquaintance of the captain, a raspy-voiced German with a sloping nose and wide blue eyes named Freisinger, who handled the boat with consummate skill.

The river ran due south as it passed the town of Baton Rouge, in

Louisiana. There they tied up for the night, because, as Freisinger told him, the volume of traffic on the river the next two days to New Orleans made it imperative to have a clear view of the whole stream and what craft were coming and going. Below Baton Rouge, the course of the river changed from south to southeast, and gradually to east-southeast, although this ancient and lazy stream turned itself to every direction of the compass, and they churned three or even four miles for every one mile of direct distance they progressed.

By half past seven of the second morning Bliven was already dressed and up on the third deck, sipping coffee as he watched the Louisiana marshes and bottom forest slip by, dark green, languid, and mysterious. Houses became by degrees more numerous, the better ones in the Creole style, set upon brick piers so high that they formed a bottom story. Whatever animals and implements they sheltered were obscured by lattice screens. The white frame residences therefore sat proof above all but the worst floods, the rooms surrounded by wide covered verandas with scatterings of all manner of furniture, for lounging, for eating, for sleeping. Clearly, much of the living here took place outdoors.

Bliven heard the splash of the *Zenobia*'s great paddle wheel slow moments before the porter appeared with a silver pot and replenished his coffee. "Are you all packed, Captain, sir? We'll be putting into New Orleans shortly."

"Yes, thank you." He was glad he had brought Alan Ross with him to manage such impediments to his attention. The porter, recognizing Ross's station, filled his cup but did not address him. Bliven lingered on the porter's words. What a marvelously large country the United States must be, for the name of the city to have so many differing pronunciations. At home people said "Orleans" with three syllables; farther south he had heard it in two syllables with an exaggerated long *e*. The porter must be local, for the whole name was contracted to two syllables, resembling "Nawlins."

At home the early snows were falling; here everything seemed as green as freshest spring, whether from the mildness of the climate or because the trees themselves were of an evergreen species, he had no idea. All his life he had heard of the might of the Mississippi, and now he had traversed it, from its confluence with the Ohio all the way down. It did not disappoint, either in the force of its flow, as he realized that it drained off all the rain that fell on the greater portion of the continent, or in its importance to commerce. At length they discerned the levee that bordered New Orleans and saw a forest of steamboats and their tall black smokestacks moored there. Farther out in the stream the larger, oceangoing vessels lay at anchor, their bows pointed south into the stream, the stretch of their cables being the only indication that there was any current to pull at them.

Almost at the same instant they saw a large warship anchored against the right bank. "Mr. Ross, look," Bliven nearly whispered. "It cannot be."

Ross joined him at the rail, and they regarded a hundred and fifty yards away a sloop of war, her too-high freeboard common to her class, but there was no mistaking the stunted foremast and awkwardly short, unpainted bowsprit. "Well," he answered, "I believe it is."

"I'll be back in a moment." Bliven ran forward, rapped on the door of the wheelhouse, and entered.

"Good morning, Captain Putnam," said Freisinger. "You will have to forgive me, I will be a trifle occupied for a few moments."

"I am sorry, I won't keep you, but I must know." He pointed ahead to starboard. "What is that?"

"Why, we call that Algiers Point."

"No, the ship, man! Do you know that ship?"

Freisinger glanced at it and returned his study to the wharf. "No, I can't say as I do. She appears to be a warship—a sloop, I think—but her rigging is wrong; the foremast and bowsprit are wrong."

But it was certain: the *Rappahannock* had come to New Orleans ahead of them. After they tied up, Bliven reviewed his orders, that he would be called for on this boat, from which he deduced that he should not leave it. He and Ross waited in their cabin; the porter brought them a pot of coffee and left it, and then a covered lunch. It seemed that everyone had disembarked but them, and it was after one o'clock in the afternoon when they heard footfalls approaching and a loud knock at the door.

Bliven pulled it open almost before the knocking stopped and was stunned at the sight before him. "Sam? Sam!"

"It's about the hell time you showed up. I have boarded every damn riverboat for the past three days fearful that I've missed you." He extended his hand, and when Bliven took it, Sam pulled him forward into a smothering embrace. "How the hell have you been, Bliv?" Sam Bandy had become as large as a bear, but without a pound of it seeming to be fat, and wore a full beard, woolly and as bright copper as a new penny, except streaked with white at the corners of his mouth. But the face was still boyish, his popped blue eyes bright and eager as ever they were.

"Sam, come in. Forgive me, I must sit down. My head is spinning."

Sam followed him into the cabin and saw Ross. He extended his hand. "I am Samuel Bandy. Your captain and I are old friends."

"Sam, this is my steward, Mr. Ross. Really, Sam, this is too much! First I get orders that make no sense, but I obey them; I leave my family at a moment's notice, and come entirely across the country. I get here to discover my old ship, which was to have been scrapped or become a hulk years ago, and now here you are, and in a goddamned uniform, to beat everything else. I tell you, I can stand no more intrigue! I must know this instant what is happening!"

Sam sat beside him on the berth and laid a meaty hand on his back as he chuckled deeply. "Well, I guess we did play a pretty mean trick on you, didn't we?"

"Trick? What trick? I had orders." He could not help himself but to laugh with Sam and lean against him. "What in bloody screaming hell?" But instinctively he knew that now, with his oldest friend in the world, it would be all right.

"Well," said Sam, "I can't tell you everything yet, because we are about to be late for an important meeting. Grab your hat and your sword: we have to make haste. Mr. Ross, you should come also. We will send back for your things."

Together they descended to the first deck and then down the alarmingly narrow gangplank to the levee. Sam walked quickly with great long strides, and Bliven and Ross had to fairly run to keep up. "May I ask at least where we are going?"

"Certainly." Sam turned to answer but did not slow. "We are going to Hewlett's Exchange. It is the principal place in the city where business is conducted. It is not far; Chartres Street is only one block off the river." They crossed a wide plaza with a cathedral on its north side and headed down the street.

"The architecture here is remarkable," said Bliven. "I have never seen its like." The buildings were fronted with porches and balconies held up not with columns but with filigrees of wrought iron.

"You haven't changed," wagged Sam. "You are still distracted in an instant by the strange and the unusual. Well, get ready to feast your eyes." He held the door open to a massive building, as tall as the others but of only two stories, its front obscured by Venetian screens. Inside was a vast hall; the ceiling was twenty feet high, the walls covered in maps and paintings of wind-blown women who clutched gossamer scarves over their still-visible bosoms. High above them the chandeliers were the largest and finest he had ever seen. There was a staging at the far end of the hall with a throng clustered around it as a well-dressed man of medium size, somewhat swarthy, spoke loudly, agitatedly, and with great force about injustices suffered, American values by contrast, and potential wealth. He spoke with a decidedly Western accent, but with a ring of the South about it as well. "That is Mr. William Wharton, from Texas. He and Mr. Archer and Mr. Austin have come to New Orleans to raise money for the war." He placed his lips almost against Bliven's ear. "Now listen: Ask no questions and act like you know everything that is going on. But, for God's sake, say nothing about yourself or why you are here, except in following my lead. Do you understand?"

Bliven had never actually taken an order from Sam before, but this hardly seemed like a time to dispute his authority. "Yes, of course."

Wharton stood down to loud applause, and another man mounted the stage and raised his hands for quiet. "And now, gentlemen," he said, "it is my duty to introduce to you a man well-known to many of you for fifteen years past. We all know him to be a man of faultless propriety, a man of integrity. It is he who first brought civilization when Texas was still a wilderness, and surely no one deserves to be heard with closer attention on these subjects of such enormous moment. Therefore, please welcome General Stephen F. Austin."

To generous and respectful applause there mounted the stage a man in his early forties, of medium size but distinctly underweight, with thinning, curly brown hair and enormous, expressive, liquid blue eyes.

"Gentlemen," he said quietly, "I believe that I may say without fear of contradiction that no man has been more faithful in his duty to his adopted country of Mexico, or placed more continued faith in her good intentions, than I. This adherence to the duty that I swore nearly fifteen years ago has proven to be misplaced. I have been confined for a year and a half, much of that time incommunicado. Indeed, I committed no crime, for no court would consent to hear my case, and I remained confined because it was the pleasure of a man who at one time was welcomed to the presidential chair by all Texans, but who has proved to be the most bestial of autocrats.

"When he confounded the nation and set himself up as absolute dictator, no fewer than five several states of the Mexican confederation rose up against him. For this act in defense of democracy, four and one half of those states were crushed in the most infamous brutality. The surviving one half of one state, the last hope of freedom in this part of the continent, is Texas.

"And so, Texas finds herself at war. We, as your fellow Americans by kinship and by the values we uphold, have come back to our native land to ask your help in this struggle. We are willing to fight to the ultimate decision, but we are a nation of farmers. We need money for arms and matériel to liberate our Texas from the grip of a medieval despot, a man whose word has proven faithless, a man who understands only violence.

"I know that some of you may offer the rejoinder to me that, in swearing our allegiance to a foreign country, we rendered ourselves liable to whatever changes in government that they might choose to impose upon us. To you I answer, first, that we swore our loyalty to a constitution that was agreeable to the precepts of an enlightened civilization. Only within the past two years was that constitution abrogated, ripped up, and replaced with the personal rule of this be-medaled maniac. I say that no freeborn American, be he ever so humble, would submit to such a dictatorship.

"Further, I know that some of you of the merchant class are invested in the Mexican economy. To you I say: Imagine the wealth you may gain from a Texas, a land hundreds of thousands of square miles in extent, ransomed from this benighted country; a Texas whose produce is made by a free and eager people and not by the downtrodden peonage of a conquered race. Imagine a Texas populated by our own Americans, perhaps even you among them, a Texas that may well join itself to the union of the United States.

"Finally, I would press upon you that the rights we seek, including the freedoms of our religious consciences and a representative democratic government, are natural rights, so basic that in any circumstance, their denial would be cause to throw off the government that denies them.

"Now therefore, just as these gentlemen who spoke previous to myself—gentlemen with whom I have not in the past always been in political agreement—I appeal for your help. You must understand that the war for Texas independence is not prospective. It has begun.

Victories have been won, at Gonzales, at Goliad, and at Concepción. Immediately previous to my coming here to raise support, I was with the army laying siege to the capital city of San Antonio. Our army is not like the Mexican army, populated by conscripts rounded up from the most desperate of the rural peonage, but an army of volunteers, each man of whom brought his own gun and powder and lead and clothing, an army deserving of your support. Word has only lately been received that the Mexican general holding the city, General Cos, has surrendered, and his army has been sent back to Mexico upon their parole, never to return under arms. This means that, as of today, no hostile troops tread on Texas soil!

"To maintain this freedom, then, is to be the genuine contest. The general in chief of our forces, Sam Houston, is firm in his opinion that the real fight is yet to come, that Santa Anna will himself come at the head of a larger army in the spring, and that we must be prepared to meet him and fight him. Gentlemen, every consideration enforces this opinion. There is time to prepare, but prepare we must.

"We ask your aid, but we do not ask your charity. The bonds that you subscribe this day are redeemable in generous allotments of land, and believe me, for no one knows this land better than myself, it is some of the richest and most healthful land on the face of the earth. We ask not your contribution but your investment, upon which you will realize a rich return. You gentlemen gathered here in the Exchange are the financial sinew of New Orleans, and we are confident that you will do your part to vouchsafe the freedom of your fellow Americans in Texas.

"Gentlemen, from here we continue on to Nashville, and Washington, and Philadelphia, and New York. By the time we are done, the success of an independent Texas will be assured, and it may then be but a formality, as the vast majority of our Texans most ardently hope, to welcome her into the Union as your fellow state!"

As he finished, Austin raised his hands in a sort of finial gesture that was his only demonstration of rhetorical style, although there was nothing of stagecraft about it. It was a genuine gesture that grew out of the force of what he had said.

There was a tumult of applause, and Bliven leaned over to Sam's ear and said, "He speaks very well."

"He is even more impressive in private conversation. Let the crowd thin down and I will introduce you."

Bliven was surprised. "You know him, then?"

"Well, of course. Remember, I was in his first arrival of colonists. When we landed, there were no other human beings, save Indians, within a hundred miles."

They held themselves at the rear of the crowd, and many sub-scribed to the bonds offered. When they saw that Austin was free, they approached him. He appeared exhausted.

"Why, Mr. Bandy!" They shook hands. "I am as happy to see you as I am surprised. How do you come to be in New Orleans, and in a uniform?"

"General Austin, it is good to see you. I rejoice in your release from prison, but I am distressed to see that the experience has left you in such a condition."

"Dungeons have that effect." The bitterness in Austin's voice was unmistakable. He tugged at Bandy's standing collar. "But what about this uniform?"

"It is quite simple, General. While you were with the army be-sieging Béxar, the government was putting together a great many other things, and among these was the beginning of a navy. Now, while I have come to be a fair shot with a musket, my better experience is in the United States Navy, and as a commercial captain. I have come to New Orleans to find a ship and a crew."

Austin's face went blank. "My God, but this is outstanding news!"

"Now, when I come back, you will not see me, for I shall be offshore, aiming to intercept your enemies before they can land."

"Mr. Bandy, I need not tell you that Mexico has the means to amass a considerable fleet of privateers. I hope to goodness you will not be alone in this."

Sam laughed. "General Austin, our odds will be no taller than what you must face on land. Now I would like for you to meet an old friend of mine, Captain Bliven Putnam, United States Navy. We were midshipmen together during the war against the Barbary pirates. Bliv, this is the man they call the Great Impresario, who led the first American settlers into the wilderness that was Texas. And a more fair or just man I never met."

Bliven found his grip surprisingly strong for a man as depleted as Austin seemed. "And a very well-spoken man," he said. "Mr. Austin, your companions provided rhetoric and oratory, but your gravity and reason, as enforced by your experience, left them far behind. Indeed, I was very moved by what you had to say."

There is a look that comes into a man's eyes when he sees that he has been perceived, and understood, by an equal mind. "I thank you, Captain. I am pleased to meet any friend of Mr. Bandy's, for he has been an asset to our colony from the very beginning."

"I do not doubt it. Forgive my directness, but your object in New Orleans seems to be to raise money, and I saw the crowd around your table. Were you pleased with the result of your meeting?"

"Enormously gratified," said Austin. He smiled a little as he spoke, revealing gums drawn back somewhat from the teeth, the look of a man in decline. "When all is counted up, we shall have received pledges of a quarter of a million dollars. Unfortunately, only about ten percent of it was gold and notes placed on the table, but that is still a powerful sum. When placed on account with our factors here, it will purchase a great deal of powder, and lead, and shoes to march in."

"And for that money," ventured Bliven, "you must have issued bonds for a vast acreage of your land."

"We shall have a vast country, Captain," said Austin. "These fellows here who pledge their money, their interest in the land is mostly speculative. They will sell it in smaller parcels to the hardworking farmers and millers who will come to Texas to make better lives for themselves—the kind of people I want, like Mr. Bandy here. Now, if you will excuse me, I must see further to our business."

The hall was quiet even to echoing their footfalls when Bliven asked Sam, "Well, did I behave satisfactorily?"

"Wonderfully well, yes."

"Where to next?"

"Not far. I got us a room upstairs. We will stop at the desk and send back to the boat for your things. The first thing that Mr. Ross will bring you—Mr. Ross, are you listening?—is a change of clothes, for your first stop is in here." He opened an oaken door beneath a tilted glass transom, and Bliven beheld inside a bathtub full of steaming water and racks of towels.

Bliven laid his hand on Sam's shoulder. "Oh, you are still my friend."

It was late that night, after a bath and an extraordinary French

Creole supper, with Sam already in bed, that Bliven sat by him and said quietly, "Now, Sam, will you at last tell me what in the hell I am doing here?"

Sam gave another deep chuckle. "Well, Captain, the government of the United States has taken a deep interest in the success of the Texas revolution. There is little they can do on land, short of encouraging people to volunteer. But just between us, and Andy Jackson, and God and maybe Davy Jones, you have been seconded to the Texas Navy. You are to cruise their coast, interrupt enemy commerce, and engage their vessels when possible. For the duration, you are a Texian; no one will know that you or your ship are American."

"Oh, my God."

"Sleep on it. You will feel better in the morning."

Sam Bandy was fast asleep within seconds, leaving Bliven sitting at his bedside with this enormous development to assimilate. "Mr. Ross," he whispered, "bring me my writing box, will you, please?"

MERCHANTS' EXCHANGE
NEW ORLEANS
NOVEMBER 17TH, 1835

My dearest love,

I must say, in lieu of the usual polite salutations, that I am so troubled by the strange nature of our parting a few weeks ago that I must address it directly, as I am confident you would wish me to do.

I was compelled to leave so suddenly at the visit of Captain Miller and in his company that you were left entirely in the dark as to the nature of my assignment, or how long you may expect me to be absent from you—matters upon which you most surely deserve an explanation. Believe me, my love, if it were within my power, I would do so. The fact of the case is, however, that I myself know little of what business I have been sent on, and what little has been communicated to me, I am most strictly adjured to tell no one. Perhaps at its end, if you write it as one of your novels, it should be a mystery in the mold of that strange young Mr. Poe to whom you took such a liking in that recent number of Godey's that you brought to my notice. However, whether my present errand should be classed among his humor output, or is a product of his darker nature, remains to be seen!

Since I am permitted to tell you nothing substantive as to my duties, my love, I shall tell you two collateral things that you will find interesting. The first, and it has fairly set me reeling, is that for many years I have been sailing the seas, and you have been writing books, and scheming how to win the vote for women and free the slaves, and while we have been thus distracted, our country has become an absolute giant of commerce. From home I was ordered to Pittsburgh, there to board a river boat and descend the Ohio River to the Mississippi, and all the way down the map to New Orleans.

My love, I challenge you, see if you can imagine the busiest street in Boston, on the most commercial day you have been there. Imagine the number of horses and carriages that you see hurrying by. Now, imagine that this street is a river, and the horses and carriages are instead river boats, of all sizes and tonnage, laden with cargo and passengers, coming and going, loading and unloading, money changing hands, people inquiring where they are from and where bound. That is what the Mississippi is like.

When we had descended so far as St. Louis, in Missouri, our vessel had to prowl the levee for a space to tie up, for I counted with my own finger one hundred and ten river boats already docked there. The breadth and strength of this stream can scarcely be described, yet I wonder at the skill of the boat captains that they avoid colliding with one another, there are so many. Several times each day we passed boats coming upstream, and the captains would blow their whistles to greet each other and passengers would wave and halloo across the water as though everyone were the greatest of friends. It was extraordinary.

And there was a further surprise, and I will close with this, for it touches most closely upon your own interests. There are here in New Orleans many, many thousands of Negroes, but unlike what you will assume about the South, as many of them are free as there are slaves. And many of the free blacks are employed in the skilled trades—they are especially esteemed as masons and plasterers. How completely do they refute any argument that those of the black race are not capable of learning a complex trade or sustaining a comfortable living. A large number of them are the same persons that the Colonization Society sent to Haiti years ago, but they determined to flee that murderous isle, settled here, and have prospered beyond what they ever dreamed. Many live in as fine houses as any of the white people, and some have done so well that—I don't know how to tell you this or how you will take it— they have gone to the market and bought slaves—yes, other Negroes like themselves, to serve them.

And now, my love, I must close, for we set sail tomorrow. I believe I would be giving away nothing secret to say that I arrived in New

Orleans to find a ship waiting for me, and I am to open my orders only after the pilot has taken us down past the mouth of the river.

If what I have seen of our Western section is representative of what happens when unsettled wilderness is brought under the aegis of our mighty country, then I must tell you it is a result profoundly to be desired. Do you remember in our youth, how provoked you were at President Jefferson for purchasing Louisiana from Napoleon, when he had no constitutional authority to do so? Well, now I have seen the result of that transaction, and I stand amazed that his vision so far exceeded ours.

And finally, and it all but breaks my fingers to have to write it, this realization has further put me in mind that even as it was Jefferson who made Louisiana American, it was Jackson who kept it American with his signal victory here in 1815. Of his crude character and unscrupulous methods I concede nothing, but if we look at the results, if we judge only the forecast of his policies, both in the conquest of the Floridas and his defense of this place to prevent it falling to the British—then I can no longer say that he has done only bad things. Perhaps there is a degree to which I have been unjust.

Farewell, my love. Whatever my mission shall prove to be, I promise you I shall effect it with the greatest speed humanly possible, that I may return to my home and my wife, who I know has suffered much from my long absences.

Your loving husband,
Bliven Putnam
Capt. USN

4

New Orleans

They awoke with the light, Bliven and Sam in the bed and Ross in the cot brought in for him. They breakfasted in the Exchange's dining room, brisk and noisy by the time they sat down to some fashion of coddled eggs in a lemon cream sauce that was new to Bliven. When he remarked on their excellence, Sam's mouth was full, but he nodded until he swallowed. "I am not often in New Orleans, but I am ever alert for an excuse to come here. I swear, it is like having the whole world contained in one city. Even the coffee"—he hefted his cup—"Martinique such as I used to procure when I had a ship."

"In those days you would send us some, every Christmas," recalled Bliven. "We have mourned its absence. It is expensive when we can find it, even though Boston lies at the opposite end of the trade route from the West Indies. I wonder that it should cost so much when the shipping is so direct."

"Oh, you don't want to tell a Texan how expensive things are.

Now Galveston is like the infant child of New Orleans, pretty much a tiny village by American standards, but ships dock there from all over the world. But unless you live right there in town, my God, the freight rates to ship anything beyond there are ruinous. For those of us who live in the interior—and that is the great majority, mind—the game has been to achieve self-sufficiency as quick as we can get there."

"Yes, tell me about your life. Have you remarried?"

Sam hesitated. "No . . . well, not exactly."

"What!" Bliven's astonishment caused Sam to shake his head and hold up his hand. "I'm sorry, Sam, I won't pry."

"No, no, it is all right. It's just the craziest thing you ever heard of. It was like this. When I and several others got to Texas with General Austin back in 1821, we heard that the Mexicans had succeeded in throwing out the Spanish, so his settlement contract with the Spanish government was no good anymore. Austin had to go to Mexico City to try and rescue everything—the poor man had to teach himself Spanish on the journey—and he was gone over a year while we poked around the land, sort of looking to see where we wanted to live. When he finally came back, the terms of the contract they gave him were such that a married man got several times the land a single person did. Well, there was this widow woman in our group, she wasn't too much older than me, and we got along all right, so we agreed to marry up, as by doing so we would get more than four thousand acres of prime land."

Bliven shrugged. "In your place I might well have done the same."

"Well, this is where it gets all crazy. In order to get the land, all of us had to become Catholic, but then in the revolution the Catholic Church sided with Spain, so they lost all their say or standing in the new country. So there we were, stuck being Catholic, and not a single priest in the whole territory to marry people, or hold church, or mass, or whatever they call it. Well, Austin struck up a system to let people who wanted to get married put up a bond as a promise to do it, if a priest ever showed up, and then they were allowed to live together. So, that's what we did. We got our land, and we stuck it out for three years, but we didn't agree on much. She wanted out and I wanted her gone, but the law is different there and she legally owned half the place, and so I had to buy her out. I repaid the bond, but I still had to pay her off, which took a few years, and then she took off to parts unknown. I honestly don't know if we are still married, or if we ever were, so you see now why I answered your question that I am not exactly married."

"Heavens. Where are your sons?"

"Pssh! They went wild as wolves as soon as they got to Texas. Sam Junior finally went back to South Carolina; he got it into his head that he could get our old place back. David—"

Bliven smiled gently. "Named for me."

"You may wish otherwise. Once he started growing some hair, he fell in with a bad sort. Austin lost control of most who came to Texas, and now the place is just thick with squatters and fugitives and hard types on the run from the law in the United States."

"Sam . . ." Bliven reached over and squeezed his forearm. "*You* were on the run from the law in the United States."

Sam pursed his lips and nodded. "For what I did to that vulture of a banker, God will hold me justified. It just wasn't legal."

"I understand that. Again, I cannot say I would not have done the same. But what about David?"

"Last I heard, he had joined up with a ranging company, hunting Indians and such. I hope they will join the Texas Army. That will put their violence to a good purpose, anyways."

"How did the boys turn out in such a way, Sam?"

Sam shook his head slowly. "Becky's death hit them like a land-slide. Once she was gone, it was like they just turned dark, and bad. They adored her. I told them so many times, this is not how she would want them to be, but"—he stared at the table and sighed—"life gave them a bitter cup, and they drank every last bit of it. I am the one who lost their fortune, so I blame myself."

"Oh, Sam. I'm sorry."

"Well, enough of that. Come! We have a hundred things to do. We have to see Mr. Toby and pick up some money, and then go find the last of the provisions for the ship. I haven't arranged for a pilot yet to get us to the mouth of the river."

"Excuse me, Captain . . ." Ross had not spoken up in a long time. "Speaking of bitter cup, perhaps we should find a druggist and see if we can find a quantity of quinine water."

"Oh, good Lord, I completely forgot about that. We left Litchfield in such a hurry."

"And it was cool weather, sir; it would not have been first on your mind."

"Quinine water?" quizzed Sam. "Have you had the swamp ague?"

"Yes, when last I was in the Caribbean. Thankfully it is not a severe case."

THEIR ERRANDS REQUIRED the entirety of the morning. On the water-front they were able to hire a lighter to carry the perishable provi-sions across to the ship, including a cow, two sheep, and a flock of chickens, all with feed, and enough fruit and vegetables to consume before they went bad. They looked across to Algiers Point and saw the *Rappahannock* taut but not straining against her cable. "She looks naked with no flag," said Bliven. "Tell me, has this revolutionary government of yours given us an ensign to sail under?"

"Ah," breathed Sam with satisfaction, "well you might ask. The last thing General Houston gave me before I left . . ." From his waistcoat pocket he extracted and unfolded a sheet of paper, on it a hand-colored drawing of a flag.

"Wait, stop right there. Are you saying that Sam Houston is behind all this cloak-and-sword intrigue to get me down here?"

Sam withheld the drawing from view as he answered. "Not you, particularly. Look, you can't have a revolution against a country that has a navy and not have some means to counter it. Texas has thousands of farmers who can volunteer for the army, but precious few sailors, so that is what I volunteered to do. We have no ships, and that meant asking Jackson for help. He said he would see what he could do. Your ship was back in port and was to be stricken from the list, so it was the most obvious candidate to disappear from the United States and show up again in Texas."

"I see." There was no denying the genius of the scheme.

"As for you, you were sort of doomed by your own history of operating independently but discreetly and, well, showing initiative. And no one knows the ship as well as you do, so here you are."

"So I was just swept up in events?"

"More or less. But we happen to think our independence is a worthwhile event. Now, have a look at the flag." He opened the paper again. "It's a funny thing about Houston. Where most of the yahoos joining the fight don't see beyond driving out the Mexicans, Houston sees the chance to create a nation and then add it to the United States. That is his vision, if you like—right down to the flag he wants us to have. He hasn't spoken of it to anyone—they would accuse him of grand delusions and chalk it up to his drinking—but he is a jump ahead of them. When the flag shows up on a Republic of Texas ship, his flag will be *fait accompli*. It's not complicated, just a large gold star on a field of royal blue. You know, the bigwigs have taken to calling Texas the Lone Star."

"Really? Why?"

Sam shrugged. "I have no idea. Possibly because she is the last hope of liberty on that part of the continent."

"Well, that seems as good a reason as any."

"Exactly. I believe our last errand is to call at the milliner's shop for the material and deliver it to the seamstress. And as a happy surprise to you, she is a seamstress only by night; by day she prepares the best Acadian lunch in the city."

"Ha, excellent!" Bliven pointed out to the *Rappahannock*. "Do you have enough crew out there to hoist these provisions aboard?"

"Oh, surely." They left the operation in the charge of the lighter captain, and Sam discharged his duty straightaway at a millinery shop with the purchase of yards of deep-blue cotton and a lesser amount of bright golden yellow, all wrapped in brown paper. It was coming upon two in the afternoon when they found the small establishment on Chartres Street, a door and three windows wide, of three stories, with a sign in script hanging over the walk that read "Regina's."

A bell suspended on a spring jangled as they entered, to be greeted by a woman so strikingly tall that even Bliven looked up a little to regard her cascade of wavy raven-black hair, eyes like sapphires, and a cream-like complexion over perfect high cheekbones. "Mr. Bandy!" she exclaimed. She held out both her hands and he took them. "We have not seen you in months! Where have you been keeping your-self?"

"Yes, well, you may have heard that things in Texas have been in a bit of a commotion."

"Yes, and we have thought of you, hoping you are safe."

"Thank you. Well, Mrs. Regina Ferraro, I'd like you to meet my oldest friend in the world, Captain Putnam, and his steward, Mr. Ross."

"Gentlemen, you are welcome."

Bliven found himself expending effort not to stare at her bosom, almost embarrassingly ample but apparently weightless, separated from her round hips by a tiny waist. No man could regard her and not think her a goddess. "A great pleasure, ma'am."

Her easy laugh told him she guessed every thought he'd had and did not object. "Come in and be seated."

"Mrs. Ferraro," said Sam, "the aroma from your kitchen tells me that one of your splendid Acadian stews is well simmered and ready to serve."

"Is that what you would like, gumbo all around? Bread and wine?"

"You have read our minds."

Bliven watched her graceful movement both as she left and as she returned bearing a large wooden tray. She set before him a large bowl of rice that rose like a white island from a thick stew, umber brown and aromatic, within which he could make out chunks of sausage, and perhaps chicken or duck, and what he took for onion and celery, and a ridged, seedy vegetable he could not name. He leaned over the bowl and inhaled deeply, its dusty pungency reaching the very depth of his lungs, and then going straight to his brain, where it awakened a piece of a memory, but he could not grasp its shape. "There is something in it," he said, "some herb or flavoring I have encountered before, long ago and I cannot place it. Can you tell me what it is, please?"

"No doubt you mean the filé."

"Filé! Oh, yes." He closed his eyes and sighed. "Years ago, I had a ship, the *Tempest,* and I took on a free Creole as the ship's cook; his name was Gaston. There was a battle, my ship was sunk, and I do not know what became of him after we were rescued."

Regina smiled. "And the filé made you remember him."

"What is it? Is it a plant?"

"We dry the leaves of the sassafras tree and grind them up. That's all. They grow wild out in the woods. When the French people got here years and years ago, the Indians showed them how to do it, and then the black people came up from Haiti and they took a great fancy to it. And they brought their okra with them, so now we have gumbo."

"Brought their what?"

Regina picked up a spoon and fished out a piece of that green vegetable, scalloped around its edges and filled with tender seeds. "Okra. It came from Africa with the slaves. And now the food here in New Orleans is all just a match and a mix of what everybody brought with them."

"New Orleans is so French, yet you sound . . . what is it? Italian?"

"Sicilian, although I have been here so long, most people can no longer pick out my accent. You have a keen ear, Captain."

"I have traveled widely."

"There are not many of us here yet," she said, "but more of my family are coming, and my family alone will do much to increase the city, I can tell you. I will leave you to your meal."

Bliven had already sampled it. "It is delicious. I have not had its like in many years."

Sated, they made ready to leave, and Regina saw them to the door. "Oh! I brought you something," said Sam. He handed over the brown paper wrap of cloth and placed on it the sketch of the desired ensign.

"Ah! You wish me to do some sewing for you."

"An ensign for our ship."

"Truly!" She lay the parcel on the table nearest the door, opened it and assayed the material, and studied the drawing briefly. "Eight feet by fifteen? That is a pretty big flag, isn't it?"

"Yes, but ship's ensigns are commonly much larger than what you run up a flagpole. We want other ships to be certain at a distance of who we are, and whether they want to shoot at us."

"I see. And this is pretty heavy cotton. Don't you think a light silk would flutter out much more smartly in a breeze?"

"Thank you, Mrs. Ferraro, but silk would whip to shreds in a very short time."

"Very well, you shall have just what you ask. Why don't you call for it in three or four days?"

"That will suit us perfectly." He took her left hand and turned it palm up, placing in it ten silver dollars. "Satisfactory?"

She closed her beautiful long white fingers around the coins. "Perfectly. Good day to you, then, gentlemen." She extended her right hand. "Captain."

Bliven bowed as he took it. "Mrs. Ferraro, thank you for a marvelous lunch and conversation."

"Ma'am," said Alan Ross.

As they walked toward the wharf, Sam began laughing. "You

know, a light silk would in fact flutter out much more smartly, don't you think."

His mirth was contagious. "Well," said Bliven, "women do see different possibilities than men do in a given situation, don't they?"

"Perhaps some curtains for the gunports?"

IT WAS FOUR THIRTY as the lighter coasted up to the *Rappahannock*'s boarding ladder. Bliven saw no one on deck as they approached, which was a very strange circumstance, but then as they tied up he heard the thudding scurry of hard-soled shoes above. Halfway up he heard the silver accolade of the bosun's whistle, and as he stepped onto the deck he was greeted with an enfilade of smart salutes, which he returned.

"Welcome aboard, Captain," said the bosun. "Are you surprised?"

"Mr. Yeakel! After the month I have had, I do not believe anything could surprise me for the rest of my life." He extended his hand. "But I am very, very glad to see you."

Yeakel took it warmly. "Likewise, Captain."

Bliven glanced among the crew but recognized no one else. "Have you been with the ship the whole time this past year and a half?"

"But for two leaves to visit my family, yes, sir."

"M-hm. And do I not remember seeing orders at the time I left the ship that she was to be converted to a receiving vessel?"

"Yes, sir, but since your illness—from which I am happy to see you so recovered, or at least *seem* so recovered—those orders were rescinded. Mr. Bandy will communicate the new scheme of things to you, if he has not already."

"Yes, he will. Would you care to introduce me to my new officers?"

"Yes, sir. Mr. Bandy of course will be your first lieutenant. May I present Mr. White, who will be your second lieutenant?" Bliven traded salutes and shook hands with an extraordinarily tall man with tightly curled ash-brown hair and a natural turn of the eyebrows that gave his face a quizzical expression.

"And the third lieutenant?"

"There is none, Captain," said Yeakel. "We came down with rather a skeleton crew. The word was that we were embarking for New Orleans for her to become a receiving ship, and those men about the Navy Yard whose enlistments were up, and who were game to relocate here, volunteered."

"And where was she during that intervening year and a half?"

Yeakel shrugged. "Just laid up in ordinary, although I was given some other duties about the Navy Yard."

"You remained aboard? That must have been a lonely vigil."

"No, sir, I rather enjoyed it."

Bliven searched again among the crew. "Is there no surgeon? No chaplain?"

"Not yet, Captain," said Yeakel.

"Well," he said almost to himself, "we surely have our work cut out for us. Where is the rest of the crew?"

"We sailed down with approximately half the full complement. Most of them are presently at liberty in the city."

"I see." He walked slowly aft down the starboard gangway, then looked over his shoulder. "Mr. Bandy, Mr. White, if you please?" They followed him until he paused just forward of the mizzenmast, where he laid a hand on the wheel. "Well, in spite of all, it is good to find myself back on the *Rappahannock*."

"Oh, Captain, you could not have known about this. I am sorry no one has mentioned this to you before. She is not the *Rappahan-nock*, not any longer. You will understand, we cannot have an American vessel involved in our struggle down here. For the duration, at least, she is the Texas warship *Gonzales*, named for the opening victory of our revolution."

Bliven stared at him blankly. "Oh, I see." He strode aft to the taffrail and peered over, but had no perspective to see down the sheer, and so pointed below. "Did you . . . ?"

"Yes, sir, they painted the new name on her stern before we put in at New Orleans. Saved people asking questions."

"Naturally. Well, since I am apparently the last one to learn anything anymore, and I realize that I am merely the captain, but could I inquire where we will be bound?"

Sam grinned. "Why, to Texas, of course." As Bliven's eyes grew wide, Sam held up one hand. "Forgive me, Captain, in Texas we become accustomed to a less formal manner of doing . . . well, everything. I have no doubt that in a short time I can regain the use of the formalities to which you are accustomed. Sir, on the desk in your study you will find a packet containing your orders, with certain sealed letters. Because of the extremely sensitive and confidential nature of our mission, you are to deliver these letters, still sealed, to Sam Houston, who as you know is the commander in chief of the Texas forces. It must pass personally from your hand to his, and to no other. You will appreciate that the capture of such a communication could not be risked in an overland conveyance."

"Wait. Did Mr. Austin not say that there are no Mexican forces now in Texas?"

"At the time he left, there were not. But we know Santa Anna is assembling an army, and there is no telling how soon he can strike into Texas. By the time we can land and seek Houston out, the country may be overrun. We cannot say."

"I understand. I assume that we have charts of the Texas coast?"

"Sadly, sir, we do not."

Bliven's face seemed to turn to stone. "Please tell me that you are joking."

"We do have a general coastal map showing the locations of our ports, but they lie mostly at the mouths of the rivers, and you could not put in, in any case, because you draw too much water to get over the bars. The whole length of our coast is very shallow and sandy."

"I had assumed that we would be bound for Galveston. Does that port not have deep water?"

"It does, deep enough, but for that reason—the volume of commerce—it also has Mexican agents keeping an eye on the waterfront. We cannot be too cautious."

"I see, but, should Mexicans not be easy to identify within the town?"

"They would be, if they were all from Mexico, but Galveston is a hotbed of Tories. Many of the merchant class there are more in sympathy with the business interests in New Orleans, and regard the revolution as the project of the lower class. Some of those who have the means to trade also have speculated in land, and they are loyal to the state government in Coahuila . . . or think they are, but that government no longer exists."

Bliven's smile was sardonic. "In other words, you are prosecuting your revolution on rather the same terms as the American Revolution sixty years ago."

"A very similar circumstance, yes, sir."

"Is no one loyal to the central government?"

"To Santa Anna?" Sam barked out a sharp laugh. "If there is one unifying factor in all of Texas, it is hatred of Santa Anna, even among the native Mexicans in San Antone. But he is all there is, and since he is marshaling his army of invasion, he is the one they suck up to."

"He is really that terrible?"

"He is a butcher."

"I was curious whether the newspaper accounts back home are truly accurate."

"If they describe him in terms of Genghis Khan, or Tamerlane, they are. Of course, he merely compares himself to Napoleon."

"Oh! Well, it is good not to exalt oneself too highly. Come with me, gentlemen, I wish to have a look about." He returned forward to the single pair of ladders in the ship's waist. Down on the gun deck he scanned fore and aft down the file of twenty-fours, their lanyards neatly coiled, their gear hung in hooks from the knees that supported the weather deck. "Good," he said, barely pausing. He continued down to the berth deck and on into the hold, which was deep enough almost to embrace an orlop deck. "Good Lord, look at all of this!" He stepped forward into the warren of shelves and nooks and odd spaces. He placed his hands flat against two chests of biscuit and surveyed the mass of them, packed among barrels of salt beef and pork, and sacks of rice and beans and peas.

"Yes"—Sam patted the top of a chest of ship's biscuit—"I believe your government loaded her to the gunwales with food and supplies before she left Boston. The crew ate somewhat into the victuals, so I replenished them after she dropped anchor here."

"Mr. Austin sold his bonds only yesterday. How in the world did you pay for it?"

"Well, I advanced them my own money." Sam greeted Bliven's

stare with a grin. "I am no longer a ruined man, Bliv. My fifteen years in Texas have been good ones. I have in my berth the receipts for what I spent, and I shall go see Mr. Toby again when I collect our ensign from Mrs. Ferraro. I want to be first in line and make sure I get paid back, now and in coin."

"Probably wise." Bliven took a second look at the stores. "Wait. No, this will not do. Mr. White, will you run up and fetch Mr. Yeakel, please?"

"Yes, sir, right away."

Bliven waited impatiently until he heard their steps clatter one after the other down the eleven ladder steps into the hold. "Mr. Yeakel?"

"Captain?"

"You have been made aware that our coming cruise is one of great secrecy?"

"Yes, sir."

"Have you noted that of these chests of biscuit, some are stenciled with the supplier in Boston, and those lately acquired have the mark of the local supplier here in New Orleans?"

"I see that they are, sir, but I did not attach any significance to it."

"In the unlikely event that the ship is taken, these chests could link her to the United States. You must have someone grind off these Boston stencils. I am not certain how best to do it."

"Well, sir, we do have holystones for'd in the sail room for scrubbing the decks. They should do, with the application of a little muscle."

"Good, do so. Then duplicate the markings of this local supplier as though all the biscuit came from New Orleans. You must go through the remaining stores and remove any marking that can identify us as an American vessel. You may exempt labeling on any such supplies as could easily be found in New Orleans."

"Yes, sir, it will be done before we sail."

"Excellent." Bliven stepped out onto the planking over the keelson and made his way forward. Just abaft the footing of the foremast he lifted up a grate, reached down into the space, and withdrew an oblong river cobble weighing perhaps three pounds. "Mr. Yeakel, the kentledge seems to have been replaced."

The bosun caught up with him. "Yes, sir. The Navy determined that they had a use for the iron scrap that could be melted for other purposes, and while she was lying up they replaced the ballast with river rocks to about the same amount. I believe they learned rather a lesson from the *Constitution*."

"Yes, I should hope so." It had caused much excitement in the service when the mighty frigate's scantling had been removed a decade and a half before and replaced with water tanks, leaving her midships too buoyant, and she quickly hogged some sixteen inches, almost enough to break her back. It took a major refitting to right the damage, and the Navy had been more careful about maintaining proper ballast in its vessels ever since.

Bliven sat on the decking and removed more large river cobbles from lower down, turning the last one over carefully in the light of the battle lantern, satisfied that it was barely damp. "This all seems very well." He replaced the rocks and the grate back into its frame.

He got onto his knees, and when he looked, Sam was there with a hand to help him to his feet. "Why in the world did you dig into the ballast?" Sam asked.

"We sprung a leak many years ago off Cuba. I just wanted to see that all was well."

Sam laughed. "Captain, all ships have bilgewater. They can't help it!"

Bliven looked at him evenly. "I prefer the seawater to remain out-side my ship. Call me eccentric." He eased himself down to the ribs and backed out to the curve of the hull, looking far forward and aft. "Yes, this all looks very well." He led them forward all the way to the sail room, where they ascended three steps, which was a special hardship for Second Lieutenant White, for he was very tall, and in the confines of the bow there was only five feet of clearance. The shelving Bliven beheld was packed tight with surely all the canvas they could need. "Mr. Yeakel, I want you to store extra lanterns in this compartment. There is sufficient space for a surgeon's cockpit should we see action, and if so I want him to have plenty of light."

"Yes, sir."

He led them again far aft, to the powder handling room, the con-struction of whose cautious partition from the magazine itself he had overseen himself before she ever went to sea. He noted the flap-covered scuttle hole into the magazine and pointed to it. "Do we have a carpenter?"

"Yes, sir," said Sam, "a good man, he came to New Orleans with me. You will meet him presently."

"Well, I think I would like not to take any boys out with us. Have the carpenter enlarge the access to the magazine enough for a small man to enter and work." None of the others were aware of the spec-ter that still haunted him, of young Turner, the powder monkey on the *Tempest* who was cut in half by a ball from the *Java*. "Or mid-shipmen. This cruise has but one purpose, and I want only men who know what they are getting into."

"Yes, sir," said Sam. "I am certain that we most heartily agree. Now, shall we work our way back up? I have papers waiting for you in your cabin."

They paused on the berth deck. "Mr. Yeakel, when will the crew be released for good?"

"Upon your order, Captain."

"Very well, thank you."

THE GREAT MAHOGANY TABLE in the sea cabin was just as it ever was, and Bliven, Sam, and White spaced themselves around it. Yeakel excused himself long enough to find the ship's carpenter and return with him, a frighteningly muscled specimen named Caldwell with dark brown hair and even darker brown eyes. "I came with Mr. Bandy, Captain," he said. "We are neighbors; I helped build his house."

"I see," said Bliven. "You are enlisted in the Texas cause, then?"

"Up to my arse, Captain, begging your pardon."

"I am glad to hear it. Have you ever been to sea before?"

"No, sir. Sitting here in the river is the closest I have come. I came to Louisiana riding in a wagon, though, and I think the motion cannot be too different."

"Ha! Well said. Welcome among us, then. Mr. Yeakel will set you to some tasks that you can probably complete by the time we weigh anchor. If you two will honor us with your company for a few moments . . ." He indicated two of the empty mates' chairs, which they took. "Now then, gentlemen, Mr. Bandy has informed me that Texians are less formal in their dealings than an Easterner like myself is accustomed to, so let me tell you first that you are at liberty to speak freely. I want to think first about a crew. Mr. Yeakel, how many did you come to New Orleans with?"

"Eighty, sir."

"Enough to handle the ship but not man the guns, was that it?"

"Exactly, sir."

"So we must find approximately another one hundred seventy men, of whom we may presume nothing in the way of skills or experience."

"I am afraid so."

"But the eighty we have are experienced Navy men, except they have mustered out?"

"That is correct."

"Is there a way they may be induced to stay?"

"I should say there is, sir!" Sam interjected. Seeing expectant eyes upon him, he continued, "Let me speak to them. Every soldier in the Army enlisted for the bounty of Texas land in payment. If most of these men came west to start over and see how fortune might treat them . . . Is that not so, Mr. Yeakel?"

"It is."

"Well, then, you let me tell them about the land. I will wager that more will stay with us than go their own way."

"When are they coming back aboard, Mr. Yeakel?" asked Bliven.

"All of them are due back tonight, sir."

"Very well, Mr. Bandy shall have his chance to see how persuasive he can be. Now, what shall we do for a chaplain?"

Sam's stomach bounced in a noiseless laugh. "Captain, of all the men I have known in Texas in fifteen years, I have known but one or two who would ever go to church, if there were one to go to. I do believe we can dispense with finding a chaplain."

Bliven drummed his fingers on the table a few times and held up his hand. "Wait. I thought that freedom of religion was a central point of your revolution."

"Well . . ." Sam smiled and shrugged. "It would be true to say that they would like to have the *freedom* to go to church . . . if they want to."

Bliven's gaze became more penetrating, and Sam realized the need for more clarity.

"And if our pleading the cause of religious liberty in the United States awakens the innate anti-Catholic sentiments among the people there, so much the better for the Texas cause."

"So you Texans have raised religious freedom more as an issue of political principle than it has been any oppression of your consciences that you have actually suffered."

"That would be more or less correct, Captain."

Bliven drew a long breath in and slowly let it out, for he had accepted what he had been told of the reasons for the Texas revolution. Sam had now just proven that false. One day he must decide how he felt about that, but for now his own opinion was irrelevant because he was under orders and he had his duty to perform. "Very well, we can do without a chaplain, but we must sail with a physician on board. That is absolutely necessary. How do we go about that?"

Sam welcomed the chance to redeem himself. "I can be more useful there, sir. There is a physician I know on Canal Street, a Dr. Sickles. In addition to his own practice, he also wholesales drugs and instruments to just about every doctor in the city. He is certain to know some physician who is game to join us."

"That would be helpful. Mr. Yeakel, when Dr. Berend left the ship in Boston, did he leave anything useful in the sick bay?"

"No, sir, he quite properly took his instruments with him, and the medicines were taken to the hospital in the Navy Yard. We have nothing on board."

"Mr. Bandy, you say your Dr. Sickles is a wholesaler?"

"Yes, sir. I am happy to say he can outfit us completely. In truth, I know of just such a requisition that he recently filled. He stocked a large trading vessel with drugs and instruments, including"—Sam traced little circles on the side of his head—"a trepanning apparatus. The total cost was about a hundred and twenty-five dollars."

"And can you draw on your Mr. Toby for that sum?"

"Most surely."

"Very well, then, Mr. Bandy has the responsibility of finding us a doctor and supplying the sick bay, and also addressing the crew when they return to exhort as many as he can into volunteering. Mr. Bandy, it does not surprise me that you are already becoming indispensable."

"That would please me greatly, Captain. Hopefully, the men will return just drunk enough to want to sign up, but not so drunk as to say they have been taken advantage of."

"Yes. With your particular history, I would not think you'd want to become known for pressing men into service."

Both the color and the amiability drained from Sam's face in an instant as he muttered, "No."

Bliven knew in a heartbeat that he should not have ventured such a witticism. "Oh, Sam, I'm sorry. Mr. White," he said, "at the beginning of the War of 1812, Mr. Bandy was kidnapped from his own merchant ship and impressed into British service, where he suffered very cruel treatment until he was rescued."

"Most unfortunate," said White. "I was just a small boy at the time of that conflict and I barely remember it."

There was something vaguely belittling, not in the way he said it, but in the fact that the younger generation no longer appreciated the desperation of that war or the sacrifices made in it. Perhaps enduring such an inane remark was just part of getting old. "A bit later we both served on the *Constitution*," he said more pointedly. "I presume you have heard of *her*, at least?"

"Oh, my God, sir, of course I have. I am envious. May I ask, Captain, under whom did you serve?"

"Commodore Preble," said Bliven. "Then Hull, then Bainbridge."

"Oh! Captain Putnam, those are legendary names."

"They are now. I knew Bainbridge when he wrecked the *Philadelphia*. I did not think him a legend then, I assure you." Bliven felt safe in saying so now, for Bainbridge had died in Philadelphia two and a half years before, bitter and carrying his grudges to the last. Had he ever learned that Bliven had said such a thing, it would likely have ended in a duel.

"Where are you from, Mr. White?"

"Mobile, Captain, originally."

"In what ships have you seen service?"

"The *North Carolina*, almost my entire period in the service."

"Heavens!" That massive ship of the line, rated a seventy-four but pierced for more than a hundred guns, including forty-twos on her lower deck, was the most powerful vessel in the Navy. "Our *Rappahannock* must seem like a very small potato to you."

"On the contrary, sir, I have enjoyed sailing in a ship on which I am unlikely to get lost."

"The other men came because their enlistments were up. Have you given up your commission as well?"

"I have, yes, sir. I still wear a uniform because I have as yet few civilian clothes."

"What were your duties?"

"As assigned, sir, but mainly I had command of a section of twenty-fours."

"Really?" Bliven and Sam exchanged knowing looks. "It might be very lucky for us if you could be induced to stay on."

"Thank you, sir. In fact I was listening to Mr. Bandy's exposition very attentively about the grants of free land."

"Take care, Mr. White," said Sam. "Once you say yes, it is unlikely I will give you a chance to change your mind."

"No, sir. I have been thinking as you spoke. If there is free land for it, I'm in."

"Not free, Mr. White. You may have to fight for it."

"Let it come."

"Well, then," said Bliven, "let's have it done. Wait, we have no—" He cast his glance about. "Mr. Ross! Are you about?"

The door to his berth opened, with a glimpse of the port quarter gallery beyond, and Ross appeared in his shirtsleeves. "I was arranging your chest, sir. What can I do for you?"

"Bring my writing kit for Mr. Bandy, will you?"

"Yes, sir," he chuckled. "I just heard Mr. White volunteer into the Texian Navy."

He returned and set the slant-topped portable desk in front of Sam, who opened it and extracted a sheet of watermarked paper. Carefully he picked up the goose quill with a steel nib inserted into its base. He held it up, turned it over, and regarded it. "Quaint," he said. "Don't see these so often anymore."

Quite familiar enough with the wording of an officer's commission, Sam dipped the nib into the inkwell and began writing, making the effort for his hand to look Spencerian enough for the dignity of the document.

Bliven watched him with fascination. "Are you quite empowered to issue a naval commission, Lieutenant?"

"We are in a revolution, Captain. I am quite empowered to do what is necessary. How about you, Mr. Ross? The ship will need a clerk and a purser. There is land in it for you, if you are game."

"Me, sir?" Alan Ross flushed. "Oh, no, thank you very much. From New England I came, to New England I return. You may have your revolution and your Mexicans and your scalping Indians and I wish you luck with them. But none for me, I thank you."

Bliven laughed loudly for an instant before he stifled it. "Now, there is an answer you do not hear often, I'll warrant."

Sam continued writing. "It is not for everyone. If everybody volunteered, New York and Boston would be depopulated, and then where would your country be?"

Your country, thought Bliven. How strange to hear that from Sam. "Mr. White," he said, "you can stage an exercise of the great guns?"

"I should say I can, Captain, and have done so many times. I have the latest edition of the manual in my bag."

"Well, you will be starting from scratch. Probably most of the new men, the ones apart from those that Mr. Bandy can hector into staying, are going to be more accustomed to pitchforks than ramrods."

"Review your manual well, Mr. White," said Sam. "Our captain is rather an expert on the use of ramrods in battle." In danger of laughing, he bit into the sides of his tongue.

Bliven eyed him coldly. "That will do, Lieutenant, thank you."

"I'll tell you about it later."

5

Texas Warship Gonzales

That evening the crew began to return, in various stages of drink, some in the lighter, some individually in canoes or pirogues that were paddled instead of poled. As the darkness gathered and the glint of lights on the waterfront became more pronounced, it was soon apparent that some half dozen of them had already commenced their new lives ashore and would not bother to return for their meager belongings. Yeakel set those who came back to cleaning the spaces around their hammocks, which they did in a halfhearted manner, feeling themselves beyond the reach of compulsion. Yeakel warned them not to turn in, that they would be wanted to assemble on the weather deck shortly.

That night, by light of torches and battle lanterns, Sam Bandy made his argument to them. With Bliven and Lieutenant White standing at the wheel, Sam pulled himself up into the mizzen ratlines to stand, one foot on the inboard rail and one on the outboard, giving him a bold and foursquare appearance. The crew was gathered close about him, down the gangways on either side of the hatch.

"Well, boys"—he tried to speak loudly enough that all could hear, but his high tenor voice did not carry—"I will tell you how it is."

Bliven listened, fascinated, for he had never seen his old friend perform such a public duty before, and it was striking how different Sam had become, how differently his loyalties had turned. It was not just that he spoke for a new nation struggling to draw breath but that he had become a different person. Even his language had changed. An American officer would address his men as "men"; to be warm or informal he might say "lads." "Boys" was a familiarity that he had ever heard only Preble employ, and he did so only rarely, to cement the loyalty of his crew. But Bliven gathered that it had become common currency in Texas, for he had heard Sam use it frequently. Nor was it the only peculiarly Texian turn of speech he had heard Sam utter—especially on the point of swearing. Hard language seemed to have grown into the Texians' daily vocabulary, cursing not held in reserve to emphasize some extreme emotion, but as a daily aid to get through a tough existence. All the evident speech patterns seemed to grow out of a new people determined to be frank and honest, guileless but not gullible, and as able to vindicate their beliefs with violence as with reason. It did not fail to cross Bliven's mind that such strong-willed people might in fact do very well to populate a new country interposed between the United States and the detritus of the Spanish Empire—even if they did practice slavery. For as Bliven had seen in Brazil and in the Caribbean, as odious as American slavery was, Latin slavery was incomparably worse.

And now that temperament was embodied in Sam Bandy, who stood on the rails in a clean uniform he had broken out, one arm steadying himself in the ratlines as the other made his gestures. He was impressive but not affected, an effective calculation to make him seem more a first among equals than a commander. "God damn it, shut up!" he shouted. "All right, now, boys, I will tell you how it is. When you left Boston, you volunteered to bring this vessel to New Orleans because you were game to relocate here. Some of you might have been washed up in the East, some of you were looking to escape the glare of a hard woman . . ." There was a ripple of laughter and Sam interrupted his cadence. "Well, come on, now, when has that ever not been the case with sailors, don't we know? Well, some of you may only have been looking to improve your fortunes among the many opportunities of the West. So you were told that New Orleans was to become a naval receiving station, and the *Rappahannock*, once stricken from the active list, was to become the point of induction here.

"Now then, you surely noticed that as we entered the stream of this great Mississippi River, that name on her stern was painted over and replaced with the name *Gonzales*. No explanation was given to you, and then you arrived here, and I came aboard and I guess maybe started acting like I owned the place." There was another ripple of laughter. "Well, after a manner of speaking, I do, and now you shall have an explanation.

"The fact is, this ship has been acquired by my country, the Republic of Texas, which has started a revolution for its freedom from the dictatorship of Mexico. This vessel is now the Texas warship *Gonzales*, named after the battle three months ago which opened our war for independence. Since then, further victories allow me to say that, as of last report, no Mexican troops stand anywhere on Texas soil. However, that hateful autocrat who now has Mexico in his grasp, Santa Anna, is not going to take this lying down. He is going to invade by land and by sea, and I tell you what: we Texians are going to throw him back right to where he came from."

At this, to Bliven's surprise, the seventy-four men gave Sam a cheer, and he continued. "Listen to me now. Thirty thousands of your fellow Americans were invited to settle in Texas, were given free land to settle and redeem it from the wilderness. Mexico had a constitution, not so different from your own, and we American Texians continued to enjoy the liberties we had known in the United States. It was a good life, and I know, because I was one of the first to go there. I have become wealthy upon my own initiative, as have many.

"But I am sorry to say, Mexico has ever been an unstable master. Since their own revolution against Spain fifteen years ago, they have had presidents and congresses, tyrants and juntas, even an emperor, and they all rise and fall. And usually after they fall, they are stood to a wall and shot. Mostly, however, they have left us alone, not having the attention to spare from their own commotions. But now that is all different. Santa Anna has dropped all pretense of democracy. He has ripped up the constitution and he rules by decree. He has stationed his soldiers among us and forced us to maintain them, and practiced other such outrages that no freeborn American would ever accept.

"I tell you, we have had enough! The contest is coming, and this gallant old sloop of war will stand like a bulwark against the dictator's cruisers and privateers, and keep our coast safe while General Houston organizes an army to meet him.

"So why am I telling you all this? Well, sober up and pay attention to me. Soldiers who have enlisted in our army are going to receive liberal grants of some of the richest land God ever created. I know, because since I have been there I have more than doubled my grant to near nine thousand acres of corn and cotton and grazing. Peace and prosperity are what we want. You boys came west to do better for yourselves. You are sailors, and I am empowered to tell you that those of you who sign up to stay on this vessel in Texian service will receive no less grants of land than the soldiers in the army.

"Now, look here. Some of you have been in the U.S. Navy for years. Aren't you sick of trying to live on twelve dollars a month, and then less after the purser holds out for your slops? A few months' service in the Texian Navy and you will be given your own empire of land on which to make your fortune. Look there—look over there! That gentleman is Captain Putnam, one of the ablest commanders in the United States Navy. I have been in battle with him, and I can tell you there is no more calm or able or determined a captain anywhere to be found than he is. He has thrown in with us! I am honored to place myself back under his command. Will you do no less?"

Bliven was so shocked at the resounding hurrah, of fists thrust into the air—indeed, he was puffed up by it at least a little—that he forgave Sam's liberty in implying that he, Bliven, had volunteered to be here among them.

"All right, then, that is what I wanted to tell you. I'm not going to make you decide tonight. You boys go below and get your suppers and think about it. In the morning Mr. Ross, the captain's steward, will be in the wardroom with a register, and those of you who want to stick with us we will enlist into the Texian Navy and he will put you in for the donation land."

"If we take this land," a voice called from the middle of the crew, "do we have to settle on it and live there, or else forfeit it?"

"Hell no!" Sam pointed at the man. "And thank you for asking that. The land will be yours as payment for your service. Once it is yours, you may live out your lives as quiet corn farmers or you may sell it as you choose, and I promise you it will be for more than any twelve dollars a month for your work! Is there anything else?"

"How long will your war last, do you think?" A rumbling was set off among the men.

Sam stood quiet until all attention was on him. "We hold Texas at present. The enemy must invade, with all the hazards of long supply lines in a hostile country. In their present disorder at home, we do not believe they can mount a long campaign, nor will their country tolerate sustaining heavy losses. Nothing is certain, but we believe that not more than three or four months will pass until the issue is decided." He listened for any more questions. "All right, then, thank you for listening."

Sam eased himself back down to the deck and stood by Bliven at the wheel as the men crowded the ladders to go below.

Bliven was smirking at him sardonically. "So I have thrown in with you, have I?"

"You're here, ain't you?"

"I don't recall reading about Texas publishing a Declaration of In-dependence. Are you quite certain about that?"

Sam shrugged. "It may have already happened. If not, it will."

SAM SPENT THE ENTIRETY of the next day in the city, accompanied by Yeakel in his best uniform up to his hard hat and silver pipe, looking like a character out of a novel. It was near dusk when they returned to the ship and called on Bliven in his cabin.

"Captain?"

Salutes were traded all around.

"Gentlemen, do sit down."

Sam was eager to ask, "How did you and Ross make out with the enlistments?"

Bliven shook his head. "Damn me if you were not right. I guess being that close to having a fortune in land handed to you was more than they could resist. Between the few who left and those who found their way out during today, we have eighty-five on board, all experienced sailors. I feared that once we got to it, we would have to take on a crew of shopkeepers and plowmen."

"Nah." Sam shook his head. "New Orleans is a big enough port; sailors get cast off or jump ship all the time. We'll do fine."

"We also had luck at finding a cook," said Yeakel. "Will you see him?"

"Certainly. Show him in." Bliven stood instinctively, and Sam stood with him. Yeakel led into the sea cabin a middle-aged Negro, short, round, a fringe of gray hair around a bald pate. He saluted in the British manner of making his respects, raising curled knuckles to his brow. "I am pleased to see you again, Captain. I was living in Haiti when you put in there. I recall your solicitude for the American Africans with great regard. I did not leave then, but I did soon after and came to New Orleans."

Solicitude, thought Bliven, *great regard*. Such a vocabulary he would not have gained in Haiti, but he had surely advanced himself by some means.

"His name is André Hoover. He was cooking in a restaurant on Dauphine Street, near the French Opera House, so he is accustomed to preparing meals for large numbers of people. The proprietors were not happy about his leaving, and they gave him no reference."

Hoover patted his ample belly. "I call this my reference," he said grandly. "As soon as these gentlemen mentioned payment in land, they had my interest."

"Indeed," said Bliven. "Mr. Bandy, is this quite . . . I mean, does his race present no obstacle to receiving land?"

"No, sir. We have free blacks in Texas, just like here, only not so many, of course. We also have free blacks fighting among our volunteers, on the same terms as the white men."

"Really? You have not said so before. Very well, Mr. Hoover, Mr. Yeakel will show you the stores and the routine of the galley, and the rotation of the meals. My steward will find you and make certain that you are regularly enlisted into the crew, and on equal terms."

"Thank you, sir."

As their steps faded forward down the gun deck, Bliven indicated chairs to Sam and Yeakel. He was keen to learn what progress they had made at finding a surgeon but then saw Sam grinning like a schoolboy. "Yes?"

"How many doctors would you like for me to bring you?"

"Ha! You are offering me a selection?"

"Dr. Sickles told me that in the last week no fewer than four had come to him for his guidance on what a complete medical office in Texas should stock. One bought his supplies and went on his way, but Sickles said he believed that he dissuaded the other three."

"Dissuaded them? Why would he do that?"

"According to him, lots of doctors from the South are making a beeline for Texas because they figure they are always going to have an adequate income because they are doctors, and if you add a big land grant to that, that will make them just about the wealthiest class around."

"Noble."

"Yes. Well, I asked him to round me up everything that a warship's sick bay would need for a three- or four-month cruise. Do you know, he already had a list prepared; he could all but sell a kit off the shelf. The stuff filled two chests."

"You brought them out with you?"

"Yes, sir." Sam reached into his coat pocket and produced a receipt of two pages.

From a waistcoat pocket Bliven extracted a pair of spectacles and positioned them carefully on his nose. "You, too?" said Sam. "That makes me feel better."

There were separate slugs of green type:

DR. T. O. SICKLES & CO.

Wholesale & Retail DRUGGISTS, 40 Canal Street

Medicine Chests Always on Hand

There followed a closely spaced list of medicines occupying almost the entire two pages. Some of them Bliven knew either from his long years at sea or from personal experience: oil of cloves for toothache and to stem infections; alba mistura for constipation; physic nut to induce vomiting; spurgewort for stomach cramps. Halfway down the first page he slapped the papers to the table. "Oh, I swear!"

"What is it, Captain?"

"Mr. Bandy, I have often been on vessels whose surgeons keep medicines to treat venereal diseases. I admit its necessity in a ship full of lusty seamen."

"Yes?"

"But this is the first time I have seen a pharmacy that stocks an aphrodisiac!"

"Are you joking?"

"You have purchased an aphrodisiac. Look. Look here. You see that? *Tincture of cantharides.* A three-ounce bottle, for sixty-three cents."

Sam squinted at it. "Tincture of . . . cantharides."

"Better known as Spanish fly! A ship's company's lusts are chronic enough without finding any reason to prescribe them this!"

Sam's smile turned into a laugh. "Well, I am sure I have no idea why that is in there, but I will ask him about it."

At the bottom of the second page Bliven regarded the grand total of $128.52 and an acknowledgment that the sum had been received of Toby and Company.

"Speaking of money, did you recover your outlay for the ship's stores from Mr. Toby?"

"I did, thank you for asking."

"When do you envision speaking to some of these doctors?"

"I asked Sickles to find me a candidate and bring him to his office tomorrow. I told him I wanted a good doctor, but equally important one who has been to sea before, if he can. A ship's surgeon is of precious little use to anyone if he is seasick all the time."

"Good. Why don't you screen off a sick bay in the bow of the berth deck and find some clean linens for the mattresses. Lay out the medicine chests as nice as you can. If you can bring a doctor aboard, I want him to want to stay. And you can show him the sail room as a surgical cockpit if we get into a fight."

"Yes, of course."

"Have you begun spreading the word that we want another hundred and seventy or eighty men for the crew?"

"Oh, naturally. There are a dozen sailors in any bar. I've put out the word for any who are interested to assemble in the square in front of the cathedral tomorrow night. There is a nice view of the ship from there, and I will stoke them. You need about another hundred and seventy, you said? If I don't return with a full complement, then I don't know anything."

"Are you certain? Are you not aware of conditions back in the East? Our merchant fleet has been shrinking for years, and those who do make good hands are in a rush to the whaling ships, where they think they might make a great deal more money. And ever since the West has started to be developed, the criminals and derelicts who used to enlist in the Navy walk into our American greenwood to see if they can make a fortune there. Our Navy is as undermanned, or worse, as ever it was."

"We should not have that problem," said Sam. "Texas offers them their very own greenwood—thousands of acres of it. All they have to do is fight for it."

"If you say so, but by beating the drum for a crew, won't our jig be over as far as any secrecy is concerned?"

"Oh, a drum! Thank you for reminding me: we can't properly beat to quarters without a drum! And I must set apart a few tough-looking hombres to serve as marines. Lord, the things we take for granted when we don't have to start a crew from scratch. Now, as to our secrecy, what you say is true, but as far as anyone in Mexico will know, Texas has acquired an old ship stricken from the American list. The fact that we are a big ship is just their misfortune. You can be sure they are looking high and low for more vessels to bring into the fight as well. I do not believe that there is any ready link for them to find between the *Gonzales* and any American collusion."

The next night Bliven thought he must go mad as he strode his quarterdeck, spyglass in hand and frequently raised, but he was unable to make out anything on the square before the cathedral but the glow of torches. It was past midnight when Sam's boat returned. "Mr. Bandy," he greeted him with undisguised anxiety, "how did you fare?"

There was a reassuring ease to Sam's walk. "Set your mind at rest, Captain: we shall have our crew, and more experienced than we had hoped. We did very well tonight."

"As I have seen, you are a persuasive speaker. You will probably wind up being president of this country of yours."

Sam considered this with a twinkle in his eyes. "They could do worse, would you not agree?"

THE SHIP'S SURGEON, when he came aboard, was a soft-spoken German named Haffner, who, if he had ever been exposed to sun and salt air, it must have been several years prior, for he appeared as soft and pale as a changeling. He did assure Bliven that the tincture of cantharides sent out in Dr. Sickles's chest was prescribed only as a diuretic, and even then greatly diluted, for it is lethally poisonous. In his own practice, he had found its reputation for sparking sexual arousal to be nothing more than sailors' lore, stemming perhaps from its unsavory but exotic origin as dried and crushed blister beetles.

Haffner's volunteering of such a complete account of the drug, and his quick facility with the other mysteries of the medical chests, won Bliven's confidence. Sam canvassed every arriving ship from the West for news of Texas; all were consistent in the intelligence that, although a violent clash must come, it had not yet arrived. They also learned that the many factions in Texas were now contending for power within the rebellion and causing Texas's first steps toward self-government to falter. One evening at anchor they were visited by a Mr. Thomas McKinney, who Bliven learned was an immensely wealthy investor in all things Texian. He had advanced their leaders everything from powder and lead to shoes—it was he who in fact stood behind Mr. Toby and the Texas factors—and if the revolution succeeded, his wealth would become truly vast. After his visit, the *Gonzales*'s hold swelled with slops for the men, supplies, and an assistant for Caldwell the carpenter—along with a suite of signal flags, for McKinney was himself a ship owner—until the vessel plumped and rounded out to her former pride.

The new year of 1836 was two weeks gone when Sam came aboard with news from a Matamoros packet of Mexican troop movements south of the border. There would be not one invasion but two, with Santa Anna to strike across the Rio Grande at San Antonio while the country's most able general, José de Urrea, would land at Cópano and cover his southern flank. Their intention was, together, to sweep all American settlement from the country.

All morning on January 15, the *Gonzales* lay, self-contained, independent of the shore and the city, waiting only the tide and a pilot to return to her wonted element, and Bliven felt nearly beside himself in anticipation. It had been too, too long. His keenness only increased when Sam joined him on the quarterdeck, a cup of coffee steaming in hand and a large piece of royal blue cotton folded over his arm. "Good morning, Captain."

"Mr. Bandy, good morning." He and Sam had never been captain and first lieutenant, yet it felt comfortable and familiar, like a fond old memory relived. "It must have been late when you came back aboard; I did not hear you."

"It was. I was waiting upon Mrs. Ferraro, who sends you this with her best compliments." He partially shook open their ensign, part of the single golden star visible upon its field of blue. "She also had this left from dressmaking." From his coat pocket he extracted a tightly wound swatch of emerald-green silk, six inches broad and almost weightless. "It is twenty feet long and tapers. I accepted it, not knowing if we had a pennant to gauge the wind."

"Excellent."

"The tide will turn before long, and the pilot will come out anytime now."

André Hoover came up the ladder before them bearing a pot and a plain white porcelain cup. "Captain, I know that your steward has already taken you breakfast, but Mr. Bandy informed me of your fondness for coffee."

Bliven accepted the cup with gratitude. "Mr. Bandy informed you correctly, thank you." He took a sip. "Sam, I am suddenly curious about something. Have you ever noticed our figurehead?"

"Well, yes, actually, I thought it was a queer-looking thing, like a pagan idol of some kind. What is the story?"

"Ha! Walk with me." Bliven strode forward down the starboard gangway, stepping through the gate down to the head with its three bare openings for the crewmen to sit on. At the very prow he leaned out and could almost reach up and touch their Hawaiian trophy, just beneath and seeming to support the bowsprit. "Hello there, old fellow! I have not had a look at him since I came aboard." They walked more slowly back to the quarterdeck. "The original figurehead was of Mary Washington, George Washington's mother, who lived on the Rappahannock. She was shot away by pirates in Malaya. Then when we were in the Sandwich Islands, my marines had to clean out a nest of heathen native priests who were holding American hostages. That fellow on the bow was one of their gods that they sacrificed people to. I had my carpenter splice him onto the plinth."

"My God, you really have had a whole life of adventure, haven't you? After I left the Navy I just became a country mouse, I guess."

"Oh, I don't know. This whole Texas revolution business of yours sounds like it could be enough adventure for any three or four men." They watched as the ship came to life; men who had come aboard in twos and fives and dozens now filed up from below to store their hammocks in the netting between the inner and outer railings, listening as Lieutenant White helped them organize into watches.

"I tell you what," said Sam, "I am almighty glad that we are sailing with an American crew. Texas volunteers don't much cotton to being told what to do. They elect their own officers; they fight like hell when their blood is up but expect to pick up and go home when it suits them. I just don't know what kind of navy they will make. Look, the pilot boat is leaving the dock."

Yeakel met him at the head of the boarding ladder and escorted him down the gangway to the quarterdeck. He made his respects to Bliven and then Sam. "Good morning, gentlemen. Andrew McKay, pilot, to take you out when you are ready." He must have been seventy, with the thin, puffy skin of the elderly, very white, with prominent crow's-feet at the corners of his eyes. He bore a mass of very curly iron-gray hair that blended to white in a great square beard. His accent was Scottish to the point of ferocity.

McKay looked up into the rigging, not in a smooth scan but in little jerks, as though he were assessing a rote list of separate conditions before he could get them underway. "Mr. Yeakel," he barked in that distinctive burr. "Where is the rest of your for'd rigging, man? You are not set for a flying jib nor fore t'gallant."

"They were lost in a storm off the Bahamas two years ago," said Yeakel.

"And the Navy could no' be bothered to repair her? Pssh!"

"They spared the expense, for she was soon to be stricken from the list. We have learned to sail around the deficiency."

"Aye," he muttered. "How much water does she draw?"

"Twenty feet at the deepest."

"God almighty! There won't be many ports on this coast where you can call!" He turned his face into the slight breeze, almost smelling it. "Captain, are ye prepared to get underway?"

"You may take us out, Mr. McKay."

"Mr. Yeakel, have you made m'boat fast to a stern cleat?"

"We have. We are ready when you are."

"Very well." He looked up again. "Your wind is southerly, and light. Set your stays'ls and weigh your anchor; that will take us into the channel. The current will bring her about, then set your tops'ls on the port tack."

In seconds Yeakel had men aloft, and the *Gonzales*'s five triangular staysails fell into place as polished pine bars were inserted into the capstan, and five men on each bar began to slowly turn it around.

When a free moment arose, Yeakel stood close to Bliven. "This man knows what he is doing, Captain. And, well, I could surely use a bosun's mate."

They joined McKay at the tall double wheel. "She moves easy, Captain. How long have you been her master?"

"I just came aboard," said Bliven, "but also I commanded her at the time of her commissioning. In fact, we have been around the world together."

"And now you are going out as Texians, to fight the Mexicans?"

"We are, indeed, Mr. McKay. She was stricken from the American list and acquired by the new government of Texas. And sort of like the dog under the porch, I guess I came with the place."

McKay gave a laugh, full-throated and loud. "Then, sir, I wish you every success."

"Do I gather you have an opinion on that subject, Mr. McKay?"

"Pah! When I was a young man I fought the dons under St. Vincent. We were outnumbered twenty-seven sail of the line to fifteen, and we made mincemeat of 'em. Worthless beings they are; I wouldn't pee on one to show mercy if he was on fire."

"Oh, my, St. Vincent. Do you not miss those days?"

"Aye, St. Vincent . . . Nelson was just a captain in those days; he went on to do some things, you know. But I have my memories, Captain. They keep me company."

"How high did you rise in the Royal Navy?"

"Rise? Shoot! In that service, sir, almost never does one rise to command. One is born into the right family, and they purchase and politic your way to command. Except ye be English and to the manor born, the ceiling for the rest of us is low and of hard timber."

"Our bosun has remarked upon your skills. Were you a sailing master?"

"That I was, sir, my very title."

"How do you come to be in New Orleans?"

"Hoot, man, I got old! A man has to sustain himself until he drops; that's the way of the world."

"Are you not married?"

"No! To share what? What do I have to offer?"

"I see. Well then, what if you were offered one last adventure?"

McKay snapped his head around and shot Bliven a look with eyes like bright blue glass. "What? To join you in this madcap sortie of yours?"

"Yes."

McKay broke his gaze to assess the banks and the channel again. "For what pay?"

"A few thousand acres of land in the new country, when it is won," interjected Sam.

"Forgive me, sir, but you mean *if* it is won. Mexico is a formidable power."

"You mean those people you wouldn't pee on for mercy?"

McKay leaned back and laughed again. "You mean you want I should just disappear without saying good-bye to anyone, with my pilot boat tied on astern?"

"That's right."

McKay stared at them hard for several more seconds. "Daft!"

"Well, I do feel badly about taking the boat," said Bliven. "What if I sent someone back with it?"

"You know, McKay," said Sam, "once the country is ours, every river will need ferries, every port will need a pilot. You will have work in addition to your land."

McKay's eyes took on a distinct twinkle. "Oh, you two are a wicked mean press-gang, you are."

"Well, what do you say?"

He held out a few seconds more. "Oh, hell. I don't even have clothes with me."

"We will manage," said Bliven as he fished a coin out of his pocket purse. "Lieutenant, please go below, find one of the men having second thoughts." He handed him the coin. "Give him ten dollars to take the pilot boat back to New Orleans and tell them that Mr. McKay will not be returning, and then he is to forget that he ever knew us. And send Mr. Ross up to me with his ledger. Tell him that we have a new bosun's mate to record."

McKay grunted and his crow's-feet deepened, his brilliant eyes unmistakably amused.

"How long until we find open water?" asked Bliven.

"I would like to make it as far as Fort St. Philip at the Plaquemines Bend by nightfall. We will anchor there tonight, and the last thirty miles should see us into the Gulf by tomorrow afternoon."

"God, after waiting so long, that seems like forever."

UNDERWAY AGAIN the next morning, the Mississippi widened until the bordering marshes seemed to disappear by degrees. They knew they were nearing open water because its muddy color altered to pale gray-green and then jade. They encountered an easy swell coming into their port bow, less than three feet, but enough to lift the ship in a slow rhythm, and it felt wonderfully familiar. By degrees the water darkened from turquoise to a deep green-blue. "Are we free, Mr. McKay?" asked Bliven.

"Aye, sir." He pointed ahead. "Now, we should maintain a southerly heading until evening to get clear of any coastal banks. That will take you a bit south of the usual coastal shipping, but with your draft you could run aground where others may safely pass. Then you can make your turn safely to the west."

"That is how we will have it, then. Mr. White will relieve you next watch. Mr. Bandy, Mr. White, if you will join me in my cabin?" Near the foremast he spied the bosun. "Mr. Yeakel, you are wanted!" And they made their way down the ladder.

In the sea cabin Bliven poured them glasses of Madeira and bade them be seated. They sat at the mahogany table, spread now with charts of the Gulf coast, the gift of Mr. McKinney, as was the excellent wine. "Well now, gentlemen, we find ourselves in a curious position. We are in the service of a revolutionary government that is not recognized by anyone else but aided in secret by the United States. My orders are no more specific than to place myself at the disposal of this revolutionary government, whose instructions will be relayed by"—he opened his hand toward Sam—"Mr. Bandy. So, then, Mr. Bandy, I am in all conscience bound to inquire of you whether you are lawfully commissioned to exercise this authority."

"I am, but it is in the nature of revolutions that not every order is committed to paper. Your own orders from your own Navy Department are sufficient warrant to ease your mind in regard to your participation."

"Very well. And what exactly are we to do?"

"First, we must land at the port of Velasco, at the mouth of the Brazos. Odds are, that will give us the shortest distance to find General Houston and learn his latest instructions. Happily, I also live near there and can make whatever arrangements we need. After seeing Houston, we will enforce an embargo on all trade to and from Mexico and engage, and capture or destroy, any Mexican cruisers that you find along the Texas coast."

"What ships do we know that Mexico has in the Gulf?"

"We don't know. Mexico has probably been preparing for trouble since last summer. We know they have money; they have surely bought and converted some merchantmen into warships and signed up privateers as fast as they can. Officially, at last report they had but two armed schooners patrolling the Texas coast, the *Moctezuma* and the *Correo de México*, maybe two guns each, but there is surely a more formidable presence by now."

"Two guns each?"

"Twelve-pounders, maybe."

It was with distinct satisfaction that Bliven could look beyond the spindled wooden partition between his cabin and the twin files of twenty-fours down the sweep of the gun deck. "Well, I guess we can assume that we are the most powerful ship in the area."

"Yes, sir."

Bliven took a deep breath. "Gentlemen, let us accept this assumption. But if we do, I believe it would be prudent to make some additional assumptions. Mexico's ships may well all be smaller and more lightly armed, but we should also assume that they are faster and more maneuverable, some perhaps even embracing the use of steam power. If their captains are competent, they can use that to offset somewhat our superior armament. We must be able to engage them on something like equal terms without having to bring our broadside to bear. Therefore, I wish you to take two of our long twenty-fours, the two forwardmost from the sick bay, and remount them as bow chasers. Mr. Caldwell will need to cut away sections of railing, and embed eyebolts for their lanyards. Mr. Yeakel, you can instruct him in the particulars."

"Yes, sir," said Yeakel, "and I will direct operating the block and tackle to hoist the guns up to the weather deck."

Sam raised a hand. "Captain, if I may?"

"Mr. Bandy?"

"Would you not desire stern chasers as well?"

"I would, but I don't want to make us top-heavy."

"If a steam-powered vessel were to get astern of us, even twelve-pounders could do terrible damage if she were able to rake us."

"True, but with our greater range, we should be able to dispatch them before they get into such a position."

"I see." Sam nodded. "Well, speaking to that point, the whole reason for chasers is to be effective at the extremity of their range."

"That is correct."

"I wonder if you would consider having Mr. Caldwell mount those chasers on some shallow ramps to raise their elevation just a few degrees. We can set blocks behind the wheels to keep them in place, and I'll bet I could design an opposing ramp to arrest their recoil. I would bet you we can increase their range by a couple of hundred yards."

Bliven nodded. "And what is the thinking that motivates this?"

"Sir, a lot of the coastal trading takes place in schooners that are bound to be faster than we are, and they can run for shallow water. I should think we want to extend our reach as far as we can."

"Mr. Bandy, you have not been to sea for many years, but you have lost none of your capacity for good thinking. Work with Mr. Yeakel and your carpenter and see what you can do to rig up with the bow chasers. We will test their range when we exercise the guns and see how easy it is to reposition them after firing. Mr. White, do you think you can conduct a gunnery drill in the morning?"

"Of course, sir."

"Sir," said Yeakel, "perhaps we should take care of this this evening so we can be ready to test them in the morning. It shouldn't take more than an hour and a half or so, and Caldwell can saw up a couple blocks to stop the wheels rolling backwards. I would bet the lanyards would be strong enough to hold the guns in place until they are fired."

"Very well, but put blocks behind the carriage wheels for good measure. Just make sure the chasers are secure in place and will not roll back down the deck. That would look very slovenly. Mr. Bandy, does your Republic of Texas have any other ships besides ours?"

"Just one, Captain, the *San Felipe*, an armed schooner, with about four small guns. She formerly sailed for Mr. McKinney in his trading business, but he sold her to the government. They have contracted for the delivery of four more small ships, I believe three schooners and a brig, but they are not here yet."

"I see."

"Now, the *San Felipe* is a tough little vessel, and her master, Captain Hurd, would sail her across the Styx itself to chase Mexicans. Last fall he actually challenged the *Correo*, beat her down, captured her, took her captain and crew into New Orleans, and charged them with piracy!"

"Good Lord," Bliven laughed. "With what result?"

"Well, an American admiralty court could not very well sustain a charge of piracy against the commissioned naval vessel of another country. They had to let her go, but the trial was the biggest circus you ever saw. The judge found both sides in contempt of court and declared a mistrial, the Mexican captain was fit to be tied, and now he's back out here somewhere, just spoiling for a fight."

Bliven threw his head back and laughed again. "With two twelve-pounders."

Sam grew serious. "Captain, there is one thing that sticks in my mind, though. Do you remember at the Exchange, General Austin made a special appeal to the commercial interests to invest their future in Texas rather than Mexico? As reasonable and hopeful as that sounded, I'm afraid he was pissing into the wind. Nearly all the large businesses in the United States—the factors, the insurance companies, and so on—are heavily invested in Mexico, and they are if anything hostile to our cause. We may well be their fellow Americans, but where their money is concerned, take it from me, they don't care a damn for our rights or freedom. In fact, it was they who filed legal motions for the *Correo de México* and against the *San Felipe*."

Bliven nodded slowly. "I can understand how they could create a nightmare on paper, but out here"—he waved his hand—"out here at least it comes down to powder and shot."

IN THE MORNING they were all up at first light, officers in their best uniforms, eating together in the wardroom as Hoover brought them eggs and ham, and pancakes with a sweet cane syrup. There was general agreement that they had done well to bring Hoover into the company. White suggested his intention to run the men through the drill once only in the motions and the second time with live fire, for he was certain that many of their former merchant seamen had never experienced the tremor of a three-and-a-half-ton cannon belching fire before them.

The wardroom's doors to the berth deck were open, and faintly above they heard the cry "Deck! Deck, ahoy! Ship off the port beam; make her a mile and a half." Bliven was first up the ladder; Ross would know to bring him his glass and speaking trumpet. It was Yeakel on watch: due to the shortage of officers, the two lieutenants, bosun, and mate all turned tricks at the wheel.

Distantly but clearly they spied a large brig under easy sail, following a westerly course. "Mr. McKay," said Bliven, "I understood from our conversation yesterday that the coastal traffic would be mostly inshore of us. What do you make of this?"

"May I, Captain?" McKay held out his hand and Bliven gave him his glass. "She is no coaster, Captain. She's got a full cargo and she's come a distance, surely has not stopped at New Orleans. I'd bet you money she is headed straight to one of the Mexican ports, Matamoros or possibly Tampico. She is the very sort of vessel you want to stop and board."

"Angle us toward her, Mr. Yeakel. Mr. Bandy, get our ensign up the spanker boom. Mr. White, I'm afraid your boys will have to have their gunnery drill with live fire on a real target. Tell them to brace themselves. Beat to quarters."

There was little efficiency to it, but over several minutes the twenty-fours were rolled in and their tompions removed; then powder and shot were brought up from the magazine and rammed gently home.

The brig took note of their approach, for when they were half a mile away she unfurled a large American flag.

They closed further, and Bliven handed Sam his speaking trumpet. "I do believe that the accents of your speech are more suitable to the occasion. Would you care to speak him?"

"Surely." Sam strode to the port rail. "Ahoy! Ahoy! Good day to you. What ship is that, and where bound?"

Several seconds later a high voice floated back in the prolonged vowels of the Deep South. "American trading vessel *Mary Ellen*, from Mobile and bound for Matamoros. Good day to you! What ship is that, and what flag?"

From Sam's friendly hail it was apparent that the brig believed them to be American, and friends. Very clever of Sam, thought Bliven, to draw him out in such a way, asking where he was bound before identifying himself.

"We are the Texas warship *Gonzales*. Mexican trade is under embargo, and you are in our war zone. Heave to, for we will inspect your cargo." It was manifestly impossible for Bliven to hear Sam's voice and not recall his friend hearing that same demand in a British accent in previous years.

"What! I will not, sir. We are an American vessel in international waters. No such country or war is recognized. Stand off, now, and let us resume our voyage."

Bliven crossed the quarterdeck and stood by him. "Perhaps if we wave our swords around and scream like the Berbers do, he will panic and surrender."

Sam could not help but laugh. "Who in hell does he think he is?" He put the trumpet back to his lips. "Now listen to me, you son of a bitch. This is the Texas warship *Gonzales*. You will come about and take in your sails or make no mistake, I will shoot." He lowered the trumpet. "Mr. White, get the most angle you can on the port chaser. If he keeps this up, we will have to put a ball through his rigging."

"Yes, sir." White ran forward to see to it.

A different voice came booming back. "Keep off me, you damned rogue. I am also armed, and I am prepared to resist your unlawful importuning."

"My," said Bliven, "what a learned vocabulary."

Sam turned and saw it was Yeakel still at the wheel. "Mr. Yeakel, you see the position of Mr. White's port chaser. Come a few points to port and give him a good line on that bastard's sails."

"Aye, sir."

Gonzales heeled ever so slightly upon coming more broadside to the swell. "I am on him, sir!" called White.

Sam put the trumpet back to his lips so the brig would hear the command as well. "Fire!"

The gun's report boomed with concussion across the water, the fire and smoke jetting upward a good fifteen degrees. Bliven studied its recoil, exultant that between the lanyard pulling taut and placing the quoins in the path of the wheels, the eight-foot recoil left the piece perfectly positioned for reloading.

All eyes studied the brig, to see a hole rip open in her main top sail. "Mr. Yeakel, come back to your course. Mr. White, run out your port guns." Sam put the trumpet back to his lips. "God damn you, I'm not wasting any more powder to warn you. Heave to, mister, or get ready for breakfast in hell!" Beneath their feet they heard the gun ports snap open and the wheels squeal on the carriages as the guns were rolled out.

For fifteen seconds all they heard was wind and chop, until they saw the brig's driver faint down the mizzen mast and saw men scampering aloft to reef the square sails.

Yeakel trimmed sail to match the brig and lowered the sloop's cutter, in it their eight marines, Bliven, and Lieutenant White, with Sam left in command. There was no resistance at the brig, and they were aided in tying on. Four marines ascended first, then the officers, then four more marines. The captain met them at the wheel before the mizzen mast, a squat, muscular man with thick hair protruding from beneath his collar; he had very straight blond hair and small, darting gray eyes beneath a single strand of brown eyebrow.

Bliven saluted as he approached and said, "Bliven Putnam,

captain—" He was within a breath of saying United States Navy as he had done for over thirty years, but caught himself. "Texas warship *Gonzales*."

The other made no salute. "I am Roger Higgins. I was master of this vessel until she was taken by pirates."

"Not pirates, Captain."

"I will see you tried as pirates if it's the last thing I ever do."

"What cargo are you carrying to Matamoros?" When there was no answer, he said louder, "What—"

"Small arms and munitions for the Mexican armed forces."

"Will you show me your manifest?"

"Under protest, yes, in my cabin."

"Your protest will be noted in my report. Mr. White, take two marines and inspect the hold. You two marines, come with me." They went below only long enough to retrieve the documents and return with them. When White came back up the ladder, he was carrying a Brown Bess musket, newly varnished, the brass work polished. "Look here, Captain, there must be fifty cases of these in the hold, plus powder, lead, and sidearms." He held it out and Bliven took it.

"Well, now, Captain Higgins," said Bliven. "I can understand why you did not wish to stop for us. And you will understand why we cannot let you proceed with this cargo that can only be meant for use against the people of Texas."

Higgins had the most sullen look Bliven thought he had ever seen, his lips thin as a pencil tracing, his gray eyes beneath that single brown eyebrow half-closed in rage. "What are your intentions?"

"You fly a neutral flag," said Bliven, "so I will not take your ship. However, I am impounding your cargo as contraband of war. Do you stand in any position of personal financial responsibility for it?"

"I do."

"Then you will no doubt have insured it before putting to sea, am I correct?"

"Yes."

"Excellent. Then ultimately you will suffer no loss and only the inconvenience of a wasted trip—or half a trip."

"Mr. Putnam, do not imagine you have heard the last of this. I am reporting every detail to the maritime authorities and the United States Navy. I do not believe Texas can send out a ship such as yours any more than if you claimed to have sailed here from the moon. I do not know what game you are playing, sir, but I will have you in a court of law, as God is my witness."

"Mr. White, is your rough inspection of the hold in substantial agreement with this manifest?" He handed it over.

"Yes, sir."

"Then use the manifest as your list of what to remove from the hold. You will transfer the entire cargo over to the *Gonzales*; it will require several trips. I will send more men over to help. When you are finished, please sign a receipt for Captain Higgins confirming what we have confiscated so that he may collect his loss from his insurers.

"Captain Higgins, I do regret the necessity of this action, and I appreciate your cooperation."

"Who in the hell are you?"

"As I have said, Captain Putnam, Republic of Texas Navy. And please do not entertain any notion to detain or harm any of my crew while they are aboard. My broadside will remain trained upon you."

Bliven returned to the *Gonzales* with the first fifteen crates of muskets, carrying one rifle up the boarding ladder with him.

Sam met him at the boarding gate. "What the hell, Captain? What have you got?"

"Mr. Bandy, let us be grateful that this day we saved many, many lives of your fellow Texians. That ship is loaded to foundering with lead, powder, sidearms, and rifled muskets. If they were bound for Tampico, they might have been used anywhere, but as they were bound for Matamoros, we can be sure they were intended for the invasion."

Sam held the new Brown Bess with wonder. "Oh, God be thanked."

"Now, does your army have any kind of arsenal where these armaments may be safely deposited until they are wanted?"

"Oh, Lord, I doubt it. In our army each man brings his own gun and melts his own balls. But we can sure make something happen."

"Well, we can keep them safe on board until preparations are made."

"We should put in at Velasco," said Sam. "That is probably the fastest way to get to General Houston. Mr. McKay, do you know Velasco?"

"Well enough to know you'll never get over the bar. We will have to mind the shallows and anchor offshore."

When the transfer was completed, they saw the *Mary Ellen* raise her sails and turn away. "Northeast she goes," said McKay. "In two days, news of this will be all over New Orleans, you can safely wager. What happens after that, I've no idea, but the Mexicans will be mad as hornets."

6

Secrets

A mighty unusual fisherman it is," said McKay, "who fills his hold on his first day at sea. But what are your intentions now?"

"To Velasco, with all speed," said Sam. "Revolutions wait for no man."

"Mr. Yeakel," said Bliven, "make all sail, course due west."

It took six days with moderately favorable winds. The mouth of the Brazos was easy to find, because with the curve of the Texas coast, the latitude of $28°52'$ indicated its only possible location, even if there were no coastal schooners to follow. They came upon it early in the morning.

Bliven was the last to the quarterdeck, dressed in civilian traveling clothes of middling quality. He found Sam better dressed, also out of uniform, McKay at the wheel with Yeakel beside him, and Lieutenant White in his best undress blues, his black shoes and brass buttons equally polished, his billed cap with its gold band snugged down; its severely flat top seemed nearly seven feet above the ground. "Well, Mr. White, you look very fine this morning."

He saluted. "Thank you, sir."

Off to their starboard lay the Texas coast, low and sandy, topped with thick tufts of beach grass and brush.

"Excuse me, Captain," said Caldwell as he approached. "I wanted to let you know we are crossing into six fathoms."

"Very well, thank you. Mr. Bandy, that is the mouth of the Brazos up ahead?"

"Indeed it is. The town of Velasco is a couple of miles upriver, which serves our purpose. We will have been seen by only a minimum number of people. You and I can take the cutter across the bar to the town and find our way to General Houston. We should be all done with our business in maybe three weeks, and we can rendezvous back here with the ship."

"Well, let us make it four weeks to be safe. It is easier for me to lie low than to keep the ship out of sight."

"I believe you can drop your anchor at any time, Captain," said McKay.

"Very well, let go the anchor." McKay relayed the order, and far forward they heard the clatter and splash.

"I will go below and get my things while Mr. Yeakel gets the boat down," said Sam.

"Yes, and have Mr. Ross bring up my portmanteau if you would. Mr. White?"

"Captain?"

"Mr. White, I need hardly say to you how much I dislike to leave my command, even in performance of a duty with which I am most specifically tasked."

"I do understand, sir."

"I have every confidence in you, and in Mr. Yeakel and Mr. McKay. You will continue the mission to disrupt Mexican commerce and engage any of their vessels that come against you."

"Yes, sir. At least we have plenty of powder."

"Ha! You certainly do. Once we are ashore, Mr. Bandy will inquire how the Texian forces can best use the armaments we have taken, but we will keep them aboard for now." From the midships they heard the canvas being taken off the cutter and the lines made fast. "Keep a good log, and remember: one month from today, on this spot. We will be watching for you."

The crewmen pulled at their sweeps toward the coast and they passed over the bar. As the surf line passed behind them the water changed from dark green to a muddy jade. "Just how shallow is this water, Sam?" With the uniforms packed away, there was no need for formality.

"Eight feet, maybe. Less after a flood silts it up."

Two and a half miles up the stream they made out the wooden shingle roofs of a small but busy town and then, jutting from the right bank, a low wooden pier that proved to be of a pine board framework nailed to cedar poles pounded into the muck. The path was well-worn, but they encountered no one between there and the outer buildings of the town.

Carrying their portmanteaus, they approached an open-fronted livery stable whose proprietor, a large man in his fifties, hurried out to meet them. "Why, Mr. Sam! We were just discussing when you might be returning. Did you have a good trip?"

"Yes, thank you, Mr. Philpott. What is the news? Have the Mexicans invaded yet?"

"Not that we have heard." He set his hat, a sailor's cap of the German style, on his head. "Good thing, too. Word is the government is all in a mess."

"Mr. Hiram Philpott, this is my friend Mr. Putnam."

"How d'ye do, sir?" They shook hands.

Sam pointed into the stable. "How is my Ranger?"

"Oh, he had a double appetite this morning, Mr. Sam. Something must have told him you were coming home."

The dim of the livery stable was not unwelcome after looking into the morning sun. Sam led them straight to a stall housing a blooded stallion, as red as cherry wood, who shook his head and pranced in his place as Sam threw an arm over his withers and heavily patted his other side. "Well, that's my good boy. Yes, sir."

Bliven's sigh was audible. "Oh, Sam, he is magnificent."

"And smart as a whip. Mr. Philpott, Mr. Putnam will also be needing a horse for a few weeks, something nice and easy that won't be any trouble. Let's get them saddled up. Now, what do you mean the government is all in a mess?"

They led the horses into the corral, slipped on bridles, and lay blankets across their backs. "What we hear is everybody wants to run the show," said Philpott. "The Council has impeached the governor, the governor has dismissed the Council, everyone is issuing orders to everybody, each countermanding the other. The Mexicans could march in right this day and sweep everybody up."

"Well, we might have known."

"Seems to me we have way too many chiefs and not near enough Indians."

"Where are all the volunteers?"

"If you ask me," said Philpott, "they're all layin' low until they figure out just who is entitled to give them orders. I guess the biggest number are at Goliad, some in San Antone, maybe a smaller garrison at the Concepción mission."

"Where is Houston, do you know?"

"Oh, God Almighty, I think that man is the center of the storm. Seems like half the men in government would follow him anywhere because he used to be attached to Jackson, and the other half want nothing to do with him because he used to be attached to Jackson, or because he drinks, or because he left his white wife, or because he had an Indian wife, or whatnot of a reason."

Bliven smiled wryly at the memory of Houston's ruin in Tennessee. "Seems like I have heard all of this before, in years past."

Sam grunted. "The point is he is the only one of the whole lot who has actually been in battle and led men in battle. These other dunderheads have no idea what they are doing. They would scatter at the first sight of a Mexican line. How about it, Philpott? Do you know where he is?"

"Nope. I think it's a fair bet the one place he won't be is in San Felipe. Someone on the Council would probably try to have him arrested."

"How much do I owe you?"

"Boarding the Ranger, and two weeks' rental on this one here— seven dollars. Would that be convenient? If you keep the horse longer than that, we can settle up when you return him."

Sam fished the silver out of his coin purse. "Well, I guess we all have to make a living. Obliged to you, Hiram."

The road north from Velasco was a well-defined trace—nothing as would be called a turnpike in the Northeast—but there was no losing one's way. As evening overtook them, they called at a house near the road; they hailed a middle-aged couple in the yard, who happily gave them a meal and blankets to spend the night on the front gallery of their house. They stayed up late in conversation, draining Bliven of news from the United States, and anything he could tell them about his life in Litchfield. Morning brought ham and eggs and coffee, but the owners seemed wounded that Bliven offered them payment.

"He doesn't know how we do things around here, does he, Mr. Sam?" the husband asked.

"No. He's never been here in his life. See, Bliv, however much we Texans affect to need no one and nothing, the truth is none of us could get by without the hospitality of our neighbors. It is freely given and cheerfully accepted. When the night comes that they knock on my door, the same will be extended to them. Now, it's true that some people have gone into full-time inn keeping, and they charge a rate just like you would expect back home, but we out here never expect payment for putting people up for the night."

Bliven's surprise was evident. "I ask your pardon, I meant no offense. How can you tell the difference?"

"Well, an inn might or might not have a sign by the road. We just know."

That second day the coastal grass gave way more and more to belts of oak forest, with taller hardwoods along creeks and sloughs—cottonwoods and pecans.

"You know," said Sam, "there is another side to that whole thing about paying for lodging. There has never been much money in circulation out here. People might live for months on barter without a coin changing hands. When you offer people money you can appear sort of high-handed."

"I had no idea."

Late in the morning they passed from one belt of oak into a meadow more elevated and rolling than the ones before. Midway through it a path extended to the left, and by it a signpost neatly but homely painted "HALCYON." "Why, this is it," exclaimed Bliven.

"Yes."

"Then this would explain the postal address I have been using all these years: Halcyon Plantation, Bolivar, Texas."

"Yes. Bolivar is just a couple of miles further up the road."

They turned from the road onto the path that led west from the sign, and Bliven pointed to a roof rising from the tall grass ahead. "That must be your house, but where are your fields?"

"Further on. My land backs up to the river. When General Austin was laying out the land grants, he thought ahead to make them long and narrow so that everyone would have frontage on the Brazos and be able to get their produce down to a market. The riverboat stops for everyone who has cotton or hides or corn waiting on the bank."

"You have steamboats?" Something so modern seemed out of place on so raw a frontier.

"Sure. What do you think, we wear skins and hunt with clubs?"

"I am happy that you can get all the goods you need. What about Indians?"

Sam shrugged. "The Kronks were a problem in the early days, but after we organized some ranging companies, they were punished so hard for killing or stealing they pretty much leave us alone now. There's some wilder tribes further up the river, but this is pretty well out of their hunting grounds. Then you get out past them, that's Comanche country, but no white man has any business up there—at least, not yet."

"I see. Now, Austin's grant was as large as most countries in the world. What led you to this location? Anything in particular?"

"Apart from being on the river, I just tried to figure out where the future business would be. I got lucky, too, because Bolivar up ahead is where the road from Brazoria to San Felipe crosses the road from Columbia to Harrisburg. That, and the east part of this land here by the road is a little higher than most. When I first looked it over I went down by the river and I looked up and saw old grass and leaves caught in the tree branches, so I could figure how high the water gets when there is a flood, and I know the house is safe."

Bliven thought it strange to converse so long while walking their horses through the front yard of a single house, but at length the grass was tamped down into a clearing. "And this is your house?"

"Yup."

"Why, Sam, it is just charming."

Sam laughed loudly. "I have wondered what you would say if you ever saw it. That is kind of you to say so, but there is no need to pretend. We both know it is nothing like what I knew back at Abbeville."

"But, like a cat, you have landed on your feet. I had so hoped for you, Sam, that life would treat you right after handing you so much misfortune."

Sam was taken off guard by such a kind sympathy. "Yes. Well, you have to take what life gives you or you get unhinged, like my first two boys. Look, now, we built the kind of house that everyone has hereabouts. It is sort of a local invention, and if there is such a thing as genius among the common people, this is its product. You see? You get your land and move onto it, and you build a single log pen to live in while you get settled. Then, when you are ready, you build a second one, just the same size, next to it but not too close. That gives you one room to live in and one to sleep in. Then you connect them with the single roof, and that gives you a nice, cool place to sit out in warm weather, or out of the rain. Then at some point you build the kitchen out back.

"Then, if you want, you can close in that open porch for a third room, and when you need to, you extend shed roofs off the back for two more rooms, and if you planned it right and made your ceiling high enough, you can put two more rooms up in the eaves, with stairs in the central hall, and add this gallery across the front. I know it looks humble, but it's as much as most anyone needs."

"My word, that is efficient, isn't it?"

"Now, some few of our rich folks have built big mansions like they had back home, but really they're just showing off. No one needs to live like that. Besides, as you remember, I was starting over."

As they were halfway across the clearing, a Negro woman wearing a blue dress patterned in darker blue exited the house, wiping her hands on an apron. "Well, Mr. Sam, praise the Lord! He has brought you safe home."

They dismounted, and Sam embraced her with a jarring familiarity. "Bliv, do you remember Dicey? She was just a little girl when you met her in Abbeville."

"Oh, my heavens, yes! Dicey, it is so good to see you. Do you remember, you brought us lemonade when I was visiting with Mrs. Bandy?"

"Oh, yes, I remember that very well." She advanced and extended her hand; he was surprised but he took it, uncertain in the scheme of things what her station might be in this household. "I remember I was so shy I liked to have died."

A black man came around the side of the house, thirty and power-fully muscled, fully but inexpensively clad in the station of the slave, but the presence of shoes told that he was a well-kept slave. "Wel-come home, Mr. Sam. Shall I take the Ranger into the barn and give him and his friend a rubdown and some supper?"

"Yes, Silas, that will be fine." He and Bliven slid their portman-teaus down from the saddles and handed over the reins. Bliven fol-lowed Silas to the edge of the house and saw a large barn with a corral beyond. When he turned back he beheld Sam and Dicey kiss-ing passionately. Then they stood facing him, arms around each other. "Come, my sweet. Let us help Captain Putnam into the house, I fear we have given him a shock. Where are the boys?"

"Can't say exactly. Romping out back with Pompey and them. They'll be around."

They mounted two low steps to the gallery porch that extended the width of the house. Dicey passed inside but Bliven held back. "Now, Sam," he whispered. He was not sure what to say. "Remem-ber, I have been all over the world. I know from my own experience that different countries have different customs."

"Ho, that was a good effort," said Sam grandly. "It is all right, you are permitted to be shocked. But I'll tell you the truth: that our ac-commodation is not at all unusual in these parts." He opened the front door. "Look down here. See this? A brass lock set! It makes us the envy of our neighbors; most of them use latchstrings. The hinges are rawhide, though; it's plentiful and doesn't squeak." They passed inside, and Sam continued, "See this floor? Sawn pine lumber. Most people use puncheons out here because wood doesn't last in this cli-mate, owing to the termites, but I brushed them on the bottom with some nautical pitch that I had saved, to see if that would stop them, and we haven't fallen through yet."

Suddenly, Bliven realized that Sam was attempting to draw him out of his consternation over Dicey and decided to cooperate. "So then this used to be the open passage between the two cabins, as you described?"

"Exactly."

"And these stairs go up to the eave rooms?" There was a staircase that ascended the right wall of the hall, as steep almost as a ship's ladder.

"Yes, and out back you see the kitchen, and that is Dicey's domain. Oh, and come look at this!" He passed out a back door opposite where they had entered, onto a small porch. "See, we have a well, and this." He pointed to a wooden frame of three shelves whose legs stood in a shallow zinc pan with an inch of water in the bottom. Around the shelves was stretched white cotton sheeting tacked into the top, the trailing edge of which rested in the water. "Here, try this." Sam pulled aside the damp cloth, and from a beige crockery pitcher poured a cup of cool, fresh buttermilk. "We have a German neighbor, name of Lederle, across the road. It's an invention of theirs: in all the summer heat, this thing keeps milk, butter—everything— just as cool as can be. He had some big word for it that I don't remember."

"'Evaporation'?" asked Bliven.

"I believe that was it. Our first German came through here about five years ago, and a few more every year since. Cleverest people you ever saw, and they work like the very devil."

"And they are good neighbors, apparently."

"Well, like with the lodging for travelers, we do help each other out. His place backs up only to Oyster Creek, so I let him use my dock on the river whenever he wants."

"He came by yesterday," said Dicey, and she pointed to the bottom shelf of the cooler. "He brought that haunch of venison that we're having for supper."

"Well, God damn! Bliv, see what I mean? Let's get out of her way. Come back inside and have a glass of wine."

"I am with you." Bliven's eyes met Dicey's for a short, deep look. "Dicey, I am very happy to see you again."

"Me, too, Cap'n Putnam. You go along, now."

The parlor lay to the right of the central hall, furnished with a settee and chairs of fine rosewood, as was a table with a marble top. At a sideboard Sam emptied a bottle of ruby-red wine into a decanter that he set, with two glasses, onto a silver gallery tray and carried it to the marble-topped table.

"Your house is very finely furnished," said Bliven. "Were you able to bring these pieces with you from South Carolina, or did you acquire them here?"

Sam poured the wine. "One big wagonload we were able to save. Good furniture out here is almost impossibly dear."

"Sam, I have a confession."

"What is that?"

"I think I like your Texas."

"Do you?"

"From everything I have seen of the people, they are frank and friendly. Consider that place we stayed in last night, this custom of yours to take in travelers and accept no money. If you are to have a revolution with the aim to join the United States, such people would be of benefit to the country, it seems to me."

Sam nodded. "I am glad to hear this."

"But you do realize the political obstacles to it, surely. The Northern states will fight like hell before allowing another slave state into the Union. That would give the South a majority in the federal senate. They will never countenance that."

"Then let the war be for independence. We must separate from Mexico, and we can go it alone as a separate country. The United States will want us in time, maybe after we start selling our cotton to the English cheaper than theirs. We're not stupid, you know." A quiet descended for several moments. "You are being so very good not to ask me about Dicey. It is all right, Bliv. You're holding a lot in, so speak up."

He shrugged. "I am just surprised, is all." Then he added, "When you told me that you were only somewhat married, and explained your separation, I assumed that was the extent of it. Now I realize that was, well, not the end of the story."

Sam leaned back in the settee. "Sometimes fate throws you together with someone, and you discover sympathy, and affection. Other people may not understand or approve, but at some point you have to decide which is harder to bear, their disapproval or your own misery."

They heard a commotion at the rear of the house, and when they went out Sam exclaimed, "Howdy, boys!"

"Papa!"

Bliven saw him clutched by apparent twin boys of about ten, whom he scooped up into his arms. In the face they looked like him, but of darker skin, and very curly brown hair. "Bliv, meet the new family, Robert and Stephen. Apparently they knew we were in a hurry to start a family, as they arrived at the same time."

In a flash the boys went storming off to the barn to play with a couple of Negro children visible there. "Goodness, what energy they have. As for myself and my modest needs, I should probably visit your head, if you will tell me where to go."

Sam and Dicey looked at each other, their eyes wide. "Lord, Cap'n Putnam," said Dicey. "You don't know? That's why God give us bushes."

Bliven stared back. "Bushes?"

"Didn't Mr. Sam tell you? We are going to have us a democracy here in Texas. I don't empty slop jars no more."

"You will see a pail of corncobs by the path, if you need one," said Sam.

"Corncobs?"

"Granted, it is a little more primitive than the lamb's wool you keep in your captain's privy, but Texas makes the whole man tough." He laughed, loudly and suddenly. "Even his arse."

Bliven nodded slightly in defeat. "Where is this path?"

"Around the side," answered Sam. "Come on, I'll show you. Be mindful of any snakes when you get down in the slough."

"And watch for poison ivy," added Dicey.

Bliven sighed. "Oh, Lord."

"You know," said Sam, placing an arm around Bliven's shoulder as he escorted him to the corner of the house and pointed the way, "our German friends, the Lederles, and the others who have settled up-country, they build a little house, maybe four feet square, over a cess-pit. They think they're so civilized, but the fact is they are positively indecent. That just advertises your business: everybody knows what you're doing in there."

"But you know why I am going into the bushes. What is the difference, except maybe the lack of poison ivy?"

Sam and Dicey's room lay to the left of the hall, the two boys slept in a shed room behind it, and Bliven was shown up the stairs to a bedroom above the parlor, having for light a single candle wedged into a brass holder. He could stand erect when under the ridge beam of the roof but had to duck to stretch out in a low bed with a mattress soft with ball moss.

Sam rode for Bolivar first thing in the morning, leaving Bliven to explore the plantation, which was on a scale that was hard for him to fathom. It did not surprise him that there were no fences as he would have seen at home. How does one go about fencing a property as easily measured in square miles as in acres? West of the house and gardens and the cabins where the slaves lived, he walked down a well-trod dirt path, gradually lower as he got nearer the Brazos, with vast plowed fields to both left and right. After two miles he began to wonder if he should have come armed in case he happened across Indians. Eventually he could see the gallery forest that he knew must define the course of the river and turned back. In New England no one would know what to do with this much land. The Germans who lived across the road must have their work cut out for them just to haul their produce down to Sam's landing.

He was curious to look into the slave cabins but did not, knowing that Sam—when he heard about it—would feel under examination, that Bliven was investigating whether the stories of neglect and mistreatment told by abolitionists were really true. The condition of the field hands he could not address, but Dicey seemed no different from any other matron tending children and a farm—she was busy, efficient, cheerful.

He did not recognize all her chores, and that evening after dinner, with Sam not yet returned, he was reading by the fire when he spied her set aside a basket of mending to screw some kind of mechanism into the bottom of a candlestick. "Dicey, forgive me. What are you doing?"

"Oh, Lord, Cap'n Putnam, out here in these parts, ain't nothing so precious as tallow. Candles are so dear, some people just can't buy 'em. So our German neighbors give us these candlesticks. See, they twist up from the bottom, so as the candle burns down, the bottom comes up, and nothing is ever wasted."

"Fascinating. I have never seen the like." In his memory he could still hear his father dressing down Clarity for buying candles of beeswax at eight times the cost of tallow.

"I got hot water in the kettle. Would you like a cup of tea?"

"I would love a cup of tea."

She rose and prepared it, pouring the hot water through a strainer. "What do you like in it?"

"Maybe just a spoon of sugar?"

When she gave it to him, Bliven slurped to cool it a bit more as he sipped it, and his eyes shot open. "Dicey! What is this tea? What on earth?"

She looked up from her mending. "You don't like it?"

He held the cup down to his lap and stared at it. "Dicey, I have been to China, I have had the best teas in the world. This beats all of them to pieces. I must know, what is it? Where is it from? Where did you get it?"

Dicey grinned. "Well, it ain't dark yet. You drink it on down, and I will show you where we get it."

After he finished they went out back and she took up a small basket. She led him down a path from the side of the house, a different direction from the path where the corncobs were destined, and in a couple of hundred yards it narrowed into a stand of gray-green bushes, most of them from four to six feet tall. Dicey walked on and the shrubs closed around them, and then she stopped and twirled in a circle. "Well, Cap'n Putnam, here we are. These here thickety yaupon bushes is where we get our tea."

Bliven fingered a branch and examined the leaves, two-thirds of an inch long and half as broad. "I have never heard of these."

"You can't buy them in no store, but when you poor and colored you learn about things." She laughed suddenly. "And some things are pretty good. White folks would have a fit if they knew we drink better tea than they do."

"How did you learn about them?"

"From some of the slaves hereabouts, they learnt it from the Indians. It's so easy. Just pick the leaves, toast 'em, and grind 'em—nothin' to it. Look here, you help me pick a bunch, and I'll fix some up for you to take with you."

"Oh! Oh, yes!"

"Now, be careful you don't pick no berries. The berries will make you powerful sick. Just the leaves, now."

"The mature leaves or just the new ones?"

"Don't matter, so far as I know, but I wouldn't strip whole branches; that might kill them."

"All right, just a few from each branch." Every time he gathered a double handful, he poured them into her basket. "Dicey, now that Sam has gone into town, may I ask you something?"

"Surely, I've been thinking you might."

"You and Sam . . . I . . . well, you can imagine my surprise to learn that you are . . ." He let the sentence hang unfinished.

Dicey dusted the detritus of yaupon leaves off her hands onto her apron. "Cap'n Putnam, did you ever have a sailor on your ship wanted to ask you something but he was so scared to, you finally had to tell him that he could speak freely?"

"Yes, in fact I have."

"Then, for the Lord's sake, speak freely!"

"If I may ask, how did it happen? How did it begin?"

Dicey resumed plucking yaupon leaves, but thoughtfully. "It's all right, I don't mind you asking. When Miss Rebecca died, I never saw a man brought so low as Mr. Sam was. I was afraid he might harm himself. Yes, sir, I was sore afraid. And I was afraid of what might happen to me without him. It was maybe three weeks after she died, one night after supper. I was putting the dishes away, and he went to bed. Even though he was upstairs, I could hear him. I went up to the door of his room and he was crying like a child. So I took off my shoes and I went in and I laid myself down beside him. And I've never left him."

"So you mean he's never forced you—"

"Lord, no! This was my doin'."

Bliven felt himself oddly on the defensive. "I'm just not certain that . . . I mean, do you think it's right . . . for you to be together?"

Dicey looked at him blankly for some seconds, then heaved a sigh, rolling her head and eyes as though she were following the sun from dawn until nightfall. "Why? Because we're not married? Because I'm colored? Because he was my master?" She shook her head slowly. "Mm-mm! Where on earth did you find such a high horse to sit on?"

Even as a Northerner, and thinking of himself now as an abolitionist, no Negro had ever lectured him so. "Now, Dicey, I don't place myself in any kind of judgment over you. But isn't it true that many of the preachers, both in the South and the North hold that God—"

"God? Pshaw! Where was God when I was torn away from my home when I was too little to have any sense? Then when I was torn away from my mama? Where was God when Miss Rebecca died? Where was God when that speculatin' banker left Sam with near nothin'? Sam and I made our vows to each other, and God can like it or He can just leave us be! Let me make something clear to you, Cap'n Putnam. Sam can't marry me—his Catholic wife seen to that—but even if he was free, he still couldn't marry me because I'm colored. And he can't free me, because slave catchers would take me unawares and sell me somewheres else. But I can tell you, as between him and me, he did free me; he just dassen't try to make it legal." Dicey opened her arms and gestured into the forest. "Look around you, Cap'n Putnam, this is as good as this life will ever get for me. And you know what? This ain't bad. I have a man who loves me, a good, snug home, all the good food I can eat, children to raise and teach right from wrong. No, sir, this ain't bad at all."

Bliven nodded in thought. "What about that Catholic wife? She must have complicated things a little bit."

Dicey smiled wickedly. "Well, I guess I did have to share him for a while. She didn't last, though." She laughed, deep in her chest, husky and victorious.

Bliven had been in the fighting Navy long enough to know when to strike his colors. He stood closer and took her hand. "Then, Dicey, if you and Sam are happy together, I will have no more to say about it. I will just be happy for you."

"Thank you, sir." She squeezed his hand. "Do you mean that truly, or are you just keeping the peace?" When he had no ready answer, she patted him on the chest. "Well, I expect you'll try, anyway. That's pretty good."

NEXT MIDDAY BLIVEN held Sam's horse as he dismounted in the yard, then asked, "Did you have a good visit? Find out what you needed?"

"Well, let's say that I learned a hell of a lot." They walked around the house and Sam poured himself a cup of buttermilk from the pitcher in the evaporator. "What Hiram told us in Velasco about the government being in chaos doesn't begin to cover it. There is no government to speak of. The one thing that everybody agrees is that it has broken down; it was a mistake to try and make a government that would please everyone, so there is going to be a new convention to declare independence."

"Where is Houston?"

"Some weeks ago he rode into town after being out rounding up volunteers, and he was so disgusted he didn't want anything to do with any of them. He told them to get things fixed, and he was going to the Redlands and make a treaty with the Cherokees to not take sides in the war when it comes. So, he is in Nacogdoches."

"How far is that?"

"Six days, if we push."

"Six days! Did you think he would be so far away?"

"No, I didn't expect that. But morning will be soon enough to start."

They rode north, the coastal prairies with their belts of trees gradually giving way to higher meadows, with large sections of a stout, short oak of a species Bliven had never seen before, and when they turned east, within three days they found themselves in a pine forest. It was thin at first, and interspersed with cedar brakes, but gradually it thickened and darkened above them.

Nacogdoches lay on the old Camino Real, so there was no danger of them getting lost, and the whole area was settled enough that they could count on being put up for the night and not have to sleep on their blankets in the woods.

"This is a substantial little town, Sam," said Bliven as they entered it at last. "How many people live here, would you say?"

"Oh, three or four hundred. No census that I know of. This road here will run right into the Stone Fort; that'll be the best place to ask where to find Houston, and we can change into our uniforms there."

Houston's camp, as they learned, lay near the Cherokee village north and west of town, and darkness overtook them so that they found the last mile by the light of campfires ahead. They dismounted when they were challenged by a sentry, and Sam said, "Two officers to see General Houston."

"Very well, if you will follow me." There were not more than fifty men in the camp, which was well organized and clean.

The sentry pulled aside the flap of a United States military regulation tent, revealing lantern light within. "Excuse me, General, two officers are here to see you." He stood aside and held it open for them.

Sam and Bliven ducked through the opening and beheld a

powerful-looking man in his early forties rising from a camp table. As he came around it, Bliven marked that he was perhaps six feet two inches tall, only slightly more than himself. He glanced down, curious whether a pair of boots added to that height, and saw he was wearing beaded Indian moccasins. He had auburn hair, thinning on top and pulled back into a queue, a strong brow and bridge of the nose, a pronounced cleft in his chin, and remarkable eyes of a brilliant, brilliant sky blue evident even in the lamplight. "Gentlemen," he said. They saluted, which Houston returned. "Mr. Bandy, you are welcome." His voice was deep and sonorous.

"General, may I present Captain Bliven Putnam, late of the United States Navy?"

He advanced far enough to shake hands. "Captain, welcome."

"I believe I am still in the United States Navy, General, but in truth I cannot say that I am certain"—he produced the letter with which he had been entrusted—"but I am sure that I have been charged to pass this to your hand and none other, for it seems to be a matter of some importance."

Houston took it with a low and deeply basso laugh. "I sympathize with your plight, Captain, for mine is not dissimilar. Pray, be seated, and indulge me, for I must read this before we proceed." As he broke the seal on the letter he resumed his seat in a ladderback chair with a cane seat whose angles altered beneath his weight, and he moved the lantern closer. He indicated camp stools for his visitors to seat themselves upon and began squinting at the letter. "As much as I esteem General Jackson," he muttered, "his hand becomes more of a curse to read the older he gets." Even across the table Bliven could tell the writing was small and crabbed and angular, the ink thick and the lines closely spaced.

"Well," Houston said at last. "Have you gentlemen been to San Felipe?"

"I was lately there," said Sam. "That's how I knew where to find you. While I was there, I thought it prudent to leave Captain Putnam at my place near Bolivar."

"Quite right."

The tent flap opened again. "I'm sorry, General, Mr. Bowie is here and says it is urgent that he—"

Before he finished, Bowie brushed behind him and into the tent. "Your pardon for the interruption, Houston. I have just come from the Cherokee camp." He glanced at Sam and Bliven. "Oh, may I?"

"James Bowie, colonel of volunteers, this is Sam Bandy and Bliven Putnam of our incipient naval department."

"Gentlemen," said Bowie, taking their hands in a crushing grasp.

"I have heard of you," said Bliven.

"I hope you don't believe it all."

So, this is Bowie at last, he thought. He wanted badly to say that he had hunted Laffite in 1817 for slave smuggling and if he had taken Bowie at the same time he would have hanged them both. Bowie had made his wealth in slaves and land fraud, and become infamous for his skill at knife fighting, stemming in part from an incident in Mississippi when he and an antagonist were locked in an icehouse from which only one of them would emerge alive, and that proved to be Bowie. Indeed, he had visited a blacksmith with a drawing for an improved weapon that could both stab like a dagger and slice, as well as being heavy enough to chop like a machete. The instrument was named for him and was ubiquitous across the whole van of the advancing frontier, but it was only now when Bliven saw one, presumably the original model, thrust through Bowie's belt that he appreciated the ferocity of its look. Its size was frightening, the blade a full twelve inches long and an inch and a half broad. The only knife he had seen to equal it was the Arab jambia he had taken in the Barbary War; he had given it to his father, and it now reposed on his mantel in Litchfield. He had left off taking it to sea with him as a youthful affectation, but at this moment he regretted leaving it at home, for he and Bowie could have held court on their respective virtues. As it was, he nodded his head at the weapon. "The famous Bowie knife?" he asked.

"It is."

"You do not use a scabbard?"

"Not when I treat with Indians. If any of them makes a threat to me, as Indians are wont to do, I want them to know what they're getting into. Now, General," Bowie said, returning to his subject, "the Bowl and the other chiefs have said they will agree to remain neutral in the coming fight with Mexico. They thank you for not asking them to join you, and they will take no action to help the Mexicans. But for this they require your word of honor that you will not again try to bring Creeks down here from the Indian Territory to settle among them. They say the land you will cede to them is only large enough to support themselves, and besides that, they don't even like Creeks. They say they always cause trouble and they want nothing to do with them. They would like some answer before they sleep tonight."

Houston stood, arms folded, looking downcast. "Very well. Tell my father—and now be certain you say it just this way—tell my father the Bowl that I am sorry my red brothers cannot live in harmony together. I believe that this must hurt the heart of the Great Spirit. But tell them that I understand, that the land we will give them is not as large as they deserve, nor as large as I would wish to give them, but it is as much as I believe the government will agree to let them have. And tell them I agree that I will have no more talks with the Creeks except to tell them they cannot come to this part of the country. Bowie, do you think that will satisfy them?"

"Yes, sir. We will draw up the treaty and you can all sign it as soon as you can arrange a big smoker to all meet."

"Thank you, Bowie. Good night."

"General." Bowie saluted and left. Houston sat heavily, shaking his head.

Bliven noted his sadness. "General, if I may?" Houston looked up. "Two years ago I was in Florida. My ship was damaged off the Bahamas, and I put in at St. Augustine to effect repairs. It was at the time that Fort King was reactivated, and I had to take supplies and a garrison up there."

"The beginning of the Seminole trouble," said Houston.

"Exactly. I had to witness a council with those Indians, and if I may be so bold, I believe you just acted as wisely as the Seminole agent acted rashly and foolishly."

"Who was that agent?"

"His name was Wiley Thompson, sir."

"Then this news might hold some meaning for you. We learned not two weeks ago that the Seminole Indians have killed Mr. Thompson and gone on the warpath."

Bliven drew a deep breath. "Oh, no, I had no idea. I am sorry to hear it, but I am not surprised. I found his lack of sympathy for the Seminoles, and the bluntness with which he told them they would have to quit their lands and remove to the west, to be quite dangerous, even reckless."

"Captain"—Houston looked at him coldly—"I knew Wiley Thompson well. He was in Congress before I arrived there and remained there after I left to assume the office of governor of Tennessee. No man was more dedicated to the advance of civilization on this continent."

"I apologize, General. I did not mean to give offense."

Houston dropped his head. "On the subject of Indian removal, however, I am more inclined to agree with you. Are you aware that I lived with the Cherokees for six years?"

"I knew only that you went to the Indian Territory after you resigned as governor. I believe that was in the newspapers."

Houston laughed lowly and grew reflective. "Yes, but long before then. I was thirteen when my father died, and my mother moved the family to Maryville in Tennessee, right on the border of the Cherokee Nation. I did not feel that I was cut out to be a plow boy and stock clerk, so I ran away when I was sixteen. I had many friends among the Cherokees, and I lived among them for three years. I was adopted by their chief, who gave me the name of the Raven, which is a totem of their religion that signifies good fortune, but also wandering. Eventually I returned home to go to work and pay debts I had accumulated. Then I joined the Army. I advanced to the rank of lieutenant, and I came to the notice of General Jackson, who took me onto his staff after I was thrice wounded fighting the Creeks in the Battle of Horseshoe Bend. After I recovered, he made me the federal agent to those Cherokees with whom I had lived. Then General Jackson made me responsible for moving them west to the Indian Territory. That was a wrong thing to do and a wrong policy, but that was not something that a junior officer tells to a general. Captain Putnam, have you yet had the occasion of feeling compelled to obey an order you did not agree with?"

"Yes, as I did even in coming to Texas." Bliven pursed his lips. "Sir."

Houston laughed again, deep and chesty. "I appreciate that. I was still quite young, and I guess I was a little afraid of Jackson. He can be rather overpowering, and those were the orders he gave me."

"Could you not have resigned?"

"Yes, but I had come to love those people as my own family. If I had resigned, they would have been removed by someone who cared nothing for them, and they would have suffered the terrible consequences that we have seen be endured by others in recent years, the Chickasaws and the Choctaws—and, yes, the Seminoles—including the deaths of hundreds. By staying, I was able to rather conspire, you might say, with the Tennessee governor, who added state money to my own budget to make sure those Indians had adequate food and clothing for their journey." Houston sighed deeply. "So my name is still attached to a wrong policy that would have been infinitely worse and caused far more suffering if I had resigned for the sake of my precious little conscience."

It had been decades since Bliven Putnam at forty-seven had felt so taken to school. "I understand, sir," he said quietly.

"Wiley Thompson was a good American, but he could be a fool. The two are not mutually exclusive. But, anyway, when I left Tennessee, I went to the Indian Territory and was welcomed by those same Cherokees who took me in when I was a boy. It was a salve to my conscience to learn after ten years that they did not blame me for what had happened to them. But now, gentlemen, it has been alleged that when I take to reminiscing, I can keep people all night, and we do not have all night. Putnam, you have been seconded to the Republic of Texas Navy—never mind whether it yet officially exists—to protect our coast while we attempt to deal with the dictator on land. You may read this, it concerns you."

PRESIDENT'S HOUSE
WASHINGTON, DIST. OF COLUMBIA

Much Esteemed Sir:

This letter will introduce you to Captain Bliven Putnam, of Connecticut, in command of the warship, stricken from our list but still eminently serviceable for your needs, to assist you in your struggle for freedom. Putnam proved his valor as a young midshipman during the Barbary War, again as a Lieut. Commdt. in the War of 1812, and on other missions of importance and delicacy to the country.

It is no mystery to you, sir, as we have spoken of this since 1832, that Texas at some date must separate from Mexico, and her American population join themselves once more to their mother country. The rise of Santi Anna as a murderous despot, while surely to be deplored by all humanity, is the perfect circumstance for them to rise up. For political reasons at home, and for diplomatic reasons abroad, I cannot be seen to aid you. But while he will invade by land, he must be supplied by sea, and this may prove his undoing.

Now, Houston, I am relying on your Cherokee wiles. Putnam is dear to us, one of the best we have. Do not let his name or nationality be known. Putnam, the ship, and provisions for a cruise of six months, I send you. Once he gets to New Orleans, he will be in

*Texian service (for all that anyone must know). Your agent there
must raise him a crew of volunteers, and use him as best you can. If
he is captured, he must share the fate of yourself or any other Texian,
may God forbid, who are captured by that rabid wolf, Santi Anna.
And now for God's sake, burn this letter.*

> *Yours sir, with great esteem and respect,*
> *Andrew Jackson, Presdt.*

GENL. SAM HOUSTON

IN CAMP

Bliven felt his face flush as he read it. He could well imagine that
Jackson had given a general order to help the Texas cause and left the
doing of it to the navy secretary and his minions. But that Jackson
himself, that figure upon whom Bliven had expended so much contempt, actually knew his name and selected him for this duty was
fresh evidence of how he had underestimated him. Bliven's face betrayed the tiniest of smiles. "I notice that once you read it you did not
burn the letter, General. There sits a candle, already lit."

Houston shook his head emphatically and pointed at him. "Nor
will I do it, until the revolution succeeds. The great object, if God
favors us, is to free Texas from Mexico and, if God further favors us,
to join her to the United States. If we succeed, there will be time
enough to destroy this letter. But if we fail, and if I am captured,
then I will see that this letter falls into the dictator's hands before I
am shot. He will declare war on the United States, which war he
must lose, badly, and Texas will be annexed just the same. That must
be accomplished whether any of us survive the battle day."

"Suddenly I perceive the depth of your earnestness," said Bliven.

"Well, keep it to yourself. For now it serves my purpose for people to think I don't know what I'm doing."

Putnam rose and regarded the map spread over the camp table. "No, sir, General," he said, pointing at the crooked inky line that was the Sabine River. "It seems to me you know precisely what you are doing. Once the Mexicans invade and come east, if you can get Santa Anna to follow you to the Sabine, General Gaines is west of Natchitoches with a large force of infantry. If you can get within his striking distance, he will cross into Texas and settle the issue once and for all."

Bliven and Sam could almost see the color drain from Houston's face as his eyes shot open, accentuating their cutting, brilliant blue. Almost before Bliven finished speaking, Houston flew to his feet, snapping shut the tent flap, and lowering his voice to a hoarse whisper. "God damn it, Captain Putnam! There are not five men in the United States who know what you just told me. How in all echoing hell have you come to know the very depth of all our intriguing so carefully kept secret?"

"I am sorry, General." Bliven held up his hands defensively. "At the time I reached New Orleans, volunteers were actively being whipped up to organize and march to Fort Jesup. It was commonly discussed."

"God damn!" Houston breathed. "I had no idea. If one of my soldiers told me what you just told me, I would have him shot before risking that General Gaines's name be attached to this campaign in any connection. Do you understand my meaning?"

Bliven and Sam exchanged looks, their eyes wide. "Our lips are sealed, General. No one will learn of it from us. But how can it matter now? If hundreds, even thousands of volunteers are joining, how can it be a secret?"

"Putnam, men are volunteering all across the United States. That is no secret. These men in Louisiana believe they are part of that movement; as far as they know they are just coming to Texas to fight. What no one knows is that for *these* men there is a plan behind it, and if Santa Anna caught one breath of it, he would never place himself within striking distance of the American army."

"Very well, I understand."

"Now, this probably won't mean anything to you, but I am engaging Santa Anna with the strategy of Fabius."

"Wait!" Bliven thought fast, trying to remember. "Quintus Fabius, who refused to fight Hannibal and his elephants head-on after they crossed the Alps?"

Houston leaned back in shock. "I underestimated you, Captain Putnam."

"I have always loved history."

"Yes. And if you remember, the Roman Senate grew disgusted with his retreat, removed him from command, and installed some braggart who said he would fight, and Hannibal slaughtered the Roman army at the Battle of Cannae. Gentlemen, I run that exact risk with the fools who are governing Texas. I cannot allow there to be a Texian Cannae. No one, and I mean no one, must know that I have planned for events beyond the forecast of the village idiots on the Permanent Council. It is imperative that they be allowed to think they are directing me. An election will shortly be held for a new convention to assemble on the first of March, at which independence will be declared and an interim government organized. I do not much believe that Santa Anna can invade before then, but I cannot depend on it, and I need you to guard our coast as much as one ship can do."

"And you have the *San Felipe*."

Houston huffed. "A ship and a half, then. The four we have bought are not here yet."

"Well, then," said Bliven, "you will be pleased to hear of our first action. We were only a day out of New Orleans when, with Mr. Bandy's assurance that our commission was good as of that moment—"

"I will guarantee that," said Houston.

"—we overhauled an American trading brig. Under his most vigorous protest, we inspected his cargo and found him to be carrying forty-eight cases of rifled muskets of the latest design, plus pistols, powder, and bulk lead for melting into balls, bound for Matamoros. Under color that he was sailing in your war zone"—Bliven shook his head—"*our* war zone, we confiscated his cargo, and he returned in a rage back to New Orleans. The factors and the insurance companies are sure to be equally put out."

"But he did not know your true identity, am I correct?" said Houston.

"Only that we were a Texas warship, but he expressed his certainty that Texas could never float such a vessel of her own resources."

"That's all right, as long as he had no certain information. What did you do with all these arms?"

"They are in my hold until we learn from you whether you have some secure arsenal in which to store them until you need them."

"Where is your ship now?"

"I sent her back out for a month under my second lieutenant to continue the hunt. I did not want her anchored off Velasco all this time, raising questions."

"Well done," Houston said softly, "well done. This is all good to hear. There is the Stone Fort here in Nacogdoches, but that is too far inland to effect a clean transfer. In the forward areas there are only two stone fortifications that could serve as an arsenal, at Goliad and at the Alamo in San Antonio. They are in our power at present, but we have nowhere near enough men to hold them in the face of an invasion. To deposit such a cache of arms there would be as good as to hand them to Santa Anna in the end. However, I do not want them on your ship indefinitely, I want them at hand for after our volunteer army has come together." He studied his map. "Galveston," he said at last. "It is at the opposite end of the country and must be the last place that Santa Anna can reach if he overruns us. It is an island and protected by the lagoon. It cannot be assaulted except by boats. I will assign a new customs collector to that port and have him prepare a warehouse to receive these weapons, with enough men to guard them. When you get back on your ship, you will go to Galveston and confer with the customs collector. I will see to it that he is expecting you."

"Yes, sir," said Bliven. "That is how we shall proceed."

Houston leaned back in his chair. "Well, this has been satisfying to sort out. However, I am afraid, gentlemen, that what we have discussed to this point is but half of the intrigue that we must employ. After Galveston, once you put to sea, you must stay there for the duration of the conflict. Do not touch our shore again except to save your lives, and if you do so, you must disappear into the brush and make your best ways home."

"I don't understand, General," said Bliven.

"Well, it's like this. There is newly in Texas an unpleasant little man, one Robert Potter, formerly of North Carolina. I have reason to doubt his loyalty to our cause, and of his enmity to me personally there can be no doubt. He is campaigning to be a delegate to the coming convention, at which he expects himself to be made secretary of the navy."

"Potter?" Bliven shook his head slowly. "That name is distantly familiar to me."

"He was formerly in the navy of the United States; never made any great shakes. He had some connection to John Paul Jones; seems like maybe he was one of the boys who boarded with him while they studied."

Bliven snapped his fingers. "Of course! I was on the board of promotions that denied him advancement. According to his captain, he was a shirker and a troublemaker, and a constant duelist. He must hold the record for length of service as a midshipman without becoming a lieutenant."

Houston harrumphed in a suddenly jovial and avuncular way. "I did not know that, but I am not surprised."

"And the word was there was no counting the bastards he may have left in dockside stews around the world. One of his superior officers characterized him as ever first in line to claim his shore leave, first in line to boast of his conquests, and, at sea, the first to excuse himself from duty."

Sam Houston seemed to relax in the comfort of exchanging dirt on a man he hated so viscerally. "Well, then, that would be a rich irony, considering his career since that time."

"I know nothing of him since he resigned from the service."

"Oh, my God." Houston shook his head. "He ran for Congress in North Carolina, but the state election commission disallowed the vote on account of the violence of his partisans. Anyone who spoke against him wound up beaten by a roadside."

"Good Lord! How then does such a man design himself to become the secretary of your navy?"

Houston leaned back and laughed, in enough lamplight for his teeth to show white and his eyes their brilliant blue. "Well, boys, the likelihood is that at the convention he will be the only man present who has ever served on a ship at all! He is a persuasive talker, and I have no doubt he will secure the appointment he seeks."

Sam had been taking all this in. "At the time I came to Texas, I had to have a judge swear to my good character and industry."

"Ha!" barked Houston. "Then you did come early! Once the squatters came in their thousands, such nice stipulations were left far, far behind. Potter came one jump ahead of the law back in North Carolina. It seems there was an elderly minister of the holy gospel whom Potter maimed on the charge that he had violated Potter's wife."

"Good God! You mean he—"

"Castrated him like a steer. The shame of it was the charge was not only untrue, it was probably impossible owing to the man's age and infirmities. But rather than admit the mistake, Potter then charged his wife with lying with a seventeen-year-old boy, and he maimed him as well. Then, when the law came for him, he sloped for Texas, where he is beyond the reach of American justice."

"Heavens!" exclaimed Bliven.

"You judged him well when you denied him advancement. He would have made the worst commander since Captain Bligh."

"Lord, what kind of country are you going to have out here?"

"Crude, at first," said Houston. "All new countries are, at first. Well, boys"—he clapped his open hands onto his knees—"is this where we can leave it? You get yourselves back to Velasco, and when you meet your ship, sail her to Galveston and unload your armaments at the customshouse. They will probably have a further instruction for you from me."

Sam and Bliven stood to go, and Houston came around the table and shook hands with them. "Captain, you asked me earlier why I did not resign rather than accept the assignment of removing my Cherokees to the West. Shall I ask why you did not resign rather than allow yourself to be sent into our fray?"

"Well, in all candor, as my boat came down the Mississippi, I did not know what my orders would be, and I was in truth considering to resign, because I suspected that the administration—"

"By which you mean General Jackson?"

"—yes, sir—was involving me in some fantastical scheme in which I would not want my name involved. But I had never seen the West before, and I had never seen New Orleans before, and although I am no partisan of Jackson's, there is no gainsaying that he was responsible for keeping them in the United States. That stayed my hand until I could learn more. And having now traveled through your country, I am content to play out the hand, for the people I have met here deserve to be brought into the United States. Only I would take it as a great favor, when we deliver your arms to Galveston, to find a Texas service commission waiting for me there so I will feel less like a pirate. In my time I have fought enough pirates to be somewhat sensitive upon the subject."

Houston opened the tent flap. "Done. Sentry, find these gentlemen something to eat and a place to bed down."

They turned to follow, but stopped when they heard Houston bark after them, "Wait!"

He leaned close to the sentry and mumbled, "Hell, let them have some of my peaches."

7

Titania

Supper consisted of beans cooked with pork and onions, and fried chunks of more pork, served on pewter plates with two-tined camp forks. As they were finishing, the volunteer that Houston had spoken to rolled onto each of their plates two halves of a preserved peach. Unlike most canned food, peaches kept much of their flavor and texture and had just a hint of the spices they were preserved with.

There was no tent, but they slept on their blankets beneath a tarpaulin, grateful in the chill of the morning to awaken to hot bread and coffee. "General's compliments," said the man who had been minding them. "Would you be so good and to stop and speak with him before you return to Bolivar?"

At different times Bliven and Sam walked out into the undergrowth beneath the pines to relieve themselves, and straightened their uniforms before returning to Houston's tent. They found him taking his ease in a folding chair before it, and he rose at their approach. "Morning, boys. Did you sleep well?"

"Indeed, General, we did." Bliven did not dare say that he had cast off his blanket in the middle of the night when he awakened in a sweat, and then again while still damp, with a chill. It was only six days back to Bolivar, and medicine, and he hoped it was not the opening of a prolonged siege.

Houston held out a folded paper to each of them. "I have here your commissions, given under my hand and personal seal. No one can call you pirates and have any legal standing for it."

Unless, thought Bliven, *we are all pirates in Santa Anna's eyes*, but he kept that to himself.

"Now, on your way back down to the coast, I wonder if you would stop in Nacogdoches long enough to hand some letters off to Captain Sterne, who has been such a leader in that community?"

"Yes, sir," said Sam, "we'd be happy to." Houston handed him a packet of letters tightly wrapped with string.

"And you, Captain Putnam, you have heard Mr. Bandy recruiting men into the service of Texas on the promise of liberal bounties of land."

"I have, yes, sir. It has proven to be a most effective recruiting technique for him."

Houston laughed, revealing large, square, cream-colored teeth, a couple of which were missing. "Captain, I understand that you are already a man of property in Connecticut, and we know that you are continued in the service of the United States service as you are seconded to this duty. That does not lessen, however, the boon that you are conferring on our country with your activity here, and you should know that you are also now entered on the rolls for land bounty."

Bliven was taken aback. "That is generous of you. My thanks indeed." He did not know whether, being in United States service, he was allowed to accept such an emolument, but for the moment he would consider it extra pay for the trouble and risk he was running.

"You can't miss the Sterne's house: it is the especially nice one on Bonita Creek, on the east edge of town. I believe Captain Sterne has returned; he was lately in New Orleans, where he raised two companies of volunteers and paid for their equipage out of his own pocket. He is a German, some years younger than ourselves, and a good man and a true friend to Texas."

Sam tucked the letters in his pocket. "We will give him your best regards, General."

"And to his wife, my godmother."

"Sir?" asked Bliven. "I don't understand. Would that not make her a bit old to be—"

Houston waved his question down lightly. "No, no, when I first came here four years ago, the only way to get land was to become a Catholic. Sterne was the town's leading citizen and we were friends back in Tennessee, but he is also a Jew and was of no help in the realm of religion! His wife, however, is a good Catholic and stood as my godmother when I got sprinkled in their parlor."

The morning was chill but not freezing, and they were ready for something hot to drink by the time they reentered Nacogdoches and arrived at the Sternes' house. It was of the same form as Sam's and most of the houses in Texas except larger, with clapboard siding and a wing that extended from the rear. They found a dozen men on the front gallery and in the yard before it, downing coffee and hot biscuits and jam as they discussed the momentous politics of the day.

"Ah, so you have come from General Houston," said Sterne when they were presented to him. He was an ample man but not fat, with a round face, an open, frank expression, and wavy brown hair surrounding a perfectly round bald spot, giving him the look of a monk in an order.

"Yes, sir, he asked us to deliver these letters to you."

"You wear uniforms, gentlemen, but not like our New Orleans Greys. What is your duty, will you say?"

"We are the beginnings of your navy, Captain Sterne," said Sam. "We had to arrange some matters with Houston and now we are on our way down to the coast."

"Ah, yes, we are familiar with Captain Hurd and the *San Felipe*. She is a brave little ship, and if you can assist Mr. Hurd it will be very well."

Bliven smiled to himself. If this was all that even the involved citizens knew of their navy, so much the better for the *Gonzales*.

"Houston?" A young man of perhaps twenty spoke up. "That stinking-drunk Indian lover?"

"Gentlemen," said Sterne, "I introduce you to my son, Charles, of whom I am not always extremely proud. Charles, Houston will be made commander of the armies that will fight the Mexicans."

"Ssht," he hissed. "Well, if he wants to help us throw off the damn Mexicans, that's well enough, but I wouldn't take orders from him, so he needn't try it."

"Young man, if you are in the army, you will take the orders of the officers over you or you will land in big trouble." He waved his hands helplessly. "And you have said this in front of these other officers, so now none of them will have you!" The yard echoed with their laughing. "And I will tell you, my little Achilles, General Houston was shot to pieces in the service of his country when he was the same age you are, by God."

"And you think that excuses his morals?"

"When we were young, he showed me the wounds in his shoulder, so that I could see the bones working out of them. I believe he drinks because he is in pain. The only thing I say about his character with women"—Sterne lowered his voice—"is that he is frank in admitting his shortcomings, unlike other men, who are hypocrites."

Charles stalked away with an oath, but Sterne raised a finger after him. "And what is more," he shouted, "Houston was shot while fighting Indians, my little hero! He was shot with bullets and an arrow, both. We shall see how you do when your time comes." Sterne folded his arms across his chest as he watched his son disappear. "Gentlemen, I tell you the truth about a thing." His accent was heavily German. "A rebellious son is a curse from the Almighty."

The other men stood in quiet sympathy until Sam lightened the atmosphere. "Hell, is he the only one you got? I have two like that."

When Sterne began to smile, the others laughed. His shoulders lifted and fell. "Then, my friend, you are cursed indeed."

"I do not wish to speak out of turn," said Bliven, "but we were just with Houston, and he was as sober as could be."

"I have known him for many years," said Sterne. "He befriended me when I was an itinerant peddler selling goods out of a wagon. I believe that reports of his wild nature are an exaggeration."

"Still," said a man who had not been introduced, "there is that wife back in Tennessee that he abandoned."

"No, my friend." Sterne pointed at him. "I will tell you a thing. Everyone believes that Houston left her to come raise trouble in Texas for Jackson. But I happen to know that it was *she* who left *him*, because she did not love him and was forced by her family to marry him!"

"Your pardon, gentlemen," said Bliven. "We have a long trip ahead of us, and we must make haste."

IT WAS SIX DAYS back to Bolivar, near Velasco, and it was the fourth night that they stayed in a well-appointed plantation, the only one that could afford them a bed in a guest room. Sam was awakened in the predawn by Bliven's shaking, and upon lighting a candle found him pouring sweat.

Their saddle horses would not take to harness, so Sam obtained the loan of two draft animals. They made Bliven a pallet in the bed of a wagon, and it was in this state that they arrived back at Sam's Halcyon. While Dicey nursed him watchfully, Sam and his hand Silas rode down to Velasco. Sam went to find a doctor with quinine water, and Silas he dispatched to the beach to keep watch for the *Gonzales* and hail its boat as it crossed the bar. He also supplied Silas with a letter to show the men who would question him that he was there at the direction of his master. This siege of the malarial fever passed, and their reunion with the *Gonzales* was smoothly effected and attracted little attention, as they met their boat on the beach, not at the little dock in Velasco. March was nearing its end when they entered the harbor at Galveston and quickly located a new armory by its flag and sentries. Bliven found this letter waiting for him.

IN CAMP ON THE COLORADO
AT BURNHAM'S FERRY
MARCH 18, 1836

Dear Sir:

If you are reading this it means you have reached Galveston, and have made contact with Lieut. Besanson, who is to receive the cache of arms lately taken by your ship.

And if you have touched upon Texas soil you have doubtless learned that contrary to expectations, General Santa Anna has made his invasion, sooner than expected, and you must have learned of the melancholy fate of the Alamo and the brave men who defended it, who were killed to the last man after a stout defense of the place that lasted thirteen days. With San Antone gone, that leaves only Colonel Fannin with perhaps four hundred men at Goliad, as the only fighting force in Texas besides the men under my command. I have ordered him to abandon Goliad, blow up the fortress, and join his force to mine so as to mount an effective defense, but he has not done it. Therefore, he must alone face General Urrea who landed at Cópano with Santa Anna's Southern Army and is covering his right flank. If Fannin and Urrea meet, it must be a pointless and unnecessary sacrifice.

Since your visit to me near Nacogdoches, we have learned items of significance regarding Santa Anna's plans for Texas that have not been widely disclosed. It is commonly believed that he has invaded our country for the purpose of punishing the guilty and restoring an order loyal to Mexico. So far from that being the case, he was overheard in frank conversation among diverse persons at a diplomatic reception as long ago as December, saying that his purpose when he should invade Texas, was to fortify the Sabine River boundary with the U. States, who as you may know recognize the Neches River as the true boundary. In so doing, it is his intention to sweep all American settlement from the country and repopulate it with Mexicans loyal to him, who will take possession of fifteen years of American improvements in redeeming a productive country from what had been a wilderness. This terrifying dispossession of thousands of innocent civilians, fleeing willy nilly on foot and in carts, has begun, and it is sickening to watch. The dictator now has divided his army into four columns, well separated, to make sure that no Americans are left behind.

In that December reception, Santa Anna made so bold as to use the exact language, that he meant to "run that boundary at the mouths of my cannon," and teach old Andy Jackson to keep his people at home where they belong. This all was recently confirmed by intelligence from Washington itself, that the dictator's Foreign Minister Señor Gorostiza avowed the same thing to Jackson's very face. This was a costly error, for it put the Old Chief into a fearful temper.

Now, Captain, how this concerns you is just this: Santa Anna entered our country with artillery enough to reduce the fortress of the Alamo, but not nearly enough to fortify the three hundred miles of boundary with the U. States. We have intelligence in hand that

Santa Anna is expecting a large shipment of heavy guns, powder, and ball, to be landed on our coast, and forwarded on to him by General Urrea. These guns doubtless will be used against me if the opportunity presents itself, before arming a picquet line of fortifications along this eastern boundary that they claim. This intelligence is enforced by the practical consideration that the huge amount of powder and ball that they expended in the protracted siege of the Alamo must be replenished from some source if their expedition is not to exhaust their ammunition.

I remind you once more that the port of Cópano is in the enemy's power, and that is the likeliest place where such matériel would be landed. It is also possible that as I draw Santa Anna eastward, the guns may be landed at some other more easterly remote point on the coast, so as to have less distance overland to traverse. I judge this unlikely, for the ship would have no knowledge of Santa Anna's location after she leaves port, whereas Cópano is safely in their hands and Urrea is in close communication with his Master.

Therefore I urge you, Captain, to direct your operation to the southern reaches of our coast, and intercept all the vessels incoming to that place. You may achieve an inestimable good for your country, and they are powerless to stop you.

As for me, I am safe for the time being, Santa Anna plays the cat and I am the mouse. The Colorado is in flood. I have crossed, and burnt the ferry, and the ogre when he arrives will find that he cannot follow. There are those in my army who grumble daily that we should turn and fight, and that as I lead them in endless retreat I am no kind of man nor commander. They do not understand that if we fight we must not only win, but win every battle against four several armies of fresh soldiers. Their abuse is

hard to bear, but all will be revealed in the fullness of time.
Remember Fabius!

Godspeed and good hunting to you, Captain Putnam.

Yours with high consideration, &c., &c.,
Sam Houston
Commdr. in Chief

BLIVEN PUTNAM
CAPT. COMMDG TEXAS WARSHIP GONZALES
GALVESTON

Bliven got the arsenal officer's attention. "Lieutenant Besanson?"

"Captain?"

"How are your men doing with the unloading?"

"Five or six more trips in the lighter should suffice, I believe."

"Good. Keep them at it, if you please. We must put to sea urgently, and I do not wish to miss the tide."

Sam came down the board sidewalk and stood by him. "We are equally impatient to be gone, I think."

"Yes."

"But as long as we are stuck ashore, there is a matter that I would like to attend to, of a personal nature."

"Of course. Can you take care of it in a couple of hours?"

"Actually, sir, it involves you. May we?" He pointed back up the sidewalk, and they walked slowly together.

Bliven found himself concerned. "What is it, Sam?"

"I believe we are both confident of a good outcome to what lies ahead, but the fortunes of war are fickle. Even in a victory, a stray bullet, or spark near powder, and disaster will befall our families."

"It is possible, yes, although unlikely."

"You are a gallant man, Bliv, but a cautious one as well. No doubt, you have undertaken all the legal steps to ensure that your wife and family will inherit smoothly if anything should happen to you."

"Of course."

"I am in a different case. You know the Mexican law here in Texas is different than back home. Women can inherit and own property here same as men."

"But you're having a revolution against Mexico."

"Exactly my point. If we win the war, there is every chance that we will adopt American law, and—more to the point—the law of the Southern states. I want my property to go to Dicey and our children, but I cannot be sure that will happen. There are those here who oppose even having free blacks stay in the country."

"I see. Look, here are chairs on the sidewalk. May we sit? I am not feeling well."

"Of course. I am sorry."

"What about your two sons with Rebecca?"

Sam turned to make himself comfortable in his chair. "I am sorry to say this, but after long thought I have to look the truth in the face and say that they are no good. They split with me years ago and have no expectation."

"So what is your answer?"

"I have my new will with me, that if Dicey and the boys cannot be freed, and be secure that their freedom will be recognized"—he hesitated—"I am leaving everything to you, on condition that you or an agent appointed by you will sell it all and use the money to get Dicey and the boys to Connecticut, where you can free her and no one will question it. Are we still friends enough that you would do that for me?"

"If we are on the same ship, we may die together. What then?"

"In that event my property will have become yours, which will go to your wife." Sam chuckled quietly. "I do believe we can rely on your wife to be willing to free my slaves."

"Ha! Yes, with Clarity that is a safe assumption. Very well, then, Sam, that is how we shall have it. But now, what about your other slaves, your field hands and so on?"

Sam shrugged. "It would probably be best to sell them along with the place. They don't know anything but cotton. I doubt they could make their way at the North."

"Well, if things do come to such a pass, and you do not come home, I do know people in the colored town in Boston who could help them find places. They may always be laborers, but they would be free."

Sam reflected for a moment, then smiled. "You mean, you are thinking back to that chamberlain, or whatever he was, in the court at Algiers?"

"Jonah, yes. He died a few years ago, but he took the Putnam name for himself, and he spun together quite some little web of trades-men who have helped Southern Negroes—forgive me, refugees—start to earn a living there. My wife and I are kindly regarded among them. I am sure they would help settle your people."

"You have eased my mind more than I can say. My God, you look like hell. Let's get you back aboard."

"I would be grateful."

"Just across the street is the office of the attorney with whom I have been speaking. Let us stop in there so I can sign the paper and have it concluded."

"Good." To perhaps do a good turn for Sam's slaves was satisfying, but the infinitely better feeling was to have brought Sam himself to the doorstep of admitting that freedom even in modest circumstances was better than slavery with its security, and moreover that it was a viable possibility for those he owned. This, however, was not to be said out loud.

"How ARE YOU feeling, Captain?"

Although it was close beside the bed, the voice came to him distantly. "Is that Mr. Ross?"

"Of course, Captain."

The dark was impenetrable, with no moonlight through the windows. "Will you bring a lantern?"

When he returned, Bliven made out his faithful, perennially troubled visage. "How is the tide?"

"Captain, we have been at sea for two days."

"No, we were just unloading the muskets in Galveston."

"No, sir, you were with Mr. Bandy ashore when you fainted, and they carried you back aboard. Mr. Bandy took command and had us put to sea as soon as the tide began to run."

Bliven stirred. "I must get up."

Ross placed his hands on Bliven's shoulders and pressed him back into his pillow. "Not until Dr. Haffner says you may."

"Well, then, send Mr. Bandy to me, if you please."

It took only a moment, for he was in his cabin, and Lieutenant

White had the deck. "Sam, they tell me I am ill and you had to take her out. My apologies."

"Jesus, Captain!" He laid a hand across Bliven's forehead and felt the sweat, at once fevered and clammy. "Will you let me send for Dr. Haffner?"

"Yes, of course."

Sam rose and leaned over to the door of the compartment. "Mr. Ross, will you tell Dr. Haffner that the captain is awake?"

"Sam, they tell me I have been out for two days."

"Yes, sir."

"Where are we bound?"

"West and then southwest, toward Cópano. I took the liberty of reading your instructions from General Houston."

"Yes, of course." He raised up on one elbow. "It does not feel like we're moving."

"I know. Calm sea, nearly calm wind. Heavy fog, like being trapped in a cotton boll."

There was an odd sort of knock at the compartment door, light, but kicked with a shoe, and Haffner entered bearing a cup of tea in one hand and an extra lantern in the other. "Well, now, Captain." He gave Bliven the tea and studied him in the extra light. "This is a little better."

Bliven took a sip and made a face. "This has quinine water in it."

"I know," said Haffner. "You have relapsed with the swamp fever. The quinine water will help."

"Mr. Ross! Some sugar, if you please. That is impossible. It is barely spring, not summer. I have been in no swamps."

Haffner sat on the edge of his berth and pressed his fingers to the inside of Bliven's wrist. "Lie still now." A quarter of a minute passed.

"Better. Swamp fever can relapse at any time; it is unusual but not unheard of. Mr. Bandy tells me that you and he traveled extensively in recent weeks, with much time out of doors and sometimes even sleeping out of doors." He lifted Bliven's eyelids and then listened to his heart through a wooden tube. "You are better. It will take time, but you will be well. Mr. Ross?"

"Yes, Doctor?"

"Will you bring some hot water and cloths? Even a captain of taste and culture will smell like a horse when he does not wash."

Suddenly they felt the slightest surge of movement and heard the ship creak somewhere in her timbers. "I'll go up," said Sam. "Excuse me."

McKay had felt it, too; he and Sam met at the foot of the ladder and went up together. On the quarterdeck they caught just the breath of wind from the southeast, which was well, for the sails were already set on the starboard tack. They never made more than two knots—not enough breeze to disperse the fogbanks that crowded together. When they encountered a crease of clear sky, it showed moonless. Four bells of the first watch had struck, the sound would probably carry for a mile into the black silence. Sam had the wheel with McKay standing by, and they beheld a wall of fog before them thrice the height of their masts.

"It's right glad I am," said McKay, "we are not near any land or obstruction."

"Indeed, so," answered Sam. They disappeared into it as into a dark room, the sheer weight of the fog seeming to quell the Gulf's habitual chop, only a low regular swell from their port quarter and the merest bellying of the courses and topsails made them believe that they had steerage at all.

"Ahoy, there! What ship is that?"

Sam and McKay both started at the suddenness of it. The voice was clipped and the accent British, loud, but calm and imperious as only they can be. Unmistakably British.

"Where away?" whispered Sam.

"Damned if I can tell," growled McKay. "In this blasted fog, the sound comes from all around." They strained and squinted, descrying nothing, but obviously they had been seen or their bell had been heard.

"Run down to the captain's cabin and fetch the trumpet, will you please?"

"Aye, sir." McKay loped forward on his toes, making far less noise in his hard-soled shoes than normally he would have. In two minutes he returned, handing Sam the brass speaking trumpet.

Sam took it and stood aside. "Take the wheel, please." He stepped noiselessly over to the port rail, thinking it more likely that they were being hailed from seaward.

"I say again: Ahoy there! What ship is that?" Nearly a quarter of a century had passed since Sam had been taken from his merchant ship and impressed into British service, but his memory of it was still as vivid as the white scars on his fleshy pink back. Despite the passage of years, his gall rose, for he had never seen justice for his treatment, nor recompense for the loss of his ship. And, his three years' captivity during which he should have been delivering profitable cargoes and running his plantation was the period from which he dated the beginning of his financial downfall. Once again his contempt for all things British, their pretense, their arrogance, swelled to the fore.

Abruptly Sam put the trumpet to his lips. "This is the Texas warship *Gonzales*. What ship is that?"

"This is His Majesty's warship *Titania*. Heave to and lower a boat!"

A hot wave washed through Sam's body like a fever at hearing the very words of that encounter long before, his impressment, the daily threat of hanging, the sting of the cat on his back, and above all that insufferable hauteur. But worse than that he could not know who it was, for false hailing was a ubiquitous tactic on the high seas. It could be an English officer in Mexican service, of whom there were some number, or it could be a privateer on the hunt for them. That captain of the *Mary Ellen* had surely put into New Orleans in high dudgeon; if he had given out the story that they were pirates, the insurers would place a bounty on them and they would be hunted. In this fog he could not know who was hailing him.

"The hell I will!" Samuel bellowed back. He lowered the speaking trumpet and noticed Lieutenant White, who had come on deck at the sound of the hailing. "Mr. White, do not beat to quarters but get the men to their stations quietly. Load the guns quicker than they ever have. Go to it!"

A full three minutes crawled by, noiseless in the fog without even the slap of the usual Gulf chop against their hull.

"What!" The English accent, clipped and amplified, came back out of the dark at them. "I say again: This is His Majesty's warship *Titania*. Heave to and lower a boat!"

"I say again: You go to hell, you lime-sucking son of a bitch!" Once more he lowered the trumpet and stood close to the second lieutenant. "Elevate your forward chaser. We can't see him to shoot across his bow, but we'll put a shot over him." Yeakel had come up, too, at the disturbance. "Mr. McKay, get ready to make a turn to port. Mr. Yeakel, be ready to trim your sails to match the turn."

In another few moments White approached again. "We are ready, Mr. Bandy."

"Very well. Mr. McKay, make a ninety-degree turn to port. Mr. White, fire the one shot when you feel him straighten out."

They barely had steerage in the near calm, but slowly they felt her come around to the south. As she did so, Sam assayed a jumble of calculations, for these were no conditions in which to fight a full action with an unknown vessel. Once they fired the chaser, whoever it was would know that the *Gonzales* mounted twenty-fours. No merchant ship would have hailed them, so it was not a vessel bearing any cargo they would be interested in. If it was a privateer or a Mexican cruiser affecting to be a British warship, they would know from the deep boom of the gun that they were vastly overmatched, and would flee. If indeed it was a British man-of-war, they would know from the report of the twenty-four that they were not a vessel to trifle with.

But all hesitation became moot when they saw the bow light up in flame as the chaser fired with a concussive blast, the masts and rigging and all the deck accoutrements silhouetted against the fireball that dimmed and dissipated thirty yards distant from the ship.

Agonizing moments crept by as they wondered whether the British captain would follow the famous Royal Navy custom of threatening to answer a single shot with a broadside. A breath of wind lifted enough of the fog to make her out, a brig, eighteen or twenty guns, two hundred yards south of them. Slowly at first and then unmistakably, they saw her turn away to the south. "Damn your manners," the voice floated over to them. "You are very unfriendly."

"Mr. Bandy, your trumpet, please, sir." He spun around to see Bliven, washed and in uniform, pale but in command of himself.

Sam's alarm approached mortification. "Did I act wrongly?"

"No, Sam! Not in the least, but I sense an opportunity. If I can go over and parley, he will put it in his log, and we will have established the presence of a Texas warship at this place and date, further masking our true identity, if that should ever prove useful."

Sam laughed softly. "Well, I'm damned if you are not smarter sick than I am when I'm healthy."

Bliven strolled to the port rail and put the trumpet to his lips. "Ahoy, British warship *Titania*. This is Captain Putnam, Texas warship *Gonzales*. Come back about, if you please, sir. We will send a boat."

"Very well!"

"Mr. Yeakel, get some oarsmen together and lower the cutter. My gig would do, but this will make more of an impression. Oh, hell! They're British—Mr. Bandy, run below and bring me some of that local tea that Dicey prepared for me. I'll see if I can't ingratiate myself to some little degree."

As a precaution, he had Yeakel lower a line for him to hang on to as he descended the boarding ladder, for he did not feel steady. One of the crew helped him to his seat in the waist as they pushed off, the oars dropped, and they crossed with stately sweeps.

"By God, sir," said the British captain as they met, saluted, and shook hands. "I have heard that you Texians are an irascible lot, and sink me if you did not bear out your reputation."

"My apologies, Captain. You cannot be unaware that we are at war with Mexico, and we could not be certain of your true identity. False hailing, I need not tell you, is coin of the realm out here. I am Captain Putnam, at your service, sir."

"Captain Wade, your servant, sir. Well, then, how could you be so certain of our identity as to come over?"

"Only a verified Englishman would swear at our manners."

Wade threw his head back and laughed. He was of rather less than medium height, with tufts of red hair curling from beneath his bicorne, and pronounced blue eyes. He was remarkably broad across the chest and showed not an ounce of fat anywhere. "Will you come below and have a drink with us?"

"I would be delighted, Captain. In point of fact, as you are English, I have brought you a little gift in apology for my lieutenant's rudeness."

"Have you, now?"

"Are you aware that there is a species of tea that grows wild in Texas?"

They reached the foot of the ladder and Wade turned, his blue popped eyes flung open wide. "I have never heard of this."

"It is not widely known, but I have a mind to open a commercial venture in it." He pulled from his pocket the folded paper Sam had given him. "Have a whiff."

Wade leaned forward and inhaled. "Well, I am dashed! I had thought you would prefer rum or whiskey, but we shall have some tea instantly. This is the damnedest thing I ever heard of. Mr. Kenyon!" he called forward to a man in a white apron at their camboose. "Tea service to my cabin, if you please!"

FOUR BELLS OF the middle watch had rung when Sam saw lanterns moving on *Titania*'s deck and then made out their cutter as it eased back with regular sweeps of its oars. Bliven mounted the boarding ladder cautiously but unaided. Sam gave Bliven a quick salute as they met at the boarding gate, and they walked slowly back to the quarter-deck. "We were getting worried. I was about to send over a skirmishing party to rescue you. How was your gala?"

"Their captain is a gentleman. I believe even you would have liked him."

"What kind of name is *Titania*? I don't see anything especially titanic about a brig of maybe seven hundred tons."

"No, no, Titania was a fairy queen in a play by Mr. Shakespeare. She is named aptly enough."

"Oh, well, then!" said Sam grandly, and huffed. "What is a dainty British fairy queen ship doing in these waters?"

"In fact, they just deposited a new consul or somebody in Matamoros. Diplomatic maintenance, dispatches, and the like."

"How did your talk go?"

"Extraordinarily well. The captain is a young shaver of a thing named Nicholas Wade. Very powerful, though—strong as a bear. If we threw him a line, he could probably hold us in tow with his bare hands. Pretty frightening, actually."

"Did you learn anything useful?"

"Well, he is a proper Englishman, but he has had cousins in Texas these past few years with whom he has been in correspondence, and he has quite a lot of sympathy for the colonists' difficulties. So I was spared the usual imperial huffing."

"Well, thank the Lord for that."

"He is of the opinion that very little in Britain is happening, politically or in foreign policy—indeed, even socially. It seems the whole country has come to a standstill waiting on the old king to die. Says he is a hateful old lecher, universally despised, as was the king before him. And next in line is his niece, a young lady named Victoria, not even close to twenty yet. There are grave concerns whether she can get the country in hand."

"Good morning, Captain." It was Evans Yeakel who met them on the quarterdeck.

"Good morning, Bosun. How are you faring deep into this night?"

"Very well, sir. I heard you coming back aboard. We are ready for your orders."

"Good man, well done. Make all sail, west-sou'west for the moment. Mr. Bandy will give you an exact course momentarily."

"Aye-aye, sir."

"Mr. Yeakel?"

"Sir?"

"That silver whistle about your neck. Does it still function?"

"Yes, sir, my apologies that I was not on deck to pipe you aboard. I was tending to something below. Wait." He raised the whistle to his lips and blew the captain's accolade, quickened to something less than a second. "There. All right, all sail, yes, sir."

Sam spun around to avoid horse laughing in Bliven's face. "Texas Navy, Captain," he said when he recovered his breath. "Less formal."

"I am well reminded. Mr. Yeakel?"

"Sir?"

"Set your stuns'ls, if you please. We are in a hurry. And tell Mr. Hoover that I am sorry to wake him but I need tea for quinine water right away."

"Aye, sir."

Sam was suddenly solicitous. "Are you all right, Captain?"

"I have been worse, but it has taken some effort to put up such a hale appearance." He coughed, deep but hollow.

"I understand. Let's get you below." They went forward to the ladder. "Back to this princess girl for a moment, I am curious. What will they do if it turns out she is not capable of governing the country?"

"In fact, Captain Wade made a very odd assertion. He says that in such an event, there is wide public sympathy to try their hand at a republic."

"No!"

"Believe it or not. I mean, you'd think one commonwealth would have been enough for them. Listen, how well do you know the port of Cópano?"

"We know it is in Mexican hands."

"Yes, but anything not within the bar is in *our* hands. Captain Wade made free to tell me that when he was lately in Matamoros, he surmised that it had become the principal staging area for the Mexicans for supporting their armies in Texas. Of the greatest interest to us, he saw a long file of field guns on the wharf that looked ready to be transported, and the only place in Texas that they could go is Cópano. If we can beat them there, they will find us waiting."

Sam looked up at the men aloft, lashing stuns'l yards and creeping cautiously out to set the canvas. "Why would he tell you such a thing? Are you quite certain he was not giving you misdirection of some kind?"

"I surely wondered about it. The English seldom take a side in other countries' wars; it is more their game to play both sides against each other and profit from the conflict. But Wade seemed quite frank in his opinions. Besides, he is not leading us into a course we would not otherwise undertake. Any Mexican arms that do not come overland must land at Cópano, and that is where I intend for us to be."

8

Beans and Flour

In his sea cabin with Sam, Bliven found himself blessing Thomas McKinney of New Orleans for supplying them with a decent chart of the long, arcing Texas coast. Without it, they might have attempted to pursue ships directly into the port of Cópano and reduce the place as he had done Tripoli thirty years before. With a chart, however, they recognized instantly the impossibility of such a scheme, for upon further review Cópano was doubly and then trebly inaccessible to a vessel of their size.

For more than a hundred miles, the Texas coast itself was shielded from the Gulf by Padre Island, a barrier of sand that was the longest of its kind in the world, and in most places from one to three miles wide. But whether it existed as a single island or was broken and breached by Gulf waters changed and shifted with the caprices of hurricanes that blew over it every few years.

Cópano, the oldest and deepest port in Texas, established by the

Condé de Gálvez in the 1780s, lay 160 miles southwest by south from Galveston. Like Galveston, it had in its earlier days been the refuge of pirates, but its situation bore a greater resemblance to Lafitte's buccaneer capital of Barataria deep in the Mississippi Delta by reason of its sheer inaccessibility from the open waters. In its northern reaches the great sand barrier broke into smaller but still formidable islands. One of the dependable cuts through them, between Mustang and San José Islands, was at Aransas Pass, a narrow, north-turning, five-mile defile that opened onto Aransas Bay. To reach Cópano then required a ten-mile sail northeast, skirting a shallow oyster reef, then a turn to the northwest into Cópano Bay, avoiding a second, even shallower oyster reef before reaching the port on the northern shore. A near impossibility for a vessel drawing twenty feet of water.

"Where are we now?" asked Bliven.

"Well, when we left Galveston you were out of your head for that couple of days. We made good time, we are proximate to Cópano now. I aimed to put us out far enough to intercept the Gulf trade but close enough to stop anyone from turning in."

"Yes, good."

With the windows of the sea cabin opened for the fresh air, they heard the cry far above them. "Ahoy the deck! Ahoy!"

"Who has the watch?"

"Mr. White, but I will run up."

"Good. I will join you in a moment." Bliven made a stop in the quarter gallery outside his berth, put on his coat and picked up his bicorne, but then felt dizzy and thought it better to sit down.

"Good morning, Mr. White," said Sam on the quarterdeck. "What do we have?"

"Good morning, Mr. Bandy. Lookout has sighted a ship about

three miles southeast. He can't see square sails; we think it may be a schooner, sir."

"Where is she headed?"

"Toward us, sir."

"Very well, keep us informed." Sam clattered back down the ladder and knocked lightly even as he entered the captain's cabin. He strode straight to the door of Bliven's berth and found him seated on his mattress. "This could be our lucky day, Captain: we have a sighting."

"Yes, I will be right up."

"How are you feeling?"

Bliven paused as though taking stock of his various functions. "Not too bad, actually; stronger than yesterday. Where away?"

"Three miles southeast, sir."

"How is the wind?"

"Fairly strong, varying east to northeast."

Bliven stood again, then stumbled. "Oh!"

Sam reached out and caught him. "Are you all right?"

"I stood too quickly, I fear. It's all right, it has passed." Ross entered the small compartment, standing in the door to the quarter gallery, ready with Bliven's bicorne and spyglass. Sam made certain to follow him up the ladder, to be able to break his fall should he stumble again. On the quarterdeck Bliven assayed things quickly as Yeakel joined them. "Helm, make northeast to open some distance, then northwest. We can angle up to him and have the weather gage. We must try to speak him. Mr. Bandy, I dislike to do this, I am sorry, but take down your Texian flag and raise the American flag. It is sure to make us more approachable and ease the conversation."

"Yes, sir."

"And then beat to quarters. I want everyone ready just in case. Where is Mr. McKay?"

"Sleeping, sir. He had the night watch."

"Well, wake him and have him join us. I want Mr. White at the guns and McKay at the wheel."

Sam was below and back on the quarterdeck in a few moments, and the blue flag with the gold star slid down from the spanker boom, replaced by the Stars and Stripes, to which he gave a long look. "Excuse me, Captain?"

"Yes, Mr. Bandy?"

"If we raise the American flag, and then if we have to start shooting, will that not cause the very incident we are ordered to avoid, in giving the appearance of American involvement in the revolution?"

"No fear. If we have to start shooting, we will show our true colors first, and they will know it was a deception."

Sam smiled, slowly at first but then broadly. "Good. If it is a Mexican ship, I want them to know who they're dealing with." As the two ships closed at a gradual angle, the schooner unfurled a Mexican flag from its mainmast. "And so now we know." Sam pointed.

When they were a hundred yards apart, Bliven put the speaking trumpet to his lips. "Ahoy, Mexican schooner! What ship are you and where bound?"

After two minutes of silence, plenty of time for the Mexican captain to have a trumpet in hand, Bliven repeated his question and timed out the continuing silence. "Well, to hell with this: our orders are to interdict their commerce. Raise your own flag, Mr. Bandy! Ahoy, Mexican schooner! This is the Texas warship *Gonzales*. Come about and lower your sails. I say again: Come about! Mr. White, open your gunports and get ready to put a shot across his bow if he—"

Suddenly the air snapped with three sharp concussions: small guns, they could tell—six-pounders. Their gazes snapped back to see the schooner's rail obscured by smoke, and they saw at the same time her profile diminish as she sheered away to port. At only a hundred yards they heard the small balls sing overhead through the rigging and heard and then saw a hole pop open in the main top staysail. "You son of a bitch," Bliven whispered in amazement, "you shot at me! Who do you think you are? Mr. White, get your guns out and fire!"

White flew down the ladder, roaring to open the ports and roll out the guns. In the twenty seconds it took for the creaking carriage wheels to fall silent, the schooner was halfway through his turn and presented to them little more than his spoon-shaped fantail. They heard White's bellow to fire, and a second later the deck trembled beneath them with eleven heavy explosions over a two-second period. The flame and smoke began to dissipate just in time for them to see a shower of splinters and spray erupt from low on the schooner's starboard quarter, and they knew they had holed her between wind and water. A second geyser of wood erupted from her taffrail, and two holes popped open in her sails. Several seconds later they saw numerous splashes several hundred yards beyond her. As quickly as she turned away, two hundred yards later she came northwest, running before the wind and straight for Aransas Pass.

"Did you see that, Sam?" asked Bliven. "Blast me if she is not a nimble little thing. She turned away to give us a smaller target; now she is making a dash for the port. That is no merchant captain. That is a naval officer who knows what he is doing, and he made a fool out of me."

"Shall we pursue?"

Bliven lowered his glass and tapped it into his open hand. "No. Damn! He is faster than we are, and he knows it. His ship is more maneuverable and can sail closer to the wind than we can, and he knows it. If we chase him, he will but laugh at us. No, he foxed me, and now we have lost our chance. Damn! Damn!" He peered upward, regarding the sails and Regina Ferraro's green silk pennant as White rejoined them on the quarterdeck. "Mr. White, you did not stop him but you hit him. Well done, sir."

"Thank you, sir."

"What the hell, we cannot catch him, but why don't you run forward and see if you can send him off with a hit from our bow chasers before he gets out of range. Helm, come three points to port and see if that gives him a straight shot."

Bliven and Sam leaned out from the port rail, keeping the departing schooner in the center of their glasses as White pointed the twenty-fours on the bow. Their deep, majestic booms were simultaneous, but they saw the balls fall one forward of the schooner and one off to her starboard. Even with the miss, it was comforting to know that they were the only ship in these waters with such guns.

Bliven pursed his lips and shook his head. "Well, hell. Mr. Bandy, resume a southerly course under easy sail. You and Mr. White and Mr. Yeakel gather in the wardroom, if you please, and have your lunch. I will join you presently and we will consider what to do next."

In his cabin he donned a fresh shirt before descending to the berth deck. In the wardroom he discovered that Hoover had served them reconstituted salt beef, sliced thick and fried in butter, served with potatoes that he had mashed and whipped into a froth and buttered, and peas. From the galley Hoover observed Bliven enter and followed him with a similarly loaded plate.

"Gentlemen, you should not have waited for me." He sat and they ate in silence, waiting to see what he would have to say. "Well," Bliven said at last, "I think that I will not be contradicted if I say that encounter did not go as we hoped. In fact we, or more to the point I, botched that rather badly." He paused for a comment, but there was none. "I had hoped that our first contact would be a ship coming out of Cópano, not going in. Perhaps we might have captured some dispatches or even some officers going back home. As it is, our presence here will very shortly now be known, and we may safely assume that alarms to that effect will be on the way to Urrea and Santa Anna, wherever they are, and a courier sent posthaste to Matamoros warning them to dispatch no more shipping to Cópano until the threat we pose has been countered."

"What else could you have done, Captain?" asked Yeakel. "I suppose you could have opened fire and sunk him by surprise even as you changed the flag, but that is the kind of thing one expects from Santanistas, not from us."

"We don't know what cargo he was carrying," added Sam, "but a two-masted schooner is not large enough to haul the amount of artillery we are watching for. Those little popguns he fired at us when he sheered off, I would bet you that's the only armament he had; indeed, they are typical for an armed schooner. I know if I was carrying anything bigger, I would assemble at least a couple of them and have them ready to use."

"Yes, perhaps," said Bliven. "Well, now, looking at things as they are, the Mexicans know the port of Cópano is blockaded as long as we are here. We know it will take a couple of days for a rider to reach Matamoros, and I am wagering that those guns were loaded and put to sea before now. My greater fear is that they may have left the port soon after the *Titania*'s captain saw them there and may already have landed in Cópano. If that is the case, then our whole errand is wasted."

"Did your British captain say what kind of guns and how many?" asked Sam.

"A couple of dozen at least, he said. He took them for twelve-pounders, but he gathered from their carriages that they were short-range field guns, not long twelves of the naval type."

"Wait, sir," said Yeakel. "If they were on their carriages, they would have to be dismounted before being lowered into a hold, and then they would have to stow them very carefully, with that much weight. From what he saw, I do not believe they could be underway in less than three days from that time. I don't see how they could be here already."

"Thank you, Mr. Yeakel. That is a comforting assessment. We shall maintain our blockade and remain hopeful of accomplishing what we were sent here for. We shall just have to ride the winds as best we can to stay outside the pass, and hope we are not blown away by a strong offshore wind."

It was in the middle of the next afternoon that the call came down. "Ahoy the deck!"

It was Sam who had the helm, with Bliven keeping him company. "What do you see?"

"A ship, sir, coming up from the south. I make her three miles off, perhaps a little more. Hard to say; she is a large brig, pretty close inshore."

Bliven and Sam exchanged stares, at once excited but cautious. "This could be it," said Sam. "What shall we do this time, sir?"

Bliven stalked back and forth, eyeing the thin line of the coast, the direction of their pennant, and the bearing of the brig. "Mr. Bandy, do you remember Gibraltar and the *Meshuda*? She was untouchable as long as she was in port, and poor Barron had to sail the *Philadelphia* up and down the bay of Algeciras to keep her there."

"Yes, I do recall it."

"Well"—he pointed out to the brig bearing distantly down upon them—"this is just the opposite case. If this is the ship we expect, he wants into Cópano; there is no place else he can go. And if we make a move to chase him, he may outrun us and do it. But he cannot go through us. Let him posture and gyrate how he will; we will cover the entrance to the pass. Mr. Yeakel?"

"Sir?"

"You have had the foretopmast that broke in the Bahamas lying at the rail ever since. Part of it is now our bowsprit. Do you think you can use the night to cut down the rest of it and rig a new sprits'l? Do you think the bowsprit is strong enough to take it?"

"Perhaps, sir. It has stood the strain of the jib and forestaysail well enough. The weight of a spritsail yard will be exerting down, however. You are thinking that you may want some extra speed tomorrow?"

"Yes."

"I understand, but I would not want to set a very large one."

"Agreed. Get busy and do what you can. And one thing further, I want you to lash on your stuns'l spars and furl stuns'ls on them. I want them there at the instant we may need them."

Yeakel saluted himself away. "Aye, sir."

"Ahoy the deck?"

"What is it?" Bliven shouted.

"Sir, I make the brig two miles away. She is turning seaward."

"Is she running?"

"No, Captain! She is still coming on but placing herself further from shore. She is slow and low in the water. She is flying the American flag!"

"Do you think it may be a false flag?" asked Sam.

"I do not. The Mexicans have no ship of that size; that would be pointless. An American trader, I'll wager, chartered to Mexican service. He is flying the flag for its protection, most likely." Bliven stalked back and forth, eyeing the shore with the pass just visible, the pennant showing a freshening north wind. "Mr. Bandy, make sure to come in toward the shore while we are still on the east side of the pass. If he tries to come in from the south, even he must tack into this wind and show us both sides to shoot at. If he gets brave and makes a run in straight from the east, his speed won't help him. He must slow down to be sure of hitting the channel. He would never survive our broadsides."

Bliven studied all their circumstances for several minutes more. With their yards on the port tack Sam steered them as close to the wind as he could, edging them closer to the shore. "Mr. Yeakel, shorten sail, if you please. I do not wish to lose the advantage of our present position until we see what he is going to do."

"Ahoy the deck!"

"What do you see?" called Bliven.

"That brig is still in sight, sir. I make him a mile and a half. His course is now northeast, sir."

"Tacking?" puzzled Sam.

Bliven found the tiny sails in his glass. "Tacking, and stalling. He is milling, Mr. Bandy! The poor bastard does not know what to do; he is coming out of the desert and we have seized the waterhole. That tells us a great deal." He stopped to think. "Although that makes a very poor metaphor, considering we are on the ocean . . ."

"It tells us that he truly wants to enter Cópano."

"Exactly. If he had business elsewhere, he would go there. If his cargo were innocent, he would come on and hail us and learn our business." He laughed suddenly. "Our flag alone should excite his curiosity. Remember, it has never been seen before."

"Well, sir, he might hail us and he might not."

Bliven lowered his glass and looked at him. "How do you mean?"

"An American ship under Mexican charter, sir, if he has to stop and be boarded, he would be expecting to have to pay a bribe to continue on. That is the way things work down there. Within the past few years the Mexican government opened customshouses at our Texas ports, and paying bribes over and above the duties became quite the required way of commerce."

Bliven stared at him. "No one has told me this before. If it is as you say, then that alone is cause enough for a revolt."

"I say it only to explain why he might not wish to be boarded."

The dance continued through afternoon and evening, the *Gonzales* patrolling the entrance to Aransas Pass, the lumbering brig milling one to two miles offshore, until as dusk approached he passed out of sight to the northeast.

"Now where is he going? Do you think he will try to get inshore of us and slip in under cover of night?"

"It is all too possible. The moon is approaching its last quarter. Do you know what time it will rise?"

"Not later than nine, as I believe, but I will run down and check the almanac."

"Yes, please do. Mr. Yeakel, my compliments to Mr. White. His gun crews are to sleep at their stations tonight, gunports open, guns run out. I want them ready for instant firing."

Yeakel saluted himself away. "Aye, sir."

Indeed, the moon rose before nine, arced overhead, and was half-way to sinking in the west at the change of the morning watch, the lookouts having searched the water between them and the beach the entire night without result.

"Ahoy the deck!"

"What do you see?"

"It is our friend, Captain! Crawling down the coast under a single tops'l."

Sam ran to the starboard rail and raised his glass. "Sir, look! He is trying to pass inshore of us. The wind is with him, but he can't trust the depth."

"Mr. White, can you get a bead on him?"

"I can, sir."

"Point your guns carefully, and when you are ready, fire a two-gun ranging salvo. That will let him know that we mean to shoot, and he can never survive a run by us."

"I don't understand," said Sam. "Why not just let him have it?"

Bliven spoke with some impatience. "We can't sink him at this range, and if he gets behind us, we can't bring our guns to bear. And if we did sink him, then those guns would be easily salvaged. No, we must drive him out to sea and deal with him there."

The flash of the two forward-most twenty-fours was blinding in the predawn gloom, and the eruption of flames had barely dissipated when the lookout cried down again. "Ahoy the deck! He is turning to sea and raising all sail!"

"Damn, I knew it!" cried Bliven. "This was his last card to play at getting into Cópano. He means to run back to Matamoros; they are going to haul the guns overland. Mr. Yeakel! Make all sail; set your stuns'l and sprits'l. I will have that little wretch if it's the last thing I ever do! Mr. Bandy, come down. Let us study the chart."

Mr. McKinney's chart of the Texas coast remained open on the mahogany table, and they refreshed their mind's eye of what must happen. The brig's captain would not hug the coast but run south by west just as fast as he could go, straight to the mouth of the Rio Grande, and Matamoros.

In the time it took to raise the sails and come to that heading, the brig had opened a lead on them of perhaps a mile. Back on the quarterdeck as morning brightened, Bliven looked above the main topgallant and saw their green silk pennant snapping straight as a ruler toward the bowsprit. He did not need to pay out knots to know that they were racing full and by, the standing rigging pulled taut as fiddle strings. He shot his glance far forward to the newly rigged spritsail and saw it bellied out into a hemisphere—and there was the ultimate confirmation that the present quarry must be the one they sought: they were gaining on her. A brig running before the wind was a swift ship; she must be very heavily laden.

Bliven stole a fitful glance down at their new spritsail, relieved to observe it regularly showered with spray from their bow splash.

"Look there, Mr. Yeakel, if the muzzle blast from the chasers does not pass completely over it, it is wet enough not to take fire."

"Yes, sir, but how do we know the blast itself will not wreck the whole apparatus?"

"Yes, you are right. Station some men forward with axes in case the whole thing is wrecked and they have to chop it all free."

"Aye, sir." Yeakel trotted back to the ladder and quickly down.

Bliven pointed back out to the fleeing brig. "What do you think, Mr. White?"

White studied through his glass and then without. "I make her a mile and a quarter off, sir; that is about twenty-two hundred yards. Still a bit far to try a shot."

"M-hm. Too far to hit him, perhaps, but not too far to fire and let him know we mean business. He can see as plainly as we that we are closing on him."

"True, sir."

"Mr. White, with your elevation ramps that Mr. Bandy devised, and by firing as the bow lifts up in a swell, do you think you can make a ball fly for a mile?"

"I think, sir, probably yes, but if not, the splashes will rise close enough to him to make him think about it."

"Good. Fire then on my order, and keep firing at intervals until he drops his sails or until I order otherwise."

"Aye, sir." White saluted as he left. Bliven walked aft, leaning into the stiff north wind that, contrary to becoming warmer as the sun rose, acquired an ugly chill.

White employed his chasers skillfully, firing them alternately every quarter hour, the splashes falling closer and closer to the fleeing brig. At six hundred yards their quarry gave up the flight, furled her courses and driver, and rolled slowly along under topsails. "Mr. Yeakel," said Bliven, "you may begin to shorten sail. We do not wish to overshoot her."

Yeakel timed his slowing perfectly, coming a hundred and fifty feet off the brig's port beam and matching her pace.

Bliven was prepared at the starboard rail with his speaking trumpet. "Ahoy, American brig. What ship are you?"

The answer came back at once. "I am Captain Carroll, American trading vessel *Five Points*! Who in hell are you and what in hell do you mean to arrest us in such a way?"

The *Gonzales*'s officers smiled among themselves. "We are Texas warship *Gonzales*. You are sailing in our war zone. Trade with the Texas ports is under blockade. You ran from us after trying to enter Cópano. What cargo do you carry?"

"I am an American ship in international trade. Your flag is not recognized, and you have no right to stop us."

The hard north wind had raised a considerable swell, and the ships each lifted from the stern as they were pushed southward. It was impossible not to take some prideful fun in having run down their quarry. "Our flag, sir," shouted Bliven through the trumpet, "will be recognized soon enough. My twenty-four-pounders give me the right to stop you. I ask again: What cargo do you carry?"

"Sawn lumber and foodstuffs, you blackguard. Do you mean to come over and steal it?"

Bliven held the trumpet away from his mouth so they could laugh among themselves and raised it again. "I thank you, we are well provisioned. We shall board you and inspect your cargo. If it is as you say, you may proceed back to Mexico, but not to Cópano."

"Come aboard, then, you rebel."

"*Five Points?*" asked Sam. "What are the Five Points? Is it from some kind of declaration?"

"No," Bliven answered with a smile. "You see, her home port is New York. The Five Points is a square in the city where five streets come together. It's in the immigrant portion of the city with a reputation for violence."

Yeakel got the cutter down, making certain that it was rowed by men in uniforms. "Mr. White, I leave you in command. Mr. Bandy and I will go over. We will take McKay with us. Have your starboard guns quoined up and trained at her waterline. If one of us shouts the order to fire, tear her side out. We can swim well enough."

"Aye, sir."

The brig *Five Points* had no boarding ladder, but netting was thrown down from their waist. Her captain and officers were waiting there as Bliven swung himself over the rail, followed by Sam, McKay, and two of their crew. "Good morning, Captain. I am Captain Putnam, Texas Navy. Do you not have any better judgment than to pile on more canvas after you are challenged by a warship in a war zone?"

"By God, you are an American!" Carroll was nearly as tall as Lieutenant White, with coarse black hair and green eyes of a calculating expression. "What right have you to stop an American ship?"

"We are Texians, if you please, Captain—although it is true nearly all of us did start off as Americans. We hope not to detain you long. May I see your manifest?"

Carroll had it in hand and thrust it out, and Bliven read it over and handed it to Sam. "What do you think, Mr. Bandy?"

"*Milagros,*" he read. "*Masa.* As he said, it's beans and flour, and I see lumber."

"Very well, Captain Carroll. Let us have a look and you may be on your way."

Carroll led them to the ladder and down. "I still say you have no right."

"Your protest will be faithfully noted." They descended through the one crew deck and entered a deep hold, where there were two lanterns lit at the foot of the ladder. They found the cargo properly stowed, the sawn lumber flat on the deck, topped by small barrels stenciled *Masa*, the beans in large sacks of burlap.

"Captain Carroll"—Bliven stood by him—"your cargo appears to be in order. I will tell you what, I will give you thirty dollars in silver for two sacks of your beans. How you report it is up to you. Mr. McKay, have your men take two sacks topside."

Carroll glowered. "Captain Putnam, you may be sure that every word we have exchanged will be reported faithfully."

"Mr. McKay, sir! Jesus, we cannot lift these sacks of beans. They weigh a ton."

McKay regarded the burlap bean sacks piled amidships against the mainmast footing. "Daft, man, that sack should not weigh more than fifty or sixty pounds."

"Then, by God, *you* lift it!" the man shouted. "I ain't giving myself no rupture trying to carry that thing."

"Oh, for heaven's sake, man." McKay strode over and bent down to heft the sack onto his shoulder, but it did not budge. "What on— Mr. Bandy, there is something peculiar about this."

Sam joined them, pulled his Bowie knife from its sheath, and slit through the burlap, and before he had finished the cut a cascade of dried beans of light brown, with dark brown flecks, flowed through the rent with a dry rattle onto the decking. Looks were exchanged around, and when the beans stopped falling he enlarged the rent. The further outflow of beans left them staring at the round leaden curve of a twelve-pounder ball. "Will you look at that," said Sam softly. He reached in and started to pull it free, but it required both hands. "Well, now, that's some mighty big beans you got here, Cap'n." He held it up for Carroll's gaze. "How long do you have to cook one of these things, anyhow?"

Carroll shifted his weight, rolled his eyes, and made no reply.

"Mr. McKay," said Bliven, "please to break open a few barrels of this flour. We shall inspect it."

McKay set his lantern on the nearest one and removed a crowbar from a stanchion to assault the top of one of the barrels.

Carroll stepped forward. "Stop! Unless you want to blow us all to kingdom come. Very well, yes, there is powder in these barrels. You do not wish to hack at them and perhaps make a spark."

"We thank you for your good sense, Captain Carroll," said Bliven. "And now finally it occurs to me that the lumber that lines the bottom of your hold rises considerably above the curve of your bottom. Could it possibly be that there is some additional commodity lying beneath these boards—something heavier, perhaps, serving as ballast?"

Carroll resumed his silence.

"Sam? Have a look, please."

Sam stepped down onto the raw boards, pulling up one and then another, leaning them aside against the ship's ribs. McKay joined him, holding the lantern. They noted the boards carefully cut, as though premeasured for reassembly. After removing lumber from a layer four boards deep, they beheld the dark glint in the lamplight of bronze, and further effort revealed the five-foot barrel of a twelve-pounder field gun.

Bliven stepped down and joined them. "Mr. McKay, will you hand me your lantern?" He knelt on the barrel, running his fingers around the breech as he inspected it closely, then stood. "Come, gentlemen."

As they rejoined Carroll, Sam asked, "Where do you suppose they got these?"

"Boston," said Bliven bitterly. "I am ashamed to say I know the foundry marks well. They are produced by the Cyrus Alger Company, a very leader in the production of improved alloyed field weapons."

"Captain Carroll," said Bliven, "will you tell me now how many of these guns you are transporting?"

"Thirty," he answered, "to unload at Cópano to forward to the Mexican army."

"Well, that is what we need to know. Let us go back up."

"Captain, sir?" asked Sam. "A word in private, if I may?" The two of them walked forward toward a small warren formed by the sail room and paint lockers. Sam laid a hand on Bliven's back and whispered, "Well, now that we've got these guns, what in the hell are we going to do with them? The barrels alone weigh seven or eight hundred pounds apiece. The cutter could never get them over to our ship."

"I know. That is not practicable, and even if we got them to Galveston, there is no transport to get them to General Houston. And further, if that awful Potter fellow has started organizing his navy department, he will be doing it in Galveston, and he needs to be kept as deep in the dark as can be managed. He surely knows about us now because of the small arms we delivered there, and if we land again he may try to extend his authority over us and expose our whole game. I am understanding now why Houston told us to remain at sea." His lips tightened in fast thought. "Go back to the *Gonzales* and tell Mr. White to follow us closely. Return with a dozen men. We will sail her into deeper water and consign the whole business overboard."

Topside, as Sam was pulled back across, Bliven saw Carroll standing sullenly at his wheel. "One thing puzzles me, Captain Carroll, so perhaps you will gratify me. What was the need to try to disguise your cargo at all? If you are going to carry cannons and shot and powder, why not just get on with it?"

Carroll looked down the deck of the ship he no longer commanded. "The *Five Points* is an American merchant vessel. We are not supposed to take part in armed conflicts. Our company, however, chartered us to the government of Mexico, and for the vessel to remain insured we were required to mask any cargoes of war matériel."

"Ah, I see. Thank you." An American cannon foundry, and the American insurance companies again. They had been a burr under his saddle since the commencement of this whole operation. Their lack of regard for fellow Americans fighting for their freedom in Texas was odious enough, and now, to know they were minimizing their risk by cloaking their cargoes on vessels in Mexican charter, made it clear that they lacked political sympathies to any party whatever. They were in it purely for the profit to be made in the war and bloodshed. Yet corporations did not act from their own sentience; they were run by men. What species of men had so little conscience?

Sam returned with the carpenter and his sounding line. There was no speaking for the next hour as they steered the *Five Points* due east with the *Gonzales* following in tandem.

"Excuse me, Captain?"

"Mr. Caldwell?"

"I just wanted to let you know, the sounding is no bottom."

"Thank you, Mr. Caldwell. Please to have Mr. McKay take in the sails and begin hoisting the bronze guns out of the hold and over the side."

"Yes, sir. It does seem a terrible great waste, though."

"I know, and I agree, but we cannot take them with us."

Thirty times, Sam and Caldwell, down in the hold, made fast lines around the guns' trunnions, with McKay cranking the windlass, each five-foot barrel slowly twirling its way up through the hatch, where other crewmen from the *Gonzales* guided it to the boarding gate, unfastened the rope, and let it fall eight feet into the Gulf waters, the bright bronze visible to a surprising depth as it shot to the sea floor. Then came the carriage assemblies, and the balls that were passed from hand to hand up the ladder, the men discovering in the doing not just solid shot but grape and canister as well.

"Captain Carroll," said Bliven at last, "our duty here is nearly finished. Your guns and ammunition are now at the bottom of the sea, and we have taken your powder for our own needs. You are a neutral ship, so I do not claim you as a prize—although I believe that an admiralty court would sustain me if I chose to do so. I am hereby returning your manifest to you."

He handed it over, and Carroll accepted it without comment.

"However, the military shipment that you went to such pains to deliver must have been accompanied by letters or dispatches to those who were expecting them. Will you give those over to me, or shall we be compelled to search for them?"

Carroll shrugged. "They are nothing to me now; come to my cabin and you shall have them. I cannot return to Matamoros now in any event. The higher up in the Mexican army you go, the more suspicious the officers become of everyone and everything, because no one knows who will be denounced and shot next. Today Santa Anna is on top; tomorrow, who knows? No, Mexico has seen the last of me."

In his cabin he opened a desk and produced a leather pouch packed tight with documents in Spanish, elegant with rubrics.

Bliven tucked them into his coat. "I am sorry for the position in which you have put yourself. If it is any consolation, I believe you have tried your best to carry out your responsibilities. You could not have known that you were sailing into the path of a vessel that would completely overmatch you, and we thank you for your cooperation. May I advise you to put into a port at your first convenience and take on some ballast? Our operation has left you high in the water. I wish you fair sailing. Good-bye." Carroll's expressionless gaze followed him as he grasped the netting and swung over the side and down to the cutter.

No sooner had they sent the *Five Points* on her way east than Sam joined Bliven on the *Gonzales*'s quarterdeck, watching her slowly recede from view.

"Mr. Yeakel," said Bliven, "we cannot go north into this wind. Let us beat eastward until it is more favorable."

"Captain," said Sam, "I know we did the right thing, but dropping all those guns overboard just rubs me the wrong way when our boys need them so badly."

Bliven rested his forearms on the railing, finally unbending from his blustering posture in this ticklish business. "I know, Mr. Bandy, I know. But it was manifestly impossible to take them with us, and certainly not to Galveston."

"Yes, sir, I do understand, of course. But now, do you think we can assume that those thirty field guns were the entirety, or nearly so, of all the artillery that the Mexican army was expecting to land in Santa Anna's support?"

"Yes, I would think so, most surely."

"Then, sir, General Houston as he retreats, either because he is luring Santa Anna within range of the American army in Louisiana or because he finds himself at an insupportable disadvantage, has no way of knowing that he can now engage Santa Anna with no fear of being slaughtered at a distance by artillery."

"Yes, that is true."

"You and I are the only ones who know what strategy he is truly following, and you must stay with the ship. May I recommend that you put me ashore as soon as we can manage it, and I can get this intelligence to him?"

Bliven considered it. "But where? We don't know how far the Mexicans can have advanced. If what we heard in Galveston about the loss of the Alamo is true, he might have already swept the country clean."

Sam thought for a few seconds. "You can put me ashore on Galveston Island at night, west of the town. I can just walk in and excite no comment; no one knows me there. If the town is occupied, I will be just one more of the citizens there; if it is still in our hands, as I believe it must be, I can learn where the army is and get to them."

Bliven thought hard about it. "Are you sure you are willing to risk this?"

"I see no other way. Besides, it is not as though my own livelihood is not at hazard."

"Very well." Bliven saw the bosun forward by the capstan. "Mr. Yeakel, a new course!"

The *Gonzales* came around east-northeast, her yards snapped hard on the starboard tack, hauling as close to the wind as she could take. Galveston Island might be four days away, two and a half days in a better wind.

THEY AIMED TO put him ashore unobserved, but close enough to Galveston that Sam would not be waylaid by foraging Karankawas who might think a man alone, be he ever so heavily armed, was worth the risk to attack. The norther eventually lightened, replaced by a light east wind that then swung to the south; they approached the western tip of the island from the south, aiming to raise San Luís Pass just at dusk, shortening sail and shortening sail again. Having lost the foretopmast in the Bahamas, the *Gonzales* crept along under main and mizzen topsails and the staysails between them. Carpenter Caldwell called out the soundings without pause until his voice took on a tone of urgency at five fathoms. With only ten feet of water beneath his keel, Bliven ordered a turn to the northeast, edging up the coast for ten miles more, ever alert to sheer back to deeper water at the first sign of an unknown shoal or wreck. These waters had had three hundred years to collect the bones of ships that ventured too close to the beach's never-ending combers; Bliven envisioned their ribs rising like fishhooks to catch the unwary.

For the last five miles Sam waited on deck in civilian clothes, with Yeakel standing by to lower the captain's gig and row him ashore. It was two nights after the new moon; the beach of fine, pale, fawn-colored sand that would have shown him in stark relief in moonlight would now offer him good concealment. He should have no difficulty blending into the town without raising comment.

Bliven came up behind him quietly and tested the knapsack

strapped to his shoulders. "Well, how do you think you're going to manage this?"

"Start with that lieutenant where we left all the small arms, I guess. Houston sent him there, so he is the safest guess to be in Houston's confidence."

"Quite right, but I wouldn't just march right in. It's been a while, as we said Mr. Potter will likely be in charge now. You might visit that lawyer of yours across the street and talk about your will. You can keep an eye out the window and see who comes and goes, maybe catch that Besanson fellow on the street and learn the lie of affairs."

"That's just what I was thinking. Have you a report you wish me to hand to General Houston?"

"No, your report must be oral. In the unlikely event that you fall into Mexican hands, we don't want any papers on you."

The inky night made the gig hard to make out only a hundred feet from the ship; Bliven and Sam raised their hands in farewells, and he ordered a lantern hung from the main fighting top to guide the gig in its return.

It was then, after Sam was out of sight, that Bliven found himself able to think more clearly about matters that had troubled him for days. He sent Ross to bring him tea with rum and sugar and quinine water. As soon as the gig returned and was hoisted up and secured, he ordered easy sail to stand south-southwest, angling away from the coast, so that by morning they would be in safely deeper water but would still be in the shipping lanes. Almost alone on the deck but for Lieutenant White, who had the watch and the wheel, Bliven sat himself on the hatch cover, elbows on his knees, his hands wrapped around the oversized porcelain cup of tea and medicine.

What cleared for him was the realization that these Texians, in their revolution fought on however shabby a scale it was, might well be acting out the very questions of duty and morality he had put to himself, though in abstract, two years previous. With the American administration now captured by the scheming, vulgar Jackson, he had asked himself then where one's duty lay when the government to which he had always been loyal became a grotesque of itself.

Could Santa Anna be such a monster as he was portrayed? According to Austin, still sick from his year and a half of confinement without trial or charge, he was. Bliven had himself heard of Santa Anna, of his abrogating the constitution, of the massacre of thousands of civilians in Zacatecas, long before he was so unceremoniously sent to New Orleans or had any connection with these Texians. Had not Jefferson himself famously written that the tree of liberty must be watered now and then with the blood of patriots—and tyrants? Surely if there was a tyrant now in power in the New World whose blood could properly water the tree of liberty, it was Santa Anna.

Yet there were elements of the Texas revolution that smacked merely of rhetoric. Did these Texians really think they should claim as a justification to revolt that they had been denied religious freedom when few of them had any intention of going to any kind of church anyway? Besides, they had accepted this condition when they entered the country. Most had never laid eyes on a priest. Might not these Texians merely be venting the same anti-Catholic hysteria that he had seen in Boston, not just shared but personified by someone as supposedly urbane and educated as Lyman Beecher?

And there were elements that remained unspoken. Slavery was illegal in Mexico, and it was the state government in Coahuila, not the national regime, that permitted its existence in Texas, so as to allow the creation of a cotton economy the same as in the American South. It caused him to wonder now whether there might have been something to the articles he had read in the Whig newspapers back home claiming that America's sympathies were being fraudulently invoked to support an incipient new slave state. If that were true, then he himself was playing a part in the furtherance of slavery, the thought of which made him nauseous beyond the malarial fever working in his blood.

Or perhaps elements of all of these things were true, just as it was true that Mexico had granted these American colonists vast tracts of land—more land than any New Englander would know what to do with—to leave their mother country behind. They had forsworn their American citizenship and pledged their allegiance to Mexico. Surely Mexico was reasonable in requiring that they leave behind as well their American expectations of the almost boundless personal liberties they knew at home, and adapt to life as it was known to millions of other Mexicans.

On the other hand, is not the right to self-government so fundamental that it cannot be bartered away? The twenty-five or thirty thousand Americans now in Texas—no one knew exactly how many, for there had never been a census—had pledged their loyalty to a constitutional government that no longer existed. The question then reduced itself to whether the American colonists' obligation to Mexico ended when that country sank into chaos and despotism.

Bliven sipped the last of his tea and nodded slowly; he could leave the argument there and perform his duty as he was ordered with a clear conscience—but with the proviso that if it became clear that

American policy was using him to aid slavery, he would resign his commission and go home to stay. More fundamentally, he recognized now how Providence had been rubbing his nose in slavery, and Catholicism, since Jamaica, and Haiti, and the Castillo de San Marcos, and the nunnery that had burned down in Boston. For some purpose, he was supposed to understand all this.

9

The Tree of Liberty

Once ashore, Sam quickly found the strip of firm sand between the surf line and the soft dunes where he had sunk ankle-deep with each step, providing him an avenue eastward to the city. The town of Galveston sheltered on the harbor side of the island, and three times Sam turned north to surmount the dunes, each time seeing only marsh and knowing he had still farther to walk. It was on the fourth attempt that he descried rooftops, and beyond them masts in the harbor.

He walked into the town from the south, nearing the harbor and at last seeing the waterfront warehouse guarded by sentries, with the flag flying before it, where they had deposited their cargo of small arms. He entered a boardinghouse across the street and bought some breakfast. Not knowing from what direction he might first see Besanson, if he saw him at all, it was a great surprise to see him pass by the boardinghouse window right beside him. He had only met the man the one time, but Sam was certain it was he: tall and swarthy, black hair, an angular face, and a big Gallic beak of a nose. Before he could pass, Sam was at the door and stepped outside. "Lieutenant Besanson, good morning."

He turned in surprise. "Why, good morning."

"If you join me, I will buy your breakfast."

"Gladly."

They shook hands and Sam conducted him inside.

"I am sorry, you have taken me by surprise, and I do not recall your name," Besanson said.

"Bandy."

"Yes, Samuel Bandy, of course. Where is your uniform?"

"I thought it best to enter the town discreetly until I should learn the lie of things."

"And it is well that you did. We are reaching a crisis here. In fact, everything in Texas is reaching a crisis."

They fell silent as the proprietress, a stout brunette virago who appeared unduly curious, brought Besanson breakfast of eggs and ham and toasted bread, and Sam handed her an American silver half dollar. "My friend and I have much to discuss, and I would be grateful if you could keep our cups of coffee full."

She closed her hand around the coin. "I guess I can do that well enough. Is your food all right?"

"It is very satisfactory indeed." When she was gone he turned back to Besanson. "What do you mean? Are you still in General Houston's confidence?"

"I am, but I am now in command only in the absence of Mr. Potter, who has been named secretary of the navy and commander of the port. You and your captain were expecting this development, I believe."

"Yes, it comes as no surprise." He nodded toward the armory. "Is he here?"

"No, he is with the army at present, and then most likely must go to New Orleans to see to fitting out our ships. He was here, and he was fit to be tied when he heard talk of a Texas warship here before he was. He has been relentless in his interrogations about you and your captain. You would think he has his hands full, with two new ships at sea and two more fitting out in New Orleans."

"Indeed? What sorts of ships?"

"Small armed schooners, about a hundred tons each. Nothing to keep a great fuss over, but they are a match for Mexico's little cruisers and can certainly take any merchantman when they like."

"What sort of man is Potter?"

"Oh, God, he is the most snotty-nosed short little turd of a man I have ever met. If I were not a Christian I would wish him struck dead. He learned, of course, that a purported Texas warship had been in port, and he saw how you supplied the armory, and he has been sniffing like a bird dog ever since to bring you under his command. He has published a circular declaring you to be pirates and licensing a vessel of any nation to bring you in for trial."

"Well, our commissions from General Houston will stand proof against that. But you say he is out of town for now?"

"Yes."

"Good. Is there a government? How goes the war?"

"Badly. You knew about the Alamo before you left here."

"That is right."

"Do you know about Goliad?"

"No. What about Goliad?"

"Fannin and his entire army are lost."

"What! How?"

"Houston ordered him to blow up the fort, fall back, and join him, but the silly man dawdled and dallied until Urrea's southern column overtook him. There was a big battle at Coleto; Fannin was surrounded and Urrea offered him terms. Said they would be treated as prisoners of war until they could be sent home to the United States. So Fannin and his men surrendered and were locked up in the presidio. Santa Anna heard about it and blew up. Sent positive orders that all of them were to be shot, and so they were, four hundred of them. They surrendered honorably under terms and then were murdered. Some few of them escaped by running into the woods or diving into the river, which is how we learned the news."

"Oh, my God."

"If people hated Santa Anna after the Alamo, you cannot even imagine the feeling about him now."

"Where are the armies now? How does it stand?"

They fell quiet again as they were served more coffee.

"As I said, things have reached a crisis. Houston and Santa Anna are both twenty or thirty miles north of here. The battle must come at any day."

"How do I get to Houston? I was put ashore last night on the western portion of the island with a report for him that is most urgent."

"God, Bandy, that is hard. I don't know. At last report, Houston was north of Buffalo Bayou, and Santa Anna was south of it. That puts the Mexican army between you and him. Let me think."

"Is there a way to get around him?"

"Maybe. Can you sail a small boat?"

"Of course."

"Do you know the bays hereabouts?"

Sam shook his head. "No, not at all."

"Then I must go with you. We have a small boat. The nearest place where we can get news is Morgan's Point; then we can decide further."

"Will you not be missed here?"

"Did you not understand? The whole issue of revolution will be decided any day now. You must get to General Houston, and I can get you pretty close. If Houston is victorious, we will be heroes. If he suffers the same fate as the Alamo and Fannin, I will be that much closer to striking out for Louisiana and safety. Let us hope it does not come to that. Come, there is a paper on my desk that you must have."

As they crossed the street, Sam cast his glance into the bay, noticing the morning light. He never knew why it happened, but the air at the seaside always seemed to shimmer; perhaps it was from the evaporation of the salt water, but sunlight through it always made objects seem to waver and float. It was a mystery that he never grew tired of, even as he marked that the earth and its beauty seem to take no cognizance of human violence and desperation.

Inside the armory, he surveyed the cases of muskets, barrels of powder, and lead bars, unmoved since they had deposited them there.

"Here, you might like to have a copy of this," said Besanson. Sam took it and squinted, for he did not have his spectacles with him.

THE NAVY DEPARTMENT
of the
REPUBLIC OF TEXAS
A PROCLAMATION

WHEREAS, the people and nation of Texas have undertaken a war of revolution against the despotism of Mexico, and we are determined to prosecute the said war according to the laws and customs of civilized nations; and

WHEREAS, there has been of late operating in the waters of the Gulph of Mexico a ship, supposed to be a large sloop-of-war, operating under the presumed name of the Texas Warship Gonzales, that has committed depredations upon the neutral shipping of the United States, and perhaps of other nations; now be it

PROCLAIMED: that the presumed Texas Warship Gonzales has in fact no connection to the Republic of Texas, and is piratical, and therefore the navies and merchant ships of all nations are enjoined to capture or aid in capturing this vessel and her crew; and be it further

PROCLAIMED: that a reward of five thousand dollars will be paid to the master, to be held in trust for his government or ship's owner, that does deliver the said ship Gonzales into the port of Galveston, to face the justice of the Republic of Texas.

BY ORDER:
Robert Potter
Secretary of the Navy
Commander of the Port of Galveston

Sam looked up and smirked. "That is not how you spell 'Gulf.'"

"Mr. Potter is not a man to brook correction on any point. But look now, these have been in circulation in New Orleans for some time now; he had a stack sent there by express messenger."

"Your two ships now in operation—are they aware?"

"Yes, they put in here for orders."

"May I have a second copy? If I live to see Captain Putnam again, he will surely want to have one."

Besanson handed it to him, then picked up a rolled blanket from the floor by the wall and took a pistol with a powder horn and sack of balls from a hook on the wall.

IN THE PORT'S twenty-foot sailing skiff, a southerly wind carried them across Galveston Bay. They kept to the western shore of Trinity Bay and then proceeded into the broad estuary of the San Jacinto River. By midafternoon they raised land ahead of them, the promontory of Morgan's Point.

"Well," said Besanson, "this answers that question. It looks like the whole settlement has been put to the torch." Numerous log cabins now stood as charred shells, each with a curl of smoke rising above it and bending to the north. Of life there was no sign, either civilian or military of either side.

Sam surveyed the destruction sadly. "I've heard about Santa Anna's sort of war, but this is the first time I've seen it. What now?"

"I suppose we must continue on to Lynch's Ferry—it's another six or seven miles—and see if that is any safer."

No sooner had he said so than he began directing Sam into a series of twists around marshes and sandbars in the middle of the stream where no main channel was obvious. Sam groused, "I thought you said this was a river."

"So it is, but it is a devilish slow and sluggish river. It may only be six miles, but we will have to navigate at least double that."

Halfway there they felt the soft concussion and boom of cannons, not greatly distant, perhaps a mile or two through the trees to their west. The reports came in a curious rhythm—one deep boom followed by two smaller; one deep followed by two smaller—for fifteen or twenty minutes.

"That is good," said Besanson. "Now we know that the armies are on the left bank. Lynchburg and the ferry are opposite on the right. I feel easier about landing there now."

"Are you certain of its location? There is no chance we will miss it? The light will fade before too long."

"No, we cannot miss it. He pulls his ferry across by hand. If nothing else, his rope will block our passage. He was the first settler here; the ferry crossing and the town are both named after him."

Their skiff emerged from between patches of reeds into open water with a clear view of the eastern bank, with a house, outbuildings, and a substantial flatboat tied to a pier. It was nearly dark as they steered for it and tied up on the other side of the dock.

A man came down from the house. He had iron-gray hair and beard and a small, pinched face with narrow-set eyes. Apparently he had once been quite strong but was in a visible decline. "Are you Mr. Lynch?" called Besanson.

"I am Nathaniel Lynch."

He saluted. "Lieutenant Alfred Besanson, Texas Army." They shook hands. "This is Lieutenant Bandy of the navy. He has important intelligence for General Houston. Can you tell us about the situation here and where we can find him?"

Lynch pointed across the river. "Well, he was right over yonder this morning, but as to this evening I cannot say. You heard the firing earlier?"

"Yes. Can you take us across?"

"Not tonight. We can look in the morning and see who is on the opposite bank. You boys may bed down by the barn."

Lynch's bearing showed little in common with the hospitality Sam was accustomed to at Velasco. "Is there any chance you can supply us with some grub? I can pay you."

Lynch squared himself. "Mister, in the last month I have pulled more than five thousand people, by exact count, across this stream, fleeing the Mexicans. Most of them had nothing more than the clothes on their backs. Some of them had some money, and they cleaned me out of every chicken, every ear of corn, and every side of bacon that I had. The only reason my family had any dinner this afternoon was that my son caught a catfish up the creek from here. Now, I am told that some of the public cattle are east of here, and I am going to go hunt one tomorrow, but for tonight I fear that we must all go hungry."

Sam and Besanson spread their blankets in the grass outside the barnyard, but after midnight Sam awakened from a sudden howl of wind, strong from the north, with a distinct chill that promised unpleasant cold when it took hold, and he pulled the blanket tighter about him.

Lynch was up before them in the morning, waving to men on the opposite bank, and then he came up to the barnyard to wake them.

"Boys, you are in luck. The sentries on the other side are ours, so I guess the army survived the artillery duel from yesterday. I can take you across now if you will go."

Sam strained to orient himself from a sound sleep. "I will cross, thank you. Lieutenant Besanson will return to Galveston." Each one walked to a different place in the forest undergrowth to relieve himself, then met Lynch at the dock. Sam and Besanson shook hands. "Can you get back in this thing all right?"

"I believe so. With this norther that's come through, I won't even have to raise the sail to blow back to Galveston."

Lynch pulled the ferry slowly across two hundred yards of water. There was so little current that the rope threaded through iron rings was barely strained by any push downstream.

One of the sentries waved at them. "Mr. Lynch, how are you?"

"Good morning, boys. I have a man here with important messages for Houston. Can you take him into camp?"

"Well, I guess we can."

The flatboat slid onto the bank, and Lynch stepped down. "What was all that firing I heard yesterday?"

"Oh, Lord, you should have seen it." The sentry grinned. "The Mexican gun started firing at our two guns, but we answered back and got the better of them. Colonel Sherman pestered Houston and pestered Houston to let him go out and take the gun. Houston didn't want to, but he finally relented rather than face a mutiny, I'll bet. Sherman made the prettiest little charge you ever saw. Then some Mexican dragoons come out of the trees at them, and Burleson's regiment ran out to help them, and there was Houston on his horse, standing up in his stirrups, screaming at the men to stop it all and come back."

"Did they?"

"Hell, no. Captain Billingsley told him to go screw himself, and Houston didn't say a thing back to him, the damn old Cherokee squaw. All our men made it back, though."

"Is that how things are now?"

"Yep. We know where they are, and they know where we are. The big fight will surely happen today if we can get Houston to fight, the coward."

"Well, I have delivered this officer to you, and I have done my duty for the day. I am going back to the other side, and when you see me get there, I want you to cast this rope loose so the Mexicans can't cross if they force you from the landing. Will you do that?"

"Yes, we will do that."

"If the battle goes your way, we will hook it up again."

Sam was led into the Texian camp of several hundred soldiers, some in uniform, others, the volunteers, dressed as they did every day. The camp lay within a grove of large live oaks, good cover from which to repel an attack if it came.

He was led to Houston's tent and was announced, and was shown in to find Houston lying on his cot. "Have you no blanket, General?"

Houston rubbed his eyes and laughed darkly. "I gave it to the gun crews to cut up for wadding. My reason was, if we lose the day, I will have no more need of a blanket, and if we win the day, I shall have a very fine store of blankets." He rose, and Sam saw he was clad in fringed buckskin. "Our brothers, the deer, keep me warm enough."

Sam thought that a curiously Indian thing to say as he accompanied him to the guard fire, Houston rubbing his upper arms vigorously. "God damn, it got colder last night than I was expecting."

"But what of your brothers, the deer?"

Houston snorted a sudden laugh. "Well, they were not expecting it, either. You have come from Galveston?"

"With a report, yes, sir."

Houston warmed his hands at the fire. "Will no man give his general a cup of coffee?" In an instant a steaming tin cup was given him and one to Sam. Houston slurped to cool it as he drank and made a blissful face. "God, I hope I am not killed this day. I wish to live long enough to enjoy more good coffee. What is your news, Mr. Bandy?"

"General, what strength of artillery are you facing, do you know?"

"Just one brass twelve-pounder is all they have used. They fired it into our camp yesterday and did some little damage: no one was killed, but Colonel Neill, our artillery commander, was struck squarely in the ass with shrapnel. He is out of the fight."

"Well, General, just over a week ago your warship *Gonzales* overtook and boarded a large American brig, called the *Five Points*, that was attempting to get into the pass to Cópano. We seized thirty new bronze field guns, intended for their army, with powder and solid shot, grape, and canister. It was impossible to transfer to our own ship, so it was all consigned to the deep, except the powder, which we retained for our own use."

Houston looked at him gravely. "Are you saying that those were the guns meant to be used against me and then used to fortify the Sabine against the United States?"

"We regard it as a virtual certainty."

Houston took a deep breath. "Then that is very good news. Have you eaten?"

"Not last night or this morning, no, sir."

"Well, come sit with me by the fire." There they were given tin plates, each with a chunk of beef cut from a hindquarter roasting over the fire, and two dough cakes made with wheat flour.

"Why, General," said Sam, "these are good. Where did you get flour? I was told that the army was near to starving. And good coffee."

"And so we were"—Houston nodded—"until on the day before yesterday, when first we reached the bayou, we came across a flatboat stocked with flour and coffee. It was abandoned, but there was a note in it addressed in bad Spanish to the Mexican army saying that not all Texians were traitors and begging them to show mercy to those who had never been disloyal to Mexico."

"God damn! Do you know whose it was? They ought to be hanged."

Houston picked a shred of beef from between his teeth. "No, but the country is full of Tories. I pray that one day they will have good cause to be ashamed of themselves, but until the government is established, and safe, we must accept that we are the insurgents, not they."

"You have declared independence, I was told in Galveston."

"That we did. I was at the Convention, in Washington."

Sam was astonished. "Washington?"

Houston laughed. "Our Washington, a new little town on the Brazos above San Felipe. Not the Washington you are thinking of."

"Well, I was about to say!"

"It was on March the second." Houston laughed again. "It was my birthday present, as it were. It was signed by representatives from every district in the country. Then they drafted a constitution, and did so in a mighty hurry, because word came that the Mexicans had massacred the men in the Alamo and were coming for them next.

massacred the men in the Alamo and were coming for them next. Now let us return to my tent to discuss more."

They left the guard tent, the morning light now full, when Sam heard a voice behind him, as high-pitched as his own. "Pap?"

He spun around in shock and beheld himself as he appeared twenty years before. "David!"

"Pap, what in—I heard you was in the navy. What in thunder are you doin' here?" He approached and they shook hands awkwardly. "How's things at home?"

"They were well when I left, but I've been at sea until a few days ago. The Mexicans may have gone through and burned everything; I have no idea."

David Bandy nodded. "I would be sorry to hear it, but most everybody here has family that has lost everything. Me and my pals"—he gestured behind him with a shy smile—"we all signed up once they called for volunteers."

Sam studied his face, not sure when he would ever see it again. "I am proud to hear that, David." He put a hand on his shoulder and squeezed. "I am very proud to hear it. But now I must go; the general is waiting."

"Yeah." He laughed, stepping back. "It is good to see you, Pap."

Sam heard their voices as they faded. "Your daddy knows the general? Damn, Bandy! That is something!"

At Houston's tent they sat on stools at a table before the open tent front, in enough privacy to speak freely. "Now, Bandy, as to that part of our plan that only you and Captain Putnam know, it worked well for a while. Santa Anna came after me like a bloodhound, straight toward the Redlands, where I could link up with General Gaines. If we could get him into the fight, he could join Texas to the United

States in an afternoon. But then our so-called government broke camp and ran for the coast, so Santa Anna left off following my trail to follow them. He figured that if he could capture and kill the government leaders, the whole revolution would be over at one stroke."

Houston stopped to chuckle. "It has been the damnedest thing ever. There I was, getting letters from General Gaines in Louisiana telling me not to risk a fight having only these yahoos supposedly under my command. 'Get Santa Anna into the Redlands,' he tells me, 'get me in on it.' And I'm getting letters from the Texas government ordering me to stand and fight, stand and fight, while their own damn horses are falling down dead from running so fast to get to the coast."

Sam shook his head.

"But now," said Houston, "*now* is the time to fight. When Santa Anna started chasing the government, he ran ahead with fewer than a thousand men as an escort. Just for these few days he is vulnerable, and my farmer boys can whip him. As of yesterday, we have marched fifty-five miles in two and a half days. Now they've had some sleep and they are spoiling for a fight. When we attack, they will be as unstoppable as demons from hell."

"What was the fight yesterday all about?"

"Oh, shht. Revolutions draw ambitious men—men who show up and right away want to take over. Colonel Sherman came down here from Kentucky and he brought those two six-pounders with him, I'll give him that. But yesterday he tried to provoke the general engagement before we were ready, in order to take some glory and unseat me as commander. Well, today he is Corporal Sherman, his men hate my guts, but I intend to turn that anger against Santa Anna, where it belongs. As to the rest of my officers, you wait a few moments and I will show you something you will never forget. Mr. Hockley!"

As from nowhere, his aide-de-camp appeared. "Mr. Hockley, meet Lieutenant Bandy of our navy, who has arrived with intelligence for me. Hockley, please to call a conference of all my officers here at my tent in ten minutes. Now," he repeated, "you shall see something. These sons of bitches have been abusing me to the limit of my patience for not engaging in a premature and fatal contest. Unless I guess wrongly, you are about to see how brave they really are."

As the officers gathered, Houston had more stools brought for them, seating himself at the head of their circle. "Gentlemen, this is the day of the great contest. Every consideration enforces it, no previous occasion would justify it, but today is the day. And now I seek your advice, whether to attack or stay under cover and receive their attack."

Sam listened attentively to the deliberation, mostly on the topic that to assault an entrenched position when they had no bayonets was unprecedented and foolhardy. Houston made them vote, and it was five to two in favor of receiving the attack.

"Gentlemen," said Houston, "I thank you for your advice. We shall attack. The front of battle will be over a thousand yards wide. The men will space themselves so thinly that their musket fire will be ineffective. We shall advance quietly and in order. General Hockley, your Twin Sisters will be in the center. At my order you will wheel and fire them to open the engagement. Colonel Burleson, your infantry will be on his left; Sherman's Kentuckians will be on your left. General Rusk, your infantry will be to the right of the artillery, and Colonel Millard, your infantry will be to Rusk's right. When we attack, the Mexicans will try to flee to the west, but Colonel Lamar, your cavalry will cover the far right and prevent their escape. The sick and the underage will remain behind to guard the camp. The attack must be made with discipline. There are two other Mexican armies out there, each of them larger than the one we are facing, and we do not know their location. They could well be within sound of the guns and come upon us at any time. The companies must be able to regroup as soon as you command it. Am I understood? Very well, go and tell your men to prepare for battle."

The others started to leave but stopped in their tracks and turned as Houston was approached by a medium-sized swarthy man with bronze skin, black hair, who addressed him in a Spanish accent. "General, you did not make an assignment for my company. What would you have us do?"

"Lieutenant Bandy, may I introduce Captain Juan Seguín, commanding our company of Mexican scouts and rangers. A better patriot and better fighter never mastered both the English and Spanish languages."

"Honored to meet you, Captain," Sam said, saluting, and they shook hands.

"I am pleased to meet you, *señor*. Now, General, where shall you position us?"

"Captain Seguín, I am sorry to tell you this, but I have thought hard about it. I am going to keep you out of the fight. You will reinforce the camp guard."

Seguín's face was a rolling kaleidoscope of emotion: shock, disbelief, insult, rage. "*¿Porqué, señor?* General, the sick and the boys must already number two hundred. They can fight to guard the camp if they have to. That is no position of honor for my men!"

"All right, Captain Seguín, I will give it to you straight. You and your company have been brave, and diligent. I could not have asked more of you. But look at this army about you. These men's blood is up to boiling, and they advance this afternoon to kill Mexicans. Their hatred is blind; they are going to shoot down anyone who is darker than they are. You and your scouts are Mexican, and I cannot risk having you killed by mistake by our own side."

"*Mi General*, with respect, I understand and thank you for your concern. However, you omit one consideration that is the most important of all to us. You forget, we hate that man worse than you do. See here. Let us suppose that you lose this battle and your army must flee. Most of your men will find their way home to your other country. We have no other country. We have no homes to go to until this man is destroyed. *Señor*, you cannot keep us out of this fight!"

Houston heard him out, his arms folded, and nodded slowly. "Did you hear that, Mr. Bandy? That is how a real man speaks. Very well, Captain, you shall fight. But how will my men be able to tell you from the enemy?"

Seguín thought quickly. "Last night my men were playing at monte. We have the cards. Let us put the cards in our hatbands, and your Americans will know not to shoot at us."

"All right. If that is what you wish, that is how we shall have it. Did all you other officers hear this?" There was a murmur of assent. "Be clear about it: Captain Seguín's scouts will be wearing playing cards in their hatbands. Do not shoot at them: Spread this word thoroughly through your regiments to the last man."

For the next hour Houston, with Bandy in tow, circulated among the camps, where the men who had been ready to mutiny cheered his decision not just to fight but to attack. "Men," he repeated in each camp, "the army will cross, and some of us may be killed and must be killed. But, men, I want you to remember the Alamo. The Alamo, the Alamo! Those brave compatriots of yours gave their lives so that you and your families may live in liberty. And I want you to remember Fannin, remember Goliad, and the unspeakable murderous treachery that happened there—four hundred good men shot down in cold blood. That would have been our future under Santa Anna's rule, but now the future that you fight for is limitless, it is brilliant. Will you not fight for this?" At each camp he was cheered lustily.

"Well, you men get your dinners, and I will lead you into the fight."

"General Houston?" It was Hockley with a dozen of his artillery company.

"General Hockley, what is it?"

"Sir, Vince's Bridge across Buffalo Bayou—you cannot be unaware that it is still standing."

"I know it is."

"Santa Anna's men were reinforced during the night by three or four hundred more."

"I know they were, and from where our last report places them, they have marched all night to get here. They will be useless. They will probably sleep through the fight, they are so exhausted."

"Sir"—Hockley gestured almost helplessly in the direction of the bridge—"ought we not to cut it down?"

"Hockley," said Houston calmly, "have you noticed the layout of Santa Anna's camp? He has the Texian Army in front of him, Buffalo Bayou on his left, the San Jacinto River on his right, and that terrible marsh of Peggy Lake behind him. He has left himself no way to escape except that bridge. Yes, Mr. Hockley, you take some men and chop that bridge down. But take care you tell no one of it until after we begin the attack. Once you see us start to cross the field, you men gallop like hell behind our line, cry to the men that Vince's Bridge is down, and it is victory or death. That will make a very nice effect, don't you think?"

Hockley hung his head and laughed. "Mr. Bandy, you do not know this, but in General Houston's youth, he was an amateur actor in a small theater. To this day, no one can equal him for melodrama."

Houston gave a courtly bow from the waist. "Thank you, sir."

"And what about me?" asked Sam at last. "What place have you for me?"

"It is good of you to offer," said Houston. "Let's see, you are a navy man."

"Yes, sir."

"I imagine you are accustomed to firing larger guns than ours."

"Rather, sir, yes."

"Well, that just makes you the better qualified. I am placing you under Hockley's command here to help with the Twin Sisters." After Sam's flash of confusion he added, "That is our name for the two six-pounders."

"That suits me very well, General, thank you."

The soldiers ate well of dough cakes made from the flour that Texas Tories had left for the Mexicans, and four public cows that were butchered. But as the afternoon wore on, the grumbling began again over when they would attack.

At last, Houston approached Hockley's crew behind the guns, carrying a spyglass, and at his order was boosted up into the boughs of a covering live oak. He lay flat on a fat branch, steadying his arm as he spied out the Mexican camp. "Gentlemen," he said when he was helped down, "of all the advantages to have in a battle, nothing is more important than to know the enemy you are fighting. Those men who reinforced Santa Anna marched all night to do it. The Mexicans have been on pins and needles since before dawn, waiting on our attack, and it has not come. And, gentlemen, in Mexico they have a custom of every day taking a nap in the middle of the afternoon. I have just studied their encampment, and there is not a creature stirring over there. They are mentally shot and physically exhausted, and they are having their siesta. Gentlemen, form up your companies quietly to attack."

Within twenty minutes they stood in a thin line, one man perhaps every four feet, stretching as far as the eye could see in either direction. It was three in the afternoon. Houston arrived, walking his horse through the trees; his large white charger was as fine as Sam's own red Ranger.

"Oh, my God," breathed Hockley. "Look at that uniform." Houston had changed from his buckskin into fawn-colored breeches inserted into polished black boots, a deep blue coat with brass buttons— a uniform from the American Revolution. The symbolism did not escape a single one of the officers.

Houston stopped his horse in front of and to the right of the guns. "Mr. Hockley, is everything ready?"

"Yes, sir, General."

Houston removed his hat, a wide-brimmed white beaver, and lowered it. "Trail arms," he said softly. "Forward."

The field was of tall grass, the ground rising gently before them, reaching a crest about halfway to the Mexican barricades. As the squeaking gun carriages topped it, Houston stopped. "Are you ready, Mr. Hockley?"

"Yes, sir, General."

"Well, then, wheel your guns. It is time to wake them up." Houston reined his charger to a halt beside them as the crews spun the carriages of the two six-pounders on their axes. Houston turned his attention to the barricade of baggage at the center of the Mexican line to see what effect their salvo would have. He drew his saber from its scabbard, held it aloft, and slashed it down. "Fire!"

There was no explosion, but Sam heard one of the gunners mutter, "Oh, hell."

"Fire, damn it!"

There was further fumbling at the breeches of the guns.

"God damn it," bellowed Houston, "aren't you going to fire at all?"

Sam raced over to see if he could help, and saw to his horror that the guns were of the olden type, with open touch holes. He also saw that they had no priming powder, and they had poured in the coarse-grained powder to the tops of the touch holes. He grabbed a twig from the ground, then blew the top of the powder from the hole and dug out the old powder. He pulled the stopper from his own powder horn and refilled it, finally handing it to the other gun crew, who had followed his actions.

Sam stood back and nodded to the two men carrying old-style linstock fuses, who blew on them until they glowed, and then stepped to the side of the gun carriage to avoid the recoil. They just started to lower them when Houston's charger neighed loudly and plunged directly in front of the Sisters.

Corporal Ben McCulloch, in charge of the near gun, cried, "God!" and knocked one of the fuses away; the other man instinctively withheld his at the confusion.

Houston regained control of his mount and got it out of the way, shock registering on his face, sensible at how close he had come to being blown to atoms, and amused at his escape. "McCulloch, do you think you would care to fire your guns now?"

"Yes, sir, General. Boys, fire!"

The brands were put to the Twin Sisters, and they jumped back in recoil from the fiery muzzle blasts.

"Well, that will wake them up. Boys, this is it: Advance! Fifers? How about some music to march with?"

The four musicians had already consulted among themselves. Each knew different tunes, and the only one that all four knew was an off-color barroom ditty about seduction called "Will You Come to the Bower?" Sam knew it well, and if it were not for the impending battle would have sung along.

The volunteers close enough to hear them began laughing, agreeing that there could not have been any more martial music to inspire them. First one and then another of the volunteers let loose a blood-curdling whoop and began to run forward, their muskets *en garde.* "Boys," roared Houston, "remember what we taught you, to stop and fire by companies!"

As Mexicans began to appear at their barricades, the Texian companies stopped and fired, but the discipline only held good for the one time. The men fired and then ran forward, screaming, drawing sidearms and Bowie knives.

"You men around me," called Houston to the left and right, "concentrate your fire on their gun crew. Keep them from firing it."

Within seconds half of the Mexican gunners were picked off and the others were fleeing as a white-haired officer attempted to rally them, whipping them with his saber and shouting, to no avail. At least two of the fleeing gunners pulled at him to flee with them, but he did not. Instead, he stepped up onto an ammunition box and stood, arms folded, glowering at the oncoming Texians. He was in a magnificent, gold-corded uniform.

War Secretary Rusk was within Houston's earshot. "I know that man! That is General Castrillon. Boys, don't shoot him, he is no Santanista; he is a brave man and I want to question him."

"Bullshit!" spat one of the volunteers, who knelt and took careful aim at him. Rusk rode close and with his saber knocked his musket up just at the instant it fired, causing the man to leap up in total fury. "You stupid piece of shit! You don't get men into a battle and then tell them who to shoot and who not to shoot! What is wrong with you?" He slapped Rusk's horse on its rump with his own saber, causing the animal to plunge with Rusk hanging on.

Castrillon stood motionless on his ammunition box, glaring, until he was blown backward by at least four balls striking him at once as though hit by a firing squad. He was dead before he hit the ground.

Houston's white charger stopped and fell to his knees with a shudder, three bright red holes in his throat and chest. "A horse, someone bring me a horse!" In the time it took to remount him, the line had outpaced him, but Sam had stayed by him and heard him utter a profanity and lean forward in his saddle, but then continued on.

Even before the time he got over the barricade of baggage carts, Sam saw the battle had devolved into a rout, into pandemonium, the Mexicans fleeing for their lives, the Texians killing whomever they could catch.

On his right Sam heard a pathetic wail, turning his head to see a boy of at most fourteen, and slight for his age, on his knees.

"*¡No, no! ¡Por María, salve mi vida!*" The Texian volunteer who was loping toward him and was almost upon him unsheathed a fearsome Bowie knife, and in a lightning-quick arc down and up caught the boy in the center of his chest just beneath his rib cage, the force of it lifting him off the ground with a plangent scream, the piercing point of the knife distending the back of his white blouse.

In unthinking terror the fleeing Mexicans ran straight behind them and upon reaching Peggy Lake, instead of turning to the side to stay on dry ground, plunged into the marsh and instantly sank calf-deep into the muck. There must have been three hundred of them struggling through the reeds, one sucking step at a time. At least thirty of the Texians reached the edge of the marsh and took their leisure, loading, shooting one down, reloading with wadding and ramrod, and shooting another one down, trading jokes and wagers while they were doing it.

General Rusk, the secretary of war, saw this and rode up in a rage, demanding a halt to the slaughter. No one paid him the least heed until Rusk again knocked a man's rifle up with his saber. That volunteer bridled and backed up a step. "Mr. Rusk, sir, If Jesus Christ came down from heaven this instant, sir, and told me to stop shooting Santanistas, I would not do it, sir!"

"By God, you will!" Rusk held his saber aloft.

"By God, sir, I won't." The man took another step back and cocked the hammer on his musket, leveling it at Rusk's chest.

Rusk backed his horse a few steps and lowered his sword. "All right, then, have it your own way."

Houston found another several dozen volunteers in the Mexican camp, looting the tents and occasionally killing a Mexican soldier found hiding there. Houston waved his saber in the air. "Men, the battle is won! Victory is ours! Form back into your ranks and begin taking the prisoners to the rear." But it was as though he never spoke at all. "Form your ranks," he roared again into the pandemonium.

Having no luck there, Houston galloped northwest from the Mexican encampment, repeating his order to cease fire and take prisoners. To catch those Mexicans who fled in that direction to Buffalo Bayou, there was no time to reload. The volunteers chased them, clubbed them down, and finished either with a Bowie knife or a rifle butt to the head.

"Take your prisoners!" roared Houston again.

"Boys, you heard the general!" bellowed one of the volunteers. "Take prisoners! You know how to take prisoners, don't you? Shoot one, then club guns and remember the Alamo! Remember the Alamo, remember Goliad, and club guns left and right and knock their goddamn brains out!"

At last Houston sat on his horse, victorious on the day but defeated by his own army. "Men," Sam heard him say to those around him, "I can win battles with you, but damn your manners."

Sam trotted over to him and held his horse by the bridle. "Mr. Bandy, these men will not listen. If Urrea or Filisola show up in the next moment with their armies, we shall all be killed."

"Well, thank God there is no sign of them, and you left such a strong camp guard, they can tie down any Mexican reinforcement until we can get reorganized."

"Maybe so. Mr. Bandy, fetch me those officers, for I have been wounded." As Houston was helped back to camp, Rusk galloped up to Sam. "Mr. Bandy, you appear to be the only sane man on the field. I am sorry to ask it, but I want you to look among the Mexicans for survivors. I will send a wagon for those you find."

"Yes, sir." He knew what awaited him. Dead men staring at the sky. Dead men gutted and disemboweled. He saw so many intestines that afternoon, he swore he would never eat sausages again. Dead men, shot in the forehead and their brains exploding out the backs of their skulls.

So, thought Sam, *this is how the Tree of Liberty is watered.* But according to Jefferson, it is watered with the blood of patriots, and tyrants. He said nothing about the blood of hundreds and hundreds of these poor, ignorant, frightened, hungry peasants, who in all probability never wanted to leave the simple labors they had always known. The Tree of Liberty was very cruel indeed to demand their lives.

The more bodies that Sam saw in their search for survivors, the more he was struck how small most of them were. One can be slight and of gracile build but still be strong. Many of these men and boys appeared to simply never have had enough to eat. There was only one man whose blood he wanted to water a tree with, and that was Santa Anna.

10

—·◦·—

Reckonings

Tasked to find someone living among so many dead, Sam found none at first, although two gurgled out the last of their lives as he knelt by them. Twice it got to be too much, and he had to look away across the river toward Lynch's settlement, or back to the oak trees of the Texian camp, or up to see the late-afternoon clouds coasting by. He was glad Bliven was not here to see this.

He knew well that Bliven could fight, and in battle he could kill, but he also knew of his conscience and his sensibilities; that he grew disgusted, and then furious, and ultimately despondent, at mindless bloodlust—and that was what had transpired here, an exposition of hatred, vengeance, and murder with no necessity for it. It was well that he did not see it.

The wagon that Rusk had promised rumbled onto the field and Sam hailed them. "Why are you pulled by horses? Would not oxen better serve your purpose?"

"Sir, we have no oxen," one said with a decided tone of bitterness. "We had two, to pull the cannons, but this damn mean old woman come up and cut 'em loose and led 'em away. Cussed out the general something fierce, the damned old blister; said he promised her when he borrowed them there would be no fight. Have you found any wounded?"

He had not, other than the two that expired before him. The rest either died where they fell, or else—and he suddenly realized what a pointless errand he had been assigned—bodies he found whose bullet wounds would not have been fatal had had their throats cut like slaughtered sheep. He realized that the Texians had already been over the field, dispatching the wounded. Still, Sam walked dogged, crossing the field back and forth, turning over those not already on their backs. The wagon rolled after him, finally loading in perhaps five or six who were still alive, although it was likely they would die before reaching a doctor.

They found no Texians, as it seemed others in Houston's army had scoured the field and taken all their own fallen with them when they finally quit the place. Sam knew that reports of battles contained some accounting of the enemy's dead; he saw no one else counting. At first he kept track by twenties, folding one finger against his palm for every score of bodies, but gave it up when he found himself walking along with two closed fists and realized they had hardly begun.

It was coming on evening when Sam made his way back to the camp in the live oaks and found the volunteers still in a frenzy of whooping, celebrating, shaking hands. To his surprise he saw Mexican prisoners, sitting on the grass before the tree line where they could be easily watched, numbering it seemed as many as the bodies he had found. He asked one of the guards where the wounded were being cared for, and was pointed to a hollow within the stand of oak trees and was told to ask for the chief surgeon, Alexander Ewing.

"Are you Dr. Ewing?" he asked when he reached the medical tent.

"I am." He was washing his hands in a basin of water.

"I was with General Houston when he was wounded. How is he?"

"He took a musket ball in his ankle. It is not a simple wound, and it is most dangerous, for the ankle bone was shattered; bone fragments went everywhere."

"Howdy, Pap." It was David's voice, coming from the nearest of the pallets of wounded.

"Doctor, excuse me; that is my son." Sam walked out to him. "David, are you badly hurt?"

"Naw, it's just a flesh wound. Had to pull a ball out of the meat of my back—probably one of ours, from someone coming on behind me. It'll hurt for a spell, that's all."

"Are you comfortable? Do you need anything?"

"Naw, Pap, I'm all right." Sam nodded and turned to go back to Ewing. David had wasted his youth, a vandal and a hell-raiser, but at least now he could know he'd been honorably wounded in the contest for the birth of his country. That was no small thing.

"How is he?" asked Ewing.

"He is not badly hurt, I am happy to say. You were telling me about General Houston."

"Well, if he lives I suppose he can add it to his"—Ewing stopped and searched for the words "—his wound collection. Before my God, I do not know how the man keeps going." From his medicine cabinet Ewing produced a bottle of whiskey, poured himself a glass, and looked quizzically at Sam.

"Yes, please, but are you not needed among the wounded?"

They seated themselves on camp stools, and Ewing took a quick swallow. "No, each regiment has its own surgeon and assistant. If Texas had as many soldiers as it has physicians, the question of independence would have been decided 'ere now, I do believe. Do you know, when I was working on his ankle, I noticed a spot of blood on his shirt, which I took to be splatter from the battle, but then I saw it increase by a little. I opened his shirt and he said, 'Doctor, do not trouble; those are old wounds.' Do you know how old those wounds are? He received them in the War of 1812! They have never healed. I opened the bandage and let them run freely for a few moments, then cleaned and dressed them. And then, by God, there is an old wound high on his thigh, from an Indian arrow, he said. It was also bleeding and has never healed."

"I had heard before that he bore old wounds, but I did not know they never healed. Could there be something in his nature that prevents old wounds from healing?"

Ewing shouted in laughter. "That is true of his mind and heart, sure enough! He is famous for the grudges he carries. But I never heard of a body refusing to heal. I swear to God, he is like some kind of Golem. He is not made of living tissue; you can just shoot him and shoot him and he keeps on coming."

Sam took a slower sip of his whiskey. "What are his chances of keeping the foot?"

"About even, maybe. If it goes to gangrene I will have to remove it or he will die. Or rather, normal men would die. He has carried those other wounds for over twenty years and somehow he manages to keep them from getting infected."

"Is he awake? Can I see him?"

"No, I have given him laudanum. Try back in the morning."

Sam stood to go. "Doctor, I thank you for your time, and your whiskey. I will—" Movement farther back in a deeper part of the glade caught his attention. "Now, who are they?"

"Them? Oh, poor creatures. As Santa Anna came on to the east, every town he burned he would round up the slave women and bring them on the march."

Sam felt his pulse quicken. "You mean—"

"To provide the services of Venus to his soldiers, yes."

His pulse became near panic. "Where are they from? Are any of them from near Velasco?"

"We don't know. No one has talked to them yet; we're just trying to make them comfortable until we can see about who owns them and send them home."

"Doctor, forgive my anxiety. My plantation is near Velasco and was in his path. I have slaves who— May I?"

"Yes, of course, go on down. If you find any that are yours, you will be welcome to take custody of them."

Sam started down the path, but suddenly he heard David's voice from the pallets of wounded. "Oh, Pap, don't! Oh, hell's bells."

Sam decided not to acknowledge him again, for he heard another ask David what was wrong. "Oh, he's got a slave woman he's been pokin' since my mama died. Makes me sick. Now he's just afeard the Mexicans have been havin' her. I'll thank you not to speak of it further."

In the makeshift camp of tarpaulins stretched over oak boughs, he asked of several slaves if they knew of a woman named Dicey, but none had, and he recognized none from the Velasco environs. At least, he thought, his mind was eased on this point, but the condition of these women irked him. Like all Texas planters, he well knew the dance that the Mexican authorities had always stepped around slavery: that it was officially illegal and that the accommodations made by the state government in Coahuila had been repudiated by the new centralist government. In fact, Santa Anna used it as one of his excuses to break up the state legislature and replace it with a military regime under his brother-in-law. But that had not prevented him from herding slave women into his ranks and forcing them into the most bestial and degrading existence imaginable.

Sam bedded down that night amid the tarpaulins of the officers and awoke in the morning to breakfast—an astonishingly good breakfast, prepared from victuals dropped off by settlers on their way back home. Of those who had fled eastward before Santa Anna, the last were within earshot of the battle. They learned quickly of the victory, and word of it flashed eastward down the trudging line of refugees. Now the movement washed back to the west, ebullient and as much in a body as a tide that had ebbed and was now flooding back. Nathaniel Lynch was busy once more at his ferry, and no doubt in a few days would be a very wealthy man. The first in the long stream of wagons had to stop and start and stop as dead Mexicans were pulled out of the road, although no trouble was taken to bury them, and by midmorning the stench began to rise.

Sam was among those who carried Houston on a litter from his tent and set him down at the foot of a live oak at the edge of the glade, looking out across the field. There he learned that he had lost eight men killed, and a few more were likely to die. He did not believe it at first, and inquired of its veracity with the chief surgeon, and Ewing confirmed it.

"How many Mexican dead?" he asked.

"Six hundred so far; we're still counting, trying not to count anyone twice."

A skinny, anxious-looking private came uncertainly into Houston's presence. "Excuse me, General, we have a prisoner you may wish to see. Says he is Santa Anna. We don't know him from Adam, but from the way he's bitching about the conditions, he must be pretty important."

Houston looked up, in pain and annoyed. "How do we make sure?"

It was War Secretary Rusk who spoke up. "General, we also captured Colonel Almonte, his second in command. He is well-known to many of us, and he is an honest and frank man. I would bring him over to translate, as Santa Anna speaks no English, and Almonte's English is probably more correct than our own."

"Well, bring Colonel Almonte first. I wish to speak to him. Then bring Santa Anna, and bring Dr. Labadie, too. He speaks enough Spanish to know if anyone tries to play a trick on us."

Sam observed Almonte when he was led up. He was a strong, medium-sized officer of about thirty, with very copper skin and an Indian's visage.

"Colonel Almonte," said Houston, "I have heard that at the shore of Galveston Bay your troops overtook our government as they fled before your invasion. I am told that you refused to fire on their boat because the president's wife was among them. Is this true?"

"Sir," he said, "I do not shoot at women."

"Allow me, then, to express my respect for your actions. Such chivalry is rare."

Almonte nodded gravely.

"Now, Colonel, Santa Anna is being brought here. You will be asked to identify him and confirm that it is indeed he."

Almonte stiffened. "Is he alive or dead?"

"He was taken alive this morning. It is my understanding that he does not speak English. Are you willing to translate for us whatever he wishes to say?"

"Of course."

Sam was shocked at the sight of Santa Anna. He looked like any shopkeeper or cobbler but for his hauteur—nothing like the butcher he was known to be. The Mexican president studied Houston's face before saying to Almonte in Spanish, "He may consider himself born to no common destiny who can say that he has conquered the Napoleon of the West. Now it remains for him to be generous to the vanquished."

Almonte was clearly uncomfortable relating such misplaced vanity from a captured dictator. Houston frowned and shifted, waiting for Almonte to finish rendering such a flowery exposition. "You should have remembered that at the Alamo!" he snapped.

"*Señor.*" Almonte launched into an English rendering of the rapid Spanish staccato from the dictator. "I had no choice in my conduct at the Alamo. My government had decreed that those taken under arms should suffer the fate of pirates, which is summary execution. I had no choice but to obey their command."

"Oh, stop it!" spat Houston. "You are the government yourself, sir. It is no use to try and hide behind the empty form of a Congress you have set up to give the illusion of some kind of democracy. And what is more, you have not even that excuse for your ordering the murder of Fannin's men at Goliad."

Word that Santa Anna was a prisoner and meeting with Houston had quickly raced through the Texian camp, and within moments the scene was observed by hundreds. One of the volunteers, backed by this solid phalanx, took encouragement from Houston's tone and brandished a coil of rope, one end of which was already tied into a noose. "Let us have him, General. We know what to do with him!" Some of those behind him cheered.

"No," said Houston loudly, "I forbid it. Now, boys, listen to me, and listen well. Alive, Santa Anna is our insurance that the other Mexican armies will march out of our country in peace. Alive, his signature guarantees our recognition. Dead, he is just another dead Mexican, so that is how we must have it. Moreover, killing him would bring the censure of the civilized world down upon us, and we cannot start our life as an independent nation under that kind of stain. He is not to be harmed, do you hear me? The man or men who kill him will themselves hang as murderers by my positive order. This I swear, so do not try me."

Writing materials were brought, and Santa Anna dictated orders to his other division commanders to withdraw, Filisola and Gaona to San Antonio, and Urrea to Victoria, and await further instructions.

Houston then gave Santa Anna his parole to live with the other prisoners, not in chains or under close arrest, an act that shocked the dictator to his core. He could not even believe he was still alive, for had the roles been reversed, everyone present knew the outcome would have been far different.

"Gentlemen," said Houston as matters concluded, "I thank you for your kind attentions. Now I must speak privately with Lieutenant Bandy."

The various officers made their salutations and drifted away until they were alone. "Pray be seated, Bandy. You may even use the camp chest throne lately occupied by His Napoleonic Highness."

They chuckled. "Where does he find the nerve?" asked Sam. "I mean, he was not just defeated but his army was annihilated, and he still views himself as a conqueror and his defeat was just the fault of others. How does he do that?"

"I believe it is simple," Houston said wearily. "I believe he is crazy. Just as I believe all great conquerors have been crazy—Alexander, Caesar, Attila the Hun, Genghis Khan, yes, even Napoleon—believe it is a species of mental disease. The question is whether the man who suffers from this disease also has the military skill to give it effect. It seems clear to me that Santa Anna suffers from the disease but lacks the skill to become a conqueror on any great scale. He is a conqueror of shirtless peasants."

"That makes sense," said Sam. Oh, how he wished Bliven were with him. Bliven would know how to talk to Houston; he would know who in hell he was talking about.

"Well now, Bandy, let us put our heads to it. How are we going to get word out to Captain Putnam that the war is won, and he may stand down?"

"I don't know that, General," said Sam, "but I do know we could have a worse problem. We could be puzzling over how to get him word that all is lost and he must sail away and save himself."

Even in his pain and laudanum, Houston chuckled. "That is true, sir, that is true."

"You will find an interest in this, General." He unfolded and gave over the proclamation of their ship to be that of pirates. "It seems that Mr. Potter has caught scent of us. He asks the help of all nations in tracking us down."

"Well, hell," murmured Houston. "That complicates the matter."

"You can do nothing?"

"No. I am the commander of the army; I have no authority over the navy. The new provisional president, Mr. Burnet, is a hateful old polecat who cheated me out of a legal fee ten years ago, and he is Potter's biggest backer. I can't touch him. Where do you think Putnam is about now?"

"Well, sir, after he put me ashore near Galveston, his intention, I believe, was to return to the waters off Cópano and continue to carry out his instructions, which were to interdict shipping."

"And Cópano is still in Mexican hands, although they should receive Santa Anna's orders to stand down in a couple of days." Houston reflected for a moment. "That is good. Any supplies that fall into his hands will come to us and equally encourage Urrea's army to go home or go hungry. But that is not what worries me."

"General?"

"If Potter can read a map, he will know as surely as we do that Cópano is the only place where Putnam would be."

AFTER GETTING Sam Bandy ashore and securing the gig in its davits, Evans Yeakel approached Bliven and saluted. "What are your orders now, Captain?"

"This needful errand is done," he replied, "but our mission has not changed: we are to blockade Cópano until we receive other orders or until we are certain that the war is over. When the sun comes up, it will be the nineteenth of April. We know that the war is in progress, and we know Mr. Bandy's estimate that the issue will be decided quickly. Therefore, my intention is to return to the waters off Cópano for perhaps three weeks and, if we learn nothing there, then to withdraw to Velasco, where we first called. There we will put a party ashore, strong enough to defend themselves until I can cover them, and find out whether the war is over and what was the outcome."

"I understand, sir."

"Come to full sail; set your course west southwest."

In the three days back to Aransas Pass their lookouts spied no other ship. They assumed a pattern of patrol in conformity to what he took to be the spring pattern of prevailing winds: light and variable for several days, then accelerating from the south before blowing cool and steady from the north, easing off, and repeating the cycle. Thus it was no difficult task to position his vessel to chase a ship coming out of Cópano or block the entrance to Aransas Pass to one coming in. But in three weeks they saw no more commerce on the sea than if they were sailing in prehistoric times.

More so by the day, Bliven grew less patient, and from the lack of shipping more certain that either the Mexicans considered Cópano closed to them and were sending no more ships by sea when supplies could be sent overland or, more likely, they knew what he did not yet, that the war was over.

On the morning of May 8 the cycle of weather entered its increasing southerly blow, and Bliven called White, Yeakel, and McKay to him on the quarterdeck. "Gentlemen, I have had enough of this. At the very least, no more ships will come here, and, moreover, my instinct is that the war on land is over, one way or another. This morning the good Lord sends us a stiff south wind to take us to Velasco. Let us take advantage of it."

They were now well past the date when Houston thought the struggle would be concluded. In two days the sextant told them that the distant thread of a shore was near Velasco, and it was time to consider how strong a party to send over the bar and up to the town.

If two men stepped onto their rickety dock from his gig, he could have well-armed marines in the cutter to cover them should they find the place under Mexican occupation and a need to flee.

"Ahoy the deck! Ahoy!"

"What do you see?"

"Two ships, four miles southeast!"

Bliven and Lieutenant White walked to the starboard railing and raised their glasses, just seeing the specks on the horizon. Bliven looked up and shouted, "Can you make them out?"

"Not yet, sir!"

"Very well. Keep a sharp watch and sing out." It was midday, with bright sun, balmy to uncomfortably warm, the wind increasing from the south, the seas running not more than four feet. If the inbound ships had unfriendly intentions and played their position correctly, they would hold the weather gage.

It was McKay who had the wheel. "Have you orders, Captain?"

"Not at this moment, Mr. McKay. Steady as you go."

"What do you think, Captain?" asked White. "Shall we run up American colors until we learn their intentions?"

Bliven lowered his glass and looked at him, always surprised at how far up he had to crane his neck. "An interesting question, Mr. White, with competing considerations. Let them show their colors first and we shall see. Beat to quarters, if you please, and let us be ready for anything."

White descended the ladder to relay the order to the men acting as marines, and in a moment Bliven heard the tattoo on the drum and the men dropping whatever they were doing. He relaxed for a moment, allowing himself to enjoy, even after so many years, the thrill of it—the scurry of feet, the orders barked by the gun captains, the squealing wheels of the gun carriages, the appearance of Yeakel armed with marlinespikes and the precious knowledge of how to repair any damage to their rigging.

It had been weeks since they sent the *Five Points* on Captain Carroll's angry way without his field artillery that was expected by the Mexicans at Cópano; even more weeks since they had lightened the *Mary Ellen* of her muskets and lead and powder. Their ship, although her true identity and nationality were not known, had been seen in New Orleans and Galveston, and speculation about them was sure to be lively. The Mexican navy had nothing to match their guns, but undoubtedly a call for privateers had brought in a fleet of fortune-seekers. If they had been declared pirates, they would be hunted by American privateers as well—not just for their value as a prize but for a large reward as well, offered by the insurers of the cargoes they had interdicted. In no circumstance did he see an advantage to showing American colors. They had patrolled their station off Cópano for three weeks, and the paucity of vessels attempting to enter there made it clear to him that their presence was deduced. That was well, for their mission was to close Cópano to the Mexicans as a port of entry to supply their army in Texas, and at this they had succeeded. Now that they had come back up the coast to try to learn news of the war, these two ships could belong to anyone. They could learn as much by flying the Texian flag as they could the American, especially since the name *Gonzales* emblazoned on her stern could give the lie to their false colors, with unknown consequences. Bliven's pulse quickened with a further thought, a variable that had not previously occurred to him: that the Texians, as Houston had told them, were assembling their own small fleet. If the approaching vessels were themselves Texian, and loyal to the secretary of the navy of whom Houston had warned him, that failed American midshipman named Potter, and if they ordered his surrender, he could be in the unenviable position of having to fight ships of the country he had been sent to help.

The *Gonzales* fell into quiet readiness, a pause that lengthened into reflecting again upon all the deafening noise and violence and bloodshed of a sea battle, and on the agonizing slowness with which they sometimes developed. Bliven loved having it among his memories that he had been on the *Constitution* during Hull's thrilling three-day kedging escape from that British squadron, but those had been three days in which their hair had been standing on end, with the issue undecided. And now here they were, bristling like a porcupine, awaiting the intentions of these two ships, which for all they knew might simply sail away and leave them unsatisfied and unknowing of anything.

"Ahoy the deck!"

"What do you see?"

"Two ships, southeast, three miles. One is rigged fore-and aft . . . appears to be a large schooner! The other, I see smoke and no sail; I think she must be a steamship!"

Such news sent White and Bliven back to the starboard railing, their glasses raised. Suddenly Bliven found himself repenting that he had placed twenty-fours only on the bow as chasers. A steamship he would outgun, but in this light wind it could run circles around him and shoot where he could not shoot back—most disastrously raking fire through his tall glassy stern.

"I can't say I like this," said White.

"Nor I," said Bliven.

"Ahoy the deck! They show Mexican colors!"

"Well, that answers everything." Potter and his call to all ships to arrest them might have presented the greater threat numerically, but if they were Mexican ships, they might have been at sea as long as he and have no more idea than he whether the war was over. He had never yet heard a sailor, lying on the deck with his blood pouring out onto the planks, ask whether a war was over. Between himself and these two oncoming Mexican cruisers, the war was very much on. "Mr. McKay, they may have the weather gage but I'll not show them my ass!" Bliven felt his blood rising, that electric energy shooting through him with such force that he wondered every time, every battle, that he did not glow in a blue aura with St. Elmo's fire. Yes, this was what kept him coming back to sea when the civilized part of his nature yearned for his wife and his farm. It was an addiction, as surely as alcohol or laudanum could be an addiction, but he would have to consider this later. "Mr. McKay, a nice northerly turn, now, then come back to the west. Mr. Yeakel—"

"I follow you, Captain!" In the instant he had men trimming the sails, laying the yards hard over on the starboard tack. With luck they could even manage a few degrees south of west.

"Ahoy the deck! The two ships are separating!"

"Are they changing course?"

"No, sir! They are coming for us but opening a distance between themselves!"

Bliven walked to the wheel. "Mr. McKay, I do not like being this close to the shore. They mean to make us fight both sides of the ship at once. The wind is not very favorable, but I wish you could open some distance from the coast; we could run with them for a while and oblige them."

"Sir." Yeakel came up with them. "If it is a schooner and a steamship, they cannot mount more than maybe three guns on a side. If they make us fight both sides, we will still outgun them four to one."

"Except one is a damned steamship," said McKay. "He will lay abaft where we canna' get to him and play hell with us."

"Then your job, Mr. McKay," said Bliven, "is to keep turning and not give him a clean raking shot through our stern windows."

McKay pointed toward the open water. "We canna' turn south, sir. We can foil him for a while, but it means turning north and west and north and northeast. Eventually we must run aground."

"Well, let us string them along as far as we can. We may inflict such damage that they might retire before that occurs." He looked up at the green silk pennant that began to fall limply with a pause in the wind, and at Houston's gold star on a blue field, wondering just for a second if the general had been able to work his will on the Texian authorities to adopt it. "Mr. White, we are opposite the port of Velasco, are we not?"

"We are, sir."

Do not touch our shore again, Houston had told him, *except to save your lives.* That could prove prophetic. "Mr. White, pass the word among the men to gather for a moment beneath the hatch.

"Well, boys," he addressed them loudly, adopting Sam's manner of informality, "I will tell you how it is. Even though there are two ships against our one, we nevertheless vastly overmatch them. In the highly unlikely event we are bested, I will get you as close to shore as we can, and the people in Velasco will take care of you. However, once these two ships count our guns and take note of their caliber, I expect they will retire and we will have to chase them. Are you ready for a chase?"

He was answered by a cheer from the gun deck, with fists thrust into the air. "Very well, then. To your stations now," he said, pointing at them suddenly. "And no daydreaming about all the land you will be awarded for making this day's fight. All right, lads?"

Again they cheered him, and turned back to their gun stations. He felt for a moment almost like old Preble, and lifted his hat to them when they cheered. He joined Yeakel by the wheel with McKay. He wished Sam were with him, for this was a very small team to command in a fight. "Gentlemen, look there. The steamship is heading upwind astern of us, where we can't turn on him, and the schooner is angling to get ahead of us to cross our bow. They mean to rake us, bow and stern. It is capable thinking; in their place I might do the same thing. Mr. McKay, maintain your course west by south. We will allow the schooner to think he will cross us. At my command, you turn hard astarboard and come to a northerly heading. Mr. Yeakel, pass this on to Mr. White and tell him to give the schooner our port broadside as we turn. Mr. McKay, after we fire upon the schooner, mark the position of the steamship and continue your turn to place him straight on our starboard beam, and Mr. White will give him our starboard broadside. Is all this clear? Mr. Yeakel, go tell him and hurry back."

As the schooner approached, it was clear that she was a privateer. She was light and fleet but built with no internal strength. Pirates and privateers—when had there ever been a half dime's worth of difference between them? They would never learn, it seemed, the folly of mounting guns on platforms that could take no punishment. It seemed a shame to wreck such a pretty craft. She cut through the Gulf swells using her speed and position to come two points off their port bow and two hundred yards ahead.

"Hard astarboard, Mr. McKay! Mr. White, get ready!"

McKay wrestled the big double wheel with all his considerable strength, and the *Gonzales* answered with a ponderous heel and gain in speed as she came before the wind and Yeakel's crew trimmed the sails to catch it. As soon as she recognized what was happening, the schooner fired her three guns, banging like twelve-pounders, and peeled off to port. But before McKay completed the turn White fired his crushing broadside, eleven twenty-fours in a rolling broadside as they bore, the entire side of the *Gonzales* erupting in flame and smoke. The guns farthest forward and aft necessarily passed on either side of the heeling schooner, but the balls fired from her midships struck home, one into her cabin, two into the hull, and one carried away part of her rudder. Through his glass Bliven saw her steering ropes fly up into the air, but with her fore-and-aft rigging she was still able to ride the wind westward swiftly until she was out of range. No doubt the crew was working frantically to get the ropes back around the wheels and get her under control.

McKay finished his turn, but the puffing steamship proved swifter than they had anticipated, and she loosed her raking broadside, heavier eighteen-pounders that tore at an angle into their stern. They heard glass shatter beneath them; they heard bulkheads being smashed. Shrieks and groans of the wounded issued up through the hatch, and then an unholy crash of metal and a curl of smoke rose through the hatch.

The *Gonzales* answered with her starboard broadside, fired all at once with a stupendous roar, and with the steamer only a hundred and fifty yards off; they could almost see the ship bend and give beneath the weight of shot that slammed into her.

Bliven dashed over to the hatch. "Mr. White! What has happened?"

"Sir, two of our guns have been unseated; six of the men are being taken down to Dr. Haffner. I do not know how badly they are hurt."

"Are your other guns all right?"

"Yes, sir."

"Reload, man! Reload!"

"We are at it, Captain!"

"Mr. McKay, I want you to go east. That steamer is by far the larger threat. I want another broadside, into his other side, before he recovers from the first."

"Aye, sir, understood." McKay muscled the wheel to starboard, but as they passed inshore of the steamer, and with White still reloading, the steamer turned as if on bearings and fired their own waiting starboard broadside, three more eighteens, at close range. They heard one ball sing as though it were coming right at them, striking and shivering the mizzenmast six feet over their heads, one holing them low on the berth deck, between wind and water, the third crashing through and wrecking the wardroom.

Bliven leaned again over the open hatch. "Mr. White, are you not ready?"

"Just now, sir!"

"Then in God's name, fire!"

Their starboard broadside thundered again, but as the steamer had finished his own turn, it presented them with a target only as wide as his beam, bow on. Then they saw a flash on her bow and the bang of a twelve-pounder, and realized that she mounted a chaser. It might be a ball; it might be grape.

"Down!" Bliven shouted, even as he dove for the deck. The ball they dodged crashed through the binnacle and straight into the wheel; if McKay had not dropped to the deck he would have been cut in half. There was a mighty crash of wood as the wheel backed off its spindle and lay flat upon the deck.

Bliven puzzled, "Now what?"

Yeakel was getting to his feet. "Sir, the sails are already on the port tack; the wind will carry us to the shore." With no steering force on the rudder, indeed, they already sensed their bow nosing around to the north, and they beheld the steamer, hurt but still dangerous, coming north also, but now several hundred yards off, wary of their overwhelming broadside. They looked ahead and saw people, several score of them now, lining the beach.

In another moment they felt the ship shudder to a halt, and with the ship no longer in motion, the pull on the standing rigging became too much for their long-suspect foremast, the lines snapped, and with majestic slowness it lay down upon the fo'c'sle.

"Mr. Yeakel, we are aground. The water is too shallow to sail and too deep to wade ashore. Get all your boats down and tie them on well. All hands to the hatch!"

Yeakel and White both took up the call until everyone still below gathered at the foot of the ladder, with Bliven above them looking into the hatch.

"Boys, they have been lucky. Our game is just about played out, but all is not lost, for we are at a friendly shore. Now, I want those of you who are good swimmers to ease yourself over the port side and strike out for the beach. Look and you will see even now a crowd of civilians waving you in to give you aid. Those who cannot swim will stay and man the guns until there is no more fighting to be done. Then you will get into the boats and we will row ourselves ashore." A thick column of smoke began to rise from the ladder down to the berth deck.

Not two minutes after a hundred and twenty men took to the water, McKay called to him: "Captain, the Mexican steamer is lowering boats as well! They must mean to overtake our men swimming ashore."

Bliven raised his glass and stared in horror at the sight of Mexican marines with their Brown Bess muskets, seated in longboats, motionless as toy soldiers on a table, being eased down to the water. "No, no, no. Don't they know I will lay a covering fire? My God, I don't want to kill all those men!"

"Aye," said McKay, "but that other captain is the one making the sacrifice, not you. You must protect your own."

"I know that, of course." He jogged to the edge of the hatch overlooking the gun deck. "Mr. White!"

"Sir?"

"That steamer is within the limit of your range?"

"Yes, sir, barely."

"Your starboard guns, how many are this moment loaded with solid shot?"

"All of them, sir."

"You have seen them lowering boats to catch our men before they can get ashore?"

"Yes, sir."

"Well, point your guns as best you can and give him your broadside. When you reload, do so with grape and train upon their boats. They must come closer to overtake our own men. Do you understand?"

"That will be a slaughter, sir."

"It is not my choice; our men must get ashore. I will take charge

of the bow chasers myself and see what I can work with them.
Mr. Yeakel!"

"Sir?"

"Take some men off the forward port battery and get them down
to the berth deck and do something about that fire!"

"Yes, sir!"

"What the hell happened, anyway?"

"One ball of their raking fire made it all the way down to the camboose and tore it apart, including the firebox. Some of the hot coals
fell down the hatch and touched off some linens and bedding."

"Bedding? Why was it not rolled and stowed? Oh, never mind!
Now listen to me. Have we taken on any water?"

"Just a little, sir."

"You must beat the fire well away from the ladder. Take ten men,
bring powder up from the magazine to my cabin and to the wardroom. Keep the fire away from there until we are ready to abandon
the ship. Can you do this?"

"Yes, sir! If I cannot, I will report it to you quickly."

"Good man."

It was too late to repent that he had allowed the crew to become
so lax in their daily routine as to leave their bedding lying about to
catch fire. If he lived through this, he resolved to become a terror of
daily discipline and cleanliness among his next crew, and he could
cite this moment in evidence.

He heard White bellow, "Fire!" and so had a second to brace himself for the wall of flame and smoke that poured out from their starboard side and the clapping booms of the guns. He took a second to
look through his glass at the steamer to see if any of the shots took

effect. He saw three strikes, one in her cabin, one low on her port side so she might take on some water, and one hole in her hull too far forward to be of consequence. If they could hit her steam drum, it would end her game, but the paramount need of the moment were the boats pulling after his own men swimming for the shore.

Bliven stole a quick glance through his glass at the beach and saw it thick now with people, women with their hands at the bills of their bonnets, the men shouting and gesturing all their encouragement.

He felt a wave of dizziness sweep over him and knew that his malarial fever was bidding to assert itself, but he could not have it at this moment. If it was in him at all to summon such a force of will as to beat back whatever debilitating humors were the cause of his disease, it must be now. Bliven loped forward to find the crew at the starboard bow chaser. "Boys, are you loaded?"

"Yes, sir," saluted the gun captain.

"With solid shot?"

"Yes, sir."

He steadied himself with a few deep breaths as he thought, *Good. Very good.* If they first fired a ball at the leading boat, perhaps the Mexicans would realize that he meant business and they would pull back toward their ship without all of them being cut to pieces. They were able to turn the gun until it pointed broad on the starboard bow, still a good distance from his men swimming toward shore. He pointed the gun himself. "Crow it up," he ordered. "Get the quoin in there."

With the barrel thus depressed, he waited a few seconds until the first boat just crossed his sights. "Stand clear now!" He yanked hard on the lanyard.

The muzzle blast boomed out its sheet of flame, and a couple of seconds later he saw to his satisfaction that the shot was even better than he had intended, for the ball carried away the boat's straight stem with a geyser of splinters, stopping them cold without actually killing anyone. Instantly the boat began to settle forward, the stoicism of the Mexican marines finally crumbling, and they stood in terror, shouting and gesturing.

The last thing that Bliven expected at that second was the walloping boom of the forward starboard twenty-four, its ball of fire flaring out beneath his feet, and his glance shot up just in time to see those Mexican marines cut to pieces in a shower of grape. Even at this distance he made out the spray of red from their backs and heads and legs. They spun and fell in all directions, over their seats, into the water.

The second and third boats' rowers suddenly backwatered, stopping them dead but making them mere target practice for White's grape-primed twenty-fours. Four and five and six and seven of them roared in a long rolling broadside. He knew what must happen and he averted his gaze, thinking, *Be it on their heads.* Instead he looked to the shore, where, one by one, the men of the *Gonzales* felt the slight press of sand beneath their feet, swam in further, and tried again, feeling it more solidly. One and then another and another of the cheering men on the beach pulled off boots and shoes, some shucking their pantaloons, and began wading out to them, catching the exhausted sailors beneath their arms, supporting them the last hundred yards to the shore.

Bliven noticed movement over to his right and saw two small sailing skiffs slap their way through the chop over the bar of the Brazos to begin rounding up any stragglers. He ran back to the hatch. "Mr. White!"

"Sir!"

"Well done. Back to solid shot now. Try to hit his paddle wheel and disable him." Then at their starboard quarter he saw the Mexican schooner making a turn, her steering ropes reengaged, to come across their stern, and he had no way to oppose their small but effective raking fire. This was even as he saw the fire lower down had gotten away from them and was nearly out of control. The ship's dry old wood, once it reached a certain temperature and was touched off, consumed itself and the fire spread along deck and bulkheads and knees with frightening speed. "Mr. White!"

"Sir!"

"Belay that last order. Get your men topside quickly and get them down into the boats. We are done. Take the men you need and help Dr. Haffner get the wounded up."

He saw the schooner's three guns run out a hundred yards away and begin her firing run at their stern. Bliven clattered to the bottom of the ladder on the gun deck, looking into the flames below. "Is anyone left down there?" he shouted. "For your lives, now, is there anyone there?" Answered only by the roar and crackle of the fire, he spied Ross through the smoke aft by his cabin, clutching a leather pouch.

"Sir, I have your log and your papers!"

"Good man, Mr. Ross, now go up and get into a boat!" Bliven climbed the ladder, again fighting down his faintness, made it to the boarding ladder, and descended to the cutter. "Pull, now. Boys, get us out of here before she blows."

Yeakel pushed them off, and once their oars were down, they swept with a will. The *Gonzales*'s hulk lay between them and the approaching schooner, so he did not know exactly when they would hear the guns raking into her stern. They were two hundred yards away and pulling hard when they heard the first one, then the second and third, and they knew the hot shot must be crashing into the wardroom and the captain's cabin. They saw the schooner's bowsprit begin to emerge from behind their ship, when they were blinded by a flash as bright as the sun overhead, and the entire aft third of the *Gonzales* disintegrated in a titanic, deafening explosion that seemed to go on and on. The concussion knocked Bliven's bicorne from his head—indeed, would have knocked him from his feet had he been standing. He leaned over to pick it up, when the cutter began to be showered with whirling, burning chunks of wood. Most were quickly tossed over the side, but one caught Bliven a terrific wallop on the back of the head, knocking him down into the cutter's exposed ribs, from where twenty hands helped him back onto the seat. "Thank you," he said quietly. "Do not trouble. I am not hurt."

"Boys," one of them said, "my God, look back there."

Coasting slowly into view beyond the ship's shattered stern, the Mexican schooner, momentarily laid almost flat by the concussion, turned tightly to port, south, into the wind until her sails luffed, and they realized that her crew must have been knocked insensible, perhaps even killed, in the full face of the explosion. They were now forward enough of the *Gonzales*'s remains to see the steamer off her opposite beam. A fresh column of black smoke issued from her stack and she entered a starboard turn, presumably to see if anything could be done to help those in the schooner.

A voice in the cutter's bow shouted, "Three cheers for Captain Putnam! Hip?"

Bliven was unsure for a moment whether he was victorious or

defeated. The third cheer ended with a prolonged huzzah, and he realized they cheered him because they were safe and in a moment would set foot on a friendly shore. "Is Dr. Haffner with us?"

"I am here, Captain. Let me see your head."

Bliven felt his hat being removed and winced at Haffner's touch on the rear of his skull. "What were our casualties?"

"There were seven dead whom I could not save. Three wounded who may live are in the boat with us. Many other smaller injuries. But for such a battle, we are very lucky."

"Indeed, yes."

The cutter's bow ground to a halt and lifted up as it slid onto the beach. "Come on, boys, hop over. This captain's feet shall not touch the water!"

Bliven felt himself being lifted up and carried and then set down ever so gently on the dry beach. Others of the crew sank down to the fawn-colored sand, sitting, lying down, curling their fingers into it, smiling at having passed alive through such a test.

Dr. Haffner was still by him. "Captain, how many fingers am I holding up?"

"Three."

He backed a few paces away. "Now how many?"

"Two."

"It is good, Captain. Sometimes such a blow to the back of the head affects first the vision, but that is not so with you. Nevertheless, I am not happy with how you look. You must retire to a bed at the first possible moment."

A voice he did not recognize came from his side. "What the hell are you boys still fightin' for? Don't you know the war's over?"

"What did you say?" he whispered.

"I say, a bunch more dead Mexicans is all to a good purpose, but the war is over."

"God in heaven!" wheezed Bliven. The firmness of solid ground beneath his feet after weeks at sea made his dizziness worse, for his guts were still rolling with the swell. "Was it won or lost?"

"Won, sir! Santa Anna's army was destroyed with hundreds killed; the dictator himself is Sam Houston's prisoner."

"My God, when did all this come about?"

"Twenty-first of April, near three weeks ago."

Bliven looked sickly back out to the Mexican steam privateer and the shattered flotsam of its launches and their floating dead. "So all those men did not have to die."

"Well, yes, they did, too, unless you and all your men wanted to die instead. May I assume from your uniform that you are the captain of this vessel?"

Bliven tried to stand straighter. "My name is Putnam, captain in the Texas Navy."

"My name is Lacey, sir, Dennis Lacey." He took Bliven's hand and nearly crushed it in greeting. He had a round face, black hair going to white, and a broad smile like the designated greeter at a prayer meeting. "Welcome to Velasco. Captain, you are not steady on your feet. Were you hurt in the fighting?"

"Mr. Lacey, I am pleased to meet you. I was not badly wounded. I have suffered from the malarial fever for some time. If there is a doctor in your town who can supply some quinine water, I—I—believe that—"

Bliven's eyes began to lose their focus even as he began to see in a blur his surroundings at once, and then vaguely he was aware of the comfortable warmth of the sand at the back of his head.

11

Dicey

It was not like a sensation he had felt before. It was not like an ocean swell, deep and rolling, nor even like the chop of a bay that buffeted him. It was irregular, surging and halting, such as he imagined the rapids of a river might be. He was aware of it for several seconds before he opened his eyes to find himself encased in a blanket laid upon straw. He saw the sides of a wooden box on either side of him and in an instant of terror thought he was in his coffin, but then realized he could see above him the purple and peach-colored clouds of either morning or evening. As he regained his senses he heard the creak of wheels and the plodding of a draft animal. "Hello? Where am I?"

He recognized above his head the seat of a wagon. "Ho, horse, ho." The motion stopped and a figure leaned back from the seat. "Are you awake?"

"Sam? Sam, what the hell! Where are we?"

Sam tied the reins to the brake handle and lowered himself into the bed of the wagon. He felt for fever on Bliven's forehead. "Are you all right?"

"I think so."

"I was on the beach in Velasco, but I couldn't get to you before you fainted. You've got a nasty knot on the back of your head."

"And the swamp fever as well, I fear, for some weeks."

They heard a horse walk up beside them. "Captain, are you all right?"

"Mr. Ross! I am heartily glad to see you. You made it off the ship."

"Of course. Do you not remember?"

"I don't—I am not certain. Sam, where are we going?"

"Home, to Halcyon, if it is still there. We should be there by noon. Will you be comfortable until we can get you there?"

"Yes. But if I was so injured, was there no doctor in Velasco?"

"Well, there was, but let's just say people began asking too many questions. All that the crew knows is that they volunteered for the Texas Navy in New Orleans, but I didn't want anyone getting to you."

"I see. Well done. Let us continue, I am all right. Help me sit up." When he could see over the side of the wagon he caught his breath, for the prairie over which he and Sam had passed the previous winter was now alive with wildflowers. Above a ground nearly solid with deep blue-violet lupines rose spikes of bright coral red, sprays of yellow, and great pillows of brilliant pink. "What in the world, Sam?"

Sam clambered back onto the seat, released the brake, and they rolled on. "April is our prettiest month, hereabouts. The flower show is a little past its prime by now. We drove all night," he said. "I stopped long enough to rest the horses, but my friends' house where we stopped before, their house was burnt down. They're not the only ones. The Mexicans came through this country for sure."

For the next six hours Bliven alternately slept and watched the clouds in the blue window of the sky above him, framed by the sides of the wagon. As the heat of the day warmed he pushed aside the blanket and felt the wagon stop, then make a sharp turn to the left. It took some effort, but he rose up again and saw the sign marking HALCYON pass by them. He reclined against the side of the wagon, looking ahead to see what condition the house might be in.

"Well, it's pretty well deserted," said Sam, "but somebody's been through here. All the animals are gone. The house is standing open. And look at this." Sam descended from the wagon and helped Bliven slide off its tail.

"Captain." Ross put in his hand a polished mahogany cane. "I acquired this in Velasco before we left there. I thought you might find it useful."

Good, good Ross; what would he do without him? Sam led them a short distance to a shallow hole in the ground with Dicey's sewing box beside it, open and empty, with needles and buttons and spools of thread scattered about it. "The Mexicans must have seen fresh dirt, figured something was hidden." He heaved a heavy sigh. "That was where we kept our money. Well, now I guess I start over again—again."

Bliven laid a hand on his back, trying to think how best to say that as soon as he got home he could send some money without it sounding like charity.

"No, sir, they only thought they took everything."

"Dicey?" Sam turned at the sound of her voice and saw her standing at the edge of their clearing, her hand against a gnarled and ancient oak.

She walked into the clearing, wiping her hands on her apron. "I left the small coins in my box as bait, where I figured they would find it. I got your gold pieces safe and sound, some on me, some buried in the cane."

"Dicey!" He strode toward her, his arms outstretched, and she flew toward him until they enveloped her, and he held her, swaying her gently from side to side. "Oh, my Dicey! Where have you been?"

After some seconds she pushed herself back, still holding him by the waist. "Pshaw, Sam! You think a colored girl don't know how to hide herself in the woods? What has happened? Is the war over? A Mexican patrol came through here weeks ago, and I been stayin' in the cane ever since. Nobody's come by to say if it's over, or who won, or nothin'."

"Oh, Dicey, we won. All is well, Texas is going to have a free government, and the Mexicans are on their way out of the country."

"Praise the Lord!"

"Where are the children?"

"They should be all right. I sent them up into Bolivar to stay with your friends the Harrises. They packed up and ran away with everybody else. If the war's over, they should all be fine and come back directly. The Lederles across the road have run away, too, but I expect they'll be back."

"Why on earth didn't you go?"

"Me? Shoot! I may hide, but I ain't running from nobody. Cap'n Putnam! Lord, if you don't look a sight. What happened to you?"

"He was in a sea battle," interposed Sam, "just off Velasco, and his ship was blown up. The boats got him and his crew to shore."

"Lord have mercy! Let's get him inside. Who is this?"

"Oh," said Bliven, "excuse me. This is my steward, Mr. Ross."

"You are welcome, sir."

"Most kind, thank you, ma'am."

The sound of it made her turn. In her own house she was accustomed to being more than a slave, indeed she was mistress of the house, but she could not remember any white man ever calling her "ma'am" before. They approached the house, whose front door stood open, the jamb splintered where it had been kicked in. Sam pointed. "They took my brass lock set, the thieving bastards."

Dicey fished in her pocket. "I don't know what good they think it'll do them when I got the key." She pressed it into his hand, their laugh expressing less her witticism and more their joy at still having a roof over their heads.

They passed inside. "The house appears to be all right. Why did the Mexicans not burn it down? They burnt out so many others."

"Well, I got one idea." She took his hand and led him through the left door from the hall into the bedroom. "Lookee there."

She had laid her red and yellow shawl across the dresser and on it two candles flanked a wooden cross, crude, of two orange-brown pieces of mahogany, whittled straight and tied together with thread. Her beaded necklace lay before it, and in front of the dresser was the footstool from the living room. Sam and Bliven both looked at her quizzically. "What have you done?" asked Sam.

"Well, all of us hereabouts got word that the Mexicans were coming, and I heard people say that sometimes, if they know that the people in a house are Catholic, they would leave it alone. I thought it was worth a chance, so I made this here little altar before I quit the place. Now, I have to tell you, I had to knock out the back of the bottom drawer to get the fancy wood. I hope you don't mind. It looks like it worked, though."

All burst out laughing in relief that Sam's home was intact. "Was it a miracle?" Bliven smiled. "If miracles really happen, maybe I need to change my religion."

"No," said Sam, "the real miracle comes if there is anything to eat around here. The Mexicans cleaned everyone else out to feed the army. What do you think, Dicey?"

She had taken the beads from the dresser and hung them about her neck. "Thank you, God, for watching over our home. Well, they took the chickens, sure enough. I turned the pigs out before I left; they may be all right, but maybe not. We can go look for them. But we got some food. I took some beans and cornmeal, and some ham, into the cane where I was hiding. I'll go fetch it. Can you boys manage to get Cap'n Putnam up into the loft to bed? He looks like he's about ready to fall over."

"Cap'n Putnam?" He heard the voice distantly, somewhere beyond the dark.

"Cap'n Putnam!" There was a pressure on his shoulder, and his eyes opened of their own accord, without will, the reflex of decades of the instant alarms of beating to quarters.

The room was dim, but slowly he came to and recognized the loft above the parlor in Sam's house between Velasco and Bolivar, and the figure that distended the mattress as she sat beside him. "Dicey."

"How you feelin'?"

He breathed quietly for a few seconds. "Better, I think."

"I made you some of that yaupon tea you like so well. Do you feel like sitting up and having a little?"

"Oh, yes, thank you." She helped him to sit up, placed the large pillows behind him, and placed the cup to his lips, hot but not too hot. "Oh, that is good." He reached up and took the cup from her. "Thank you, I can hold it. How long was I—"

She placed her hand against his forehead, then on his throat. "Why, your fever's broke. Oh, Cap'n, you was out of your head most of a week. You was thrashin' and talkin' crazy."

"Oh, no." He sighed and took a second sip of yaupon tea. "Not very dignified, was I?"

"No, sir, not so very. You was shoutin', 'Hard astarboard,' 'Fire at the turn,' all that navy talk, like you was still fightin'."

"Well, that's not so bad."

"You thought I was your wife part of the time."

"Oh, no! What did you do?"

"Well, sir! I told you we was both married." She lowered her voice. "But I said if we wasn't, I'd jump on you like a duck on a june bug."

He coughed and snorted tea when he started to laugh. "I wish I could remember that. I am sorry; I must have been so much trouble."

"No, not so much. That nice man, Mr. Ross, he been lookin' after you most of the time. Not too much for me to do."

"Oh, Ross! Is he here?"

"Of course he's here. Don't you remember?"

"Oh. Oh, yes. He rode up here beside the wagon, didn't he?"

"That's right. He's not here just at the moment. He's gone into town for a few things."

"It was the swamp fever again, wasn't it?"

"Yes, sir, and that knock on the head you took. The doctor came down from Bolivar; he said to keep giving you quinine water, stronger than before. You fought it, but he said keep givin' it to you—said you was too insensible to remember how bad it taste once you come around."

"He was right, I don't. This tea is good, though."

He looked up and saw Sam ducking through the door. "Well!" He stood up to his full height as he got under the peak of the roof. "Welcome back to the land of the living."

"Sam!" He held up a hand and Sam took it. "Are you all right? What all has happened, can you tell me?"

"I can, but it will take a while. Do you feel up to it?"

Dicey stood up to leave. "I'll let you boys talk about the fightin'. Cap'n, I'll bring you some more tea in a little bit, if you have a notion for it."

"Yes, Dicey, thank you, I would love some more. Sam, you can just tell me the main points, but I must know. I believe that I remember, someone told me on the beach, that your war has been won. Is this the case?"

"It most surely is. I guess the easiest explanation is Santa Anna chased Houston until Houston caught him. After he wiped out the Alamo, the Mexican army chased Houston almost to Galveston Bay, and drove all the Americans out of the country before him. Then Houston turned and whipped the living tar out of him. Now all those people are turning around and coming back."

"Oh, I am glad to hear it. Did you get him our message, that we intercepted the artillery before it could be used against him?"

"I did, for a fact. The Mexicans only had one cannon at the big battle, a brass twelve-pounder, they said."

"Did the American army cross the border and join the fight?"

"No, they did not. You remember the plan was, Houston would lure Santa Anna into the Redlands, and if the Mexicans crossed the Neches, General Gaines would come west across the Sabine. Well, as the Mexicans came on, the government in San Felipe broke and

ran for the coast like quail scattering out of a bush. Santa Anna
figured if he could catch them, that would end the revolution at
one stroke, so he left his army behind and ran ahead with less than
a thousand light infantry. Houston got wind of it from captured
dispatches, and he drove his volunteers near sixty miles in two and
a half days. The two armies faced off and had a skirmish, and I
reached Houston that evening. Once he knew he wasn't facing a
line of heavy guns like something out of Napoleon, he attacked the
next day."

"I see."

"But now listen to this. He didn't attack right away. He knew the
Mexicans were ready for it, and he let them wear themselves down
in expectation all day. It was three in the afternoon, the Mexicans
decided he wasn't coming after all and were taking their siesta, then
he swarmed them. My God, you never saw such a slaughter. He in-
flicted casualties of maybe a hundred to one."

Bliven smiled. "I am certain it must have seemed so."

"Oh, now, listen here, my man!" Sam rolled his eyes. "I'll have
you know, I was one of those tasked with searching for survivors in
the Mexican army. By my count, Houston lost eight dead and about
thirty wounded. The Mexican dead were north of six hundred, not
counting those that sank in the marsh and were not found. Lots of
wounded, but I do not know that count."

"God almighty, how did he achieve such a thing?"

Sam's gaze cast down as he pursed his lips. "Well, Bliv, that is less
praiseworthy. I heard one of the boys say before the attack that after
the massacres at the Alamo and Goliad, their blood was up so high,
Houston was dreaming if he thought prisoners were going to be
taken. It was obvious to me that many of their wounded were fin-

ished off where they fell—throats cut, stabbed through the body—then they moved on."

"My God, I am sorry to hear it, and sorry that you had to see it. But wait a moment. I heard about the fall of the Alamo, but what is Goliad?"

"Oh, Christ, you won't believe it. That was where Fannin surrendered his southern force. General Urrea offered them terms and treated them as prisoners of war. When Santa Anna heard about it, he went over the moon. By express order, he censured Urrea and had Fannin's whole army lined up and shot—something like four hundred of them."

"Oh, good God."

"So Houston's men were in a wicked mood when he formed them up to attack. He gave them a talk right before they crossed; he said some of them would be killed, but they should remember the Alamo and remember Goliad. He had tried for weeks to discipline them, get them to march and wheel and fire by companies. They got off one volley, then they just went at 'em, every man on his own. That whole sight must have been terrifying, for the Mexican line broke in an instant. The whole battle was over in less than twenty minutes. The Mexicans just turned and ran like hell, but there was no place to go."

"How do you mean?"

"Santa Anna made his camp with Houston in front of him, a river on his right and a swamp behind him. Hundreds of them ran into the marsh and got stuck in the mud and cut down like target practice. Some ran north, which was the only dry ground, and our cavalry was right there waiting for them and chased them down."

"Houston couldn't stop it all?"

"He tried; I was right by him. He rode up and down, hollerin' at men to regroup and take prisoners, and they just defied him and went right on killing."

"Heavens. He led the attack?"

"He did, for a fact. Got one horse shot from beneath him that I saw, got shot in his left ankle by a musket ball, but he sought no medical attention until the battle was over. It was a very dangerous wound; his ankle was shattered and bone fragments went everywhere. The chief surgeon did what he could for him, but he realized they had to get him to New Orleans for some expert treatment."

"I see."

"Then listen to this: Do you remember in Nacogdoches we learned what a lightning rod Houston is, how some people love him and some just hate his guts?"

"Yes."

"Well, his enemies in the government refused him permission to leave the army to get treatment. By God, they were hoping he would die of his wound."

"They could be that petty?"

"I met the chief surgeon, a good man named Ewing. He got Houston down to Galveston and onto a boat for New Orleans. Ewing was cashiered from the army, and they tried to charge Houston with desertion, but after winning such a victory they realized the army might mutiny if they did, so they backed down."

"And *that* is the government that they fought to establish?"

"Ironic, huh?"

Bliven lay back on his pillows and sighed. "Well, it's all over now, I guess. You have your country, and I get to go home. Except—"

Sam laid a hand on his shoulder. "You rest now. There is more to tell you, but we need to get you well just as fast as we can."

Bliven so surprised himself that tears welled up. "Sam, I blew up my ship."

"Yes, I was on the beach, remember? They told me you moved all that powder you captured from the magazine up to your cabin and the wardroom. She burned to the waterline, and all that powder touched off. Blew her stern halfway to Caracas."

Bliven nodded sadly. "I suppose I should confess that I prefer she have this ending than to be broken up or sit in some muddy harbor as a hulk."

"You won't like this so well, either: one of the Mexican ships sent a prize crew aboard, to see if they could put the fire out, see if they could find the log or any other papers. They didn't get off in time; they were blown to atoms."

Bliven shook his head. "Poor bastards. There weren't any papers on board that could tie us to the United States, anyway. Ross got them all."

Sam stood to go. "Really, now, you get some more rest."

"What is the time of day?"

"Late morning."

"Well, since I have proven somewhat hard to kill, and my body is still functioning, I probably need to go explore your bushes sometime soon."

"Oh, yes. There is a jar here by the bed if you need to make water. If you need to do more, I'll help you downstairs. Do you feel strong enough?"

A chamber pot would have been a great convenience, but Bliven's instinct was to be as little trouble as possible. "Yes, why don't you help me down."

It was curious, but taking up a corncob and walking into the brush with its spice-scented air seemed to wake him up, and he returned to the house feeling better than he had since the whole onset commenced.

Sam met him on the back porch of the house, where he was seated with an empty chair beside him. "Here, Dicey has made some beef soup and some cornbread. Can you eat?"

"Oh, yes, I am very hungry. Where did you find the food?"

"Some of the public cattle were up between here and Bolivar, and I hunted one down. We will have a big fat catfish for dinner. Your friend Ross has proven to be quite a fisherman. A boat came into Velasco with a cargo of meal and other things. I was able to get what we needed, since Dicey was sharp enough to keep the damn Mexicans from getting their hands on my money. We'll be all right until I get a new crop."

"Oh, there are potatoes and carrots in this soup. This is very good."

"Yes, the Lederles across the road had some vegetables when they came back. I had more beef than we could use, so we made a little trade. Now, my old friend, there is something I have not told you yet."

"Why? I have not been strong enough to bear the news?"

"Something like that. As much as I enjoy your company, we have to get you out of here and back home just as fast as you are strong enough to travel. It seems, *Captain* Putnam, that the whole Texas government has situated itself right down in Velasco. The president, the cabinet, part of the army, and Santa Anna with them as their prisoner."

"I don't understand. Why ever here?"

"I guess it was because Santa Anna didn't come through there. This was Urrea's area of operation. Santa Anna's intention was to burn all of us out of the territory and start over. Washington is burnt, San Felipe is burnt. Urrea had more of a conscience about it."

"Maybe he should have been president."

Sam pulled the sheeting back from the evaporator and poured a cup of water from a pitcher. "Maybe if he had been, we wouldn't have had to fight. We got along for years under all the different governments they threw at us, but this murdering son of a bitch was just too much. Anyway, Velasco is still here, and the mouth of the Brazos is sure to remain an important port. But then it's also remote enough that the government can keep people away from Santa Anna until they figure out what to do with him. Most of us would like to hang him from the highest tree we could find. I'd like to offer you some buttermilk to follow your soup, but they took our cow."

Sam took a sip of water and handed Bliven the cup. When he drank he looked up in surprise. "That contraption really works, doesn't it? Your water is nice and cool."

"Yeah. Now listen: there is a schooner that's come into Velasco, the *Comet*, leaving for New Orleans in three days. As much as I hate to get rid of you, it would be wise for you to be on it. The first thing Potter did when he got here was walk down to the beach and have a look at the wreck of your ship. He doesn't know where you are, but it won't take him long to figure it out."

"It's all right, I think I can stand the trip. Can Ross go with me?"

"Yes. Dr. Haffner has already vamoosed, but he was able to leave the ship with his medicine chests. He gave the store of quinine water to Ross, so you should get to New Orleans all right."

Vamoosed. It made Bliven smile that Sam should be aware of the new slang. "That all sounds very well, Sam. I thank you for your trouble."

"You take it easy today and we'll hitch up the wagon and leave in the morning."

That evening Sam moved chairs out to the front gallery and they drank Madeira. Bliven looked back into the hall. "Where is Dicey?"

"She said after she got the kitchen cleaned up, she and Silas were going to plant some corn and peas, get the garden going again. I don't know: it may be too late for peas, but maybe it won't get too hot too quick. Maybe . . . maybe . . ." His voice trailed off. "Seems like everything is a maybe anymore."

"Sam, I don't know quite how to say this. I know we are not as close as we used to be, and I won't pretend to understand everything about your life here, but I am very glad that we have had time together."

Sam laughed softly. "Remember old Commodore Dale?"

Bliven smiled and nodded. "Friends forever, he made us swear."

"As watchful for your honor as my own." They reached out and touched their glasses together.

WHEN SAM PULLED his wagon to a halt at the riverbank just outside Velasco, they found it in commotion, and not one but two small schooners at anchor in the stream. Sam braked the wagon at the top of the rise, away from the crowd. "Bliv, you just pull your hat down and wait here. I'll go find out what is going on."

He made his way through an angry crowd to an even angrier man shouting at them, and he heard someone address him as "Mr. President."

"You are Mr. Burnet?"

"I am."

He was moderately short and of truculent bearing. He carried his shoulders back and his head high so that he could affect to look down at people despite his stature. His mouth was wide and set like a rat-trap.

"Then shame on you for the way you treated General Houston after he was wounded—and Dr. Ewing, too. That was all nasty business."

Burnet harrumphed. "Stand away, sir. You are not helping this situation."

"I can if you will let me, you old fool." He caught the attention of Velasco's liveryman. "Hiram, what is the meaning of all this?"

"Mr. Sam, on one of those ships they mean to send that butcher back to Mexico, and after what-all he's done, we won't have it." He gestured to the head of the wooden pier, where a medium-sized Mexican in dirty civilian clothes stood with his back to a piling, within a square of four armed sentries. "We mean to string him up."

"Well, I am sure sorry, Hiram, but you can't. All right, now, listen to me, all you people!" called Sam loudly. "I was with General Houston at the battle, and I was with him when he questioned this prisoner. Houston understands your anger. Texas is a new country now, and Santa Anna alive guarantees our safety. He has recognized our independence, but if you kill him, all that goes right out the window. If you kill him, all those Mexican armies still in Texas will turn around, burn the whole country to ashes, and you could never stop them. Houston's positive order is that he is not to be harmed."

"And we say he ain't leavin' this place," a voice in the crowd hollered.

"All right, then, keep him a prisoner here, but don't you harm one hair on his head." He turned to one of his guards. "Where are you boys camped?"

"Just east of town."

"Well, get him through the crowd; you can use my wagon up

there. Let's just get him out of here. Hiram, which one of those boats is the *Comet*?"

He pointed. "That one on the left, there."

"Can I use this boat long enough to row a passenger out there? He is expected."

"Sure. If anyone asks, I'll tell them you'll bring it right back."

The mob parted for them, and back atop the rise he helped Bliven down from the wagon. "Here," he whispered, "lean heavily on your cane like you are really sick. Don't speak to anyone."

When the sentries and the dictator followed, Santa Anna's eyes met Bliven's for just a moment before he and Sam walked down to the river.

"What a common-looking man," said Bliven quietly. "You could never picture him doing all he has done."

"Well, I'm sure the forky-tailed devil will say the same thing when they finally meet."

IT TOOK THE *Comet* a week to reach New Orleans, but in all of Bliven's years in the Navy it was the first time he ever felt seasick. The schooner's small size and cruising just off the shore rendered her broadside to the Gulf swell, exaggerated her roll into a deep and rapid wallow. What a hellish way, he thought, for all those immigrants bound for Texas to sail off to a new life.

Once afoot in New Orleans, it took little time for him to be directed to the firm of McKinney and Williams, which when he entered he found in commotion.

"Mr. McKinney?"

"Captain Putnam! I am glad to see you again. I understand that you played your role most nobly in winning the freedom of Texas. Both the present and future generations will owe you thanks. I regret that you find me in great haste. How may I help you?"

"My steward, Lieutenant Ross."

"Your servant, sir. It is good that you gentlemen found me, for in another three days' time you should have walked into an empty warehouse."

"You are not going out of business!"

"Certainly not, Captain! With Texas safe, thanks in no small part to you, we are relocating our main operation to Quintana, at the mouth of the Colorado, to be proximate to the line of settlement as it spreads to the west."

"My steward and I find that our duty is accomplished, we need passage to get home, and we find ourselves in New Orleans with little more than the clothes on our backs. I am myself a man of some means, however, and if you can advance us the fare through to Cincinnati or, even better, Pittsburgh, I can draw on a bank there for the rest of the means to continue and remit your outlay back down to you."

"Of course. This incipient Republic of Texas is already into me for over eighty thousand dollars, so adding your passage to Pittsburgh will not make a noticeable difference."

"My word, Mr. McKinney, when I was ashore in Texas, I saw very little in the way of cash in circulation. Do you believe you can recover such an outlay?"

"No matter." McKinney waved it off. "With an American population safe in an independent Texas, and with statehood sure to follow, I calculate on recouping my investment just in commerce to supply the growing population, over and above hoping for satisfaction from their government. Mr. Tomlinson!" McKinney shouted, drawing the attention of a man at the rear of the warehouse. He approached, very tall, with high, raw cheekbones and thinning blond hair. "Mr. Tomlinson, write a note, run it over yourself right away, to Captain Furlow of the steamboat *Boadicea*. Tell him to reserve passage for two officers who will board shortly. He may charge their passage to our account. Gentlemen, he will sail early in the morning, but I recommend you board at once, just dressed as you are, and avoid being too much seen between here and the wharf. Someone might recognize you."

"Still an object of inquiry, am I?"

"Oh, God, Captain, you have no idea. Perhaps you are not aware, the vessel that you lightened of so many field guns, the *Five Points*, was insured by the Boston United Maritime Company. Of all the financial concerns in the North, none are more heavily invested in Mexico and its economy. Directly after your encounter, she put into New Orleans and reported you and the *Gonzales* as pirates and posted a five-thousand-dollar reward for your capture, either alive or for your dead body. At least four armed privateers went out after you. I shouldn't be surprised if some are still hunting you."

Bliven was seized with a curious notion. "Do you know, was one of them a steamship, two large guns, either eighteens or twenty-fours?"

"Yes, the *Umbria*. The Mexican consulate here had her armed and at sea within three days of the *Five Points* coming in."

"Did she fly the Mexican flag?"

"Yes, she registered as a Mexican privateer, conformably to law. I heard that she carried a note from the Mexican consulate to put in at Cópano and take on a couple of heavy guns and soldiers to operate them. The other ships I could not say one way or another."

"Then I would believe it likely that she, operating in conjunction with a Mexican naval schooner, were the vessels that destroyed my ship."

"Oh, I am sorry to hear it. Were any of your crew captured?"

"No. We managed to damage them both so heavily that they retired. We fought just off Velasco, and my crew made it to shore and were pulled in by a friendly crowd. It was her steam engine that made the difference. Her course was not limited by the wind, and she was able to outmaneuver us, rake our stern, and set us afire. It makes me believe, in future, that steam power will render sailing ships obsolete and useless in combat against them." Bliven allowed himself a moment to assimilate all that he had been saying. "Well, Mr. McKinney, I am unsure whether to regret or celebrate my status as a wanted man. But I will say that I regret to hear of a Boston firm so financially engaged with a regime dedicated to repression and dictatorship."

"Hardly the only one," said McKinney. "The Eastern financiers have not been our friends. In fact, when General Austin and Wharton came through here raising money, he got a quarter of a million in New Orleans, somewhat less in Nashville, but Washington and New York, he hardly raised a half dime."

"I am sorry not to be surprised. Back in my days as a young lieutenant, I was confronted with our economic hypocrisy once before."

"Really?" In the face of such a story, McKinney seemed to forget his haste for a moment. "In what connection?"

"New Englanders are supposed to be so hostile to slavery. It was a great shock to discover how many of those slave ships operated to the profit of Boston owners."

"Well." McKinney said the word with a finality that signaled his time was exhausted. "I am sorry for the loss of your ship, but of course officially she was broken up and no longer existed anyway."

12

***

Old Hickory

WASHINGTON, DIST. OF COLUMBIA
JUNE 10, 1836

My Ever Dear Love,

It has cost me more anguish than you can imagine, that my lengthy cruise at sea, and the delicacy of my duties when on shore, have prevented my sending you even so much as a line to let you know that I am unharmed.

I send you these tidings now, with the additional news that I am just returned to the capital city, and I do not anticipate being detained here more than a few days' time, after which I shall find the first coach—bound for home. And let me tell you, the horses have not yet been foaled that could carry me there fast enough!

I do not know whether the following will be good news or bad, that I am released to come directly home, which is good, but the malarial fever that first took hold of me in the Caribbean has once again made its presence known. Let me hasten to assure you that I am under the most expert care, for upon arriving in this city I reported to the hospital in the Navy Yard, where I will rest for a short time before resuming my journey. I am nothing like dangerously ill to any degree, but my vigor is sufficiently affected that I am permitted to come home and recover, before being interviewed on the subject of my duty just completed. Do not be overly concerned, my love, but it would be a good thing to contact our valued Dr. Allison in Worcester for a quantity of his quinina, as I fear that a good portion of the tea that I shall consume during the summer will be spoiled with its bitter, though beneficial, physick.

This missive comes with the love of

> *Your husband,*
> *Bliven Putnam, Capt. USN*

MRS. CLARITY PUTNAM
PUTNAM FARM, SOUTH ROAD
LITCHFIELD, CONNECTICUT

The coach kept its pace as it entered the southern environs of Litchfield. Old Mr. Strait from the former days would have known to slow and stop at his house, but as it was, Bliven kept a watch from his seat at the familiar landmarks as they rolled by, marking the presence of a few new houses farther away from the center of town than his own. Spring was still soft and green, early-planted flower beds were now coming into the height of their bloom, and he was not unaware that in his best uniform of deep blue, brilliant white, and gold lace and epaulets, he showed very fine against June's emerald landscape.

He noted a familiar bend in the road and looked ahead, then knocked on the rear of the driver's seat. "The house just ahead on the right, Coachman, if you will please to let me off." The driver reined in the team and handed him his portmanteau as soon as he touched ground. "I thank you for your kind attention, and you must take this for your extra trouble." He pressed a silver dollar more than the fare into his hand.

He no sooner turned around than the door opened and Clarity stood in it wearing a dress of deep garnet red and black plaid, its throat closed with a gold brooch. She descended the single step to the grade and entered his open arms. "Oh, God be thanked," she said into his shirt. She looked up at him and they kissed.

"Dear Lord, how I have missed you, my love." He rested his chin on the top of her hair.

They stood still, swaying gently, before it occurred to Clarity that unlike their former days when she felt swept up in his embrace, now it was he who was in some degree leaning on her. It was a subtle difference, but one that communicated a change in their positions. "What is your pleasure, dearest? Are you hungry? Do you wish to lie down?"

"I believe I will lie down presently. But now, walk around the house with me. I wish to remind myself that I am home."

They walked leisurely, arm in arm, around the side and to the rear of their house. "You are traveling alone, dearest? Where is your Mr. Ross?"

"He is coming by a different route, as he wished to visit relatives whom he had not seen in some long time. He will be along later in the summer and will send word of exactly when. Where are the boys?"

"Still in their schools. I have written them of your imminent arrival, and they will hasten home at the end of their terms."

"They are well?"

"They are splendid; you will be so proud of them."

At the rear of the house he found the near yard planted in flower beds, with the addition of an arbor with a bench beneath it. "Will you look at this!" he said with a soft exclamation. "Oh, but I do approve. Let us see it." They entered the arbor, where she eased him down to sit on the bench. "Why, is this not much like the arbor at the Misses Pierce's old school, where we first met?"

Clarity laughed with a note of triumph. "I win."

"How do you mean?"

"I wagered a dollar with Mr. Meriden that would be the first thing you said. And, dearest"—she held his hand tightly—"this is not similar to it. This is the very arbor where we had our first conversation."

"What?"

"Yes, I am afraid the dear old Female Academy has closed and the property been sold. I made an offer to obtain the rose arbor, which was dismantled and rebuilt here. Are you pleased?"

"It is brilliant." He gaze shot suddenly to the bases of its pillars. "If I know you, you had the rosebushes dug up and transplanted as well."

"The very ones."

Bliven shook his head. "You are a marvel of the age. How is Freddy? Did he get everything planted this spring?"

"Oh, this will surprise you. Mr. Meriden is recently married."

"No! Well, it was high time. He is not going to leave us, is he?"

"That occurred to me. He mentioned nothing about wanting to leave, but for his wedding present I gifted him a few acres next to our own. I know that you enjoy his association beyond his being our employee, and I thought I would give him some incentive to stay with us. And, yes, the planting was done, with some improvements, as he will show you when you are feeling up to it."

He put an arm around her and pulled her close. "Oh, this is wonderful. Promise me, my love, you will never permit me to leave again."

Clarity laughed lowly. "Would that were within my power. Come, let us go in and make you comfortable. I will make us some tea."

"Oh, that reminds me, I have a surprise for you." He set down his bag and withdrew and opened a small wooden box. "A new tea that I am certain you have not had before. What do you think?"

She sniffed it carefully at first, then fully. "Oh, my, yes! Where did you get it?"

"New Orleans. I thought you would like it."

In the keeping room she lifted a paper from the dining table and folded it to show the story. "And here is a surprise for you, dearest, if you have not heard it. It has led the news of late. Texas seems to have won its independence from Mexico. Your friend Mr. Bandy will be pleased."

Bliven took the paper and examined it closely. "Well, for heaven's sake! What do you know about that?" He returned it to her. "You know, I think I will just go refresh myself after all." He entered their apartment behind the keeping room, but as he closed the door he felt an unexpected wash of emotion swell over him. The secrecy of his mission was paramount, and he thought he could deceive Clarity, and what throttled him now was the injustice to her. After thirty years together, could she not tell when he was concealing something from her? Would she question him on it, or would she wait for him to confide in her when it was safe to do so? It was incomplete, and unfair, but he was powerless to alter things at the moment.

THAT SUMMER OF 1836 was a halcyon time. Their sons returned, Ben from Yale and Luke from his preparatory academy, both strapping but so very different. Ben took a full part in running the farm, and Luke evinced such an ardor for study that he virtually camped in the library. Bliven and Clarity provided him an allowance, to acquaint himself with the bookshops in Hartford and Providence, and even Boston, and to add to the library the latest significant volumes of history and geography and the sciences. It was from Luke's own observation, without prompting, to question why Litchfield had no bookshop of its own, and thus from the age of sixteen found what he took to be his calling in life.

As Bliven learned, the addition to the farm was a large field, almost but not quite contiguous with its main block, which was planted to wheat. There would be more than enough for themselves, with the remainder ground on shares at the mill to sell as they wished.

Dr. Allison called from Worcester every couple of weeks, monitoring Bliven's recovery until he could declare that the malarial fever had passed. However, this time it was not without leaving some shade of itself behind, as Bliven, even when he felt well, saw in his visage in the mirror a certain darkness beneath his eyes, a certain hollowness in his cheeks, which if they were visible to him must be noticeable to others. Clarity noted it, for as they lay late in bed one morning, she ran her finger down his cheek. "Dearest, do not be cross with me, but you will have noticed as well as I that this round of sickness has been different from those before."

"Yes, I know."

"Do you believe there is anything to be done about it?"

"Done about it?" He traced his finger down the curve of her cheek. "My love, I shall do exactly what I have done before. The summer is nearly done, and autumn is coming on. I shall let the farm heal me. I shall pick and crush apples, and carry pumpkins and parsnips into the root cellar. When I am up to it, I shall help Ben mend fences."

She tapped her open hand on his chest. "That's the spirit." She had seen it all her life, that those who kept to their beds and coddled an illness so often wasted away there. It was those who got up and doing—she thought of her mother—those whose vigor returned by activity, and, more than that, from the enjoyment of activity—who made old bones.

As winter came on they judged his regimen a success, for Bliven seemed his old self again, strong, vital, alert. In another recollection of their earlier days, Clarity acquired a pianoforte for the parlor, upon which she renewed her acquaintance with music when the house was otherwise empty and there was no one to annoy with her practice. They entertained, as neighbors and old friends of her family recognized in her what they had once seen in her mother, a connection to the town's earliest history. The boys attracted friends, who often as not were importuned to stay for supper. Bliven recognized it as a meaningful step for himself when he had two new dress uniforms tailored, and indulged himself in the recognition of being a celebrated naval figure, but was not anxious to be recalled to sea.

The season culminated in a Christmas of hospitality, of food and singing, of gifts given and received, of mulled wine with close friends by the fire. The day after Christmas was cold but brilliant, and Bliven and Clarity decided to bundle up and partake of the sunshine with a stroll into the town center. The packed snow crunched beneath their feet as at length they came within sight of the Beechers' old house, high and grim, now occupied by a reclusive tenant of whom little was known. "Many a day and evening you passed in that house," he said to her, even as he marked the door to Beecher's former study, where he had sought refuge, the one time that Beecher had actually been useful to him, when he was so haunted by things he had seen in the War of 1812.

"Dearest, may I confess something to you?" She looked up into his eyes. "This has been the Christmas of which I have dreamed."

He pulled his head back in disbelief. "What? When you were a girl, as I remember, you did not believe in Christmas."

Clarity looked away and shrieked, shaking in laughter. "Oh, do not remind me!"

"You held it to be a heathen ritual."

"Yes, that is true. Well, I suppose a long enough acquaintance with Reverend Beecher has taught me a few things about what doctrines are essential and what is merely pompous."

He squeezed her shoulders closer to his side. "Speaking of old Beecher, what news have you heard from the wilds of Ohio?"

"Oh, my dearest, you don't know!" She pulled back and faced him, holding both his hands. "His seminary has splintered as though hit by one of your twenty-four-pound balls."

"You don't mean it!"

"It seems that the students and some of the faculty demanded that there be a series of debates on the subject of slavery versus abolition.

Such a series of debates were indeed held, and tempers ran so high that the pro-slavery faction in Ohio threatened violence against the school and its teachers. Beecher sought to tamp down the flames and calm the feelings—"

"Really? He should have had such a care for Boston."

"Well, perhaps he learned that lesson after all. But he forbade any more discussion on the topic. With that, a large portion of the students who were passionate on the subject of freedom for the slaves withdrew from the seminary, and some of the faculty resigned. And that is not even the most momentous result."

"Good heavens, what remains?"

"Well, dearest, it seems that one of his dissenting faculty, a Reverend Stowe, up and married our dear young Harriet and accepted a post at the new Oberlin College."

"Good Lord! Where is that?"

"Also in Ohio, but at the opposite end of the state, near Lake Erie." She regarded him with a look of appraisal. "I can tell that you have persisted in your opinion that no man would have such a homely young woman."

"I said nothing."

"There is too much astonishment in your face for it to be about the seminary alone." His smile betrayed him. She went on, "Stowe is a widower nine years her senior, and by her account a very godly man."

Bliven pulled her back to his side and they continued walking. "She is well matched, then. I wish them happiness."

"There is one thing more, dearest. Their new college of Oberlin had its own fierce discussions, at the conclusion of which they determined to admit qualified Negroes along with the white students."

"What!"

"What, indeed. What do you think about it?"

"They sound like revolutionaries. We should send them money."

She stopped again and looked at him, searching. "Do you mean that?"

"My love, in the past two years I learned more about slavery than ever I desired to know. Five years ago I would not have said so, but now, yes, I do mean it."

"I am heartily glad to hear it, for I answered their subscription appeal by pledging a hundred dollars per year."

"Ha! Of course you would." A chill gust cut through their cloaks, and Bliven snuggled her against him. "Well done. It is getting colder. Let us go back."

Polly brought them tea in the library, and on the tray they found a letter with the all-too-recognizable red wax seal of the Navy Department, at the sight of which Clarity bridled just a little. "No fear, my love." He patted her hand. "Let us see what they want."

WASHINGTON
DECR. 28TH, 1836

Dear Sir:

The Secretary of the Navy is pleased to have been informed of your recovered health, which was in a state of some delicacy at the time of your return from your mission last June. By direction of the Secretary, you will please to make yourself available in this city not later than the 16th of January, 1837, to be interviewed on the matter of your duty undertaken earlier this year.

A room has been reserved for you at Brown's, where you will be lodged, along with other persons of importance in the same undertaking. This will include a delegation from the Republic of Texas, which will soon be extended diplomatic recognition, if it has not already, by this Government. This delegation will include at least one cabinet level secretary appointed by President Houston in that country. However, you should not assume that he, or the other Texian members, are aware of the confidential aspects of your late duty, therefore you are to consider yourself enjoined to the same level of secrecy as you formerly observed.

You will be further directed from that place.

> *Yours with all considerations, &c.,*
> *Nicholas Dalton*
> *for the Secretary*

BLIVEN PUTNAM, CAPT. USN
LITCHFIELD, CONNECTICUT

The dark apprehension on Clarity's face did not lift for a second while he was reading it. "Am I not to know the present business, as it was a year ago?"

He thought on it. "You are setting my loyalties into conflict."

"Well, please do not let your mere wife cause you any disturbance."

He thought longer on it and held the letter over to her. "These contents are not to leave this room, ever. Agreed?"

"Very well, agreed."

"My love, I am in earnest."

"Very well, so am I." She took it and read it avidly, closely. "Texas? What have you to do with Texas?"

He made no response, letting her work on it until at last she heaved a sigh of recognition. "That is why you were in New Orleans, isn't it? You were seconded to their navy, to aid in their rebellion, weren't you? Well! That is a curious duty for my in-house abolitionist to undertake, I must say! Just recently I was shown a pamphlet by Mr. Lundy, and Representative Adams, showing that that whole enterprise was really a conspiracy to add territory to the slaveholding states."

Bliven held up a hand to stop her. "My love, there are yet many things I cannot tell you, but I can tell you of my own knowledge that that particular accusation is false. Set your mind at ease on this point, I beg you."

"Very well, upon your assurance. But they have a nerve to call such a recently sick man to Washington in the bitterest depth of winter. Perhaps they really wish the cold to kill you and then their secrets would truly be safe."

BLIVEN'S PREVIOUS VISITS to Washington had centered about the Navy Yard, which lay southeast of the governmental center, and had once embraced a visit to the President's House. He had never before seen its most prestigious public lodging, Brown's Indian Queen Hotel, which reposed on the east side of Eighth Street, with its south wing fronting on Pennsylvania Avenue. This placed it halfway between the executive mansion and the national Capitol. Bliven found its architecture remarkable, as its long west front displayed five symmetrical sections, the largest and central one of four stories, plus dormer windows to attic rooms and a widow's walk atop the roof. It was flanked by wings of three stories, also with surmounting attic dormers, and outlying them small brick extensions of three stories, but of lower ceilings within and a more humble appearance overall.

Bliven timed his arrival for the sixteenth of January, as he was directed, and upon giving his name to the desk clerk heard him respond, "Ah, yes, Captain Putnam. You are expected already. Here is your room key. The porter will take your portmanteau up ahead of you, but if you will come with me, please?"

They crossed the lobby and entered the restaurant, and at their approach men seated around a large table stood to greet him. "Captain"—a young officer saluted him—"I am Lieutenant Ricks. These men have lately arrived from Texas; they will make their own introductions. The President will receive you on the morrow. Please present yourselves at his house at noon. Until then, your time is your own."

The boyish lieutenant departed and one of the Texians, a great four-square man with piercing blue eyes and a full beard, approached Bliven and extended his hand. "We have not met, Captain Putnam, I am G. W. Hockley, secretary of war to President Houston."

Bliven took his hand. "Your servant, sir."

"This is Colonel Patton, who has looked after Santa Anna since his capture last April, and this is Mr. Barnard Bee, who will see to Texas's diplomatic standing here in Washington. Now, Captain, you will not be acquainted with His Excellency, Antonio López de Santa Anna, the President of Mexico."

Santa Anna smiled at him amiably and extended his hand, which Bliven had no desire to take, so before he could reach completely out Bliven stood to attention and saluted. "I have not had the honor." But then the man left his hand hanging in the air until Bliven had to take it. His grip was reasonably firm, but his hand was distinctly sweaty, which spoke volumes.

Santa Anna spoke in Spanish to an officer at his side, who said to Bliven, "Captain, I am Colonel Juan Almonte, traveling with His Excellency as aide and interpreter. The President asks whether he has met you before, perhaps in Texas. You seem familiar to him."

Bliven shook his head slightly. "Please thank the President. I am quite certain that we have never met. I have not been to Texas."

Even for state reasons, he found lying disagreeable. "General Santa Anna," said one of the Texians, "Captain Putnam is newly designated as the American naval attaché to the Republic of Texas, who will be attached to the consulate there."

The hell I am, thought Bliven.

"I see," said Santa Anna through Almonte. "In regarding the snow outside, I will warn you to expect a great change in climate." Bliven felt lucky that before the conversation got even further beyond him, two men came from behind the hotel's desk. "Mr. President, Colonel," said one, "your rooms are ready, if you will be pleased to follow us."

When they were out of hearing Bliven nodded around. "Gentlemen, forgive me asking, but what in the hell is Santa Anna doing here? What business can he possibly have?"

"Captain"—Hockley placed one hand on Bliven's shoulder and with the other gestured to a vacant chair—"let us have a drink."

When they were situated, the three Texians with glasses of whiskey and Bliven with red wine, Hockley continued: "The fact is, Captain, that letting people know we were bringing Santa Anna to Washington to repeat his guarantees of Texas independence to Jackson himself was the only way to get him out of Texas alive. We have been trying for months to get him back home, but the army and the citizens still want to see him hang."

"Well," said Bliven, "there is no denying that his crimes merit it, but I applaud your government's determination not to begin its existence with blood on its hands."

"That is it, exactly," said Hockley. "We even got him on board a ship once, bound for Veracruz, but before it could raise sail, a mob of citizens stormed the vessel and seized him. That was a close call, I can tell you. We only just got our hands back on him. One of the prominent local fellows, a Mr. Bandy, was able to talk the crowd down from a near riot."

"I understand. Gentlemen, if you will forgive me, I am just alighted from my coach, and I would like to go to my room and clean up."

"You are in the south wing, third floor, near us. Come on, we'll show you." Bliven's third-floor window overlooked Pennsylvania Avenue and gave him a fine view of the triple-domed Capitol, the very heart of the government in whose service he had expended his life. As they would not see Jackson until the next day, Bliven and the Texians used the afternoon to gratify their curiosity about the seat of government with a visit. The outer two domed blocks had been built separately, the south one in 1800, the north one to be identical and finished in 1811, and then connected by a colonnade—the whole burned by the British in 1814 but then rebuilt to expand into a central bloc with a fine high dome to overlook the others. The whole now housed the Senate in the south wing and the Representatives in the north, with the Supreme Court, Congressional Library, and cabinet departments within such nooks and corners as could be found. They ran their fingers over the exotic colored marbles and tried for themselves some of the fine furniture.

"Somehow," observed Bee, "I am not anticipating that our own government will be as well housed." Indeed, at the time they left Velasco, the government was considering to locate in the town of Columbia, to the northeast, not far from Harrisburg, one of the few that Santa Anna's columns had neglected to burn during their Hun-like rampage to the east. Of special mention had been an intact house of two rooms flanking a hall—one for the House and one for the Senate—and behind them and beneath the lowering roofline two sheds that could serve for committee meetings, if walls could be finished to close them from the weather.

They returned to Brown's in the early evening, encountering in the lobby Almonte, still in uniform, and Santa Anna, who had undergone a remarkable transformation. After visits by a barber, a tailor, and various merchants who supplied him with personal articles and toiletries, Santa Anna emerged in immaculate civilian attire. He who in former days luxuriated in being an imperious and bloody autocrat—who could and did order the execution of hundreds with a wave of his hand—now appeared as a visiting head of state who would be extended every civility that the government could bestow.

No PERSON WHOM Bliven had met who had been celebrated enough to have had paintings or engravings made of him matched those representations in such full measure as did Andrew Jackson. His shock of white hair was brushed back and fluffed to such a volume as to draw stares, which were then drawn to his eyes, which seemed to hurl thunderbolts and inspire nothing so much as dread. His whole bearing was taut and angular to such a degree that he seemed incapable of relaxation, as though he were ever ready to strike out. The softest thing about him was his voice, its harshness ground down by his seventy hard years on earth, his native Carolina drawl given some edge by the Tennessee frontier.

Bliven saluted, which Jackson answered with a slight inclination of his head. "In previous years, Captain, when I returned a military salute, people said civilian officials are not allowed them, and I must imagine myself a dictator, but when I did not return a military salute people said I was being arrogant. To this good damned day I am not certain what I am supposed to do."

"I appreciate your dilemma, Mr. President."

Jackson extended his hand, and when Bliven took it, he found it skeletal but astonishing for its strength. He discovered Jackson and Hockley already acquainted, and found Patton and Bec also in attendance, the latter of whom the President gave special attention as Texas's diplomatic representative. They were still standing when there was a knock at the door and Santa Anna and Almonte were admitted. Jackson strode over to them and gave Santa Anna his hand. "General Santa Anna, we have been a long time in meeting. I wish it could have happened sooner."

Through Almonte, Santa Anna said, "Mr. President, this is an occasion of high significance, for the leaders of our two great nations to finally greet each other in friendship."

"I appreciate that, General. Gentlemen, let us all be seated. Did you have a pleasant journey, General Santa Anna?"

"I regret that I did not, Mr. President. You will understand that I come from a tropical country. In your ice and snow, I have suffered from colds and influenza, and we were nearly sunk by icebergs on your Ohio River. I am lucky to have reached this place, and this after escaping Tejas with my life."

Jackson nodded. "I am familiar with events in Texas. Indeed, you are lucky they did not execute you. This I attribute to President Houston's determination to establish a temperate government."

"Mr. President," Almonte related carefully, "speaking of Tejas, there is a matter that I wish to discuss before any others, for it reflects upon yourself. My agents in New Orleans, in whom I have the utmost confidence, informed us that during the late war, one, perhaps two American ships and crews operated in the Gulf of Mexico, against our country under the false flag of Tejas. Can you impart to us any information about this?"

Jackson leaned back in his chair, his face grave. "Well, General, I would suggest that if your agents were as reliable as you suggest, you would have known better than to invade a country whose people were as angry and determined as these Texians."

Santa Anna's lips narrowed as Almonte rendered Jackson's answer. "Mr. President, I regret that your explanation is not satisfactory. One of our vessels of supply, sailing from Veracruz, was piratically overtaken in the Gulf by a ship whose crew was certainly reported to be American but flying a flag purported to be that of Tejas, which had no flag at that time. This was reported to us by the ship's insurers, an American company very familiar with maritime matters. This gives us much cause to believe that the United States of the North was covertly aiding the rebel effort in Tejas."

Jackson seemed to mull this for a moment. "Well, now, your campaign having intended to drive the American colonists out of Texas, you must know very well that nearly all its population are Americans, and sound like Americans when they talk, so their speech alone does not signify. What do you allege that you lost on this vessel?"

"Cannons, powder, and shot sufficient to have effected the opposite result in the last battle at San Jacinto. With such batteries of artillery, Houston's army would have been destroyed before they crossed halfway on the plain."

Jackson frowned, suddenly pointing a crooked finger at the dictator. "But for the fact that your whole army, as I understand, was taking its siesta at the time of the attack. But more to the present point, those must be the cannons at whose mouths, according to your foreign minister, Mr. Gorostiza, you imagined to define the boundary between our two countries. Well, sir, I have been wondering if you would venture to allege something so outrageous." He turned in his chair and shuffled through papers on the credenza. "As it happens, I have proof that your allegation is unfounded. You can only be referring to the ship *Five Points*, whose insurance agents have already submitted a claim to this government for this alleged pirate attack, which claim by law had to include—ah, here it is—a manifest of its cargo." He flipped over one page and then another. "Beans, rice, flour, sawn lumber, dry goods. Here, see for yourself." He handed the sheaf across the desk to Almonte. "Now, if you knew anything about the political situation in my country, you would know that the wealthy business interests, including the large insurance companies, are inimical to my administration. Do you not imagine that if they could bring my government into disrepute by showing I had aided the revolution in Texas by seizing your guns, they would do so? Yes, sir, they would, even to the point of fraudulently listing those imaginary guns on the manifest of the ship. But they did not, sir, because it did not even occur to them to alter the cargo list in any such falsely incriminating way. Moreover, I happen to know lately from my own agents in New Orleans that that cargo of foodstuffs and dry goods was safely offloaded in New Orleans."

"With respect, Mr. President," protested Almonte, "no. The ship *Five Points* carried thirty of the latest improved field guns, with carriages and full kit."

Jackson tapped a gnarly finger on the document he had displayed. "No, Colonel, this is the ship's own verified manifest. There is no indication of armaments on board of any kind. By God, sir, those guns are the invention of your President's imagination."

"Perdón," interrupted Santa Anna, *"muy estimado señor."* He continued at length in Spanish to Almonte, who related, "You and I are both men of affairs, and heads of state. You and I know how some things must be said for the public to hear even while we know in private that the truth, for reasons of policy, must remain private. You may say what you will for your Congress and your people to hear, but you and I know the depth of your collusion with the rebels in Tejas, and it would be a kindness not to insult me by asking me to believe it also."

Jackson's voice became unmistakably scolding as he rose, and all the others rose with him. "General Santa Anna, I can well imagine that it would salve your wounded pride to believe that you were defeated by some power greater than that mob of angry farmers at San Jacinto. But by the Eternal, I can assure you that the United States played no part in the Texas revolution."

Santa Anna's mouth became very small as Almonte translated, but he stood straight, for as the captured general in the enemy capital he had no alternative. He spoke as soon as Almonte had finished. "Mr. President, it still remains, I believe, for us to discuss the matter of the boundary between our two countries, in dispute these past thirty years."

Jackson took a more relaxed posture, folding his arms. "Actually no, sir. You are correct that the boundary is not settled, but that is a matter now between the United States and the Republic of Texas, whose independence you pledged yourself to recognize, and influence your government to recognize, in the treaties you just signed in Texas, copies of which have been given to me to consider, in extending our diplomatic recognition to the new government."

After Almonte translated, Santa Anna snorted. "The papers that I was compelled to sign in order to escape the hangman will never be ratified by my government."

"Well," huffed Jackson, "wars have consequences. And when you lose a war, the consequences are seldom pleasant. I'm afraid you will have to get used to the idea that you have lost Texas. But there is one more matter that indeed we are bound to discuss. You were allowed to leave Texas alive to come here and repeat to me your pledge to recognize the independence of the Republic. Will you gratify us by giving your word on this point now?"

"*Señor,*" Santa Anna said through Almonte, "a captive head of state can promise nothing that his government is bound to accept. Surely you understand this. But when I return home, yes, you have my word that I will lend my influence to making peace between Mexico and Tejas."

"Well, then, that is good enough for me; I hold your pledge fulfilled. And now, gentlemen, I beg you to excuse me. I have not been well, and it is time for my medicine." Jackson gestured to his aide. "Mr. Donelson, if you will show these gentlemen out, and bring in some of that infernal decoction? Mr. Dickerson, if you will tarry a moment, and you, too, Captain Putnam." Santa Anna rose, bowed stiffly but only slightly from the waist, and spoke in a tone that sounded distinctly high and formal. "My President," said Almonte, "expresses his gratification to have met Your Excellency and hopes that you may speak again soon, and of greater substance."

Jackson bowed in return, in equal brevity. "General Santa Anna, I hope that between your embassy and the hotel, your comforts are adequately seen to. For your comfort, we are moving you from Brown's Hotel to Mrs. Ulrich's boardinghouse, which is directly across the street from here. You will find it more convenient for our future meetings. If you want for anything, please to inform Mr. Forsyth, the secretary of state, and he will see to it. One more thing you may think about until we meet: rather than repeat that difficult and dangerous journey, I am willing to send you home on the safety of an American frigate."

Santa Anna nodded as Almonte finished speaking. "*Muchas gracias, señor.*" They turned and left.

"Now, Bee, I might recommend that you boys start investigating properties to let, as you will be needing some storefront in which to house your consulate."

Bee had almost reached the door, but stopped and returned a few steps. "Mr. President, our hope and our expectation is that Texas will join herself to the United States in less time than would make a consulate necessary."

"Yes, as I am very well aware," rejoined Jackson, "and I will do everything I can for you. But you need to know, opposition to Texas here is pretty damn strong. John Quincy Adams, the infernal little weasel, already has his people spreading the story that your whole revolution was a conspiracy to spread slave territory so as to gain the majority in Congress."

"Not a bit of it!" snapped Bee.

"Mr. President," said Bliven, "if I may add, I believe Mr. Bee is correct in his assertion. General Houston's officer, who involved me in this whole campaign, is also my oldest friend; we were midshipmen together during the Barbary War. He is a Carolinian and a slave owner. We have exchanged words on the subject many times over the years, not all of them amicable. If adding to the power of the South lay anywhere in the Texians' calculation for the war, I have no doubt that he would have said so straight out."

Jackson gave him a long look. "I appreciate your saying that, Captain." Jackson peered at him so long that Bliven's blood suddenly ran cold with another possibility: that there was a conspiracy, and that it began not with some vague collusion among Southern states but with Jackson himself.

Barnard Bee thanked him and left, and when they were alone Jackson motioned between the two remaining. "Captain, have you made the acquaintance of Mr. Dickerson, our secretary of the navy?"

"Only by his name, sir." Again he saluted, and they shook hands. Dickerson was as old as Jackson but better preserved, and it was apparent from what remained that he must once have been very dashing, as he had a full head of white hair and a quick eye. Beneath his tightly done-up uniform he might have sagged and bulged as all old men do, but thus hemmed in, his trim and erect bearing subtracted many years from his appearance.

Jackson strolled to the window and gazed down, saying at length, "There he goes, the Napoleon of the West. Can you imagine, calling himself that? He's proud, but if there is one thing I cannot abide, it's a man who can't admit when he's been whipped. At least he's not wearing one of those gaudy uniforms of his, looking like some Emperor Almighty."

"No, sir," ventured Bliven. "You may be aware, Mr. President, that his wardrobe was captured along with the Mexican camp. The last I heard of his uniform, it was being shared among the privates who captured him."

Jackson barked out a laugh that extended until it became a cackle, then a wheeze, and finally a deep cough. "Donelson!"

Jackson's personal secretary dashed into the room bearing a small brown bottle and a silver spoon. Jackson reached out. "Never mind that thing. Give me the bottle." He drew a long swig from its tiny mouth, then squinted and screwed up his lips. "Shit! Oh! I tell you, the best thing about this damn brew is the laudanum in it. My God, that is foul." Donelson had already poured him a glass of whiskey that Jackson reached out and traded the bottle for. Jackson took half of it in his mouth and held it, then leaned his head back and gargled loudly before downing it. "Oh, God Eternal. Sit back down, gentlemen. Well, Putnam, you had quite an adventure, didn't you? Have you had enough of a chance to rest up?"

"I have spent the summer at home, yes, sir. In Texas I was stricken with a relapse of malarial fever, but a New England winter is very bracing, and the swamp fever has largely passed."

"I am told that after your last battle you came ashore at that little town of Velasco. That is where Santa Anna signed these two treaties?"

"Yes, sir. I was there when he was brought down from San Jacinto."

"Would you say that he was threatened or abused into signing them?"

Bliven thought on it. "I cannot speak to abuse, sir, but it is true that there was widespread demand among the army that he should be tried and executed. I am certain that, considering what his course would have been had the roles been reversed, he was indeed surprised not to have been killed."

"No doubt."

"That was in May, and I made my way home. I have no knowledge as to the conditions of his confinement since then. I heard that the army did seize his camp kit. Many of his furnishings were of solid silver, even his chamber pot. And they tell me he had a fantastical saddle, mounted with gold and platina. I believe their intention was to auction it off in order to pay the soldiers something."

"I see. And you passed time with General Houston, I believe. What was your impression of him?"

"I did not see him at the time of the battle or after. I understand that he was most dangerously wounded."

"He was taken to New Orleans for treatment," said Jackson in a thoughtful change of tone. "I am told now that he will recover, although he will limp. He is a hard man to kill, as we learned back in fourteen."

"I did see him in Nacogdoches during the last winter," Bliven added. "In all candor, Mr. President, I found him one of the most capable men I have ever met, not just in managing his army but in foreseeing consequences of competing courses of action and preparing for the future."

"I am not surprised. Was he well?"

"Perfectly, so far as my observation extended."

"Was he sober?"

"Entirely, sir. He never offered us liquor and indeed averred that there was none in the camp."

Jackson chuckled quietly. "In our former association, when he was much younger, I never saw him sober for two hours together."

"Yes, sir, that is surely his reputation. It seemed that everyone else in Texas accepts that he is a drunkard whether or not they support him politically. But by legend some of his sprees must have been epic."

"Well, if you had been through everything that he has, you might drink, too."

"I heard this also from some of the more fair-minded men down there."

"Well, this is a good thing." Jackson paused, turning something over in his mind.

"Sir?" Bliven cleared his throat and looked dubiously at the secretary of the navy.

"Be at ease, Captain. You may speak freely, Mr. Dickerson is in our confidence."

"Thank you, sir. Mr. President, there is one point that has raised itself since my arrival in the city on which I would be grateful if you could gratify my curiosity."

"If I can, yes."

"My whole late mission in the Gulf, sir, was shrouded in great secrecy. I lay ill in Velasco for a time, and Santa Anna was brought there for a longer time. We never engaged in conversation, but I was with a crowd of citizens that once viewed him while he was chained to his tree in Velasco. I cannot be certain that he never saw me or heard of my presence. Considering the almighty secrecy, I am wondering why you would risk bringing me into the same room with him when he might make a connection between me and losing those guns that cost him such a disaster?"

Jackson tightened his lips and nodded. "A fair question, Captain, and, more than fair, it shows an admirable alertness to the dangers of an encounter. Do you play at cards?"

"Only when I must, sir, and when I judge that it would be in my interest to lose a small sum of money to someone particular."

Jackson's belly bounced twice in silent laughter—the first sign of ease that had escaped him. "Captain Putnam, a man like Santa Anna lives to exercise power over people and to abuse them with it. It is as important to him as his food and water. In playing against such a man, it is important to take not just enough tricks to win the game but *every* trick, leaving him with nothing if at all possible. If he had seen you in Velasco, or heard of you, he could prove nothing by it. For all he knows, you are merely attached to the Texian delegation. But if his suspicions are aroused, it will heighten the sense of injustice that he has been tricked, which will feed upon the impotence of being unable to do anything about it. His possible humiliation is only a small trick to take in the hand against him, but it could be a highly useful one."

"Is there no risk of provoking him into eventually attacking the United States, as that artillery would have been positioned to do? Once he is back home he can easily obtain all the ordnance he wants."

Jackson laughed quickly and tightly. "Well foreseen, Captain; you've got promise. Now, do you suppose for a moment that if he goes to war with the United States that he will emerge victorious?"

"No, sir."

"And what do you suppose that we could exact from a prostrate Mexico? The Rocky Mountains? Perhaps even Alta California? No, sir, I would not grieve for a moment if he acts so rashly as to attack the United States! It would be his ruin and add immeasurably to the future glory of this Union."

Bliven took this in silently, for it was the first moment that he realized in full the nature, the measure, of Andrew Jackson—that he was a man who wore his reputation as a ruffian as part of his costume that won popular appeal, that he was a man of proven violence, but also that he was a man capable of foresight. That he was a man capable of deep plotting would have rendered him even more dangerous had that ability been harnessed to his personal ambition, but now he realized that Jackson's dedication was to the country, however different his vision might have been from his own.

"And what is more," said Jackson, "by adding western lands to the United States, it will cut the influence of Southerners like that lunatic Calhoun who want to split the Union in two because they imagine it will protect slavery." Without warning, Bliven erupted in a pure horselaugh. "What in hell is so funny?"

"Forgive me, Mr. President." Bliven smiled. "I met Mr. Calhoun many years ago; he was a law student in my hometown in Connecticut. I thought he was barking mad even as a young man."

"Did you, now? Well, that is good to know. And now, Putnam, we must talk very seriously."

"Sir?"

"You are a military man. You take orders and you give orders. I was also a military man, and I know the comfort of having a defined position in a hierarchy. You follow me?"

"I think so, sir."

"But now I am a political man, and I have in my hands the welfare and the advance of the nation. It is not news to you that to many people in this country I am too wild and uncouth to be entrusted with such a responsibility." Jackson gave him a searching look with his raptor's eyes, but Bliven forbore to respond. "You are a New England man; I guess I should not flatter myself to think that you have relished my rise to this station."

"As you say, Mr. President, I am a military man. I have thought it better not to complicate my duties by clinging to political affiliations of any kind."

"Mm. Well said. But look now, of late your military duties have brought you into, shall we say, some glancing contact with the heady world of international politics. And in that world, which is now *my* world, sometimes secrets must be kept. Indeed, some secrets must be so closely held as never, ever to be imparted to another mortal human being for as long as you live. To fail in this could be to endanger the standing, even the security, the safety, of your country. Do you take my meaning?"

"You may rely on it, Mr. President, that I feel no need to tell anyone of my recent experiences, especially since I lack the conceit to believe I have seen the whole picture. To tell my small part of it must surely convey only a small and perhaps prejudicial portion of the entire story." What he might confide, and must eventually confide, to Clarity in the warmth of their embrace was not for Jackson's approval. Jackson was foolish if he believed himself the only one who could play a game of confidences.

Jackson ran a gnarled hand through his shock of white hair. "Mm. I like you better and better. In all these matters, Captain Putnam, you have performed as admirably and honorably as your previous history led us to believe that you would. So let us think of your future. Is there any posting, any command, that you would like to have?"

"I had not thought on it, sir, although Mr. Hockley introduced me as the naval attaché to the Republic of Texas, which I am not nor have any desire to be."

"Hm! That Texas post is yours, if you want it."

"I thank you, sir, but no."

"Well, maybe now that you have had a taste of international affairs, there is some foreign post where you would like to gain some experience. For instance, that young boy who is now king in the Sandwich Islands would benefit from some enlightened guidance. I know you have a history there with the old queen, God rest her soul, and I need a consul to represent us there. Would you be interested?"

Bliven thought instantly, *Where better for you to make sure that no one learns of your doings in Texas than by sending me back to the other side of the world?* "Mr. President, I am deeply gratified by such an expression of confidence. Perhaps you are not aware that my wife was once a missionary to that country. Will you allow me to consult with her about perhaps returning there for such a posting before giving an answer?"

"By all means, Captain!" Jackson rose, and Dickerson and Bliven as well. "Now, you take a couple of days, Mr. Dickerson will talk to you a couple of times to make sure he understands all your activities in the recent months, including, of course, any personal expenses that you incurred in performing them, and we will see you again before you leave for home."

* * *

WASHINGTON CITY
JANUARY 21, 1837

My love,

I send you a few lines to say that my business here is fairly well concluded, and I shall be home again in a few days.

I do not believe I am wrong in harboring a suspicion that you have some worry over my having been recalled to Washington, and whether I have succumbed to some attraction to the high affairs in this place.

My love, let me allay your fears in this way. If you have ever read the history of Cleopatra, and if you can visualize that bowl of delicious figs presented to her upon her last day, then you can see in your mind's eye, the delicious and attractive fruit, and the moving curl of the snake within. That is how I feel about this place.

Further, it is my intention when I arrive home to bring you such a present, that if I had been to India, and raided the diamond mines at Golconda, you would not be more pleased. I shall spend the next couple of days in pleasure at the thought of your being perplexed as to what that gift could be.

Your loving,
Bliven Putnam
Capt. USN

MRS. CLARITY PUTNAM
PUTNAM FARM, SOUTH ROAD
LITCHFIELD, CONNECTICUT

January was nearly spent when he descended from the coach in front of his house, and Clarity greeted him as she always did on the front steps. They kissed and he held her quietly. After a long moment he said, "Do you recall," and she felt his throat against her temple, his voice vibrating, "I said I would bring you a mighty gift?"

She stood back and smiled. "Something about a diamond from India?"

"Ha!" He pulled a folded paper from his coat pocket and handed it to her with some show of formality. She opened it and squinted a little in the light.

WASHINGTON, DIST. OF COLUMBIA
JANUARY 22, 1836

Dear Mr. Secretary,

In the normal course of duty, I would address this letter to my immediate superior, but in his absence, and looking toward our imminent second meeting, I take the liberty of writing to you directly.

In the year 1801 I tendered my services to the Navy of the United States as a midshipman, and embarked upon the schooner Enterprise to make war upon the Barbary Pirates. In the ensuing one-third of a century, and more, I believe I may say that my career has not been uneventful. It shall always be the pride of my life to have played a part in the furtherance of my country's course, and honor.

I am mindful that numerous fellow officers of my similar age and experience remain in service, and I am deeply grateful to yourself and to President Jackson for evincing in me such confidence that I might have a choice in my future assignment. However, I now feel that my higher duty unites with my personal desires, to return to my farm, and to my wife, who has waited for me without complaint these many years, while I still have something left of strength and vitality to offer her.

Thus, sir, as you may imagine, it is with the greatest stir of competing emotions that I tender this resignation from my commission, effective this date. Ever mindful of the great privilege it has been to be useful to my country, it is now my intention to subscribe myself for the final time,

> *Yours, sir, with great respect,*
> *Bliven Putnam, Capt. USN*

Hon. Mahlon Dickerson, here present
Secretary of the Navy

> *Endorsed, with regret—M. Dickerson, Secy.*
> *Accepted, with the gratitude of your country. A. Jackson, Pres.*

As she held the letter with one hand, her other rose to her lips to mask the tremble in her chin. "Oh, can this be true?"

He held her, rocking her gently. "Every word, my love. Your Cincinnatus has come home to plow his fields and to savor the company of his wife"—he lifted her chin and looked into her eyes—"who has never once the first time scolded me for the career I had."

He hefted his portmanteau and they entered the house together, and the keeping room he had known since a boy. She pointed into their apartment beyond. "You will want to wash and change. I will put some water on and make us tea."

She closed the door after him, set a kettle of water atop a new Thompson cooking stove, and then crossed the house to the library that had been his parents' bedroom. She took a seat by the window and donned her spectacles to read the letter again, with the satisfaction of seeing it more clearly. She allowed a tear to fall before she held the paper gently to her chest.

She smiled slowly and shook her head. "A very fine effort, my dearest," she murmured. "So very sweet, but surely we know this will never last."

ACKNOWLEDGMENTS

———•◦•———

This fourth installment of the Bliven Putnam Naval Adventures brought me home to my native history, and thus was more in need of a sure editorial hand to keep the story sculpted and not let me rove off into collateral history lessons. Once again my treasured editor, Gabriella Mongelli, proved her worth.

I also bend the knee to the series' godfather, Ivan Held, president of G. P. Putnam's Sons, and my agent, Jim Hornfischer, who initially brought the idea of the series to me, and who has regularly enriched it with his interest and suggestions.

And as always I am indebted to the few readers whom I trust with raw manuscript, in this case most particularly Greg Ciotti of Austin.

FURTHER READING

———————

Brands, H. W. *Andrew Jackson: His Life and Times*. New York: Doubleday, 2005.

———. *Lone Star Nation: How a Ragged Army of Volunteers Won the Battle for Texas Independence—And Changed America*. New York: Doubleday, 2004.

Haley, James L. *Passionate Nation: The Epic History of Texas*. New York: The Free Press, 2006.

———. *Sam Houston*. Norman: University of Oklahoma Press, 2002.

Jackson, Jack, ed., and John Wheat, trans. *Almonte's Texas: Juan N. Almonte's 1834 Inspection, Secret Report & Role in the 1836 Campaign*. Austin: Texas State Historical Association, 2003.

Jordan, Jonathan. *Lone Star Navy: Texas, the Fight for the Gulf of Mexico, and the Shaping of the American West*. Washington, D.C.: Potomac Books, 2006.

Moore, Stephen L. *Eighteen Minutes: The Battle of San Jacinto and the Texas Independence Campaign*. Dallas: Republic of Texas Press, 2004.